CROSS *the* STARS

BOOK ONE

عبر النجوم

a novel by

VENESSA KIMBALL

writing as V. ANGELIKA

رواية من تأليف
فانسا كيمبل
أنجيليكا .و كتابة ف

Library of Congress Cataloging-in-Publication Data

Angelika, V
Cross the Stars (Book One, Crossing Stars Duet) — 1st edition
ISBN-13: 978-0692633830 | ISBN-10: 0692633839

عبر النجوم
عبر النجوم
عبر النجوم
النجوم عبر
عبر النجوم

~ I always thought it romantic the way people would describe their last moments. Stand-out moments framing their existence here on earth. My moments; my sister Jilly, Allison, Grandma Wallace, attending Georgetown University. Meeting Tom for the first time about the program and the decision to travel to the other side of the world, Jordan. The moment I met my host family, the Ba'ashirs, and the family they gave safe haven to, the Ahmadis. My girls, the moments I had with them. Learning Arabic, something I never imagined doing in a million years. Above all, the moment Raj looked into my eyes and told me I was his forever; no matter the pact fate had made with the universe ... we would defy it. Cross the stars and steal the moon, risk everything to be together. This is what frames my existence as I lay here among the ruin, hovering between two worlds just before the darkness finds me. ~

جوم عبر ال

م عبر النجوم

عبر النجوم

بر النجوم ع

ر النجوم عبر

النجوم عبر

Chapter 1

Ella

The knocking on my door at eight o'clock in the morning, courtesy of my roommate Allison, would normally be a rude awakening if I wasn't already awake. "Are you up, El?"

"Yeah."

Technically I am awake, no longer slumbering, even though I am still lying in bed with my blankets pulled up tight around me. Even though it's April, spring has not found its way this far north, and wrapping myself up in five or six blankets to keep warm is getting really old.

"When I say up, I mean in the literal sense. Meaning rising from the catacomb, El," Allison calls from the other side of my door. Up until now my eyes have been closed, taking in the last of the small moment in time between wake and sleep, when my door opens.

Bundled tightly, I turn only my head to acknowledge her. "Is it ever going to get warm again?"

She has a cup of coffee in hand as she leans against the doorway and smiles snidely at my rhetorical question. The steam wafting from her mug calls to me with both the promise of warmth and liquid adrenaline.

"Come on. It isn't so bad," she says as she tucks her arm close to her body, idly looking around my room. "It does seem colder in your room though."

Ignoring her observation, I wonder how we had made it through another cold Washington, D.C. winter here at Georgetown University in this small, tight, quartered yet affordable two-bedroom apartment. I look up at her over my covered body. "It is fucking cold in here."

Allison opens the drawn curtains, letting in some of the dull pre-spring overcast sunlight. "They say it's supposed to start warming up this week. Thank God!"

The overcast light fills the room, making me squint.

Allison and I have been roommates since our freshman year. Last year we pooled our money together and found this apartment. It's a longer distance from campus than the dorm, but a hell of a lot cheaper, and every penny counts when you are living on financial aid.

I sit up, bringing my tightly wrapped blanket with me. Cocooned in fabric, I reach down to turn up the space heater when I notice the illuminating "on" switch is not lit. "No wonder it's so cold in here. My heater is off," I mumble as I flip the switch off and on, off and on with no reaction from the heater. "What the hell?"

"What is it?" Allison calls to me, now down the hall clanking around dishes in the kitchen.

I glance over at the outlet to make sure it's plugged in; check. I flip the switch off, on, off, on a few more times without any solution. "My stupid heater is broken!"

"Damn, that sucks," she replies. "You think you can be ready in fifteen minutes?"

As I rise and stomp in my long socks to my dresser, half of the blankets wrapped close to me begin to fall away loosely to the ground. I open and shut my drawers hard as I grab for each article of clothing. "No! I'm just getting out of bed! Sorry, I'm just pissed about the heater. Just go on without me."

As I stand there, a blob of blanket, she smiles at my fluffy attire and the frustration melts away, leaving me wondering why she is going in so early. "It's only eight. You don't have class for like two hours."

Allison pours the remainder of her coffee down the sink and talks as she rinses her mug. "I have a makeup lab from last week when I was sick. This is my last chance to make it up and I can't let some stupid lab keep me from getting an A."

She is aiming for medical school, so every A is a necessity where GPAs are concerned. I, on the other hand, have just moved from "Undeclared" to an English major, and I'm not sure if I am going to stay with it or change again. I'm barely keeping my head above a 3.0 GPA with my time divided between studying and my job on campus.

Allison puts her jacket and gloves on and tosses her backpack over her shoulder as she speaks. "Yeah, well I need to turn in my financial aid packet for next year."

Shit, I have to turn in mine. I filled it out two nights ago, just haven't had the time to make it over to the financial aid office to drop it off.

"Next week is the deadline," she warns. "You are going to apply, right?" We are sharing an apartment and I can understand her need for me to take care of my financial end of the bargain, but I can't help thinking maybe I am wasting my time. Yeah, I know, how could I fucking be wasting my time by going to Georgetown University? It might just be me, but I can't see me doing anything with purpose beyond graduation at the rate I'm going; it's disturbing.

Before I can relieve her concern, she probes, "Or are you going to talk to your parents tonight about helping you out?"

I cut her off before she can go there. "The paperwork is already filled out. I will drop it off this week."

Avoiding any further interrogation, I go into the bathroom, shut the door, and turn on the shower faucet. I can't blame her for asking. I mean, if I knew my friend's parents had money and were in a political position like my father, yet she chose to put herself through college with work and financial aid, I would want to know what the hell brought it on. She never straight out asked me my issue with them, just indirect comments and questions like the one she just posed.

Allison's voice sounds full of apology as she calls to me over the running water. "Want to meet for lunch?"

I drop the blankets around me and get undressed. A hotdog or a burger is the best lunch option I could find in college on a tight budget.

"Yeah, lunch truck at one?" I call back as I get into the shower, lather up, and rinse quickly, leaving a few short seconds to soak up the remaining hot water.

The bus stop is three blocks down from our apartment complex, with the ride to campus being just over thirty minutes with stops. The neighborhood is not the safest, but we don't mind. My parents don't approve of the part of D.C. where I live. They make it known at every family dinner. I don't expect them to understand, since money is no object for them. Having come from two well-bred families, they have never experienced wanting for anything.

Grandma Wallace was the only one who could truly understand having grown up with no money until marrying Grandpa Wallace. Even then, she kept things real. She would always come to family dinner on Fridays and talk about all of the things she did in her life. Even at the age of ninety, she would recall the moments of her life as if they had occurred yesterday. My last memory of her is asking me, "Is it worth the risk to cross the stars and steal the moon for something greater than yourself? Something greater for someone else? For love?"

"Always do something with purpose, Ella Marie. Something greater than yourself. Risk for love, risk for life. Cross the stars and steal the moon if you have to."

Those words ring fresh in my mind and have been with me for days now, haunting me, reminding me I need to do something with my fucking life. I'm sure it has to do with tonight's dinner at my parents' house. Dad said he had an offer to discuss with me and I have been debating canceling just to avoid any fucking confrontation with him.

Dad is a Congressman serving his third year as a prime example of our roots. Mom is the ideal congressman's wife, having been groomed by her own mother, who was the wife of an influential prosecution lawyer who turned into a judge in his later years.

There are very few Wallaces and Cromwells who haven't made a name for themselves up and down the east coast of the United States. Those cast aside Wallaces and Cromwells, the deadbeats left for no mention, were considered a sore on the family names. What if they just took the road less traveled? The tucked-away road, the road of the fucking "undeclared," not yet purposed? They still could prove themselves.

My parents see this as the direction I am heading, since I haven't made as many advances and wise decisions as they expected. My mediocrity isn't something that just happened one day; there were reasons for it.

Mine started years ago in high school. I had become tired of not fitting in. The phrase "If you can't beat them, join them" somehow became a necessity in my naive mind. Dad was a newly elected senator and Mom was finally enjoying the fruits of their labor by decorating our new house on The Hill, also known as Capitol Hill.

It was a lapse in judgement with me trying to fit in. A lapse leading me to believe the finest schools, the prettiest clothing, the best-looking boyfriends, the most popular and well-to-do friends, and the most elite and influential people in the district were what I had to surround myself with.

Try it. You will like it.

The best tutors for the highest GPA. Getting accepted to the best universities. Losing your virginity to the most popular senior in high school and son of one of the most influential families in the district.

Try it. You will like it.

Sex in Logan's parents' cabin, my bedroom, the backseat of his car. Nowhere was off limits because we were Logan and Ella and it was expected since it was inevitable in everyone's eyes that we would marry and live happily ever after with little Bristols running around.

Try it. You will like it.

Attending the National Debutante Cotillion and Thanksgiving Ball for only a few of the hand-picked juniors "coming out" with Logan on my arm; a preparation for his and my parents to brag about us being the most pedigreed couple of the entire event.

Try it. You will like it.

All of it was a putrid pool of overindulgence, entitlement, and extreme privilege invisible to me until the night I came home from the ball, my five-thousand-dollar Emilio Pucci dress rumpled from the clumsy and haphazard sex Logan and I had in the backseat of the limo paid for by his parents, with my Jimmy Choo heels linked in my fingers. My mother and father sitting in the living room waiting for me to tell me my grandma had passed.

Her death was my awakening. That night was when the rose-colored glasses of living under my parents' endowments, my parents' great expectations, and our family's influence in the elite circle of friends we kept came off. Actually, I threw them down and stepped on them, completely shattering and rejecting everything that reflected the privileged and materialistic lifestyle I had focused on for far too long. One of my many rebellions widening the rift between my parents and me was choosing to pay my way into Georgetown University without their help.

That night the rift between us became so wide, I never expected to fill it again. It still hasn't been filled, just calcified over the bitter co-existence. That is what the high society does, covers the rifts and makes nice like everything is perfect and undamaged.

My wait at the bus stop is cut short when a white BMW pulls up to the curb.

"Hey, El." It's Natalie, my sister.

"Hey, what are you doing here?"

"I was in the area and thought I would catch you before you got on the bus. Get in, I'll give you a ride to campus."

Okay, first off, she would never be caught dead in my neighborhood, let alone at eight thirty in the morning, so I'm skeptical from the start to get into the car. I hesitate, wanting to question her reason for being here, when she leans farther across the passenger's seat and raises her eyebrows.

"It's cold and I have to get to campus. Look, I thought I was being nice by stopping by."

She rolls her eyes then forces a smile. "Come on, get in." The smile she holds on her lips is full of unvented sarcasm, I can feel it. I get into the warmth of her car and barely get the door shut before she takes off.

"What are you doing all the way over here?" She lives in Georgetown in an apartment she is renting with another graduate. There is no reason for her to come all this way unless something is up.

She concentrates on the traffic. "I had to drop off a document with a client. Hazards of being an intern for a corporation, I suppose. Could be worse," she says and starts to giggle, "I could live here," then she realizes her comment went a step too far. She glances at me briefly, then back at the road. "Sorry."

I glance out the window to hide rolling my eyes and try to change the subject. "Yeah, so we have dinner tonight at Mom and Dad's."

"Yeah, but I need to head back right after. I have this thing with a couple of friends," Natalie halfway explains.

"That's fine." If the evening at Mom's and Dad's is too long, the conversation turns against me and I don't want to deal with that shit. It's hard enough bringing myself to go every week as it is.

I hear my mother's voice ringing in my ears, *"It's family tradition, Ella."*

"Want to come tonight?" Her question doesn't register right away, until she peers over at me.

"Me?"

She gets this stupid look on her face. "Yeah, you, El. Who the hell else? Are you okay? Don't tell me you are sick or some shit. I don't have the time to catch anything from you, let alone bring you to Mom and Dad's sick!"

I shake my head, more to diminish her credibility to myself than answering her. "Just thinking about classes."

"How are they going? Are you keeping up? You know, since you chose your major late in the game, things are going to get more challenging. What's your major again?"

This is how deep our disconnection is. She doesn't even remember my major. She is as big of a pain in the ass about my shortcomings as my parents.

Being a year ahead of me, Nat earned a bachelor's degree in Communications from Georgetown University on my father's dime. That wasn't enough for my mother and father though. "Aim higher, Natalie," they said. Fitting the Cromwell-Wallace mold, she was accepted into and enrolled in the master's degree program for Public Relations and Corporate Communications. What kind of job will that get her? I have no fucking idea, but it sounded prestigious to have been accepted into the program at GU. Hey, it might earn her a husband, you never know.

She was the perfect Cromwell-Wallace package all wrapped up into the nicely dressed, perfectly made-up and bejeweled eldest daughter of Byron and Nannette Wallace.

Suddenly, the car jolts as a taxi cuts her off and stops to make a pickup, sending Nat into a conniption fit as she lays on her horn. "Are you fucking serious! Move out of the way, you fucking asshole!"

Minor flaw: for a pristine daughter, she has a mouth like a sailor; just like me, the affected daughter. The taxi moves on quickly and Natalie swerves around it as she stares over at me. "What is wrong with people?"

I can't help but grin.

"What?" she asks, noticing my smile.

"Nothing, it's just that I don't see why it is such a big deal."

After I say it, I regret my words.

She takes turns looking at me and then the traffic in front of her. "Well, El, maybe if you did think things were a bigger deal then your life would be a little fucking different for you. Maybe your choices would be smarter."

Damn, I set up that opportunity for criticism. I choose not to look at her as I defend myself. "My decisions are fine and I'm happy with my life."

Not entirely true, but I will fake it to save face in front of my holier-than-thou sister.

"Really, El. You are happy scraping by on financial aid, working on campus when you could have had Dad pay for college and possibly be on your way to a paid internship somewhere?"

I shift uncomfortably, wishing myself out of this car as she continues to bombard me.

"You are happy living in the ghetto when you could be living on campus comfortably with no worries of walking to and from a bus stop? I lived on campus and I—"

"I do not live in the ghetto and Allison and I are careful. Don't compare me to you! You are fine with their guidelines and opinions, Natalie. You like them telling you what to do, but I sure as hell don't."

"God I wish you would, El. It would make life so much easier for you. Maybe you would find direction. Tell me, do you like life being difficult? Do you like torturing yourself like this? Or is it solely to prove yourself to Dad and Mom?"

Hell, she sounds just like Dad. I wouldn't be surprised if Dad sent her to pick me up and start shit with me this morning; in preparation for tonight's dinner. I close her off and stare out the passenger's window at the peppering of students starting to come into view as we get closer to campus.

"El."

I don't want to even look at her right now. "What?"

"I shouldn't have said what I did."

"Why did you? Are you seasoning me for tonight or something? Getting me ready for Dad and Mom's line of fucking questions, suggestions, advice, and criticism. Is that why you swung by to pick me up this morning?"

She stares at me for a long time before turning back to the road. She raises her chin and tightens her lips. "Look, you are lost, El. You have just decided on a major and it is your junior year at one of the best universities in the United States. Yes, you are smart, you got into fucking Georgetown University on your own merit, but what do you have to look forward to after college? What is your plan?"

Mind you, Nat didn't get into Georgetown on her own. I overheard her and Dad talking my senior year of high school, telling her he had gotten her in.

"Ella, you have to plan ahead, play the game, and right now you are just drifting. Mom and Dad are worried about you and yes, I wanted to talk to you before we went over there tonight so I drove all the way over to get you in that ... your neighborhood, to maybe talk some sense into you. Give you some advice about taking Dad's offer tonight."

The fucking offer. They are going to corner me with some ridiculous offer and I will reject it because it will be both demanding and commanding, which will totally fucking piss me off, ruining yet another family dinner.

I can't help my sarcasm. "Offer, yes, the main course of tonight's menu. I was wondering when they would plan an attack again. I'm sure this one will be just as demoralizing as all the others." I shake my head and release a low laugh. "Unbelievable. I should fucking cancel right now."

Realizing she has pushed too far, she starts backpedaling. "Damn it, El, don't start this shit. You skipped last week's dinner and if you skip this one..."

"I had to skip! I had papers and an exam to prepare for!"

She shakes her head. "Fine. Whatever. Look, this offer is not an attack, believe it or not they are wanting to compromise with you."

Okay, that is a word I have never heard my family use before.

Seeing she has my attention, she eases into it as she pulls into the student parking. "I don't know the exact compromise Dad has to offer, but Mom told me he wanted to come to an agreement with you on things."

Holy shit, it's a miracle!

She turns off the ignition and shifts her body to face me. "Dad doesn't do compromise, but for whatever reason he plans to with you. Whatever he has to offer, just please listen to him. He is your father, for God's sake. It is the least you could do. Just hear him out tonight, all right?"

Picking up my backpack from the floorboard, I take a deep breath then settle my eyes on hers as she stares at me with a small sense of pleading. Pleading is again something my family doesn't do, and the only thing making me more curious about what Dad is going to offer as a compromise.

"Fine."

Her entire body visibly relaxes and the concern on her face disappears as she perks up. "Thank you. Meet me here at five. Traffic is going to be hell."

"Yeah."

Getting out of the car, Nat adds, "Oh, and think about going with me to meet my friends tonight. It will be fun."

Fun with Nat. I can't fathom.

"Hey, did you want to meet for lunch?" Her question is unexpected.

She has never asked me to lunch before.

"Oh my treat." I know she has added this because of my budget. "Promise no talk about Mom or Dad. Just sister stuff, I guess." The questioning look on her face mirrors my thoughts as I don't think we have had a "sister stuff" talk since middle school.

I consider it for a half second, when I remember I'm meeting Allison for lunch after work. "I can't, sorry."

She shrugs. "No, it's fine. Meet me here at five."

"Okay."

I head toward campus wondering if I have sacrificed a chance to turn a corner with my sister because of work or fear. I could always ask to switch days and find Allison before we meet. I turn around to change my mind, but notice she is on her phone already, walking in the other direction.

"Hey, did you want to go to lunch still? I'm free after all. Yeah, she couldn't make it."

I don't call to her, realizing I am second place to the person on the other line and Nat always thinks of opportunity before family.

As I exit the Southwest garage, the chill in the air from earlier has nearly vanished and the sun has finally pushed through the blanket of clouds covering the city. I can't help thinking about tonight, dinner and this looming offer. There are two reasons I still attend the family dinner. The lesser of the two is my hope that one of these days my parents will magically accept my choices and the way I want to live my life. The number one reason is for my little sister, Jillian, Jilly. She is a junior in high school and the most level headed and mild mannered out of our entire family. She reminds me of Grandma Wallace, another reason I look forward to seeing her every week; seeing her keeps Grandma's spirit alive for me.

I take the last bite of my sauerkraut, mustard, and sweet relish dog just as Allison asks details about the surprise ride to campus with my sister. "So she went all the way to our hood to pick you up out of the goodness of her heart?"

The rhetorical question is laden with sarcasm; one of the many reasons I love Allison. I nod, unable to immediately speak through my chewing. "Hmmm. She had to drop something for a client."

"Yeah, sure. I don't buy it. Something is up." She takes a bite of her hotdog, then crumbles the wrapper in her hands. I take a sip of my drink, then collect my own trash, tossing it in as she holds the bag out to me. "Yeah, well, I guess if there is, I will find out tonight at dinner."

Rising, I pick up my backpack from the ground. With the sun shining now, we couldn't resist sitting out on Copley Lawn just like all the other students scattered around us.

"So, are you heading work?" Allison asks.

"Yeah. Why?"

"It's Friday and there is this thing going on in Red Square. You don't have to be to work until one, right?" This is Allison's way of asking me to go with her.

"Yes, why?"

Red Square is a huge open area students gravitate to on Fridays. It is not uncommon to see student organizations promoting causes, spontaneously putting on a dance performance, or spur-of-the-moment celebrations for national holidays. The organizations on campus also like to advertise for events and performances on good weather days, like today.

She shrugs and stares off in the distance as she explains, "I wanted to look into something for the summer. I just happened to pass a table offering an internship after leaving my last class to meet you. I didn't stop, but wanted to go back after lunch."

I glance down at my watch; it's only twelve ten and while I wouldn't normally go to Red Square, Allison appears desperate to go back. "Sure."

As we get closer to the Intercultural Building, the distinct red-brick walls, the roaming students, the sound of live music, and the smell of grilling hamburgers are evidence we are entering Red Square on a Friday afternoon. I totally forgot about the GU Grilling Society and burger on Fridays. Allison and I look at each other at the same time as she says, "How could we forget about the burgers!"

Our freshman year, we ate hamburgers from the society every week, weather permitting. We both laugh a little at the fond memories. "They kept asking us to join."

"And we always had an excuse not to," Allison adds, smiling, "except that one time those two guys asked us out."

My smile sours a little. "Yes, the date."

It was one of the few dates I agreed to go on as a college student and a one-night stand in his dorm room I would rather forget.

"What? They were cute," Allison chides.

"Yeah, well, cute can only get you so far."

Table after table, student representatives talk and laugh with passerby stopping to chat, when Allison stops. I look down at the banner—"Georgetown Summer Medical Institute"—l then up at the cute guy standing behind the table smiling at Allison.

"You're back," the guy says. Allison's grin is as wide as his. Okay, so there is more to this possible internship than what she originally let on.

Seeming caught in a white lie, she shrugs at me, then looks at him. "Yeah, I wanted to find out about applying for the Institute for summer!"

Allison is a brainiac and has her heart is set on med school, but her uppity voice and ear-to-ear smile tells me her heart is set on more than the Institute.

"El, this is Bradley. Bradley, El." Her introduction and his, "Hi nice to meet you," are vacant as they continue to stare at each other. Allison had no problem hooking up with guys and from time to time they would stay the night. Yeah, I hooked up with a few, but never let them sleep over. I always kicked them out right after, security I suppose. That vacant, faraway expression she has right now, this one might be spending the night soon.

"I'm going to just be over here for a minute, okay?"

My comment seems to get Allison's attention as she looks at me for a split second. "Sure. I'll be there in a bit."

I slip away behind her, passing by students eating, talking, and laughing when I notice a banner that reads, "Go Abroad! Make a difference with WorldTeach."

I turn around to see how far I have strayed from Allison, just as she turns my way. I point to the table, letting her know I will be here, and she give me a nod.

As I walk up to the table, my eyes are immediately drawn to the laminated pictures displayed: children in a rundown classroom raising their hands, sitting in small desks with a woman leading them in classwork. Another poster on the desk shows a group of children leaning against a concrete wall, having been lined up for a picture with their volunteer teacher standing with them. Another picture shows a group of volunteers standing among statues; looks like a foreign landmark.

"Hi, would you like an information packet?" the man behind the table asks.

"Uh, sure."

I can take a brochure, no harm, no foul. The words "WorldTeach" are written across the brochure in red. "Is this only for people who want to be teachers?"

As the man smiles wider from my question, I feel stupid for asking all of a sudden. He shakes his head, still passing out brochures to the few students pausing long enough for him to give them one. "No you just need to have the desire to make a difference. You know, get out there, take a stand for something bigger than yourself."

I'm not a superstitious person, but hearing him share a sentiment so similar to Grandma Wallace's, my gut tells me to linger and find out more.

He passes out another brochure to a student, then focuses on me. "Are you interested?"

Somewhat put on the spot by his direct question, I look down at the brochure, then at the pictures of places and people representing something bigger than me.

"Yeah, I think I am."

The man at the table introduces himself as Tom Stern, then takes down my name and email address, telling me he will be in contact to set up an appointment for next week. I thank him and walk back toward Allison, who is already approaching me. "Hey."

"Hey." I fold the brochure in one hand and hold it by my side.

Allison looks down at the brochure in my hand, then at the table. "Go abroad? You thinking about going abroad for the summer?"

I keep walking and answer her nonchalantly, "I don't know. Just looked interesting."

"Oh, can I see the brochure?"

Feeling self-conscious about something I might not even do, I frown at her. "It probably won't turn into anything."

She smiles menacingly. "Okay, just let me read it. I might be interested."

I shake my head and smile as I hand it to her. Feeling the pressure of her scrutinizing the hell out of the brochure, I ask, "Don't you have somewhere to be, like class?"

She looks so serious as she reads through it, answering me softly, "No, I have an hour break. Summer programs available for undergraduates interested in making a difference in another country; Chile, Amman, Jordan, Morocco. Says they are looking for students interested in volunteering to teach English."

I nod, recalling the similar points Tom the director made. He said I would be an asset to the program. Abruptly, she swats me with the brochure. "English major, Ella. That is you!"

I nod and smile mildly, attempting to diminish her excitement.

"What?" Allison asks.

"What do you mean, what?"

"It's just you nod and smile like that when you have already made up your mind." Her expression of worry is foreign since I come from a family lacking much of it.

"Well, you're wrong. I'm supposed to meet with the director next week."

She seems shocked. "Really? God, Ella, traveling to a faraway land, discovering a new culture, using your abilities to help teach others the English language while learning a new language and culture yourself. That is an amazing opportunity! A chance of a lifetime!"

Feeling the pressure of not being everything this program might need, I divulge, "Yeah, well I'm not sure I will be a good addition."

"Don't you even do that shit, Ella," she says, nudging my shoulder then handing me the brochure. "See, aren't you glad you came with me to Red Square today? It wasn't a total loss, right?"

I turn my eyes up to the sky and change the subject from me to her. "Yeah, it was entertaining watching you flirt with Mr. Med School."

She swats my arm and squeals. "I was not flirting! It is for an internship!"

"Yeah, sure. When is he spending the night?" I ask playfully.

"Ha, ha, ha," she says, finding no humor in my attempt to distract the focus. "Seriously, El, keep the appointment.

What do you have to lose?" As I collect books from each study room on the fourth floor, I think about traveling abroad and Allison's question. *What do you have to lose?*

I have nothing to lose. I mean, what are the chances of me going to Red Square today of all days and stumbling upon Tom's table to talk about going abroad? South America, the Middle East? At least ten thousand to one. It would just be three months. Nothing to lose for a small risk of putting myself out there to find something more.

Nat's car is already running when I get to it after my shift. I overhear her phone conversation as I get into the car. "Yes, she just got in. We will be there in about twenty minutes depending on traffic. Okay, bye."

Hanging up, she looks over at me. "Hey."

"Hey." I toss my backpack into the backseat and put my seatbelt on.

"How was it?"

Her question throws me off a little. "How was what?"

"Your day," she says, running her hand through her golden-blonde hair as she weaves around traffic, almost rear-ending a car. I want to close my eyes as I cringe from the anxiety.

"Uh, good. Yours?"

Nat takes my simple polite question as an invitation to unload her entire day on me she drives. By the time we pull up to my parents' house, she has maybe stopped to breathe a handful of times in between telling me about the counselor she is working with on her dissertation and her over-demanding boss.

"This is a fucking internship. I shouldn't have to take this shit from him, right?" Is she really asking me?

As she turns off the car, I reach into the back, grab my bag, and open the car door, and pacify her rant, "Right, you shouldn't."

As I walk up the steps to the house quickly, Nat follows close behind me. "I know! You would think he would be more appreciative. I mean, Dad telling him about me. My taking the internship and giving my talent. I am a fucking asset!"

Correction, Dad got you the internship and you aren't a fucking asset, just a fucking ass.

"Yes, Natalie. You are so right. You are a fucking asset," I say, smiling perversely.

I pull my jacket close around me as I ring the doorbell. The house's stately prestige from the outside could be intimidating to any visitor not of upper crust caliber. It just made me fucking uncomfortable. Before I can pull back, Jilly opens the door and smothers me in a huge hug. For being smaller and younger than me, she packs a wallop. "Ella! Oh my God! I have missed you so much!" Even though she is in high school, her soft child-like voice seems to chime when we are together.

I hug her back and laugh. "It's only been two weeks, Jilly! You act like you haven't seen me in months."

She steps back letting us pass through the front door, "Yeah I know. It just gets so boring with just Mom and Dad here."

I set my backpack down on the high end marble flooring and notice Winston, our white Siamese, slinking around the corner curiously looking at my bag. "What about Winston?"

"What about Winston? He is a cat, El. It isn't like I can talk to it."

She rolls her eyes dramatically and crosses one leg in front of the other, folding her arms roughly. I can't help but smile at her angsty teenage posture.

I pick up Winston just as he rubs his jaw against my backpack. He lets out a low meow. "Sure you can. See?" I hold him close, his face next to mine, and move his small white paw in a waving motion to Jilly. Clearing throat, I throw my voice, "Hi, Jilly. Will you please talk to me? I am so lonely."

She rolls her eyes again and giggles. "You are crazy, El."

Natalie passes in front of me, lacing her arm through Jilly's, pulling her away from me and Winston deeper into the pretentious abode my parents have surrounded themselves with. "So, tell me how everything went."

I put Winston down and follow after them as they walk through the lavish foyer. "How what went?"

Natalie glances back at me briefly before she tosses her head back. "Seriously, El. Debutante? Hello? What is going on with you today, El?"

She moves on with Jilly by her side. "I am so excited for you. Have you decided on your dress? I remember when..."

I feel a burn in my stomach twisting and gnawing as Natalie reminisces about her fucking debutante days to Jilly.

Natalie stops in the living room and pulls Jilly into a delicate hug. "You are going to have the time of your life, Jilly, mark my word."

Jilly nods as Nat disappear through the dining room doorway. "Hi, Mom. Dad."

With her gone, Jilly and I look at each other. She is still smiling, but it is different than the one she gave Nat just now. "Is it really going to be the time of my life, El?"

I don't know if she remembers much about the night of my debutante ball. It was rightfully overshadowed by Grandma Wallace's passing. I badly want to tell her not to do it, not to give in to what they expect of her. Instead, I lock arms with her, walking side by side into the dining room. I don't want to change her mind, but I also don't want to glorify it like Nat and Mom obviously have. "Jilly, just take it with a grain of salt. It is just a dance. Plus, it's like six months away."

"I know, but Mom and Nat talk about it all the time," Jilly whispers to me, just as Nat comes into sight sitting to the left of Dad, still dressed in his suit. Mom is buzzing around in a dress and heels as she sets the table. A suit and dress attire isn't what you would expect at a normal family dinner, but sophistication always trumped normalcy in this household. Jilly and I were the only two under dressed for this joyous occasion. I pull her close and lower my voice. "Jilly, just don't try to be someone else for them. You are perfect the way you are."

She pulls back and smiles softly, her blue-gray Grandma Wallace eyes thanking me before the words pass her lips. "Thanks, El. I won't."

I let her go and move to the opposite side of the table just as Mom stops me by the shoulders, air kissing me. "Hi, honey. What were you two whispering about over there?"

Mom doesn't wait for my response as she continues to buzz around the table, straightening napkins and silverware.

"Nothing."

Jilly and I exchange a quick glance at each other as we sit.

Dad is talking to Nat intently, barely acknowledging me. "Ella."

"Hi, Dad."

That is about as tender as our greetings get nowadays.

Dad takes the lid off the dish to his right. "Mmm. Chicken stroganoff!"

I smile, remembering how much I love Mom's chicken stroganoff. She hasn't made it in years.

"Isn't that your favorite, El?" Natalie asks as she takes the dish from Dad to get her serving.

I take the dish of green bean casserole Mom is passing me. "Yeah, it is."

I notice Mom smile. "I figured why not. It has been a while since I made it. Just thought it would be nice."

Mom can definitely cook, but one thing she was really bad at was lying. I look across the table at Nat, who is busy pouring herself a glass of wine, giving me a level eye and smirk.

The sound of silver forks and knives tapping porcelain plates fills the room, as the tension in my stomach rises.

Fuck it.

"What's the special occasion?"

Dad wipes his mouth with his napkin, reaches for the bottle of Pinot Grigio and pours me a serving. "New opportunities, new endeavors. Let's just enjoy this meal, shall we?"

Dad sounds genuine, not wanting to rush into a discussion, which makes me consider the offer even more.

Taking the glass of wine, I nod then take a hefty sip as the conversation starts around me.

Mom talks about Tibby Nelson, president of the Junior League of Washington, and how she is finally going to relinquish her position and pass the torch to Mom. Dad congratulates her and, right on his coattails, Nat tells Mom how she is so happy for her, but not without asking if there are any open chair positions she could inquire about. Jilly talks about her day, the exam she needs to study for, and the term paper she is struggling to complete on landfill issues. Dad gives her the "just stay focused and power through" talk just as Nat forms a link of commonality with Jilly's term paper and her striving to get the acknowledgment she rightly deserves at her internship.

"Natalie, you are very lucky to have found the internship. Don't burn any bridges," Dad warns as he sits back, savoring his wine.

Nat tilts her head; she does that when she gets pissed at him. "I don't intend on burning any bridges. The internship is over in three months."

Dad sets his glass down and folds his hands in his lap as he feeds her his thoughts. "And then you are done. You will have experience behind you to use for your career."

She nods, fiddling with the edge of the butter knife.

"Have you been in contact with Hank Bristol?" my father asks.

Hank Bristol is uncle to Jasper Bristol, and great uncle to Logan Bristol. Hank is also the owner of one of the biggest corporations in America, Bristol Holdings.

Nat stops fiddling and folds her hands together in her lap. "Yes, I have. We had lunch last week."

Dad sets his glass down. "Good. Just put on your charm and your Wallace confidence and you will do fine, Natalie," he says, smiling. It is obvious Dad has swooped down and positioned Nat in a job. She is glowing, having Dad's full attention and approval, until she shifts her gaze to me; it quickly fades as she realizes I have seen through their conversation.

She brings the rim of her wine glass to her lips, sipping generously. "What about you, El? Anything to talk about? New possibilities?"

Well played, Nat.

I reach for the bottle of wine as everyone's eyes shift to me. "No, just wrapping up classes, getting ready for finals."

"How are your grades?" Mom asks.

As I continue to pour a robust serving, I nod. "Good."

Nat probes, putting me back in the spotlight, "What are your plans for the summer, El?"

I'm about to tell them I don't have any when Dad clears his throat. "Well, I suppose this is a perfect time to discuss a proposal I have for you, Ella."

Nat looks at Dad, Jilly, then Mom with pure surprise, acting like she has no idea what he is talking about. Dad angles his body toward me. "Now I know you and I haven't seen eye to eye on many things lately, but I want you to know I respect what you have accomplished."

Is he complimenting me? If I could see myself now, my jaw is probably hanging on the floor.

His tone changes suddenly. "Ella Marie, I won't pretend that it has been easy to sit back and watch you struggle. Your mother and I have wanted to step in many times and I know I have been demanding on several occasions trying to talk you into letting us help you."

He pauses for a moment, appearing to collect himself, then clears his throat as he leans his elbows onto the table. "Tonight, I am offering not with an ultimatum or demand, like I have so many times before."

I would be lying if I said his expression of emotions isn't making me consider what he plans to propose. It is said to be innate in politicians to have top-notch negotiating skills. This could be the case, or maybe the effects of a glass of wine before dinner. Either way, he has my attention.

"Your mother and I had dinner with Jasper and Liz Bristol a few nights ago."

Before Dad can go on Mom interrupts, "Remember how we used to have family dinner with them years ago, El? Natalie, Jilly, you and Logan. You two ... Ellie and Logie." Her voice drifts off as she smiles and looks down at her food before she takes a small bite of stroganoff.

I know she is angling for me to take a walk down memory lane, but I'm not into it. Daydreaming about Logan Bristol is long gone, a past I would prefer not remembering.

Seeing my lack of enthusiasm, her smile fades as she continues, "Anyway, Jasper asked about you specifically, right, Byron?"

Dad sets his wine glass down. "Yes, he has a paid internship available through his law firm and he thought you would be perfect."

How would Jasper know if I were perfect for an internship? I haven't seen him since my senior year in high school, and the way I ended things with his son cold turkey, I would expect him to remember me as the girl who hurt his precious son's ego, not perfect for a paid internship at his multi-million-dollar law firm.

Dad continues to sell the offer. "I told Jasper you were an English major and law wasn't something you were aiming for. Still, he insisted I tell you about it since the internship was research based and you would be working alongside law students. With this being a paid internship, maybe it could help alleviate some of your expenses with the apartment, food, etcetera."

"Who knows, it might give you some direction for your future." As soon as Mom speaks, she backpedals. "I mean, more options."

Nat speaks up, "El, opportunities like this don't come around every day. He is asking specifically for you."

I have had two glasses of wine on a near-empty stomach, but I'm still able to see through the bullshit being served. What is Jasper Bristol's angle in all of this? I know Dad's and Mom's is to give me direction because they feel I am fucking flailing here through the last year and a half of college. Yeah, it is true, but I'm not going to fucking admit it to them; I have my pride.

Nat purposefully goads, "You would have to be crazy to not consider this. I mean the only other paid internship he has offered was to his son, so he must think highly of you."

Of course! There it is! The ultimate reason for this offer! Insert Logan Bristol, the one they all think I let get away.

"She is right, Ella. Logan was offered the same internship a year ago, just before he started law school. I believe he is still working there. Byron?" Mom asks.

The clarity is blinding.

"Yes, Nan. He is still there and showing great promise of heading the firm once Jasper retires." Dad doesn't dare look at me as he seasons the offer with show of Logan's ability to provide greatly for a token wife, AKA me.

I pick up the bottle of pinot grigio and pour as I respond to their strategic proposal. "I'm not interested."

You aren't even going to think about it?" Dad's aghast laughter is all too familiar; years of disappointment with me has been great practice at perfecting it.

"Ella Marie." Mom's tone is saturated with criticism and disappointment. "Don't rush into any decisions without thinking this through."

"You need to think about it, El," Nat adds. "I mean, what else are you going to do this summer? You haven't attempted to look at any other internship options."

I take a long drink of my wine and think of the option that opened up to me today. "Yes, I have actually, Natalie." My voice slurs her name a little; the sweet elixir is doing its job nicely.

Dad sits back in his chair arrogantly and folds his hands together, resting his elbows on the arms of it. "What do you plan to do this summer that could possibly give you opportunities like Jasper Bristol's?"

"I plan to go abroad and teach English."

You know the dizzy feeling you get when you have said something you know is going to lead to more chaotic bullshit? Yeah, I just did it.

The resounding "What?" from Dad, Mom, Nat, and Jilly obliterates my confidence. I take another savory drink of my wine before I state my case. "You asked if I had plans giving me opportunity. I believe this program will open doors for me."

Did I really believe it? Huh. It's funny how alcohol can bring clarity and make you say what you really feel.

I lean back in my chair and stare back at the eight eyes targeting me, confused and bewildered.

Dad's eyes bounce from Mom to me. "And this program will pay you?"

"I'm not sure."

"You aren't sure?" Mom asks, then Dad chimes in, "Did you not think to ask such an important question?"

"Ella, if this program doesn't pay, it is a waste of time and energy." Nat's superficial logic is a typical response, but it still fucking pisses me off.

"I don't think you have much to go on, Nat."

"Well, she has a point, Ella." His chuckle is patronizing. "I mean, how long have you considered this program? Did you just up and decide this weeks ago, days, hours?" His voice is getting louder as his own scenario of what I have considered to do this summer eats away at him.

"So typical!" Dad heatedly tosses his napkin onto the table.

My lips finally loosen to his rant. "Typical, disappointing Ella, right?"

"Byron," Mom warns, sensing the slow build of tension between him and me. "Jilly, help me clear the dishes, honey."

Jilly puts her napkin onto the table and pushes out her chair slowly.

"Jilly," Mom says more curtly now, moving her into motion as she collects her dish.

"It is typical for you to turn your back on something valuable, like a paid internship that could become something ... more," Dad says.

"Like a potential partnership with Logan Bristol. Playing matchmaker with the two high school sweethearts. This isn't fucking high school and I have no plans on returning to that time in my life, thanks!"

Dad pushes back from the table, shaking his head at me. "That is not what this is about, Ella."

Nat makes sure to say her peace. "Seriously, El, you are being so dramatic. After how you acted with Logan, you should be thankful Mr. Bristol is considering this internship for you."

I peer straight into her eyes. "Thankful?"

As I rise from the table, Dad starts in. "Where do you think you are going? This conversation isn't over!"

"Yes, it is!"

I place my napkin on the table just as Mom walks back into the room. "Ella, don't leave like this, please."

She shakes her head and furrows her brow as she starts collecting utensils from the table. "Volunteering abroad? A foreign country? You aren't thinking straight. Let's just sit down and talk this through, logically."

I look from Mom to Dad, then to Nat, taking turns shooting daggers at each of them. "Oh, I'm thinking straight, but just to humor you, answer one question for me. Is Logan Bristol one of the law students I will be working with at Bristol Law Group?"

Their silence is the most honest they have been all night.

"I take that as a yes." I move around Mom, and just as I get to the open doorway, Dad calls after me.

"You are still throwing your life away on ignorant decisions, Ella. After three years of struggling, trying to make your own way to prove some kind of point to us, throwing the help we offer back in our faces, and not having any direction for your life, you still do not get it! You are a Wallace, like it or not! No matter how much you fight it, eventually you are going to realize the mistake you are making! I am giving you every opportunity to save face!"

I stop in my tracks, turn on him, and snicker, "Save face?"

He retaliates immediately, "Yes, and you just throw it away, choosing to go to another country to volunteer over taking a paid internship! Okay, enlighten me! What are you going to do there? You will be working for free and live in meager surroundings at best. You will be putting your life in danger! Tell me, where will this 'philanthropic' mission take you? Where are you going since you have thought this through so thoroughly?"

I shoot back from the hip, "I have options. Chile, Morocco, Jordan."

His eyebrows rise high on his forehead as his jaw works overtime, pushing a bitter scoff from his mouth. "Jordan! Perfect, the Middle East! Do you realize what is going on over there? The fighting, the terror? Hell, our military troops are leaving, refugees fleeing the civil war and unrest and here you are blindly going over there to teach English!" His face has reddened to a ruby tone I have only seen when he has reached a level of anger nothing can stop.

Nat makes sure to include her two cents. "Terrorists, militants, poverty, war."

Her list stirs the pot already boiling over for Dad. "I doubt you are aware of any of this. You aren't aware of the most obvious gifts being handed to you right here by your own family! Tell me, Ella, what are you putting your life at risk for? What reward are you searching for by doing this? Because I can't think of a single great fucking reward!"

"Byron, please," my mom pleads for his language.

"A purpose greater than myself!" I doubt he remembers his mother speaking those words before her death.

"Goddamn it, Ella!" He hits his fist against the table, making my body jump. "Risking your life to gain some greater purpose! You don't have to take risks with Jasper's internship! It is a gift to simply take!"

"It isn't a gift. It is a give and take. I take, but what am I giving up in return?"

He looks at me wildly, like I am the most ignorant person on the planet, and shakes his head in disgust. "Please tell me you are smarter than the choice you are about to make, Ella Marie."

Standing at the doorway, holding my breath, emotions, and tears on the cusp of overflowing, I think about what the smarter choice would be and I know in my heart I'm right.

"I am. I'm not taking the fucking internship. Goodbye."

I storm through the living room, and as I pass the kitchen I see Jilly coming toward me. Her embrace is one someone would give if they were afraid of never seeing the other again. "I love you, Ella."

"Love you too, Jilly."

Nat picks up her bag and mine and opens the front door, then walks to her car talking over her shoulder. "Another glorious family dinner! Look, I have somewhere to be, so let's go!"

Following after her, I glance back at Mom standing with her arms folded across her chest and Jilly wiping tears from her eyes as I get into the car. As soon as the car door is shut, Nat pulls away from the curb without hesitation. Speeding from the house, she starts her rant.

"Unbelievable. Well, I guess this turned to shit after all. Turning down an internship to volunteer abroad? What the hell is going through your head?"

"I am not going to take a fucking internship because of Dad's and Jasper's fantasy of me marrying Logan!"

"He has your best interests in mind and so do I! I tried to redirect the conversation! Oh and by the way, I didn't appreciate your patronizing look when Dad and I were discussing my job opportunity with Bristol Holdings." Nat weaves through traffic, then enters the freeway.

"Redirect? That is fucking bullshit!"

"Mouth of a sailor," she mumbles under her breath.

"Yeah, well it must be a family trait."

Magnifying a sigh, she changes lanes. "Look, we both are pissed off right now." Her eyes shift to me. "Difference of opinion. Maybe you just need to relax a little."

I breathe out, expelling every ounce of heated anger inside. "I am relaxed."

"Yeah, sure you are. How long has it been since you let loose?"

My eyes move to hers questioningly. "You mean like go out with friends?"

She gives me an over-exaggerated eye roll. "Yes."

Nat puts on her blinker and exits the freeway.

"Wait, why are you exiting? My house, remember?"

Without answering, she slows down enough to turn onto Wisconsin Street. "Yeah, I remember. We will only stay for a little while."

"What? Stay where? What the fuck, Nat! I don't want to fucking go to your party!"

She glances between me and the restaurants, coffee shops, stores, and buildings we pass.

"We are just making a party pit stop!" She grins from ear to ear, hoping I will cave to her idea.

"Pit stop? The last thing I want to do is be at some pretentious and superficial party with a bunch of fucking unappreciative rich kids!"

Her smile fades as she turns stiff. She turns down a side street, then onto another. "You can either sit in the car, or you can be polite and come in for a quick drink. I need to show my face before driving you all the way home to your fucking shanty town."

She pulls the car into an open spot along the curb, leans across the center console, and looks out my window past me. "This should be it."

I don't bother following her gaze as I fold my arms over my chest. I am not fucking getting out of this car.

She digs through her purse, turns on the interior car light, and starts applying lipstick in the rearview mirror. Pouting her lips, she smiles, closes the lipstick, and tosses it in her purse. With her hand on the door, she gives me another onceover, making sure to avoid my stare as she asks, "Are you fucking coming or not?"

"No."

Her keys jiggle as she turns off the interior lights. "Fine, sit in the cold car."

"Fine!" I shoot back, not letting her have the satisfaction of the last word before she tosses the keys onto my lap and shuts the doors. Crossing in front of the car, she walks toward the lit entrance of an apartment building. Looking out my window now, I see how massive it is. She is about to open the glass entrance doors when a suited man opens it for her instead.

A doorman? I have been to a few college parties, but definitely not to onc in a hoity toity luxury apartment building equipped with a fucking doorman. Even though I want nothing to do with this shit right now, I can't help being curious about what my sister is walking into.

"Shit."

Getting out of the car, I tap the alarm and put the keys in my jacket pocket as I follow after her. The doorman sees me coming and opens the door, not without giving me a onceover. In comparison to my sister's dress and heels, I am underdressed in jeans, sweater, and peacoat.

"Nat, wait!" I step into the elevator just as it's closing.

She looks at me sideways and grins. "Sitting your ass in a cold car doesn't appeal to you?"

"A doorman? Really? What kind of party is this?"

She is texting on her smartphone, smiling as she gets a ping back. "Not sure, a friend of a friend invited me. This place is pretty amazing though, right?"

Would it be wrong to say when my sister gets this excited, it is either because she plans to befriend or sleep with the person in question?

"So you are crashing the party?"

She furrows her brow at me, then goes back to texting. "No, it doesn't work that way, El. God, I swear it is like you have lived under a fucking rock since writing off being a socialite."

I lean back against the elevator as it rises.

"Sorry, I shouldn't have said that," she says dolefully, but it lacks luster as she continues texting.

The elevator doors open and Nat puts her phone into her purse as she steps out into the hallway. Exiting after her, I hear the low, pumping bass of a party reverberating off the walls. There are only five doors total on this floor. With all the bells and whistles and a doorman, these are probably suites. Nat is not far ahead of me as she looks at the suite numbers, passing one door after another until she comes to the one at the end of the hall. "It must be this one."

What kind of college kid would live in a place like this? Has to be Mommy and Daddy's place, borrowed for the evening. Nat looks down at her phone, texting as she stands in front of the door as I slowly approach. Suddenly the door opens, releasing the sound of the music and party into the hallway as a drawn-out, annoying "Hi" spews from her long-time friend, Serena Atwood. Her shrilling vocals are almost as annoying as fingernails scratching a chalkboard.

Nat and Serena hug and rock back and forth together as my sister mimics the annoying "hi."

"This is like the best party ever," Serena says, releasing Nat and looking me over. "Ella? Is that you?"

"Hi, Serena." I haven't seen her since high school. Serena glances at Nat, then back at me, scanning my attire. "I didn't recognize you."

Nat takes her hand, leaving Serena to take mine and pull me into the apartment.

Thinking Serena knows more about this party than my sister, I ask, "Hey, whose party is this?"

Serena releases my hand as Nat stops pulling us along. "It is some Sheikh or prince's party."

"What?" I don't think I heard her right. "A prince? What would a fucking prince be doing here at GU?"

Nat hands Serena a green glowing drink, then she passes it to me, giggling, "Many royals have passed through the doors of Georgetown, Ella. He is some Lawrence of Arabia or something."

I take a sip of the green liquid and feel the heat instantly as it slides down my throat, taking my breath away. Clearing my throat, I spot someone I wasn't expecting to see: Logan Bristol.

I turn away to avoid him just as Nat catches him in her sights. "There you are!"

Shit, she knew he would be here. What a bitch.

"I'm going to find somewhere to sit." I start to walk away, when she pulls me back to her side and talks through her toothy grin. "Don't be rude."

I look at him and, God help me, he still is gorgeous, maybe even more chiseled than he was in high school.

"Hey, gorgeous," he says as he keeps his eyes on me while hugging Nat. She eagerly obliges, hugging him back, a little too eagerly in my opinion.

As a new song begins, Serena and the people around us start bouncing around as a guy comes up behind her and sweeps her into the crowd, dancing and laughing.

"Hey, Ellie." Logan's deep baritone voice is just as I remembered as he calls me by the nickname he coined when we were eight years old. His voice is smooth and disarming enough to make me lighten up.

"Hey."

With one arm draped over his shoulder, Nat's eyes widen as she tilts her head toward Logan. Shit, what the hell does she want me to do? Jump him?

She nudges him. "How long has it been since you two have spoken? All you have to say to each other is hey?"

I had seen him on campus a handful of times over the three years I've been GU, but it is a big fucking campus and it isn't like the law school is on my radar for frequented places. Logan has kept up with Natalie obviously.

He looks at Nat then smiles at me. "Too long, right, Ellie?"

Without warning he puts his arms around my waist and lifts me up like he used. Nearly spilling my drink down his back, I have the sense to hold it away from us until he brings me back down to earth. I would be lying if I said I didn't feel my stomach tense like it used to. You know, the type of angsty, sex-starved tension you get when a guy touches you a certain way. And yes, I was sex starved. It had been months since I had a meaningless one-night stand.

Logan isn't quick to let go as he focuses on me, but I manage to slip out of his hold. "Uh, yeah. It has," I say as I shift on my feet nervously, my eyes moving everywhere but at him. I force another gulp of the sour green stuff in my cup, letting the burn it provides numb the coiling tension his heavy stare is producing. Damn him for being so good-looking.

His smile is more than casual as he continues to stare at me. "Wow, you look just as beautiful."

I nod and bob my head, pretending to ignore him and enjoy the thumping bass of the music. "Thanks."

"So, I guess you heard about the internship," Logan says smoothly as he puts his own cup to his lips.

Talk about putting a fucking damper on things. Of course he wants to talk about it! Dad, Jasper, Nat Logan, all of them are in on it; it's a conspiracy.

"Uh, maybe we should talk about this later, Logan," Nat suggests, nervously glancing back at me.

He takes in what she is saying, then tries to save face in typical Logan fucking Bristol fashion. "Oh, yeah, sure. Maybe over dinner this week. Sound good, Ellie?"

Avoiding his question and his hard stare, I slowly drain the liquid from my cup. It burns all the way down, aching at the pit of my stomach. Scenarios of my sister, Dad, Jasper, and Logan Bristol meeting to devise this plan to put me in arm's reach of Logan again run rampant in my head, as my sister interlaces her arm with Logan's. I wouldn't put it passed Natalie to make a play on Logan, knowing how disinterested I am in him and the internship now. Yeah, it's cold and callous, but so is Nat.

"I'm not taking the internship. I have other plans this summer."

Logan gives me a glare I remember all too well. The type of glare one gives when they don't get what they want. The kind of look Logan would give me when I would turn down sex with him. The kind of look a kid would have if he had his candy stolen from him.

I blurt out senselessly, "I'm not candy."

He steps to me, coming so close I can smell the whiskey on his breath. "Excuse me? Candy?" His condescending tone is something I hated back in high school and I hate it even more now.

Still having her arm draped in his, Nat leans in close to him as she looks at me. "Logan, leave it alone. This isn't the time or place."

"I want to leave, Nat. Now!"

As I walk away, she calls to me, "Wait, just give me a minute!"

I look back long enough to glare at her. "Fine."

Their argument is voluminous, but is quickly enveloped in the rhythmic music as I flop down on the cushion of a nearby sofa. I run my hand over the soft material. Velvet? Almost immediately the seat cushion next to me shifts, followed by the annoying, sing-song "Hi" only Serena can achieve.

"Ooooh, is this velvet?" she asks, touching the cushions beneath her ass, and laughs. "Of course it is. He is the fucking prince of Persia."

I put my elbow on the arm of the sofa and rest my temple on my hand, watching her pet the fabric next to her. Laughing at her antics would be nice if I wasn't so pissed right now. She does manage to get my mind off of Logan and Nat as I screw with her. "I thought you said he was Lawrence of Arabia?"

She giggles, "Arabia, Persia, whatever. He's a fucking prince!"

I survey the room searching for Nat and Logan, but I have lost them now.

"Have you seen him?" she asks as I continue to my search for them.

"Who?"

"The prince, crazy!" She elbows me, then snorts.

I shake my head and roll my eyes. "No, you?"

Why am I even entertaining this stupid conversation? I want to leave and my sister and ex have disappeared. Together.

She continues talking and I halfway listen to her until she says, "He is here somewhere. His brother just flew in like yesterday with a bunch of bodyguards. Correction, hot body guards and hot brother. How do you think he knows all these people?"

The music suddenly shifts to something more chill, and as I inspect the room, I notice the mix of people around me: college girls in high-end cocktail dress, most definitely bought on Mommy and Daddy's Amex, reaching to the ceiling with their drinks held high, no care in the world. She said the prince was Persian or Arabian. I notice the cultural mix in the room; some white, mostly Middle Eastern. All elite, of course.

"He probably doesn't."

I feel her look at me. "What?"

"Status," I huff the words out through bated breath. "High society. It isn't who you know, it is who you are seen with. Who people think you know."

Serena sits back with me now more casually. I notice her scanning the crowd like I was moments before. Her voice changes, becoming less uppity and careless. "Yeah, you are probably right. Status means everything to everyone."

She doesn't appear happy with the statement she has just made.

"Does it bother you?" I ask.

Shrugging, she continues to watch the crowd. "It is what it is. If you want to be something in this life, status has a lot to do with it. Like it or not."

Even though I have always considered Serena to be some airy elitist twit, she has given me a glimpse of what she really thinks and I feel sad for her all of a sudden. I was her once.

"It doesn't have to be. Don't you want to have a purpose deeper than this?"

She doesn't say or do anything to signal she is listening. Like a polar shift, she rolls her eyes and smiles as she rises from the sofa, turning to me quickly. "Not tonight!" Airy elitist twit Serena has resurfaced, hiding what she really thinks. She tugs on my hands, trying to get me off the couch. "Not tonight. Tonight is for dancing!"

Feeling the contents of my stomach lurch as she pulls me halfway off the couch, I fall back and shake my head. "I don't think it's a good idea."

Her smile fails a little.

My stomach would hate me. Plus, I'm waiting for Nat. "I need to get home."

Her smile lessens even more and she puts on this pouty face suited for the fake Serena. "Party pooper."

She slowly releases my hands, holding my gaze for only a moment more before she turns and bounces off onto the dance floor disappearing into the moving bodies.

Would my fate have been much like hers if I had never pulled back from this shit? Would I be one of these girls in the sea of over-indulgence, dancing without a care in the world?

I don't want to be here anymore. I start searching between the gaps of swaying people for Nat when I'm drawn to the sofa on the other side of the loft. This guy is loosening his tie, pulling it from his neck and tossing it to the other side of the sofa. I can tell he is as done with this party as I am. Everything about him has me curious as to why this attractive guy would not be having a good time. Everything about him also has me entranced—the black suit with the loosened white-collared shirt beneath, exposing just enough of his exotic, tanned chest. The way his long, muscular arms stretch along the back of the sofa as he casually sits back and surveys the room.

I haven't come into his sights yet, so I greedily stare for as long as I can before he looks my way. His dark, thick hair hangs over his brow in the front, while it's nice and tight on the sides and back. He isn't trendy, but classic. My eyes blur and I blink a few times, wondering if he is just a hallucination from the alcohol. Nope, I am buzzed but he is still there, perfectly stationed on the sofa, giving me an eyeful of his beauty as he scans the crowd. Who is he looking for?

As I watch him, I rest my elbow on the arm of the sofa, propping up my heavy head. The contrast of his bronze chest against his stark-white shirt holds my attention far too long. I make my way up, following the angle of his strong jaw, his full lips; they beg for the most attention, rightfully so. It isn't until I meet his penetrating gaze, I realize I have been caught.

I divert my eyes and pretend to rub the back of my neck with the hand propping up my buzzing head.

He isn't staring at you, Ella. You aren't much to look at, especially in jeans and an over-sized sweater. He has probably moved on. It was just a passing glimpse.

This is definitely my intoxicated head giving me reason to look at him once more. As I do, I am captured, held in place, by his intense stare. A deer in fucking headlights, unable to pull from this invisible hold he has over me, unable to breath, unable to comprehend why I would ever want to leave his gaze. Suddenly, he shifts his body forward, removing his arms from the back of the sofa and bearing deeper into me. His stretched arm leaves the back of the sofa to come to rest on his thighs as he pulls me deeper into this gloriously tantalizing trap. A trap I want to remain in for as long as possible.

Suddenly, I'm cheated, let go from this sweet capture by a black suit stepping in between us, dissolving this invisible tryst.

It is ridiculous to think anything just happened between this guy and me from a simple look across the room. It is more likely the amount of wine at dinner and the conspicuous sour green concoction I downed are hallucinations of an obscure seduction.

Results of too much alcohol and not enough sex.

I sit up straight and try to think soberly. I need to find Nat and get out of here. Rising from the sofa intent on seeking her out, I find myself wanting to go back to those mesmerizing eyes.

The suited interrupter has shifted over, revealing this extraordinary man, but only for a second as he follows the other suit, bringing any substance of a mystic rendezvous to a halt.

With my head swimming now, I lose him, the ensnaring, warm, comfort of his gold-flecked, brown eyes. Through the crowd, Serena resurfaces, bouncing back toward me, her eyes as wide as saucers. "Did you see them?"

"Nat and Logan?" my mind now refocused on getting out of here.

"Duh, the princes!" she exclaims, somewhat annoyed by my disinterest. After the night I'm having, a narcissistic prince high on himself, throwing some luxury end-of-semester party, is not my thing. There is only room for so much arrogance in this fucking room. Speaking of arrogance, I'm about to give up the search for Nat and just leave when I spot her in a corner on the other side of the loft. Her brows are furrowed in frustration as she argues with someone hidden behind a column. Just as I leave Serena's side to get Nat's attention, a hand darts out from behind the column, taking her arm.

Truth be told, I hate my sister right now, but if someone is starting shit with her I am going to protect her. I'm only a short distance from her now and about to call for her when the owner of the hand comes into view, heated and intense.

Logan?

Their dueling frustration is obvious in his hardened jaw and narrowed eyes as he pulls her flush against him. Caught in the moment with them, I'm unable to take another step as I watch the exchange unfold; the seductive stare, the deep breathes, the desire, the lust. Slowly Logan moves in and kisses her. Wrapped in the disbelief of what I am seeing, I stand there, staring at them as the kiss turns ravenous.

I was right; she made a play for him. The air around me is too thick to breath. If I don't get out of here I am going to pass out. Turning to escape a little too quickly, I stumble. Serena takes hold of my shoulders before I crash to the ground. "Whoa, Ella, are you all right? Here, let me get Nat."

I shake my head, making the room spin. "I have to go."

I try to move past her, but she tugs on my arm, keeping me from escaping. "Wait, she's right there. Let me get her."

Of all the reactions I could have right now, tears are the ones to surface. I half-heartedly laugh. "Don't bother. She's busy closing a deal."

People like Serena can be easily confused and my words have done the trick as I pull free of her hand and rush for the front door.

I pull my coat tightly around me, buttoning it quickly as I step out of the building and see my sister's parked car. I don't give a shit about the stuff I left in it. I just need to go home.

Poor Serena; she had no clue what I meant by Nat closing a deal. As I walk on, I glance behind, checking to make sure Nat or Logan aren't following. If I see either of them, I don't know what I will do. In all honesty, I don't give a shit about Logan. But Natalie, looking out for herself, my own blood doing that sneaky shit to me? It can really fuck with the faith you have in the world when your family turns against you.

As the leftover winter wind presses against me and no way of getting home other than the bus, I walk to the nearest stop for the long ride home.

Chapter 2

Rajaa

As my brother follows close behind, I'm still distracted by that girl sitting on the lounger across from me. Something about her made her more interesting than anyone else in the room. More interesting than anything about this fucking party my brother insisted we throw before ending the semester. Something about her made scanning the room less intriguing than what was going on behind her eyes, a sea of blue green I could get lost in. While I have spent time with plenty of blue-eyed, green-eyed, and brown-eyed women both here and back home in Jordan, the way this girl seemed lost among the backdrop of the guests attracted me.

"What is it about?" I ask my brother in Arabic as he walks ahead of me. With my father's health, receiving a call from him this late is worrisome.

Zaid runs his hand over his rough unshaven chin, then shrugs as his eye is caught by the American woman exiting the restroom to the right. As she walks in the opposite direction of us, Zaid half turns and follows her with his eyes. I'm not blind; I like looking at tight asses, but not when I have a waiting call from my father in Jordan. His lack of concern himself is frustrating. "Zaid."

He glances at me, then back at the woman. "I don't know. He said it was important. I told him I would get you."

Zaid motions to one of the guards and lowers his voice. "Get her for me."

He glances back at me as he slows his backward walk. "I will be there in a moment. I need to tend to a guest." His wry smile gives his motive away.

I watch him follow after the guard already stopping the girl for him. Zaid slides his hand down her back as he speaks to her. Discretion is not his strong suit. My brother is many things: commander of the Jordanian Armed Forces, well educated at the best schools and university in Amman, a persistent socialite, and owner of a perpetual sexual appetite and fiery and daring temper are a few. Zaid is ten years older than my twenty-three.

Two of the five bodyguards my brother brought with him when he arrived yesterday are sitting in my room when I enter. While it is necessary for us to have security at home in Jordan with the climate of crisis at our borders, it is not necessary here and I think my brother insisted upon it more for the show of pageantry rather than safety.

The men rise and one of them hands the phone to me. Taking it, I dismiss them and bring the phone to my ear. "Baba, As-Salamu alaykum."

"Wa-Alaykum as-salaam Rajaa," my father responds shakily.

Knowing my father's comfort with English, I speak freely, concerned for the early-morning call. "Are you all right?"

"Everything is fine," he says, clearing this throat.

"Mama? Is she safe?"

With the way Islamic state fighters have brought terror to those advocating for the refugees and women in the Middle East, it supports my concern.

"Fine. Everything is fine, Rajaa. Don't worry so much. It shows weakness."

He knows it's something I can't help when it comes to family.

"I spoke with Zaid again about your decision to be benefactor for the center in central Amman, Makan Lil Amal."

Of course he brought up the center with my father again.

I know how he feels about my decision to support the center, but calling to discuss at this hour, I could only think my brother rekindled concern in his mind. Zaid does not approve of the proposal for the program, or any involvement for that matter. He calls it a foolish attempt to save Amman by giving asylum to those with no loyalty.

"They don't register with us, do not follow our beliefs, yet you want to feed them, clothe them, give them money, and take from our own people? We need to feed our own people's mouths and fight back against these terrorizing pissant militants," Zaid says.

While I would expect my brother to successfully lead attack with the power of the Jordanian Armed Forces, I fear he is underestimating what would result from it. I see more benefit helping stabilize the refugees we have brought into our country, changing the climate of Jordan from within. I know programs like the one I have proposed will bring sustainability rather than a temporary adjustment building a crisis on top of a crisis.

I can't blame on Zaid for his narrow views. He is my half-brother, and while our father and mother tried to rear him toward a more progressive Islamic way of living, her majesty Yaasmeen al Hashemite, the first Queen, held a more doctrinal view of ruling and living within Islam and instilled it in Zaid at a very young age. He idolized his mother, as any son might, and when she passed, it broke him, from what my mother and father have explained. He was only nine years old when she died from complications due to pneumonia. A few short months after her passing, my father and mother fell deeply in love and within a year married, crowning her the new Queen of Jordan.

My father was fifteen years older than her, she of a new generation of Islam. A queen that would be known for her progressive views of human rights, women's rights, a Jordanian valuing education for all women, giving aid to the impoverished, and safety to those seeking refuge. She believed we could be a faithful Muslim family in a new age of the Middle East, and while her vision was one my father, sister, and I embraced willingly, my brother rebuked the ideals, maintaining the old ways of Islam and the Middle East were the righteous ways.

I had finally gotten through to my father, with my mother's persuasion, to become the silent benefactor for the Makan Lil Amal center, established years ago through Caritas. I envisioned the program two years ago at a lecture on foreign humanitarian aid and diplomacy hosted by Mr. Tom Stern, director of WorldTeach Washington D.C. branch here at Georgetown University. While it was expected to encounter such a topic in my major, Bachelor of Science in Foreign Service - Culture and Politics, I didn't anticipate the passion it stirred in me, to find a way to fund his program and partner with Caritas, a non-profit humanitarian relief organization in central Amman.

In recent months, Jordan's funds and ability to support the copious amounts of unregistered Syrian refugees have dwindled to nearly nothing. They have been unable to offer many services through the Makan Lil Amal center. In speaking with Mr. Stern, I knew his passion for the cause was just as strong as mine, and when I proposed it to my father, the King, he immediately refused. My mother had her hands in many humanitarian programs, and while my father was already concerned for her safety, he didn't want to have me in danger as well. Shortly after my first proposal to the King, the Queen's safety was compromised, putting a stop to all humanitarian relief funded by my family. A bounty had been placed on her head. Zaid fed my father's fear for his Queen's and family's safety, making any compromise impossible, just like the one he was trying to put to a stop right now.

It wasn't until six months ago when I visited home and asked him late one night to reconsider my being a silent benefactor for WorldTeach and Caritas when he agreed to my proposal. He made sure I knew he was only agreeing because of my being a silent contributor.

"You are truly passionate about this cause. Almost two years you have been after this."

"Yes, I am."

"Your mother, she says while you have the heart for the people, you have the focus and training of a steadfast leader. My little flower is rarely wrong, but many in our country do not feel the same as we do. It is hard for me to say, but your brother is one of them. Day by day I see the old views of your grandfather, his mother rising within him. The near attack on your mother was a sign we must be vigilant about our influence, our presence. I can't have you at risk, Rajaa."

Remembering his words, I respond, "You know where I stand on this, Baba. While my heart is for the people, my focus is steadfast and safety is key. I have already talked with Mr. Stern about my anonymity and the funds have been transferred. With my returning home after the semester, I can remain watchful over the program—"

My father interrupts, "But removed! See, this is why I am unsettled. You say you want to remain watchful over the program, but how is it possible without physically being there?"

"Baba, it isn't completely possible. If something happens at the center, I need to be present. The staff and volunteer there are serving on our behalf; they need protection."

"And then again our family is at risk for attack! You are at risk!" I hear my mother's passive voice in the background trying to calm him as he loses his temper again. He starts to cough, then clears his throat.

I breathe in deeply. "Look, Baba, I have been trained to protect myself. I have gone on four military missions with you and Zaid as a First Lieutenant. If I am trusted to defend the King, then I will be more than capable of protecting myself at the center with guards present."

He could not argue my ability to defend myself and those around me. From an early age, he made sure my brother and I could defend ourselves because of our status. At one point, Zaid continued the pursuit of military defense, while I turned to learning about the diplomatic influence and the power it held.

Zaid walks in and I want to throw the phone at him for starting this cyclical discussion with my father. Zaid shrugs, feeling the brunt of my glare, mouthing the word, "What?"

Forcibly holding back my frustration with Zaid, I add to my conversation with my father, "Maybe my brother will accompany me to the center."

Zaid's gaping mouth shuts tightly, realizing what I might have just assigned him to.

"He is a decorated commander of the Jordanian Armed Forces with countless tours," I boast, then smile cleverly at Zaid.

He rolls his eyes and leans back against my headboard, crossing his legs and grinning ear to ear, not denying my praises with any modesty.

"Only if you need to become more involved with the center," my father clarifies.

"Only if I need to be involved," I repeat. "Sometimes risks need to be taken to gain the security we need for our country, Baba."

My father breathes out deeply into the phone receiver. "With your knowledge, your heart, your passion for our people, I sometimes wonder what kind of king you could have been, Rajaa."

By all rights, the firstborn son will always be heir; that is how it has been under the house of Hashemite and how it will continue to be. My father's comment is a whim, but it's troubling that he could consider me over Zaid for any reason. "Zaid will be a strong leader."

I wait a moment for him to agree, but it doesn't come. I ignore the uncomfortable silence and my brother's glare from hearing his name being associated with his ability to lead. As he lays on my bed, watching me, I end the call. "I will see you soon, Baba. Maasalama."

"Maasalama," he says before I hang up.

"What was that about? Why did you mention me being a strong leader?" Zaid's curiosity and defensive nature are immediate as he crosses his hands behind his head.

Feeling trapped by his question and stabbing eyes, I challenge him by changing the subject. "No, let's talk about why he called. Why is Makan Lil Amal center in question again?"

Zaid shifts off the bed and walks toward me with his hands in his pockets. "I am worried you will put yourself at risk the moment we land in Jordan, Rajaa."

"My intention is to help our people and you know how I plan to do it."

I turn away from him and glare out the frameless windows lining my bedroom, overlooking the city. "The funding has already been transferred, the deal is done. Since you are concerned, it would make sense for you to visit the center with me."

I look back at him and repeat the declaration to feed his ego and hopefully end this discussion. "I would never put the future King of Jordan at risk. That is how strongly I feel about this, Zaid."

My brother folds his arms over his chest and rocks back on his heels as he grins. "Yes, I know how strongly you feel, but feelings are transient and a weakness."

My grandfather's and father's view of weakness shine through in him and is meant to diminish my resolve. Not going to fucking happen. "Mine are not transient."

Unifying Muslims and Syrian Christians in the inner city of Amman and making a path for the new Middle East to rise once this maddening civil unrest ends in Syria is what I see.

He raises his finger with exception. "You will only become involved when it is necessary, just as our King has said," he warns.

"Agreed."

Chapter 3
Ella

"Hi, Ella. It is nice to see you again."

"Yeah, nice to see you too," I say to Tom.

I follow Tom Stern, the local director for WorldTeach, into his office.

"I have to tell you. I was kind of surprised by your call this morning," he says, setting his keys down on his desk.

After a sobering two-hour bus ride home and no sleep last night, I decided I didn't want to wait to change the path my life was taking. "Yes, well, I have had plenty of time to think about this since meeting you. I'm sorry for bringing you into work on a Saturday."

He sits down at his desk and opens his laptop. "No, don't worry about it. I was planning on coming up today. We just received a generous amount of funding from our benefactor, so I had to work on the accounting."

He leans back in his chair and folds his hands in his lap. "So, you are wanting to move forward with applying for a summer placement."

"Yes."

"Have you considered which placement you would like to apply for?" he asks.

I really hadn't thought about it. "Where would I be the most useful?"

He smiles, then leans and taps on the keyboard of his laptop as he browses the screen. "Well, we have a few summer placements available in Chile, but we have a large amount of placements open in Amman, Jordan."

The one place my father openly admonished.

His eyes move from the screen to me. "I don't want to persuade you one way or another, but it just so happens funds were granted by our benefactor specifically for volunteers of this program. We are partnered with Caritas, which is a humanitarian organization..."

Before he can continue, I interrupt him. "Funding for the volunteers?"

"Yes, the placements through WorldTeach have a commitment fee. Summer placement fees hover around $2,500.00 and that is to cover the visa sponsoring, literature on preparing for the placement and arrival, orientation, teacher training, cultural and language immersion, as well as needed safety and security."

"Oh." I didn't realize I was going to have to pay for the placement. I can't afford to pay a placement cost.

Tom explains, "Chile will have a placement fee, but Amman will be covered with the granted money. Again, I don't want to pressure you in any way. It's your choicc."

There really is no other choice. If I'm going to do this, I need to take Jordan.

"Yes, it does help with my decision. I would like to apply for the program in Amman."

"Are you sure?" he asks somewhat warily, which makes me put up my defenses.

"Why wouldn't I be sure?"

He sits back in his chair again. "Amman, Jordan is an extreme culture shock for many volunteers. I just figured you might want a placement not so ... contradistinctive to our society."

"You couldn't be more wrong about me, Mr. Stern. You don't know my story and I would appreciate it if you would let me decide what I can handle."

I have stumped him, maybe even shocked him by my response. "I'm sorry. I didn't mean to offend you."

With all the events transpired over the last twenty-four hours, I can wholeheartedly say deciding to volunteer abroad is the one event in my life bearing a silver lining to the darkened clouds in my life. Maybe a complete culture shock is exactly what I need.

Not wanting to dwell on the awkward moment, I move on. "It's all right. I'm sorry if I came off rudely. I'm just solid in my decision and want to do this. What's next?"

The actual application was lengthy and some of the questions I couldn't answer since things like my immunization records were at the apartment. Once I was done I handed the application back to him. Ready to leave, I put my purse on my shoulder. "Thank you again for meeting me so soon after speaking. I will wait to hear from you."

"Wait, where are you going?" he asks, holding my application in his hands.

Confused, I answer him, "Don't you have to go over the application, then get back to me in like a couple of weeks?"

He smiles. "Yeah, but there is no point in handling this later with you sitting in my office right now. You are here on a Saturday before ten in the morning. No college student would get up before noon and drive to a recruiting office unless they wanted to speed up the process."

I set my backpack down on the ground next to the chair. "I didn't drive. I took the bus."

He reads through my application, pausing to make tick marks at certain spots. He looks up at me, noticing I'm still standing. "Please have a seat, Ms. Wallace."

I sit patiently as he reads through my application. When he finishes, he flips back to the first page. "Do you have your immunization records up to date?"

"Yes, I left them at home, but I can get them to you."

"Clean bill of health? Regular doctor's' visits?"

"Yes."

"Is it through the University?" he asks as he readies to write.

"Yes."

"Then I can get it directly from them." He pulls out a form from his desk drawer and hands it to me. "Just give me authorization to access the records."

I sign off on the sheet after adding my school and student ID.

He continues, "I think I told you this yesterday. With you being an English major, it will be a great benefit for this placement in particular. However, you will be teaching students English, which is somewhat different. Do you feel you can handle this?"

How hard can it be? "Yes."

He nods and reads on. "You put Allison Brown as your emergency contact. What is her relation?"

"She is a friend."

He glances up from the paper. "We usually like to list the first of kin, like a parent if they are living. Are they living?"

"Yes."

Fuck, I really didn't want to put Mom or Dad down.

He clicks his pen to life on the desk, then readies himself to write. "Okay, which parent will you put down?"

I sit there for a moment, thinking about my father getting a call in the middle of the night explaining there has been an emergency with his daughter in Amman, Jordan. If I survived the emergency he would do everything in his power to remind me how he warned me about doing this. My mother would break down emotionally, but it would quickly turn to frustration for always choosing the hard road for myself.

"Ella?"

Tom is staring at me, waiting for my response.

"Oh, sorry."

Seeing my visible concern, Tom tries to calm me. "Ella, let me reassure you, emergencies are rare since we have an extensive in-country field staff to assist with security and safety for the volunteers. In my ten-year experience of being abroad with WorldTeach, I have never experienced a dire emergency."

His confidence that contacting my parents will be only circumstantial eases my concern. "My father, Byron Wallace."

His eyebrows arch upon hearing his name. "Byron Wallace, the congressman?"

I nod as he stares at me with surprise. I can almost see the questions stirring behind his eyes.

"That is interesting," he says as he writes my father's name. Many times I have heard people consider it "cool" or "amazing" that my father is Byron Wallace, then ramble off questions about how it fucking makes me feel to have a political figure as my father, but Mr. Stern's response of "interesting" is a first.

"Does he know about you going abroad?" Mr. Stern asks directly.

"Why?"

He stops writing and looks up at me. "It is just most students going abroad tell their parents, so they can share in the experience. I would suspect being that your father is involved politically he would have some opinions on your traveling."

Yes, he definitely has opinions.

I answer cut and dry, "They know and if they have an opinion it doesn't make a difference to me."

Unsure of my readied answer, Tom returns to my application but remains watchful as he reads on. Shit, what if he attempts to call Dad to make sure he knows about this? It will only cause problems and if he screws up my chances of being selected I swear I will go ape shit. "Are you going to call them? I mean you don't need his permission or anything. I am pretty much supporting myself so he really has no say in anything I do."

He clears his throat and goes back to my application. "No, there is no need to contact them unless it is necessary. It says here that you are on financial aid and you just said you support yourself."

"Yes."

He writes a note to the side. "Your parents don't pay for your education?"

"They wanted to, but I declined."

Once again, I have gotten Tom's attention as he places his hands down on the desk. "You declined?"

Barring the long story, I explain quickly. "Yes. We don't agree on what I want in life."

He gives me a stiff grin, then goes back to the application, flipping page after page onto his desk until he gets to the last one. "Okay. Looks good. Do you have any questions for me?"

"This decision to do this is on me and I want it to stay that way. Can we just put aside that my father is a political figure and stick with the reason I am doing this? No one needs to know who I am or who my family is. I'm just another volunteer. Okay?"

Tom folds his hands over my application, his expression tender. "Your application is confidential and only seen by Caritas and upper-level staff. I have not stated anywhere on the application your father's political influence and I don't anticipate saying anything more about your family's history beyond this room. Now, one more thing. You said your decision is on you. Tell me, why did you decide to do this, Ella?"

Too many reasons to list, but one stands above all the others. "To find a purpose, something greater than just me."

Mr. Stern smiles, seeming content with my reason, unlike my father's reaction.

"When will I know if I have been accepted?"

Tom puckers his lips as he looks at his laptop, scrolling down the screen with this mouse. "The deadline on this placement is this Friday, but with all of the openings still available I don't see why you wouldn't be accepted. I can give you a confirmation call on Monday to make it official though."

I want to make sure I am hearing him right and not reading into anything. "So, the possibility that I am going is high."

Trying to relieve my anxious curiosity, he smiles widely and says, "If I could stamp approved on the form now, I would, but for the sake of rules, I need to wait to welcome you into the program until Monday. We depart for Amman three weeks from today."

"We?"

Was he going with us?

"Yes, I'm going to help staff this placement. We need all the hands we can get over there."

He rises from his chair and I follow. "Thank you again for allowing me to apply today, Mr. Stern."

He nods and we shake hands. "No thanks necessary. Thank you for wanting to be a part of the program. And please call me Tom."

"Okay, thanks."

Walking down the hall to the elevator, I open my bag to put the copy of my application and the book Tom has given me on traveling abroad with WorldTeach. As I hear the doors open, I misplace the book in the bag and it falls to the ground.

"Shit," I hiss, grabbing it quickly, then rise, walking right into a foreign-voiced man talking on his cell phone. His broad chest sends me backward, but before falling, he catches me, pulling me to my feet.

"Whoa," his voice drops, and I feel like such a fucking idiot. I push the book into my bag and escape onto the elevator. Just as I turn to face the closing doors, he picks up his phone and looks up at me. The familiarity of his light-brown eyes and gold flecks against bronze skin to the guy last night is uncanny. As he tilts his head with recognition, I reach for the button to delay the closure, but the space between us is already sealing.

Descending, I consider riding back up for a half second, then decide how idiotic it would be, like I'm some creepy stalker or some shit like that. Plus, I could have totally been imagining the gold flecks in his eyes. Three hours of sleep and a hangover can do that shit to you.

Opening the door to the apartment, I see Allison standing in the middle of the living room with her arms crossed, hair sticking out in all directions and still in her pajamas. "Where were you?"

I haven't seen her since yesterday afternoon and last night I didn't bother to wake her to tell her what happened. I walk toward her and start to speak when I see a figure in the corner chair; Jilly. "Hi, El."

"Jilly? What the hell are you doing here?" As I move to her quickly, thoughts of her running away from home and coming here race through my head.

I pull her too me and hug her tight. "Are you okay?"

"Yeah, I just needed to make sure you were okay and return your stuff," she says softly.

Allison walks to the kitchen as Jilly pulls away and points to my backpack next to the chair. "Nat came by this morning."

Of course she did. Rather than coming to drop it off here, she wanted to stir more trouble to get back at me by running to my parents.

"She told Mom and Dad you left her at the party, just ran off," Jilly says. I'm worried she believes the lie.

Allison speaks up from the kitchen, "You went to a party last night?"

I roll my eyes and keep my focus on Jilly. "Do you believe I would just run off?"

She shakes her head. "No, I don't. I was just so worried. I know Mom and Dad would never bring your backpack. They would expect you to come and get it yourself, and with the way things went last night at dinner, I don't think you will ever come home again."

Jilly starts to sob and I pull her to me. "Jilly."

Her sobs taper and she pulls back from me. "You are still going to go abroad, aren't you? You haven't changed your mind?"

I glance over Jilly's shoulder at Allison, who is standing in the kitchen blowing on her steaming cup of coffee. I hadn't told her yet, which will be a whole other lengthy conversation I'm sure.

I know Jilly desperately wants me to change my mind, but I can't. I won't. "I need to, Jilly. Too many arrows are pointing me in this direction."

"You mean forcing you," she says as she wipes her nose on the sleeve of her oversized sweatshirt. Her understanding of my circumstance makes me realize how grown up Jilly is becoming.

I shake my head, surprised by her being here. "How did you get here?"

"My friend brought me. I told Mom and Dad I was going to breakfast and the mall with her. She is going to pick me up out front in ten minutes."

I'm sick she had to lie to come see me, her own sister, but I'm glad she did at the same time. "This isn't the safest of neighborhoods, Jilly."

"It is safe enough for you and Allison," she says between sniffling.

I don't want to fight with her, especially with only ten minutes to spare before she has to leave. I notice Allison leave the kitchen and walk into the hallway back to her bedroom, giving us privacy.

I move away from her and sit on the futon. "Jilly, remember how free spirited Grandma Wallace was? How she felt she needed to have purpose?"

Jilly comes to sit down next to me. "Yeah."

"She took risks to find purpose in her life and I don't want to live my life without meaning. Right now, I feel like it doesn't have any."

"What are you saying, El?"

"What I am saying is I need to find myself."

She nods and looks down at her folded hands. I place mine on top of hers and squeeze them tightly. "How will I talk to you while you are gone?"

"It will just be the summer, Jilly, and then I will be back."

"Can I write letters. Do they have email?"

I remember reading something in the application about email being accessible to volunteers and use it to cheer her up. "Yes, we can email back and forth."

The crease in her forehead softens now, knowing we can still communicate while I am away.

"It will be like a pen-pal thing."

I smile widely in an attempt to raise her spirits.

She laughs again, then shakes her head. "I'm going to miss you, El."

I swallow the lump forming in my throat. "Me too."

Three weeks later...

My bedroom looks like a fucking bomb made of clothing has been detonated, fabric shrapnel scattered on the ground and bed where I sit taking it all in. Two open suitcases in the corner of the room, waiting to be filled with the long list of items from the orientation and information packet I received on the first day of training two-and-a-half weeks ago. Once Tom confirmed my being accepted to the program, I have barely been able to come up to breathe.

I hear the phone ring in the living room, then moments later a swift knock on my door before it opens. I expected Allison to hold the phone out to me and say it was my mother or father, or maybe Natalie wanting to speak to me, like a last attempt to ask me to stay. Instead Allison is phoneless, looking down at my bed, then up at me as I sit there holding this damn packing checklist.

"Uh, you are leaving for the airport in like two hours, right?" she asks cautiously. "You are not backing out, El!"

I can see why it would still be on her mind. Processing my visa, vaccines and immunization, language and culture training, safety and security training, and add in the last week of school and finals, I was bound to blow. It just so happened to be hours before leaving for Amman, Jordan.

What was I thinking? I mean, really. Who am I? I'm just a college student with no clue what she is getting into!

"I rushed into this, didn't I?"

Allison marches over to me. "Stop it. You did not rush into anything, El. It is just cold feet, completely normal. Remember, it's an opportunity of a lifetime!"

I want to speak up, ridicule myself into believing this is all wrong when I know in my heart what I'm doing is right. That would be easier, less scary now that this journey is staring me right in the fucking face.

She rests her hands on my shoulders, pulling my attention back to her. "Don't give in to what they have told you your whole life."

She doesn't have to call them by name for me to know she is talking about my parents. Her voice becomes softer as she continues, "You've got this, El. You are one of the strongest, bravest motherfuckers I know. Just like your grandma, you are going to..."

Allison pauses and stares off in the distance. "Wait, what is it she said again?"

"Cross the stars and steal the moon," I mumble.

Her voice is strong and baritone when she looks back down at me and repeats the words. "Cross the stars and steal the moon, Ella."

I laugh a little as she pulls me into a hug.

An hour and a half later, Allison is pulling one suitcase out of my bedroom to the front door while I pull the other behind her. I hear the ominous sound of a horn; the taxi I asked Allison to call while I finished getting dressed. He's early. "Shit."

"It's fine," Allison tries to calm my nerves. "He will wait."

I let out a very sarcastic, "Ha, yeah right," as I follow Allison out the door of our apartment. "Taxis don't wait, especially around here, Allison."

She stops in front of me and pulls her keys from her pocket, going back to the door and locking it.

"What are you doing?"

She peers over her shoulder as she locks the door. "Just go. I will be right behind you."

I shift my backpack higher on my shoulders and pull my suitcase behind me. As I rush down the hall and out the front door of the apartment building, I see a yellow cab pulling away.

"Wait!" I holler after it. "Shit, shit, shit! Mother fucker!"

Allison is giggling behind me.

I whip around. "What the hell is so funny?"

I notice a guy standing next to her. Mr. Med School from Red Square.

"Brad is your taxi. Did you really think I would not go with you to the airport?" she says in jest. He steps toward me and takes hold of my backpack.

"Hey, Ella. Allison said you could use a ride."

His smile is genuinely sweet and I can see why Allison likes him. "Thanks."

He pops the trunk and puts my backpack and suitcases in. Allison walks over to me and in an attempt to avoid any tender words, I busy my mind with deciphering Brad and Allison. "So, Mr. Med School and you?"

She smiles and nods discreetly. "Yeah."

"You two ready?" Brad asks from his side of the car.

I would normally worry about his intentions with her and if he is a good guy or not. It's just what good friends do. None of it matters as I watch their exchange. I'm happy for her and strangely relieved she has him while I am away. I won't worry about her being alone for the summer.

As we pull up to the curb under the United Lufthansa sign, I tell myself not to cry as an annoying knot forms in the back of my throat.

"Okay, thank you for the ride," I say as I open the car door.

I try to avoid looking at Allison, knowing if I see her cry I am done for.

"Like I said, no problem," Brad says as he opens the trunk of his car. I search for Tom. He said he would be standing outside near the main entrance waiting for all the volunteers. Just then, I see a group of people with Tom standing in the middle holding up a sign that reads, "WorldTeach."

Brad hands me one bag, then the other, placing them onto the sidewalk and extending his hand to me. "Have a safe trip, Ella."

I shake his hand, delaying the goodbye between Allison and me as long as possible.

The lineup of cars begins to increase around us as people drop off and collect travelers. Someone honks their horn a few cars back and Brad says apologetically, "Sorry, but we have to go."

Giving us a few seconds alone, he quickly gets back into the car. I turn to Allison, immediately noticing her red eyes. It's all I need to see to make my own waterworks start.

"I'm going to miss you," we both comment simultaneously as we hug tightly.

"Stop it, you bitch!" I demand jokingly, trying to make light of the moment.

"Okay, Okay!" she demands, then tries to laugh but executes as a sad whimper. "Get out of here, bitch."

Another horn honks from behind us, pulling us apart.

"See you in three months," I say as I take hold of the handles on both of my suitcases, my backpack on my shoulder. I don't look back. It will just be another cycle of emotions for both of us if I do, so I instead focus on getting to Tom and the group. Spotting me, he waves and quickly adds a tick mark to his clipboard.

I am the last to arrive as Tom leads us all into the airport entrance now.

Bumping into someone next to me, I look up and recognize the girl's exotic dark eyes and curly hair. "Sorry."

"It's all right," she says.

I can't seem to place her, but she seems to remember me. "English class. Eras in 20th Century American Lit."

I nod as it clicks into place. "Good to see you again."

"Yeah, you too..." Damn, I don't remember her name.

She extends her hand, "Analise Diaz. Just call me Ana."

I shake her hand. "Ella Wallace. El."

The airport security line weaves snakelike and seems dauntingly endless as Tom glances at his watch, then looks at the line ahead of us nervously.

"So, what made you sign up?" I am not expecting her question and I guess she realizes it as she grins and explains, "We are going to be here a while. Just making conversation. You know, chit chat."

I take in the line ahead of us and behind us and concede to the fact we will be here a while, but don't offer an answer to her question. I barely know her, and while it is an obvious question, it's still one I haven't come to terms with completely other than the clichéd answer of wanting to have a purpose; she might think it is a line of bullshit or something.

She doesn't push as she turns around in line and moves forward a few steps, starting up a conversation with the girl in front of her. The line continues at a snail's pace for a whole hour, forcing us to run through the terminal to catch our plane. Once I am sitting at my seat I am able to breathe and feel reality settle in as I watch the tarmac disappear from my small window. I am leaving the country, going to a country I have never imagined setting foot in, and I am so fucking afraid.

It will be worth the risk.

Through the small pocket window, I watch the flashing light on the wing of the plane against the backdrop of night as we speed along the runway, then take flight. I close my eyes and let sleep take hold, envisioning white sands and the possibility of a new beginning.

Chapter 4

Ella

Amman, Jordan
Two weeks later...

The two women sitting across the table from me are eating their meal quietly as I reach under the veil I have worked into a makeshift hijab to scratch my dampened scalp, my hair not fully dry from the quick washing I was able to do this morning. Both mother and daughter look at me to watch what I am doing, then turn back at their food and speak softly in Arabic. The mother's name is Hoda and the daughter's name is Ameena.

My Arabic isn't great, even though I trained before leaving the States and the two weeks since being here. The integration classes here, plus assistance from Hoda and Ameena, have been the most help.

I take a generous bite of my dolma, enjoying the grape leaf-filled wrap. It isn't something I have mastered in the two short weeks I have been here, as part of the leaves give way, breaking a little.

"Shit," I hiss under my breath. Curbing my cursing has been the biggest challenge, and while Hoda doesn't know what I have said, Ameena does, having bluntly asked in my past slipups. She covers her smile and looks away from her mother's curious stare.

I set my Dolma to the side and pick up the Manakeesh with two hands like I would a hotdog. You would think a flatbread with minced meat and delicious flavor would have me more satisfied than a hotdog, but God I miss them. Thinking of them reminds me of Allison. I need to respond to her email when I get to the center this morning.

Hoda asks me a question in Arabic. I catch the gist of what she is asking, if I like the way it tastes. I don't dare consider saying what I want, which is that it would have tasted better piping hot, but since it's customary for men to eat their meal first here, I nod and smile, bringing life to her eyes and a small reserved smile to her lips as she focuses again on her plate. Both the patriarch of the house, Ismad Ba'ashir had left for work, while Ghalib, their six-year-old son, had eaten long before us. Mr. Ba'ashir works for a food delivery service for the wealthy here in Amman; the Abdoun area, which is a completely different reality from this side of town.

"Jayyid Jiddan," I say choppily in my functional, yet poor Arabic, which means "very good."

Ameena, almost twelve, bows her head and smiles, releasing just a hint of laughter at my lingual butchery before her mother gives her the discerning look of warning to show respect. I want to tell her I'm not offended, but I have made this error before in trying to explain her comment wasn't harmful. The conversation ended with Hoda walking away angrily and speaking very harshly in Arabic. I had obviously said something wrong.

Ghalib walks around the corner, gently wraps his little hand around my arm, and looks at me with intended sternness as he slowly enunciates every syllable of my broken expression. "Very good," drawing each letter out. I want to laugh at his adorable animated face, but I smile instead.

He smiles at his mother and sister across the table, drawing out the word again. "Very good."

Both Hoda and Ameena entertain him with their English in unison, "Very good."

He smiles proudly, thinking he has taught his mother and older sister something, then skips off to the other room.

Looking across the table at Hoda, I tell her slowly in Arabic that he learns quickly.

Delighted by her son, she smiles wider, but only for a brief moment as the familiar sound of the call to prayer brings a deafening silence over the house. The Adhan is is sacred in this house and throughout much of Jordan.

I continue to eat as the call to prayer sounds and Hoda, Ameena, and Ghalib move to the room next to the living room. I notice Jasara and her eldest daughter, Laila, ascend the stairs. They are Syrian refugees the Ba'ashir family has given asylum to for the past two years. Jasara Ahmadi has one daughter, Laila, thirteen; a son, Rushdi, six like Ghalib. Her husband did not make the journey with them. He was killed just before they fled Syria. Before arriving here in Amman, they had stayed in two of Jordan's refugee camps, but the overcrowding, lack of supplies, and violence within the camps sent them to the streets to look for shelter. That is when she found Caritas and the Ba'ashir family.

The Ahmadi family does not participate in Adhan since they are Christian, not Muslim. When I read the host family profile Tom handed me on the bus the day we arrived, I asked him if it was a typo. A Muslim family taking in a family of refugees is rare, and more so if they are a Christian family. He said it wasn't a typo and that is one of the reasons the Ba'ashir family was chosen by Caritas, because of their desire to assist those in need, no matter their religion.

Hoda and Ismad are good people and have lived in this neighborhood since they were children. Jasara and her daughter show respect for the time of prayer as they silently sit with me at the table waiting for Hoda, Ameena, and Ghalib to return.

It has only been two weeks since my group clustered and trailed through Amman Queen Alia International Airport. I remember feeling overwhelming regret. I wanted to run, dart out of the Arabic-speaking crowds smelling of cigarette smoke. I remember thinking *6.4 million people, 6.4 million peo-*

ple over and over again as I shuffled, stopped, maneuvered around, clustered together, then shuffled some more.

Caritas, a humanitarian charity non-governmental organization, had sponsored a private bus to take all of the volunteers into Amman. Tom had spoken to us in more detail about Caritas and how they were a partner organization during orientation after I was accepted into the program. He said Caritas had been handling humanitarian work in Jordan since the 1960s due to the effects of the wars having displaced Palestinian people to Jordan. Where many of the volunteers through WorldTeach are working with the education needs of the refugee population coming mainly from Syria now, Caritas assists with medical, financial, and counseling needs of the refugees in Jordan.

As I walked out of the airport with the group, a hot gust of wind hit me, taking my breath away. I could feel the grains of sand against my cheeks, tingling as they hit my face, along with the smell of waste. I quickly lifted the shawl Tom had given us on the plane and realized he wasn't giving it to us to be generous, he gave it to us for the purpose of Middle Eastern custom and protection from the elements. I commented to Tom on the smell and he said it wasn't uncommon since many foreign countries do not share our sanitation practices. He said I would get used to it.

The bus was large, with plenty of room for each of us to have our own section of seats. I didn't care to socialize, so I sat in the rear in the very last row, hoping to isolate myself. I just wanted to get to our destination, meet my host family, thank them for their hospitality, and hole up in my room. Tom came through handing us our host family descriptions along with the names of the family members. When he got to me, he gave me my packet then sat down in the seat across from me. He asked if I was okay. I told him I wasn't sure. He smiled and said it was the cycle of traveling abroad, that acclimation worked differently for everyone.

"The first time I came ten years ago I wanted to hop a plane straight back to D.C., but then I met the people," he said. As he continued to explain, I looked out the window at the sparsity of trees, and the density of golden sand cut-aways and cliffs as he wound through a highway. "It will come once you meet your host family and see the center with the volunteers and the children. A feeling of duty washes over you that is hard to explain. The desire to serve will transfer at some point to a fulfillment you can only get from knowing you have met your match, your purpose here."

The landscape changed drastically as we entered the city, sand hills and limestone rock quarries turning to lush green landscape among the valleys, or wedyaan, then to villas and mansions tiered through the hill tops called jabal. At first it was hard to believe this city was suffering as we passed the residences with well-manicured greenery, iron gates, and luxurious amenities.

As Tom spoke about the city landscape, he told us this was the area of Abdoun, which was west of the center of the city. The widened streets of Abdoun, high above the city of Amman, quickly narrowed as our bus moved down into the wadi of Amman's inner city. The mansions were replaced with aged cement buildings tiered along the jabals. As I looked up into the dense populous of concrete buildings, Tom explained they were being used as subsidiary camps for the refugees and those who didn't register with the UNHCR would need to find more meager housing, if any. Many unregistered refugees were in poverty and homeless. Passing the buildings, I notice segments missing, having broken away and slid down the edge of the jabal.

Deeper in the city, narrow streets were lined with vendors, shops, and open doorway inlets for what I would suspect are homes. Some of the businesses and homes we passed were dusty and aged, but kept as best as they could by the people living and working within them. The Arabic signs above the shops moved too quickly for me to read, if reading them were a possibility with my rudimentary Arabic. The faces of men sitting on stools, the veiled women, and the children playing and running around them brought a fragment of the culture to life for me as we got closer to the center of town and closer to the Makan Lil Amal center, which was located in the middle of Amman and the only center supported by Caritas with assistance from the WorldTeach volunteer program. As we exited the bus, a wave of heat washes over me, having been spoiled by the air-conditioning. As I followed the group through the narrow, gated passage the center, I heard the distinct sound Middle Eastern music carried with the light mewing sound of children singing just beneath it. Their voices crooned in their native language. While exotic and so different from music in the States, it was beautiful as the tones welcomed us.

As we stepped into the courtyard, the singing stopped and many of the children surrounded us, taking our hands. The adults stood back, leaving room for the children to see us. Many of the women covered their faces with their traditional hijab, but those partially unveiled showed us the joy we brought to them by being here. Two of those faces were Hoda's and Jasara's.

Tom was right. That was the first time I felt like I had a calling, a purpose for being here, and it isn't the last, as I feel the same calling sitting before Jasara and Laila right now.

"Sabah el-khair," Jasara whispers.

"Sabah el-noor," I whisper back.

"Good morning," Laila whispers and smiles brightly. She is always so eager to use her English.

"Good morning."

Once the call to prayer has ended, Hoda, Ameena, and Ghalib come back into the kitchen.

Hoda comes to us speaking in Arabic, telling me I must go as she exchanges a small embrace and kiss on either check of Jasara, then Laila.

I watch Ameena greet Laila like a sister would, as they exchange a small embrace and a peck on each cheek. They are almost the same height and could easily pass as sisters. Ghalib wraps his arms around Laila's leg as a little brother would to an older sister, then darts off into another room.

While they are two distinct families from two different nations, even two different religions, they seem to have found their oneness as a unique unit. Every day since I have arrived, they have given me no reason to think otherwise as they depend on each other, care for each other, and, in instances, love each other like a true family.

Ghalib runs back into the room and takes the lunch Hoda is holding out for him. She holds one out for Ameena, then me. She has been packing my lunch since the first day at the center, and while it is strange since I've never had my lunch packed for me, even by my mother, I accept her expression of respect warmly.

I smile and bow my head to her graciously. "Thank you."

Hoda bows her head in return and replies, "Welcome," then quickly moves on to distributing the remaining food in the kitchen for Jasara and Laila to take down stairs to their small space in the house.

Hoda shuffles behind Ameena, Ghalib, and me, speaking in Arabic as we follow them down to leave for the day.

"Allah maakun dayman," she says at the top of the stairs, hugging Ameena and Ghalib before they descend.

God is always with you.

Watching her close her eyes when she tells each of them this phrase is beautiful. As I come up to pass her, she says the same to me, placing her hand on my back, kissing both of my cheeks. My cheeks instantly flush and my heart softens as this is the first time she has included me in this family routine of goodbyes.

"Shukran."

I adjust my veil on my head to conceal most of my hair and stay close to Amani and Ghalib as we walk to their school. While the more exclusive parts of Jordan are more liberal with the wearing of hijab, our part of Amman holds utmost respect for this custom in concealing modesty. I learned all too quickly the first few days of being here in the city, if anything was exposed too much I was looked at as if I was a harlot or whore. I could get away with it in the Ba'ashir's house and in class with the students, but anywhere else the veil was on.

Even though it fucking itched like crazy with the heat, I had to suck it up. Like I said, I didn't take it seriously at first, until the day Ana and I went to the corner market to get some items for the center. The hot winds picked up and there were warnings of a dust storm approaching.

"Do we need anything else?" Ana asked before we walked out of the small room meant to be an Ammanian convenient store.

I rewrapped the veil over my head with little success and nodded, confirming we have everything on the list. Ana saw me struggling with the veil. "Here, let me help you."

She adjusted my veil over my ears, then opened the door. I walked quickly, following behind Ana as the rough wind whipped against my face, stronger now than it was when we left the school. It felt gritty, like sandpaper rubbing against my cheeks, so I kept my head down and pulled my veil tighter. As soon as I did, the plastic bag of goods started to slip from my hands.

Holding it tighter in time with holding my veil in place, one of them had to give and it happened to be my veil. Wanting to get back to the school quickly, I ignored its absence and kept the pace with Ana as we passed a group of men sitting along the sidewalk.

The cat-calls were immediate and brazen, having me spinning around fast, ready to give them a piece of my American mind when Ana grabbed my arms and pulled me to her, saying firmly, "Don't say anything. Just keep walking."

A few of the whistles got farther away as she pulled me along, but hard foreign words were close on my heels as two of the men hadn't let up. One of the men I recognized from the neighborhood near the Ba'ashir's house.

Ana tried to put my veil back my head as she moved alongside of me, but it fell down to my shoulders again.

Suddenly, I felt a tug on my veil, pulling me back. It was the man I recognized. Motherfucker! He was yelling and spitting at me. I stopped walking, my anger pulling at hot tears in my eyes, and yelled at him, "Leave me alone!"

Ana grabbed my arm and tugged me again as I pulled my veil up away from the ground. My confronting them made the spitting and yelling worse as we hurried to the center's courtyard only a few yards ahead. Ana and I ran the last few feet as the men give way at the entrance, knowing they have met their barrier.

"Are you loca?" Ana barked at me loudly once we were behind the closed doors of the center.

With all of my senses coming back to me now, I realized what a mistake I had made by speaking out to those men like I was ready to start a fight or something.

Hushed, she continued, "We are not in America. We are in a foreign fucking country with customs we have to follow. Some of those people out there do not want us here and you are giving them more reason to attack us with your mouth!"

I nodded the entire time she berated me, knowing I was wrong, but refusing to surrender to this bullshit. "Don't you think I fucking know," I hissed at her as we caught our breath in the hallway. "It just blew off and I couldn't put it back on! I didn't think it would be a big deal."

"It isn't about the damn veil, Ella. Your mouth is going to get you in trouble. You yelled back at those men!"

"What happened?" Tom's baritone voice caught me off-guard as he walked toward us.

Ana folded her arms over her chest, clamming up and giving me the floor to explain.

Fuck.

The last three weeks posed a challenge for Tom with my line of questioning during integration classes. It wasn't that I didn't want to integrate, it was just hard to stomach all of the shit I had to relearn as a woman in this culture. Tom and the staff didn't hide their frustration with my constant questioning and my slip-ups of foul language.

I speak quickly, "My veil, it fell off my head. There were a few men. They didn't like me uncovered. We are fine though. Nothing happened."

"And?" Tom asked, expecting more. "What else happened? What did you say to them?"

He knew me too well to know I tolerated this without speaking up. Ana and I stared at each other and I was fully expecting her to tell him I mouthed off at a man in the streets.

"Nothing. That was all," Ana said as she looked directly at Tom.

I could see Tom suspects more, but he didn't push. "There are many people happy we are here to help, but there are some who would rather us leave. We are outsiders. They will find any reason to intimidate you, even if it is a fallen veil, which might I remind you is custom to the Muslim people. We have been over all of this, Ella, and we have been over how to blend into the culture."

Realizing he is coming off domineering with his reprimand, he spoke more calmly now. "This part of Amman holds tradition sacred when they have little else to hold onto, Ella, and while being progressive, liberal, and somewhat outspoken are commendable traits of women in America, they are not looked upon similarly here. I don't think I need to remind either of you again. Am I right, Ms. Wallace?"

I nodded, my mouth burning from the unspilled words I wanted to send his way.

"Ms. Diaz?" Tom asked.

"Yes, sir," Ana responded.

Once he was out of earshot, Ana reached for my fallen veil gently and leaned in close, whispering, "You need to wrap it like this so it won't slip."

"Okay."

As she tucked my veil under my chin and swung the long part over my shoulder, I thought of the reason Mr. Ba'ashir always told his children and I to be very careful. Did he fear I or one of the children might be attacked in retaliation for them giving asylum to the Ahmadi family? While he agreed to let me do this favor for him and Hoda, did he fear for our safety? Did Jasara choose to bring her own children to the center separately from me, so I wouldn't be targeted if they were? The man that pulled my veil from my shoulders, he was from the same neighborhood as the Ba'ashirs. Could he be watching me? Or is it just my mouth and my non-conforming attitude causing all the trouble?

"There," Ana said, pulling back to hold the bag of supplies out to me.

I took the bag from her as she added, "If these were the streets of D.C I would have had your back with that asshole, mi hermana. This isn't our world and while you seem tough, I don't think you have seen what I have, been where I have been, to take on a son of a bitch like that. What I can tell you is neither of us are tough enough for this world, so don't go and try to be a hero, all right?"

Her words made it apparent that while I haven't divulged anything about who I was or where and how I grew up, she has caught on to the fact I haven't seen the hard world she has experienced and even that world doesn't compare to this one.

Holding my backpack tighter, I look around me as I wait for Ameena to say goodbye to her brother at the boys' school he attends. She hugs him then he rushes into the concrete building before we move on to the girls' school she attends a block away. As soon as we are close to the entrance she turns to me and says, "Bye," with a small smile hidden behind her very traditional hijab.

"Bye," I say, waving as she turns and quickly walks into the school.

The center is a few blocks away from Ameena's and Ghalib's public schools. The refugees at the center aren't allowed to attend public schools because they haven't registered with the Jordanian government, and while Jasara's family was once registered, when they left the camps, they were on their own, receiving no assistance for her family. I have offered to walk Laila and Rushdi with me to the center, but Jasara refused the offer. Tom had told us many of the refugees refused to register with the United Nations for fear of retaliation from the Syrian government, and with Jasara's family having been registered she feared retaliation on anyone she comes into association with.

The name of our center, Makan Lil Amal, means "place of hope" in Arabic. It was erected almost three years ago, just a short time before the Ahmadi family found its doors. I sit down at one of the six outdated computers in the concrete room turned technology lab. These are the only computers in the center and are used for email and for accessing resources for instruction. I pull up my email account and an unopened message from Jilly catches my attention. Though, if anyone were to scroll through my inbox, they'd see Allison and Jilly's names all the way down. I got into the habit of saving all of their messages for the days I really miss home.

"Hey." Ana walks in and lets her veil fall from her head as she sits down to the computer next to me.

"Hey."

Typing on the keyboard, she enters her username and password to access her email account. "I can't wait until the weekend. Hey, a few of the volunteers and I are going to do some touristy stuff on Saturday. Want to go?"

I open the email from Jilly. "Like what?"

We continue to scroll our emails side by side. I don't see an email from Allison, so I open a new message and send her a quick note.

Hi! Doing great. Settling in finally. The Ba'ashir family is so nice.

So are the Ahmadi's. Love the girls I teach. Miss you.

"Um, going to Roman Amphitheater I think. Then some restaurant. Hashem. It is supposed to be popular," she says as she scrolls her own emails.

El,
I need to see Amman! Send pictures soon!
Miss you, Love you.
Jilly

Her emails have become shorter and more playful after the initial heartfelt ones, which has made opening her emails less bittersweet.

"Roman Amphitheater?" I ask Ana.

"Yep. That is what we are thinking."

I smile as I type quickly.

Jilly,

I will send pics of the Roman Amphitheater in a few days. Everything is going well here. I love my class of girls. Love the family I live with. Miss you. Love you. El

I sign out of my account and glance over at Ana. "What time are we leaving?"

I notice the waiting room to the medical clinic has started to fill as I walk down the hall past the section. The medical staff and volunteers are through Caritas. One of the clinicians I see every day is checking the temperature of an elderly woman. She looks at me just as I'm passing and smiles. I smile back lightly and move on. The next few sets of rooms are where the physicians and nursing staff see the patients. Through the corridor is another section designated for financial assistance and registration with Caritas. The section beyond is for counseling families. Trained staff and volunteers help counsel children and adults experiencing trauma, depression, and other symptoms resulting from their life as refugees. It is also the last section before entering the area WorldTeach has made into a temporary school.

Each room represents grade levels, starting with the youngest, six-year-olds. The rooms in the building have been divided by accordion-like partitions to make room for multiple classes. Like the schools in Amman, boys are separate from girls in the classroom, with one hall being for male teachers and boys and the other for female teachers and girls.

One of the male volunteer teachers exits a room and walks toward me with a cup of coffee in his hand. "Hi, Ella." David has been with WorldTeach for three years. He has been to Chile and to Morocco, choosing Amman this summer. "Did Ana talk to you about the Roman Amphitheater?"

"Yes, she did."

He nods and walks on, surely going to get fill his cup with Turkish coffee, the richest fucking coffee I have ever tasted. Don't get me wrong, it is good, just too strong. One sip and I am buzzing with adrenaline.

While we have a stout number of male teachers through WorldTeach, we also have a few through Caritas who are native Jordanians. Just like the host families, they have lived here their whole lives and want to help the Syrian people displaced due to the war.

I pass through the intersecting corridor leading down a hall, doorways lining each side. This is the girls section of classrooms. Ana and I are separated by a partition in the classroom we share. Her girls are nine and ten-years-old and mine are six through eight. We each have ten girls and I have already claimed mine as "my girls," when I talk about them. The first day of classes made for a tough audience as

I tried to break the ice in broken Arabic. That got a few giggles, but no instruction. For all, this was their first experience in a classroom and a completely new place with some strange American girl trying to speak Arabic. These girls had seen things I could never imagine seeing: the death of their brothers, fathers, or sisters. They had been forced from their homes because of a war they did not start and cannot stop.

In the first two weeks of being with the class, my spirit broke as I read their files, experiencing on paper the traumatic events they endured as they found passage to Jordan, into refugee camps, then into the city of Amman. It was my fault; I asked Tom about each of them. Ana didn't ask. The girl who taught in the room across from us, Laura, she didn't ask. They didn't understand why I wanted to know.

"It makes things more complicated, Ella," was Laura's reasoning to avoid hearing her students' life stories. I couldn't be expected to teach English and math not knowing what they had experienced.

When I approached Tom about it during lunch, he said it wasn't standard practice to share certain information, which made me question what he chose not to share with me about the Ahmadi or Ba'ashir family. Had Jasara Ahmadi's family been through worse than the informational packet I was given stated? Had the Ba'ashir family been condemned for giving refuge to the Ahmadis? I told him it wasn't standard practice to expect me to teach girls having never set foot in a classroom. Children who had experienced so much trauma in their lives that reading, writing, and math are mundane compared to their existence.

After the third go around with him, he knew I wouldn't let up, so he introduced me to Samara Hallal, a counselor through Caritas. He told me she could tell me more about my girls. She had a stack of files on her desk and told me she was going to get a cup of coffee and speak with the director of Caritas. She placed her hand on the stack and told me, what I read in that room, stayed in that room. I sat and read their stories, some similar and some more horrific than I had imagined.

Fleeing death with only the clothes on their backs and a bag or two of the belongings they could carry. Running, crying, begging, as they crossed the border from Syria, watching death take those not strong enough to make safe passage; too sick, too old, too frightened of retaliation from Syria. Too painful to look back. At first finding hope in a refugee camp, until it became too crowded, or the abuse too harrowing, or the attempted rapes too terrifying.

These traumas, the damage, had peeled away their dignity, self-respect, and self-awareness, leaving each of them spiritless in some way. Story after story, they leave a camp and find a new one, just for the fucking cycle to start over again, peeling, stripping away layer by layer of life until there is only an outer shell of a father, a mother, a son, a daughter, a little girl who has seen too much in her short life.

After reading in Samara's office, I walked Ameena and Ghalib back to the Ba'ashirs' home without speaking. I looked at Hoda and Ismad differently, as saviors to the Ahmadis. While the two families carried on with their night, I ate in silence, then excused myself to my room, where I found solace in crying for the first time since arriving, not for myself in being frightened in a foreign country, but for my girls, Jasara, Ameena, Ghalib, Hoda, Laila, Rushdi, and Ismad. I heard the echo of my father's voice telling me I didn't know what I was doing. After, I wiped my tears and swore I would not teach my girls English or math until I got each of them to smile at least once. That was my new rule.

It took me three days to get all of them to smile, but once I did I knew there was hope for them finding their spirits again. While I think about it every day, I haven't found the courage to ask the Ba'ashirs or the Ahmadis their stories beyond the packet I received on them.

Walking into the classroom, I turn on the lights and set my bag down on the metal chair behind my small metal desk. There are only two desks and chairs in the room; one for Ana and one for me. We are supposed to receive student desks sometime soon; funds from the mystery, silent benefactor who funded my getting here. Tom said we would have them two weeks ago, but still nothing. As I straighten the thin scraps of carpet we are using to cover the concrete floor for the girls to sit more comfortably, I look up in time to see the first of my girls enter into the classroom, Muna Sulaiman. She was the last to smile for me.

"Salaam, Muna."

"Salaam, Ms. Ella," she says softly as she holds her notebook to her chest and finds the small scrap of carpet closest to me.

She opened up easily after that day, wanting to hold my hand as we walked to and from lunch, choosing to sit with me in the courtyard while the other girls played, never wanting to leave my side and always being the first in the classroom in the morning, like she is today. Samara said once a child like Muna has latched on to someone, they never want to let go. I could accept that, fully knowing what I know. Her mother and father were murdered the night her older sister and brother fled with her from Syria. They found passage with an aunt and uncle fleeing with their two children. Samara said Muna shared a room with her parents and witnessed the massacre. Her sister and brother hid, but once the intruders had fled, they searched for her and found her buried under the blood-soaked bedding between her mother and father's bodies.

Muna holds my hand tightly, looking up at me with her big brown eyes as we walk to the cafeteria for lunch. The girls giggle and squirm in line, but straighten up as soon as I look back, only to giggle and squirm once again after I have turned around.

Only women are in the cafeteria now. The men and boys have already eaten. The women serve us Dolma, Shrak, and hummus for dipping. One of the many foods I have come to love is the Shrak, which is a pliable pita-style bread. Even though Hoda makes my lunch every day, I find myself getting in line for a round of Shrak when my girls line up for their lunches.

Most of the girls in my class spread out, sitting with girls from other classes, sisters, and cousins. A few of their mothers help around the center and come to visit during lunch, like Jasara does with Laila.

One day at lunch, I asked Laila in Arabic why Jasara helps, knowing she won't be paid. She stared at me like I had grown a third head and told me in the best English she could that she was thankful for what they have done for them. "Not ... eh ... um ... maal."

I deciphered what she was trying to say. "Money. It isn't about the money."

She nods and continues to eat her lunch. "They give food. Help when sick. Teach." She smiles at me tenderly. "I am thank."

Decoding her words, I say what I think she is trying to. "You are thankful."

She nods eagerly and speaks slowly in English. "I am thankful."

Muna sits in between Jasara and me, dipping small pieces of Shrak into the creamy Hummus. She is so petite and I watch her take little bites, hoping those bites eventually get bigger, making her stronger. I wonder if she worries this might be her last meal. Is that why she takes small bites?

She never finishes her food, but always asks me at the end of lunch, "You keep?"

At first I didn't understand, but Laila's perception was keener than mine when she told me she wanted me to hold it for her. Save it for the end of the day.

Everyone starts to clear their plates and Muna gazes up at me, holding out her nibbled Shrak, whispering as if anyone discovered the bread would disappear. "Keep me?"

I smile at her effort to ask me to hold onto it and place both of my hands under and on top of the bread. "I will keep for you."

She smiles and whispers, "Shukran."

"You're welcome."

The girls get a thirty-minute recess after lunch. As my girls walk behind me, with Muna's hand in mine, we enter the section of the center housing the Caritas and WorldTeach directors' offices. I turn to the girls and put my finger to my lips for them to be quiet as we pass the offices. As we turn the corner, I notice two armed soldiers standing guard outside of Tom's door. The door is open, so without being too obvious, I look in only to catch a glimpse of two dark-haired men sitting side by side across from Tom. Tom is usually a very happy and smiling type of guy even when things get frustrating for him. He isn't smiling now and it leaves me wondering if something is wrong.

My girls' light chatter distracts me, and just as one of the guards glimpses down at me, I look away from the room and turn to calm them again as we walk on, eventually making our way outside.

I usually play hopscotch with my girls. They loved learning this game and it has been the game of choice this week.

"Ms. Ella, come play," one of the girls calls to me, waving me down.

Preoccupied with the soldier standing on the other side of the courtyard gate, I smile and wave. "You play."

Yes, we have a guard walking the courtyard when the children are at play and the gate is always locked when we are out here, but never a soldier. Two soldiers within as well. Something is going on. The front door of the center opening catches my attention and I see Tom walking toward me as he watches the girls play. I adjust my veil, feeling the wind creeping under it, pushing it back.

"They love hopscotch, don't they?" Tom asks, making conversation as he comes to stand next to me.

I watch the two separate hopscotch games they have created to accommodate all nine of the girls except Muna, who is by my side drawing with chalk on the concrete. "They do." I smile, remembering the day I taught them how to play and how they have come such a long way since then.

"Why are soldiers here?" I ask openly.

Tom is still smiling at the girls at play as he responds, "The benefactor paid a visit today. Wanted to see how the program was coming along."

"Oh, and he requires soldiers to visit?"

"Yes, it does," he says flatly, obviously not in the mood for my interrogation.

That didn't seem to explain the heightened security fully. "Is he still here?"

Realizing my questions were going to continue, Tom shifts his attention to me. "No, he left."

"Hmm."

I give room for Tom to settle from my questions before another one begs to be asked remembering the two men in his office. "Was the silent benefactor one of the men in your office?"

I scratch the tip of my nose, attempting to seem casual about my perpetual chain of questioning.

"Yes, we were discussing safety precautions."

A red flag goes up immediately. "Safety?"

We have gone over safety and what to do if the center was under an attack. We knew where to hide, but we were reassured since the center was established nothing has happened to put the refugees, the children, or the volunteers at risk. Refugee men volunteered to be trained as guards. I'd felt safe under their guard, but now we had soldiers?

Tom nods casually. "We will be discussing added security in a mandatory meeting after classes today in the cafeteria. Could you tell Ana and the other volunteers? Spread the word about the meeting?"

"Yes."

I'm about to ask more questions, but Tom is already walking back to the doors, preoccupied with the soldier standing guard at the courtyard gate.

Chapter 5

Rajaa

As we get into the car and drive away from the Makan Lil Amal center, Zaid breathes a deep, throaty sigh of relief before drinking the cold bottle of water we each have waiting for us. I don't open mine. I had hoped my first visit to the center would be about raising security measures for the volunteers and refugees, but with the increase of attacks surrounding us in Beirut, Iraq, and north of Amman, the need for heightened security is necessary.

It had been three weeks since returning home and both Zaid and my father had done an excellent job keeping me busy and away from the center. With the conditions worsening at the borders, I demanded coming down here. Zaid insisted on coming, only because he didn't want me staying any longer than I should.

"Thank you for going with me." He places the lid back on the bottle and glances over at me, but says nothing. "It would be irresponsible for me, our family, to leave them vulnerable if an attack came."

"Yes, and putting our own safety at risk in the process is fine with you?" he adds as he looks out the window. Our black SUV winds through the labyrinth of Wust El-Balad, downtown Amman. We are led by a car ahead of us and another SUV identical to ours behind.

"We were not at risk. No one was aware of us being there other than the directors." We made sure to keep ourselves hidden as we entered the center through a side door and alley rather than the main entrance through the courtyard.

Zaid takes another drink of his water, then clears his throat. "We could have sent word with a soldier. One of the handfuls I have stationed there temporarily. I have trained those men personally. They know how to deliver a simple message."

My brother's arrogance and selfishness is relentless and has become more acute since my returning home. He has changed since I last saw him and I'm not sure what it is. "Send word with a soldier? Like you would send a greeting card or a gift? Is that how you would handle notifying the center of a threat, brother?"

Zaid leans his head back into the headrest as he glares over at me. "There is no threat, as I'm sure you would know if you spent more time focused on the state of our security rather than daydreaming of ways to save people increasing our risks. They are the real threat. Make no mistake, I have complete control over my area of expertise, brother, where you have none."

"Two bombings at centers in Mafra last week, an attack at a city camp in Jaresh yesterday. While your defenses are bulletproof, the attacks are coming and it is not from within. A handful of soldiers dispensed to these centers would not break our defenses Zaid. Show some fucking compassion."

"You are a prince, Raj! We have people to do these things for us, risk themselves so you can remain safe and help lead our country. Yes, I will be king, but I will expect your advisement on diplomatic decisions. You can't very well do that dead, can you? Your mind needs to be on the state of Jordan, not running around being some savior for illegal immigrants!"

My father had made the comment about me being an advisor a few times since my coming home.

"Jordanian, Syrian, American, they are all people at the center, Zaid. Just because they are not pure Jordanian, or registered refugees, does it make them less human to you? Fuck!"

Zaid shakes his head and turns away from me. "Listen to you, I thought I was the one with the temper. That is what the King always says," he laughs and looks after me, hoping I will join in his humor. "Remember when we were little, how you would always try and hush me when I would curse?"

I force a half grin of the memory as I look out my side window. "Yes, I guess it is your turn now to hush me."

The walk down memory lane is lost when he returns to our discussion. "Raj, the Americans at the center are the only reason I agreed to relinquish a few soldiers for the center. Well, that and the King's demand. Apparently, he sees this grand vision of yours, as does your mother."

I run my hand over my face. "You say you agreed like our father's opinion is just something to side step. If you just gave this center a fucking shot, you would see what it's worth to our country."

Zaid ignores my suggestion. "You have always been a daydreamer, Rajaa. Peace and love and poetry. Is that what the American university has taught you?"

He shoots me a glare. "You used to have your head on straight, now all of that shit has weakened you and your philanthropic desires are bringing weakness here to an already ill king. A father wanting to appease his son upon his return since he may not make it to another."

As Zaid shakes his head and looks away, I am dumbfounded by his cold and callous regard of my father's decision to carry through with the center and the way he considers my father's death as something quickly approaching.

"You don't know what the fuck you are talking about, Zaid. I haven't changed, just grown wiser."

"In the few months you are here, I suggest you spend most of your time with our father and studying the current state of Jordan, and less time worrying about this center. Reacquaint yourself with your home, your people, our ways, rather than the way of the West clouding your mind." He doesn't look at me as he gives me this advice.

"Should I remind you our father attended Georgetown University and my attending was under his advisement."

Zaid shoots back, "Yes, and as the eldest son, the one that will be crowned heir to the throne, I chose to stay here and serve my family, my country, learn the ways of leaders, form allegiances, relations. If I hadn't, who would be here to help the King make decisions affecting the future of Jordan? Your mother, the Queen?"

He shakes his head. "No, it has been me!"

"What about our Prime Minister, Shafar Badran, the Cabinet. The weight of rule doesn't fall completely on the King and Queen. I'm sure they have been..."

Zaid smirks and jumps in before I can finish. "Yes, well they have done what they can by law, and I do everything else."

His double talk strikes a nerve of concern, but I leave it for now as he continues.

"I have proven my worth to both the King and our executive office. Let's not forget I have been working by his side while you have been off fucking American coeds at Georgetown."

Once my brother gets this way, it is pointless to continue a logical discussion.

The tension between us has grown too thick, as it has many times since being here. The endless media coverage of my being home and the apparent delay my father has placed on crowning the heir apparent to succeed him as king has only added to Zaid's maddening personality shift. He sits back and turns to his side of the window just as his cell rings. Picking up, he speaks quickly, saying he can't talk. It's because of my presence, I am certain. He continues his conversation by text as I look out my window.

Driving through the center of Amman as a child with my brother, my father. and mother, the streets didn't look like this, desolate from a palpable fear of attack on the capital of Jordan. The entire Middle East suffers from this symptom of war and terror transfixed by the extremist revolutions peppering the Arab states.

Home is west of Amman. As soon as we arrive, we silently exit the car and walk through the entry toward my father's office, the strain between Zaid and me tangible.

"As-Salaam-Alaikum," my brother announces sharply to my father.

"Wa-Alaykum as-salaam," my father responds as he closes his laptop, sensing the tension in my brother's voice. "Mal Khatab. What is wrong?"

"Nothing is wrong," I say quickly while my brother takes his question as an open invitation. He speaks quickly in Arabic, telling our father he and I shouldn't have gone down to the center today. That our presence wasn't necessary when a soldier could have easily been sent with the message to Mr. Stern.

"Nothing happened, everyone is safe. Zaid and I just disagree on the responsibility I hold for the center, that is all."

Zaid sits down in the chair across from my father. "Really, Raj, then what is it you were saying to Mr. Stern about wanting to take a more active role at the center?"

He raises his arms high, like he is calling upon Allah. "You said you were compelled!"

I did not think being at the center would affect me if I remained disconnected while we were there, but somehow the children, the woman in the courtyard, unraveled my separation. I meant to go in there, talk to Mr. Stern, and leave; that was my intention.

Little girls in the courtyard hopping and playing with a stone. I have seen girls on the streets of D.C. play this game. As Zaid exchanged more details of how the soldiers' presence will relieve any worry and how the staff and volunteers should be briefed, I watched the girls through the small, dusty window behind Mr. Stern.

I noticed the soldier guarding the gate as Zaid and I had instructed; all entries into the center were to be guarded at all times now. There was a woman standing near the children, watching over them with her back to the window. I couldn't see her face, as she was shielded by a blue veil, a hijab. I noticed a piece of blonde hair escape from beneath it, like a ribbon of gold as it rose and fell to her shoulder over and over again. The dance it had taken on was seductive, making me look away; the veils purpose is to preserve modesty and there I was staring.

I attempted refocusing on Zaid's and Mr. Stern's exchange, but my thoughts drifted back to the woman and how she reminded me of my mother. She used to wear the veil every day of my childhood, then one day she stopped. She would tuck her hair in quickly when it would begin to come loose as she played with my brother and me. She would chase us and my brother and I would laugh until we couldn't breathe. The woman in the courtyard didn't tuck her hair back, or even acknowledge it had been freed from the veil.

I was nine when I saw my mother's long, dark head of hair for the first time. The dark mass fell around her oval face, like the waves of the sea at night. I'd asked where her hijab had gone, but she didn't explain. Now I understood it was a choice that didn't frame her internal or spiritual relationship with Allah. It was a choice she made, but not afforded by all. Those in impoverished areas of Amman, and among the refugees, traditions and faithfulness was strong, and so was hijab. The woman in the courtyard, with her liberated hair, she was not a Jordanian or Syrian. She was not from here at all. Min Barra, *an outsider.*

"Is she a teacher?" I asked Mr. Stern

The weight of Zaid's immediate stare in my direction was heavy as Mr. Stern shifted the conversation. "Yes, she is," he said as he looked out the window behind him.

I looked at the silhouette of the woman once more, just as she turned her head to the side, seeming to sense my heavy gaze. Her profile, her nose, lips, she seemed familiar to me. My brother adjusted the conversation back to the safety of the center, expecting my undivided attention. When given a moment's leeway, I searched for her again through the window, but she was gone, having moved away.

As we walked from the office into the hall, I felt the compulsion to find this familiar woman, but not in mixed company. "I'm compelled to have more involvement in the center. I'm not sure to what capacity, but I would like to visit again regularly, Mr. Stern."

Seeming stumped and confused, he cleared his throat and stepped closer to my brother and me. "Whatever way you see fit, we would love to have you, Prince Rajaa. I know you want to maintain anonymity, and I know your time should be spent working closely with your brother and father, the King."

Zaid quickly spoke up, "Yes, I'm glad you say that, Mr. Stern."

"Oh, Tom, please," Mr. Stern corrected him.

My brother nodded, "Well, Tom, you understand we need to protect ourselves as much as we need to protect the center. His presence will have some division."

I noticed Mr. Stern shrink away a little, and smile respectfully as Zaid took control of the conversation. "Of course, Prince Zaid."

My brother put out his hand in kind for Mr. Stern and Tom accepted it graciously. "Zaid is fine, Mr. Stern, but let's just keep that between us, all right?"

Zaid's stout laughter outweighed Mr. Stern's timorous chuckle.

Sitting next to me and across from my father, Zaid's smug smile and accusatory glare is infuriating, and I could easily rise to his level, but I manage to keep my anger in check as he continues to stir it with his words. "Did the teacher in the courtyard compel you?"

I choose to speak over Zaid. "Baba, if you had been there and seen how this program is helping heal this people, bringing the refugees together with the volunteers from Caritas, the teachers from WorldTeach with the children." I shake my head, not wanting to deny my duty as the son of the King. "While Zaid's duty is to be your right hand, I feel it is mine to not leave this project as untouched as I had originally planned. Not with the recent attacks near us threatening their safety. It is our responsibility to protect them while they are in our country."

"It is not my duty, Rajaa," Zaid says smugly, reinforcing his position. "Baba, this is what I was talking about, his complete delusion and loss of touch with our ways here. The West has influenced him too much."

My father mumbles in Arabic, then quickly shifts to English. "I suspected this would happen," he says, looking at me. My brother is thriving on my father's agreement when he says, "Your principles for human rights are too strong to relinquish your involvement."

Carefully, he rises from his chair and walks to the window, his hand seeking the support of the cane he is using today. His right hand wobbles as it pushes down on the top of the cane. He stops at the window and looks out onto the courtyard below before speaking again. "Your mother is the same. Now, her life has been threatened; she has had to back away."

Zaid speaks to my father like I am not even in the room. "We can't afford to have him making poor decisions,

Baba. This whole thing is bad ... kul eshee! Just as it was for the Queen."

"Everything is not bad." I bring his awareness back to my being in the room. "To someone who has no sense of humanity it may seem bad!"

"Raj, you are wanting to mingle among refugees, a prince among the poor, the outsiders from another land. They have no loyalty to us!"

While my brother's argument is valid, it is only to an extent. "Loyalty is earned. Tell me, would it be more likely they give loyalty to the country that has flushed them out or the one that has given them safe haven?"

The argument between us becomes a rally back and forth, Zaid next to volley. "Do you know them, Raj? No! This program will not change them or anything about this crisis!"

"We will not know until we try."

"We have to secure it, feed it, house it, give it medical care, schooling. This program is a dream, brother, one soon to become our most painful nightmare if we aren't fucking careful!"

I shake my head. "You are wrong, Zaid. I can see this program succeeding, transforming the people and the crisis!"

Zaid flutters his hand as if to brush off my defense. "You are wasting your energy and your mind on this small, insignificant stepping stone when you could be using the skills you have received at that big American university to influence policies, change sanctions, and give us the upper hand to fight back against the revolution pushing the crisis here! Rajaa, I don't think you have the wisdom to speak on this matter. While you have been off at college, I have been in the depths of what you are reading about over a cup of coffee with friends."

"That is enough, Zaid!" My father's raspy voice attempts a yell, but falters.

"Ana asif, Baba," my brother quickly offers his apology.

"I'm tired of this chatter. It is pointless, especially among brothers who should be bound together no matter their differences."

Zaid squirms in his chair, and angles to my father as he clears his throat. "Father, I didn't mean..."

My father interrupts again with rising anger, his quivering voice exposing his decreased health. "Chatter is for women! Are you a woman, Zaid? I would hope not, as I would never make a princess a king!"

I can see the anger from the verbal slap my father has given brewing in Zaid's downcast eyes. "No, father, I am not. My apologies. Ana asif."

Looking between both my father and brother, I can see the resemblance they share; the thick jaw snapped shut because of anger, the long nose flaring from displeasure.

My father puts his cane first as walks back to his chair. "Going to the people, being at their side, it is something your mother and I have always tried to instill in you both and Tamanna."

He watches Zaid as he sits. "While strength can come from a powerful leader in war."

Shifting his eyes to me, he adds, "It can come from a vision of peace and act of humanity just as swiftly. The combination of both is necessary."

My father's eyes move from mine to Zaid as he says, "A king must have both; if he doesn't the land will eat itself alive."

The silence between the three of us is broken by the heeled footsteps of my mother and little sister, Tamanna.

"I didn't know you had returned," my mother says as she walks to my father and places her hand on his back. My father's temperament shifts as soon as he looks upon her. My mother is beautiful, and while her beauty should make any man's temperament calm, I know he has calmed only to disguise the conversation we were having.

Zaid pushes his chair away from my father's desk and rises, quickly turning to leave.

I notice my mother's eyes follow him, then she looks at my father, concerned. "Is everything all right?"

My father pats her on the hand. "Everything is fine, zahrat baladi. Everything is fine, my flower."

Even with his soothing words and my explanation of it just being the difference in the way we see things, my father brings up his concern for Zaid's changing ways again.

"He doesn't see things as we do. I have spent years trying to break down the walls he keeps building around himself! Lately, I have watched Zaid change. He is always gone, says he is in meetings, talks with influential people that can help with this civil unrest, but I know nothing more. He tells me nothing of these people!"

"He says he helps you, has been by your side as an advisor," I comment.

My father nods. "Yes, he has been by my side and has done all I ask of him, but when he isn't..." He shakes his head. "I don't know if he is doing things in the best interest of our country or for himself."

This doesn't sound like Zaid. My brother has always been wise, focused on the best for our country, never putting any of us or our people at risk. I give my brother the benefit of the doubt. "He loves our country, would do anything for it, Baba. Maybe he is trying to eliminate stress for you."

His brow furrows, lost in my logic. "Why?"

He is already angry from my highlighting his weakened health and I wish I could take it back now, but it is too late. "Because of your health."

He pounds his fist against the table. "My health is fine! It hasn't affected my mind, Rajaa! What is affecting it is how Zaid is undermining my rule." He leans over the desk toward me, his eyes reflecting both fear and worry as he lowers his voice. "Undermining the Prime Minister, the Cabinet by going behind our backs!"

My father looks at my mother, then back at me as he grabs his chest. "I have this feeling inside he is involved in something that could destroy all of us."

Growing up, Zaid and I worked hard to be the most competitive, most accomplished, and most daring in the family; racing motor bikes in the Wadi Rum sand dunes, rock climbing, playing football, known as soccer in America. Weight room challenges of who could bench press the most became a daily competition in the recent summers. Athleticism has always been a strength for both of us and so has achieving what we set out to do. Since being home this summer, I can see Zaid's extreme focus on the security of Jordan.

My mother rests her hand at my father's shoulder. "While I am only half a mother to Zaid, I have loved him as my own and tried to talk with him, but he has rejected me. He only sees one half of what it takes to being a strong king. Your father is a strong leader, a faithful follower of Islam, and a man of hope, dignity, and honor. That is what your brother should be trying to accomplish. His late nights ... sometimes not returning for two and three days. His eyes bloodshot and his temper shifting from moment to moment. I fear he is dealing in things over his head. Over our heads. It frightens me. I swear I have tried to be good for him." The pain in her eyes is saddening. I know she has tried with Zaid and been faced with rejection of not being his mother, the woman he idolized and loved so much.

My father looks up at her, puts his hand on top of the one she has left on his shoulder. "Layaali, you have been as much of a mother to him as you have to Raj and Tamanna. Do not blame yourself, little flower."

The exerted energy this conversation is taking on my father is apparent as he inhales deeply, leaning back into his chair. "Rajaa, while he won't turn to us, he will turn to you."

My brother, turn to me? "I'm not sure that will happen."

"Your brother will turn to you, Rajaa," my mother adds. "He speaks highly of you all the time, has talked about your return for months. He has even discussed the vital role you both will have in the future of Jordan. He wants you by his side."

My father speaks up, "She is right, Rajaa. He has talked to me about your involvement after graduating. Even if you don't believe it, he is so happy you are home."

I lean forward, my elbows on my knees as I observe both of them. "He isn't too happy about what I am doing at the center."

My father assures me, "What you are doing, the difference you are hoping to make for the refugees and the people of central Amman is good, Rajaa. I know your brother feels otherwise, but he doesn't see the possibilities. I am counting on you being the one to show him." He suddenly lowers his eyes to his desk. "Time is not on my side, as you can see."

The King's orders are for his private staff of doctors to not discuss his health publicly under any circumstance. Parkinson's disease has begun its consumption of my father's body over the span of two years. Each time I see him, I find a new tremor or tick he has developed and it seems like every time he gets a cold or virus, he adds a new symptom. The latest being the nagging cough from the cold he caught in December. While it isn't a direct symptom, it is still one I associate with his weakened immune system from Parkinson's. With my father's age, sixty-seven, the symptoms of the disease and other illnesses he may contract are heightened and even worsening quicker due to the final stretch of mortality.

My mother chides him in Arabic and he reprimands her for it, telling her that even though he is keeping his illness hidden, it must be discussed among our family. "Don't you think I despise not taking long walks with my wife? Standing by my family's side in front of our people when Rajaa arrived?"

He has become very private due to his visible symptoms, not wanting to show weakness in front of the people. We have told him it isn't a weakness, but it only angered him, as he demanded he wouldn't have his people feel they were being led by a weak man just because his body was wearing. "My body may be weak, but my mind is strong! Something you all keep forgetting!"

"We haven't forgotten, Baba. We know your mind is strong," I say to him as he shakes his head.

Since being home, it is apparent Zaid, my mother, and sister have had to endure observing his bad days while celebrating his good days. While I'm here, being a support is the least I can do for him.

His head begins to shake, a tremor taking hold, as he brushes my other hand from his shoulder and looks at me wearily. "Rajaa, he is to be king. I do not want to spend my last days fearing for his reign. Please keep your eyes open for me."

My father's plea holds the weight of a king's dying wish. I can't deny my father. "I will, Baba. I will."

My search for Zaid after leaving my father's office isn't long. He is on the phone in the courtyard. He sees me, says a few remaining words, then hangs up. "These phone calls don't stop. You would be surprised how many I field in a day for our father." He shakes his head and smiles as he tucks his cell phone into his pocket.

I had noticed the number of phone calls. The times I have come into the office, interrupting him mid-call, having him quickly find reason to get off so I won't hear the conversation.

"Well, it is good our father has you to take them."

Zaid looks at me with a hint of surprise and curiosity. "You think so?"

"Does my saying that surprise you?"

Zaid starts to walk along the pool, as I fall into step with him. "I don't know I am what they expect," he says, laughing a little, then quickly changes his tone. "As you have seen, our father's health rises and falls from day to day. I have tried to relieve as much of the stress as I can."

I nod. "I have noticed."

"Raj, I may not lead like him, but I do everything he says, handle all the affairs as he commands. I am working to make Jordan a better place." Zaid's declaration is sincere, but to what degree of sincerity, I'm not sure. He places his hand on my shoulder as we casually walk. "I have a dream of you and I working together to make Jordan rise above this crisis. Help the entire Middle East transform."

He pulls me closer to him. "Ah, I've missed you, brother. We have not been out since you have come home."

My brother and I have always celebrated my returns to Jordan. In the past there have been parties held at one of the palaces or a small intimate gathering at my cousin Anwar's, or even at one of the clubs here in Amman. It always seemed to get the media going, but I was hoping to keep this return subdued with my involvement in the center and my father's desire to remain reclusive.

"There is a party tonight," he says, smiling from ear to ear as he puts his Versace sunglasses on.

Knowing my brother's social needs and desires, it doesn't surprise me. "Ah, of course there is a party. With you, there always is," I say jokingly as I recall the party at the penthouse before leaving D.C. I heard him fucking that woman from the hallway all night long.

He plays along, laughing loudly. "What? There is a time to work and a time to play!"

"How big is this party?" I ask, hoping it isn't a large, indiscrete party at a nightclub.

He rolls his eyes. "Answering your question isn't important. You are going to say no."

"I may surprise you." It had been a stressful day and relaxing over a couple of drinks sounds good actually.

He looks over at me and grins. "It is very private, the host has made arrangements. There will be a certain princess there."

Ah fuck.

Zaid continues, "One the Queen and King hope you propose to sooner than later." His singsong, teasing voice annoys the shit out of me. He is talking about Daya, the Amir of Kuwait's daughter.

"Princess Daya," he says in a high-pitched voice. Zaid is completely aware of my aversion to the idea of a planned marriage. Even though my parents have transformed many traditions during their reign, one that has stuck with both of them is for me to marry a Muslim woman with royal lineage to ensure the longevity of our Islamic faith and the forming of a political alliance with other Arab countries.

Kuwait is an ally my father has wanted to form stronger ties with for years, something my grandfather wanted, but couldn't achieve. When Daya was born two years after me, the Amir, Husaam al-Sami al-Akram al-Satar, and my father vowed to have their two children form ties for Kuwait and Jordan through marriage.

I stiffen as I momentarily consider the custom. Feeling my tension under his hand, Zaid laughs. "You know this is inevitable, Raj, and it doesn't have to be bad. I mean, Daya has become a beautiful woman. Fucking her won't be so bad."

He pulls out a cigarette and lights it as I look at him with astonishment. "Really? Fucking her won't be so bad?"

The lengths he goes to with his crudeness continues to surprise me. "What?" he comments through his teeth clasping the dangling cigarette. "It is true. I would fuck her."

His narrow mindedness is irritating. "Fucking her isn't the point! The point is we don't know each other, and while I know we would get to know each other, it isn't love."

He takes a long drag then pulls out the cigarette and hands it to me. I shake my head and he immediately responds. "When did this happen?"

I had only smoked one summer. "For a while. That shit will kill you, Zaid."

In the past he has smoked here and there, but since being here his chain smoking has become excessive.

He looks at me like I have just pissed all over his dream or some shit. I laugh at him staring at me through his fucking blinged -out Versace's. "What?"

He puts the cigarette back in his mouth and looks up into the sky. "I know a lot more shit that can kill you here in the desert and it isn't fucking cigarettes." He puts the cigarette back in his mouth, then abruptly stops walking and turns to me. "Hey, so do you want to go to the party or not? Because I'm going. Raj, it is important to be seen together at these parties. There will be influential and powerful people there tonight and this is how connections are made here. Not behind some fucking desk in some office. Seeing you and I together, the two Princes of Jordan, bound by blood and our country is what we need. ALittifaqiya?"

"Naam." I nod, understanding what he means.

We leave just after dusk. Two of our family's guards follow us as Zaid drives us farther beyond Balq and As Salt in his white Pagani Huayra, one of the rarest cars in the world. So rare it is no longer available being manufactured. "While you are here, you can drive my Pagani, Raj."

He had offered his Lamborgini about a hundred times since being home. "No, I'm fine with the guards driving me," I tell him.

"Suit yourself." Zaid shifts gears, taking the car faster. Out here in the desert, the roads are pitch black. Rural until you come into a well-occupied area, like the one we are approaching. We turn off the main road, drive along a side road, before turning into a set of gates to a private residence. I'm surprised how well the two guards tailing us have kept up with the speed Zaid has been pulling tonight.

This is a new area that has developed within the past year. Everything west of Amman is new development and very expensive as Jordan's expansion continues to thrive. "So who's party is this?"

"A friend to Sheikh Tariq bin Qasim," he says, somewhat distracted as we are permitted by the guards through the gate. "He is the son of..."

I finish his sentence, "The son of Sheikh Qasim bin Khaddam of Syria."

It's rumored Qasim fled his country to London while his son Tariq stayed behind to hold down their palace in Syria, defending their territory from the civil unrest, revolutionaries seeking takeovers. Other rumors have spread as well. Rumors that the Khaddam family has been involved in funding the revolutionaries involved in the war within the Syrian borders. I'm curious why he is here in Jordan if the rumors say he is defending their territory.

"So Tariq is here," I state flatly, not thrilled about his presence.

His glare is cutting as we drive on beyond the gates. "Look, while you cater to the impoverished refugees of Syria, I attend to the influential ones when they need our help.

You haven't had to experience unrest in your cozy penthouse in the States."

His dig is meant to shut me up, but it has the opposite effect. "You know the rumors, right?" I ask.

He nods. "Yeah, fucking rumors from the media, just like the rumors this bullshit war is contained in Syria. It has a long reach and it is spreading, Raj. Poor or rich, royal or peasant, it is all around us. And to be clear, I sought out Tariq, invited him to come to us whenever he needs to, not the other way around."

He lights up a cigarette hastily and I grab for the steering wheel. He brushes my hand away, already having lit up. "I got it. Look, Samir Fadel is a good friend. This is his house and Tariq is his guest."

"How long is he staying?"

Zaid pulls up behind a red Ferrari. "As long as he wants."

I think of how our father reacted to this, if he even knows. "Does the King know?"

He cuts the engine. "Is it law to inform our King of Syrian houseguests? If that's the case we should report every illegal refugee at your fucking center." He laughs maniacally.

He opens the car doors and we get out into the chilled desert night air. His voice is calmer, more controlled when he speaks. "Rajaa, The King is aware of what he needs to know, so is the Prime Minister and Cabinet." He comes around the car to me and places his hand on my shoulder. "We can't expect him to make decisions like he once did. Some days he does not think straight and while he says he is strong in mind, it's weakening ... I see it. I made the call on this when Sami offered his home. I have met with Tariq many times and he is someone we can trust."

"Who knows he is here?" I can't help questioning him for fear of the unknown with Tariq.

"Only the people close to me."

Zaid walks away toward the staircase leading to the estate entrance, leaving me standing there with a swarm of questions.

Zaid looks back at me. "Are you coming?"

"Yeah."

I follow behind him just as our guards pull up in the SUV, watching us ascend the steps. As I catch up to Zaid, he speaks quietly, "It is easy to tell someone else what to do and when to do things when you are not walking knee deep in this fucking shit crisis on our side of the world. That is why I wanted you to come tonight. So you will learn how things are done, not in some political arena where everyone pretends crisis can be worked out on pen and paper, some fucking resolution. Words that have no meaning here. This is how things get done, Raj and the sooner you learn this the better."

He stops at the top of the steps. "You said it yourself not too long ago. Sometimes risks need to be taken to gain the security we desire for our country."

He smiles, the desire to set me straight by using my own words achieved. "Come, let's not keep our host waiting."

Security opens the doors to Sami's grandiose estate. Modern, and very American, music resonates beyond the foyer where only a couple of people are mingling. My brother knows the man, as he walks over to him, kissing him on either cheek. "Sami!" my brother announces him jovially as he pulls away gesturing to me by his side. "My brother."

"Prince Rajaa!" Sami announces my name as if he knows me. "So nice for you to come. Your brother talks about you endlessly." He pulls me in and I reciprocate, kissing him on each cheek. "The semester at Georgetown has come to an end?" Sami asks.

"Yes, I will be here for the summer, then finish my final semester in the fall."

Zaid moves back around to the man, gesturing for me to give the woman the customary kiss. "This is the beautiful Rima!" Zaid says, stepping toward her and exchanging a peck on either cheek. I watch Sami's reaction, thinking Zaid kissing her cheeks is bold in our culture, but he doesn't react.

She laughs delicately. "Thank you, Prince Zaid. That is very kind of you," she says somewhat flirtatiously. She leans over to me and I hesitantly kiss her cheeks as Sami continues to make conversation with me. "So when you finish, you will return home to Jordan."

My head is swimming from the strong perfume Rima is wearing. Before I can respond, Zaid answers, "Yes, that is his plan."

It is my plan, but I don't like to be answered for. "Yes, I will return."

"Good, good," Sami says as he holds Rima close to his side now.

"Tariq?" my brother inquires about his whereabouts.

Sami signals behind him and grins. "In the courtyard ... entertaining, of course."

Zaid's smile matches his tooth for tooth as he moves past the couple.

"Nice to meet you," I say, left to close the conversation.

They both smile at me as I follow my brother into the heart of the estate.

The adornments of Sami's family have been overrun with Tariq's display of mosaics, alabasters, and busts of his Syrian royal lineage. I try to give credit to Tariq for finding pride in his family's bloodline, while intruding on Sami's home like he has, but this isn't a typical fucking house guest.

"Looks like he has moved in?" I comment.

Zaid's eyes, filled with caution, flit back at me, then keep moving ahead.

Massive floor-length windows and doors are entries from the courtyard into the dining hall and living spaces of the house. Sheer window trappings sway in the trivial breeze, filtering through them the sounds of laughter, mingling bodies, and small talk among the guests.

Walking onto the portico is like walking into another domain. The sound of splashing and laughter draws my attention to the pool on the far side of the courtyard. Dressed in slacks and a collared shirt, I suffice that my brother and I didn't come prepared for a swim.

"I see him," Zaid announces.

As we walk toward the source of the music and the largest cluster of women, I see a man much shorter than Zaid and I emerge. "Z!"

"T," my brother announces with open arms.

Tariq holds his tumbler of milky liquid aside as he dances to my brother. It is hard to not notice the bright-red speedo donning the Jordanian flag. Having seen more than I want, I divert my eyes to the mass of women ogling both Zaid and me. The stares and whispers among men and women come with the territory of being royalty, but it's concerning as to what is being said about us, especially in the company of Tariq, a man wearing our country's flag on his ballsack.

Some of the women are dressed eloquently in sequined and embroidered jalabiya dresses, while others are wearing see-through wraps to appear modest in their scant bikinis and thongs. A few men and women are in the pool, splashing and swimming.

"Rajaa!" Tariq is standing next to my brother, smiling with his arms open to me. Reluctantly, I walk over to Tariq and move in to give him the traditional greeting of a kiss on both cheeks when he takes hold of my face, guiding the greeting, then pulling me into a hug. "As-salaam 'alaykum!"

"Wa 'alaykum Salaam," I manage to get out through the forcible pats on my back he is giving. He holds me at arm's length, seeming to look me over. The smell of hard liquor on his breath is overwhelming.

"Ah, Zaid, he is just as you described. Young, but he has the eye of a man that will make a great advisor to the King of Jordan someday, yes?"

He points at me with the hand holding the drink and nearly spills its contents onto me. "You need a drink, Rajaa. Come with me."

As he turns to walk away, he calls on his entourage, "Come, ladies. Taalo!"

Smiling and dancing to the rhythm of the music, a few of the women fall into step on either side of him. My brother drapes his arm over my shoulder and pulls me closer. "He's a good guy, Raj. You will see."

As Zaid and I follow behind Tariq, I notice him place a free hand on the ass of one of the girls, squeezing and making her squeal. It sends the other girls around him into a frenzy of laughter. Zaid notices, laughs savagely, and nudges me for approval.

"Come on, Raj. This is a place we can enjoy our royal indiscretions. T?"

"Yeah, yeah," Tariq says, pausing to look back at Zaid. He seems nervous and hyper, like he is on something.

"Is Daya here?"

Ah shit.

Tariq looks around the courtyard aimlessly in an attempt to find her. He speaks quickly to his security detail walking along with his crew.

"Zaid, just leave it alone," I say under my breath to him.

"What? If she is here you should say hello. It would be rude for you not to," Zaid says as he searches for her as well.

Tariq pats his guard on the back, then calls back to us. "No, Daya left a while ago."

I breathe a sigh of relief for Daya's absence. One less encounter to have. Noticing my relief, Zaid comments, "There, she isn't here. Now you can let go relax a little. Remember two summers ago, those girls I surprised you with? They were perfect; tight asses, tight tits, tight everything, yeah?"

I don't know why the fuck he is bringing this up now, but it isn't the time or place.

He continues to speak though. "The one you had, she was not cheap. I made sure you received the best for your first time."

I continue to ignore him as we walk on, only to remember the situation vividly. Zaid surprised my cousin Anwar and me with three beautiful women delivered to Anwar's private residence for my first time two summers ago. While sexual encounters outside of marriage are an obscenity, a disgrace in the eyes of Allah, both my cousin and brother coached me on how the mores and cultural rules bend for royalty. I had the safety net and guidance of my brother and cousin; my first time turned into multiple times that summer.

While my indiscretions were free in Jordan, I kept my desire at bay back in the States. I didn't care that Zaid had paid the women to have sex with us then. I was fucking naive, just looking for sex, invincibility even. My sophomore year, invincibility became fragile and conquerable when my father was diagnosed with Parkinson's. Eternity wasn't an option and the way I lived meant more to me. I fucked a couple of women at the beginning of that summer, but it had lost its luster, unlike my brother and Anwar, continuing to screw like rabbits.

Anwar got married the fall of my junior year, so my brother was left to his own sexual deviance with me out. I always made an excuse and he always had a reason to party. Fuck, looking back at it now, he was starting to change then and I hadn't realized it. He was less reserved about his escapades with women, so much that the media caught him in rather compromising situations, his pants literally around his ankles as he fucked a waitress in the back alley of a club.

The more I observe the atmosphere of this party, the women, the alcohol, the music, the seclusion in Sami's magnificent mansion outside of Amman, hidden from tradition, the more I'm led to believe this party isn't as dignified as Zaid made it out to be.

One of Sami's servers comes up to my brother and me with two glasses filled with a milky liquid. "Ah, Arak! Shukran!" Zaid takes one of the glasses, handing the other to me.

I take the drink and raise it to my nose, taking in its aroma. Arak is unlike the average American gin, whisky, or scotch.

With Zaid watching me as he takes a hefty gulp of the absinthe-like drink, I man up and match his sampling. The cooling effect of the ice is smooth and the taste of anise settles onto my tongue before I swallow the spiced fire of the drink.

He raises his eyebrows as he pulls the drink away from his mouth, licking his lips as if the drink has quenched a thirst he has had for far too long. "Arak!" he bellows.

Tariq continues to march on ahead of us with his harem of women, calling back to Zaid, "Arak!"

My brother takes another long draw of the creaming alcohol and I do as well, the fiery burn now doused with the numbness it provides with potency.

"Too strong for you, Raj?" Tariq prods.

Pretending to ignore his comment and accepting his challenge, I drain the rest of the Arak in my glass, making my brother cheer again, "Arak!"

The waitstaff is waiting at my side to take my empty glass and hand me a freshly prepared iced glass of Arak. I take it from the server and drink half of it as I walk on, following Tariq and his women disappear beyond the glowing candescence of white curtains. Once on the other side, the mood of the parlor-like lounge is clear, erotic. Men and women exercising their sexual escapades occupy the deep burgundy chaise lounges, the darkened plush sofas, and the enormous ottomans spread around the room, fucking, riding, and writhing in ecstasy. I can't help staring at the show going on around me. Zaid continues past me only to pull me along with him.

We descend a stairwell to a lower floor. Once at the bottom, Tariq kisses each of the women by his side before they retreat back up the stairwell. Tariq sits on a lavish oversized chair. "This is the wing Sami and his beautiful wife have given me when I come to visit. Here, let's talk ... eh chit chat as they say, right, Raj?" He gestures to the two chairs across from him. He drinks down the rest of Arak, then sets it to the side of him.

Tariq smiles widely as he looks at Zaid, then me. "I need to thank you, Rajaa. When my father fled our palace in Al Raqqah, he told me to go with him, seek asylum in Europe. A palace in London was waiting for us to run away to, but I refused to leave." He shakes his head and waves his hand aimlessly. "I do not run."

He covers his mouth as he belches, then continues to speak. "He is old and I understand his reasons. He has done what he can for his territory, he does not have the strength to do any more. We have similar situation, right, Zaid?"

Zaid nods and raises his glass to Tariq before gulping another hefty portion of his Arak.

Tariq looks back at me as he explains, "He feared death by the hands of those fucking bastards. Fucking President Faraj."

President Faraj Al-Dawood, the notorious president who has built a regime of torture and devastation to the Syrian people for over two decades. Tariq's disgust is evidence of his feelings toward the regime and maybe the reason for him seeking partial refuge here in Jordan. Either way, it is fucking bullshit Zaid is keeping him a secret.

Tariq shakes his head, "While Faraj has many enemies, my father's vitality was his; he was afraid of losing his life because of the revolution. But I, I wouldn't leave our land without a fight. If I ran, I would be showing weakness," he continues, glancing from Zaid to me. "Running away from the Middle East, our history, the birthplace of my royal bloodline thousands of years before me ... How can you run from that?"

He shakes his head, seemingly affected by recalling the history his statement entails. "I met Zaid shortly after my father left. Sami introduced us. From that day, your brother promised my safety and I promised to aid in the rise of both of our countries."

He settles back into his chair. "You have done right by me and I plan to assist your family any way I can, Rajaa."

Tariq downs the rest of his Arak, licking his lips for any remains.

I speak freely, the Arak giving me loose lips. "Assist our family. How exactly?"

Tariq looks to Zaid, then leans forward in his chair. "Your brother and I, my people, we have it under control."

His avoiding my question strikes a nerve. And who the fuck are his people? He scratches the back of his neck, then stares at me with his own curiosity. "Your brother tells me you are promoting a center for refugees from my home."

I nod, but clarify where he is mistaken. "It is a program to support and aid the refugees that would otherwise would be living on the streets with no food, no shelter. I wouldn't call it a promotion. It is a necessity."

Tariq looks at me queerly. "Ah, a necessity, yes, I am aware of necessities during war and crisis."

I'm not sure of the purpose of his comment, but he continues, "I suppose you could say that what I am doing is like your little center."

His confidence that he is like me is provoking, and his diminishing the center fucking pisses me off. "Really, how is that?"

"Your brother says you are acting as a silent benefactor. I am also a kind of silent benefactor."

"For what?"

He sits back and takes me in, studying me. "Well, then I wouldn't be so silent if I disclosed that, would I!" He laughs maniacally and looks at Zaid, exchanging a nod and smile. Tariq settles back in his chair and settles his laughter. "It wouldn't be wise of me. Ah, look at him, Z! So young and eager, like a baby learning all of these things for the first time." The glimmer of excitement in his eyes is menacing and his condescendence is unnerving.

"Well, I'm sure I can handle it."

He leans forward immediately, his excitement no longer present as he narrows his eyes on me. "That remains to be seen, Rajaa. For now, I can tell you the new Middle East will start with Syria and Jordan under your future king and," he tilts his head from side to side, "whomever will be in control of Syria."

He breathes in deeply and sits back as he shifts his gaze between Zaid and me. "As the storm comes, we will be ready."

He suddenly glances at the stairwell behind us. A guard has descended and come into view. Tariq snaps his fingers. "Nursil lahum fi. Send them, oh, and drinks. We need more Arak!"

My brother joins in on the call for more alcohol. "More Arak!" They both feed on the other's laughter as they rise from their seats. I follow in suit and rise as I puzzle over this phantom plan lingering in the air around us.

The room spins a little and my feet feel heavy suddenly. Shit, it's hitting me hard.

I glare at my brother, the future King of Jordan being motivated by Tariq, the man laughing maniacally drunk on Arak, a Syrian Sheikh wanting to show his daddy what a brave motherfucker he is by being the first to return home if this crisis ever ends. I am not sure which of the two poses a greater threat, but I fear a threat is coming either way.

I look down at the half-drank milky drink I'm still holding and down the rest of it. Tariq and Zaid applaud my stout consumption of Arak as I notice three women come into the room holding a fresh glass of Arak each. They are dressed in lingerie, covered only by the sheer mantle they each wear. Nothing is left to the imagination as they parade toward us, silencing both Tariq's and Zaid's laughter.

One of the women focuses on me with her deep-set eyes and moves in handing me my fresh drink. "Drink, prince, and let me take care of you," she says as she guides me back to my chair.

Even though my mind is against her offer of pleasure, my dick says otherwise as it twitches against my trousers. I down the new glass of Arak this mistress has given me like water; the sting of it no longer exists with it flowing in my veins now.

My brother and Tariq both yield to the commanding hands of their consorts as they slowly sit down in the chairs they rose from moments ago. They take the glasses the women have brought them and raise them to each other in a silent toast, one I am not a part of. The mistress stands above me as I sit back in my chair. She slowly lowers the sheer blue mantle, letting it drop to the ground just before she moves in time with the music rising in the room.

The elixir ebbs and flows, making the room hazy and her movements a seductive smooth tease meant to arouse. My cock is pushing against my zipper as she runs her hand against my tensing thighs. As her hands feather upward, she slowly unbuttons my shirt and runs her hands over my bare chest, over my abs, my nipples. Tariq's seducer has wasted no time on seduction, having straddled his legs and given him full access to her as she starts to ride him.

I look back down at my seducer, just as her hand slips down beneath my belt, reaching and teasing my cock with her touch. She asks me if I'm ready for her in Arabic, but I don't answer. My head is heavy and my tongue mute from what has to be the Arak, but it has never affected me like this in the past.

Something isn't right.

I pinch my eyes closed and let my head fall back, hoping that will help. As soon as I do, images begin to flash in my head, like an electric storm. The courtyard at the center, fast-moving children running and hopping, then a shift to an empty space with the blue-veiled woman, her golden hair blowing in the wind. The sky is darkened and she turns to face me. As clear as day, it is her, the same eyes, the same presence as it was far away from here that night. The mixture of her seduction, her veil slipping from her head, down along her fair skin, and the persuasion of Tariq's mistress' hand loosening my belt blends too easily, too tempting, too arousing.

Groans from the other participants in the room get my attention as I pull my paramour's hand away from my throbbing dick. She slithers along my chest with her tongue, her lips brushing against my skin. She works her way up, her almond-shaped eyes targeting mine as her tongue fondles my nipple.

Zaid groans with pleasure as the woman buried between his legs moves in rhythm with the forcefulness of his hand wrapped in her hair. Tariq growls with pleasure as his riding concubine rises and falls above him faster and faster.

"You like your whore, Rajaa?" Zaid's gasps and groans as he looks over at me.

"Of course he does, Zaid. My whores are the best money can buy. We will have them all night long." Tariq hisses and slaps his concubine's ass, making her writhe faster. "Do you feel the difference with it, Zaid? It's Qaa'ed."

Captain?

Zaid pulls the woman sucking him off up with him, bends her over the chair like a rag doll, then takes her from behind as he pulls her hair. "Yes, I feel it. Do you fucking feel it, whore?" he asks the woman, who winces as he yanks her hair harder. He peers over at me. "Do you feel it, brother? The Captain and Arak coursing through your veins, mixing, energizing you? It is fucking amazing, isn't it?" His words are enunciated to match each thrust as his invincible rage to take her harder and harder becomes his only obsession.

What the fuck?

The scene I seem to be watching from above, the game they are playing, the prostitutes, the warped pleasure, the fucking drug Captagon, they fucked me up.

I look back down at the woman beneath me; she has already undone my belt and unzipped my pants, partially setting my throbbing dick free. I'm not sure if it is the shock of being drugged by Tariq and my brother or the disgust of almost surrendering to this sick fucking orgy Tariq and my brother have devised, but either way I gain enough strength to push the mistress off of me before she takes me any further.

The words I push from my mouth come out slurred, almost incoherent. "You fucking drugged me. I can't do this."

"What the fuck, Raj?" Zaid's voice is full of disappointment and anger as I stumble forward, almost falling over the woman beneath me. "Get back here and fuck her!" If not for the pain of my hard-on, I might not have sobered enough to focus on getting the fuck out of here.

Tariq growls from behind me as I find my footing and ascend the stairwell, "Get back here, Rajaa!"

I nearly fall at the top of the landing and somehow make it through the maze of loungers and sofas draped with men and women and sex. Once I'm beyond the white curtains of the indulgent carnal congress, the chilled night air of the desert hits my face, rousing me from the influence. Ignoring the stares and whispers, I move through the courtyard, the interior, the entry, and out the front door.

Our guards are waiting at the SUV that followed us. As they see me approaching, they look at each other questioningly. "Where is Prince Zaid?"

"Busy. I needed to get out of there." As I shut the car door, I submit to the darkness and close my eyes. Both doors in front shut and one of the guards asks me if they should wait for my brother in Arabic.

I let my head lull to the side and look up at Sami's estate. "No, let him stay."

Chapter 6

Ella

The classrooms are closed on Saturday and Sunday, so walking there this morning to meet Ana and the other volunteers to catch our ride to the Roman amphitheater and a late lunch is off beat. Faces I don't normally see peer back at me as I walk along the less-busy sidewalks. An elderly woman is sweeping the sidewalk in front of her home. Two boys about Ghalib's age are sitting on the step watching her, eating what I would guess is breakfast.

Hoda got up early this morning to make me something to eat. I hadn't expected her to and thanked her. In Hoda's own way she appreciated it, even though she waved her hand, dismissing me. "Thank you, no! Ana bikhayr!" she whispered sternly. Her saying it's okay in her native words made me smile as she guided me by my shoulders to the door as I ate my favorite carb overload of Shrak, the best bread ever.

The small tour bus Tom offered us yesterday has already pulled up to the center and the soldier posted at the entrance to the courtyard is visible. As I walk past the bus and soldier and into the courtyard, I see Ana and five of the other volunteers chatting near the front door to the center.

"Hey," she says casually. "We are just waiting on a couple more volunteers. There is coffee inside the staff work room if you want some." She holds up her Styrofoam cup for effect.

The food has definitely grown on me, but I can't get used to the bitterness of the Turkish coffee. "I'm okay."

"I know," one of the volunteers comments. "I'm waiting for the Starbuck's near the Amphitheater."

"No shit," Ana's statement is hushed.

Tim laughs a little. "Yeah, just a few blocks supposedly."

David, the volunteer spearheading our outing, comes out from the center and looks beyond us. "Ah, there they are. Let's get going."

I turn to see Isabel and Laura, the two volunteers we were waiting on, walk through the gate past the guard.

I have Ana take a picture of me standing in the center of the Amphitheater with the center's borrowed digital camera. Tim brought it along so we could send the pictures to our family once he uploaded them after we get back.

Here at the site we appear to be average tourists, not volunteers at a refugee center with specific guidelines and code for dress. It gave some lenience and it was really nice to let my veil fall around my neck to be worn as a scarf today. It is strange running my hands through my hair in public.

The green and white logo of Starbuck's is a sight as we walk from the amphitheater to the coffee shop. All of us opt for a cold coffee instead of hot with the Eastern heat. After trekking back to the bus at the amphitheater, we drive a short distance south to Hashem Restaurant. Tim has been talking Hashem up all day and I can't wait to taste the stuffed falafel he keeps bragging about. I'm not disappointed; heavenly. Our waiter is so nice and welcoming, and even sends me away with an extra order of falafel before we leave. I try to pay for it, but he refuses to take my money. He keeps saying, "A gift, A gift."

The entire day is a win, but after lunch I'm really feeling the drain from the dry heat here in Jordan. I am more than grateful when we get back on the air-conditioned bus. On the ride back to the center, I close my eyes and think of how this day was bittersweet.

I had the opportunity, the freedom, and resources to travel and visit centuries-old landmarks here in Amman, while the families living along these deteriorating streets, the families I live among for the next two months, don't have the luxury of travel or touring. Their perspective is focused on putting food on the table and holding their family and faith close to their hearts. There is no money nor time to spare on site seeing. As for the refugees, there is no money period, many of them not getting paid for their work around the city. I feel the guilt of not knowing the Ahmadi family's situation again and tell myself I need to ask. I want to know their story.

When I left this morning and Hoda shooed me out of the house, she rushed me along like I was going off to work at the center. Did she realize I was going for leisure, not work?

The sun is setting as I walk back home. My veil is wrapped over my head now that I am back in our neighborhood. A few children are playing on the sidewalk, running back and forth while being watched by a woman from a high window. She smiles gingerly beneath her hijab then turns her attention back at her children, telling them it is time to eat in Arabic. "Waqtul Akil!"

She looks beyond me, her smile buried with suspicion at whatever she sees. I turn around quickly to see what she has, but there is nothing. Looking back up at the window, she has already retreated, the children running through the door of their home, shutting it tightly behind them.

I look back again and see only a handful of passersby making their way toward me now from around the corner, but nothing to cause suspicion.

Once home, I pass the large room the Ahmadi family occupies and notice Jasara and Hoda along with all the children sitting together within it. I am about to ask what's going on when I hear Ismad arguing with another man upstairs. They are speaking too quickly for me to attempt understanding them.

Hoda takes hold of my arm and pulls me into the room. "Come, come!" she hisses.

The volume of the men above suddenly rises, then tapers off into a long discussion. I sit down next to Ameena and Laila. Ameena smiles over at me timidly, then bows her head back down and continues to write in the journal she received at school. She is writing in Arabic, so I don't linger too long on its content.

I lean over to her and ask, "What is going on?"

She stops writing and closes the journal with her pencil inside to save her place before speaking. "Laila's uncle, Jasara's brother, has made it across the border. He crossed two weeks ago and has been looking for us."

I can't imagine how he could have found them. It would be like searching for a needle in a haystack. "How?"

Ameena shrugs, then opens her notebook and begins writing again. Laughter from above draws all of our attention as we all look up at the ceiling. Jasara and Hoda look at each other with smiles on their faces and I trust the fast-talking Arabic the men are exchanging now is good news.

"Hoda, Jasara, atfal tallo! Come! Ella, please come up!" Ismad calls to us. The sound of a smile on his face conveys with the tone of happiness in his voice.

"What is going on now?" I ask Ameena. She closes her notebook, smiling widely and holding Laila's hand tightly as cries tears of joy.

"He can stay," she says.

He can stay? I didn't understand.

"Why wouldn't he be able to stay?"

"My father. It is not respectful for a man to come into another man's home without permission. With Jasara, Laila, and Rushdi staying down here, Nazeer has to claim his responsibility for them and ask for permission to stay here. They have been talking up there for hours."

"He has accepted?"

Ameena smiles widely as we climb the stairs. "Yes."

Nazeer Ahmadi, Uncle Nazeer, is equal in age to Ismad, Hoda, and Jasara. I instantly see the resemblance that Nazeer and Jasara share as they stand side by side, tears streaming down their faces. The long embraces of Ameena and Rushdi with their uncle and the numerous kisses on the cheeks between the four of them were so overwhelming I couldn't contain my own tears. The Ahmadis clung to each other while Ismad asked Hoda make dinner in Arabic.

"This is a happy occasion, Ella!" he says, smiling under his heavy beard. I haven't heard him speak this openly with me before; it's kind of disarming. Ismad lifts Ghalib up into his arms, as does Nazeer with Rushdi, and they walk into the other room, leaving the women in the kitchen area.

Ameena, Laila, and Jasara jump into action, helping Hoda prepare food. Since being here, Hoda has always shooed everyone out of the kitchen, but tonight it seems like a family affair. I step aside, feeling out of place, when Hoda notices me. "Ella, tati al-musaaeda!"

Tati al-musaeada, tati ... I'm not sure what that means.

I notice Ameena mouthing to me from behind her, "Come help!"

I jump too, realizing she is asking me to help! "Oh, yes, help. Musaaeda. Shukran."

Hoda smiles at me as she kneads the dough for a fresh batch of Shrak.

Once the men and boys have eaten, the women sit at the table and eat our fill of Shrak, Tabbouleh, Fattoush, and

Hummus. I'm nearing my food coma when I remember the stuffed falafel from Hashem's, the extra order the waiter gave me.

Remembering him saying it was a gift, I tell them, "Oh! I have a gift! Laday hadiyya!"

With a spring in my step, I rise from the table and rummage through my bag at the top of the stairs and return with the white paper back. All the women are looking at me, then at each other curiously, which only builds my excitement to share this with them. I open the bag, remove the Styrofoam container, and open it to reveal the stuffed falafel. "Laday hadiyya from restaurant ... mataem," I say in broken Arabic mixed with English, mostly to clarify my choppy pronunciation.

Hoda reaches for the Styrofoam plate, rising from her seat, then looks up at me seemingly for permission. I hand it to her happily. She turns to the kitchen counter and places the falafel onto one of her own plates and takes it into the men, as it is a rule for the men to be served first. I hear her talking to them and catch the Arabic words for restaurant, gift, and my name in English. Seconds later Ismad appears around the corner with a falafel in his hand.

His dark, deep-set, almond-shaped eyes find mine and even though his beard hides his mouth, his smile is more than visible as he bows his head and holds the falafel out to me. "Shukran, Ella."

I bow my head as he has. "Al afo."

He disappears around the corner and Hoda comes back in with the remaining falafel, smiling from ear to ear. As she sits down across from me she reaches her hand across the table and squeezes mine, then pats the top of it. "Shukran."

Getting thanks from them for something so small compared what they have done opening their home to host me and give shelter to the Ahmadi family, I can't seem to form the words past the knot in my throat. I bow my head and lower my eyes instead. The eyes of all of the women are wide as they take their first bite of the stuffed falafel, then they seem to melt a little into their chairs from the flavor, just as I had at the restaurant.

Hoda finishes chewing the small morsels in her mouth then begins telling a story. From the few words I gather, she is talking about the restaurant, Hashem. She sees I am listening intently, so she pauses. "Ameena," she says, peering at me.

Ameena holds the falafel in her hands mid-bite, then sets it back down on her plate. "Oh, she is talking about my father taking her to Hashem just after they married."

Ameena's English is impressive, but it shouldn't surprise me; she is a smart girl. "Oh."

She continues to translate as Hoda tells her story. We all ooh and aah when she tells us King Amaar was there that night and he greeted everyone at their tables. Hearing Hoda speak seemed to open the levy for me to want to know more.

"Were you and Ismad in love?" I ask in English, hoping Ameena will pick up and translate for me just as she has for her mother. Instead I find all of them staring at me like I have asked something off limits. "Ana asif. I'm sorry, I shouldn't have been so bold."

"No, it okay," Hoda says. I guess she is getting better at pairing together English words as I am with Arabic. "Eh," she says as she appears to find the English words to explain, but can't. "Eshroon sanah."

Ameena starts to translate, but I repeat her response in English, knowing the translation, "Twenty years."

I stare into Hoda's brown eyes as she nods and says, "Yes. Love."

These two small bits of information and the youthful look in her eyes as she says the word *love* builds a story in my mind for Hoda. It makes her life hold more meaning for me.

"You love?"

Her question has me a little confused. "Do I have a love?"

She looks at Ameena then speaks quickly in Arabic.

"She is asking about your family. She says she is sorry for her English," Ameena translates loosely.

"No, it's okay. Yes. Naam Feaalan."

Laila adds a question; I think it is one from her own curiosity. "Do you have sister, brother?"

I answer her, explaining I have two sisters, Natalie and Jilly; all the while Ameena translates for Hoda.

"Do you have pictures?" Ameena asks curiously after translating.

I think about it. "Uh, yes, I think I do."

I rise from the table and go to my bag as Ameena translates my going to get a picture. If I have any they would be in my wallet. As I file through my billfold I see Jilly's smiling face. It is two years outdated, but still a picture nonetheless. I take it out and notice a family picture. It was taken five years ago, my junior year in high school, before Grandma Wallace passed. A flood of memories come back as I take it out. We were not estranged then.

I close my billfold and walk back to the table and start with the picture of Jilly, passing it to Ameena. "This is my sister. Okhti, Jilly."

Ameena studies the picture for a moment then passes it on to Laila, then Jasara. "Jamil," Hoda says once it is in her hands. As she hands it back to me I place the picture of my family on the center of the table. We took this picture in our backyard.

I point to my father and say, "Baba;" then to Mom, "Mama;" Natalie, "Okhti Natalie;" then Jilly again, "Okhti Jilly."

As I name off each of them, everyone is smiling with intrigue except Hoda, who is looking at me somberly.

"Write?" she asks expectantly then repeats her question in Arabic.

Ameena translates, "Do you write them? Since you have been here?"

Feeling in the spotlight, I fiddle with my fingers as I answer, "I write Jilly."

Decoding my words, Hoda presses with another question, one I knew she would ask. Especially with the way she watched me as I pointed out my family. "Mom, Dad?"

I know Hoda enough that she is a woman with expectations and she expected me to have written my mother and father out of respect. I also know there is no hiding lies from Hoda, even if it is the smallest one like not writing my parents. "No."

She takes her napkin off her lap and sets it on the table next to her, then leans forward. I don't know what to expect, a reprimand in Arabic? A slap across the face? I wouldn't put either past her. She is one tough mama. She takes hold of my hand, turns it over to my open palm, and points her index finger firmly in the middle of it.

"You write!" As she says each word, she pokes my palm softly, seeming to embed the statement into my hand, my heart.

My hand is easier penetrated by her words then my heart when it comes to my parents. I don't give her a promise; instead I nod, then pull my hand away.

Chapter 7

Ella

I look down at Muna's small hand, wrapped around my much larger one, as we walk back into the center from the courtyard. It is the same hand Hoda marked with her expectation last night. Write my parents.

When I got to the center this morning, I sent Jilly the digital picture of me at the amphitheater and at Hashem Restaurant. I almost included my mother and father on the email chain, but then had second thoughts. I quickly typed under the pictures:

Me at the Roman Amphitheater and eating stuffed falafel at Hashem with the volunteers. Love you. Miss you

I log out before I change my mind about adding my parents. Hoda would be so pissed if she knew I left them out.

With my free hand I shift my veil, feeling the itch of sweat on my scalp from standing out in the courtyard. The girls had been extra excited to go out and play today when I told them I would show them how to jump rope. They were impressed I knew what I was doing. Even Muna gave it a shot and stayed with the girls while I looked on. I noticed the guard watching them a few times. He even smirked when the girls would get caught up in the rope and giggle. He wasn't so stoic after all.

The girls' chatter increases in the halls, as it always does, and as I always do I stop walking and turn around to hush them. As I do, a thunderous boom echoes in the distance. The slight tremor it creates slides beneath my feet and the girls stand before me deathly silent. Their eyes are wide and the smiles are wiped from their now fear-filled, ghost-white faces.

The crackling break of an eruption closer now, setting a larger tremor over the ground beneath our feet, sends me to my knees and the girls immediately to the ground as they scream and muffle their cries with faces buried in their hands. I try to huddle close to them, touch them, let them know I am here.

"It's okay. I'm here," I say with a shaken, out-of-breath voice. I start to rise, trying to pull Muna up in my arms, just as another crackling explosion strikes even closer, sending Muna squirming, fighting to get free of me. For a little girl she is pretty fucking strong. I scramble after her, pulling her down with me, huddling again with the rest of the girls. I know I need to get them away from here, but as I try to pull on them to rise, they yank away from me and remain flat to the ground. I can't leave any of them just to take one at a time. It will never work.

"We have to go!" I call to them, my own panic setting in. I try to scoop up two of my girls, Kameela and Sahla, but clinging to each other like they are, it is impossible for me to lift their dead weight on my own.

"Ella!" I hear Tom's yell come from behind me as I continue to tug at the girls to get them up off the ground.

"Help me! I can't get them up!" I call out just before the sound of bullets and shattering glass fill my head. Something hits me from behind, a body, sending me straight to the ground, flat like a pancake. The rain of glass pelts my arms and the back of my head as my body is covered by another, the hard breath from him in my ear now.

I try to wiggle out from under his body, but he takes hold of my hands with his, keeping me from moving. "No! Stay down!"

His Arabic accent takes dominance over my plea. "The girls! Save them!"

I hear the static of walkie talkies and heavy boots around my head. My human shield commands, "Khodhum! Take them! Go!"

Their screams are becoming wails of agony, if not for physical pain, then for the trauma of living again what they thought they had fled far away from here. I keep telling myself, *They're screaming. They're alive.*

I can hardly breathe from the combined weight of my defender and the anxiety of what I can't see, when he suddenly lifts away from me, taking me up with him and hoisting me over his shoulder in one swift motion. I open my eyes and see the shattered glass on the ground where we laid get farther away as I am taken from the scene.

No blood on the ground. They aren't hurt.

"Where are the girls?" I yell, begging for an answer as I crane my neck to look around the front of us. "I need to see them!"

As we turn the corner and pass through a corridor, a door slamming behind us, the light from the outside world is shut out. Gunfire peppers beyond the door again. Is it our soldiers or those attacking? Is it the guard in the courtyard? The one who finally smiled at the girls playing today? Has he been hit? Is he dead? Are the girls in here with us?

With adrenaline pumping through my veins, I writhe and squirm to be released as my mind continues to assault me with questions. "Put me the fuck down!"

In one swift motion he abandons his hold on me, dropping me to my wobbly legs and cupping his hand over my mouth, holding me still. His height towers over me and his mass engulfs me as his angered golden-ember eyes search mine.

It's like an ambush, a familiar capture as he holds me captive with his furrowed brow, his eyes darting between mine, a symbol of his recollection. He is searching my eyes for something he's discovered before. Something we both succumbed to. How is it possible? We are in Jordan in the middle of a fucking attack. My golden-eyed stranger was in D.C. at some fucking rich-ass party then again in a fucking elevator! As his hand loosens over my mouth, I don't fight his hold like I had seconds before, as I consider how any of this is happening.

"'Eh enta."

I don't think his deep-voiced whisper was meant to find its way into the open space between us, because once he said it, he quickly closes his mouth, tightening his jaw as he backs away from me completely, leaving me to free fall in the release of golden amber having captured me before, in another place far away from this world.

It is him.

"Ella!" Ana voice permeates the door.

Tom brushes past us, breaking the soldier and I apart further as he opens the door halfway. "Ana! Get in here! Quiet!"

Pulling her in, her eyes go wide as soon as she sees me and she starts rambling in loud whispers. "Oh my God! I thought you and the girls! You were out in the courtyard!" She pulls me into her arms and hugs me with every ounce of trembling force remaining within her. I notice the girls huddled in a corner with two soldiers standing beside them and Tom huddled near them, speaking to them in Arabic as their sobs are contained to small whimpers. I want nothing more at the moment but to go to them and hold them.

Once Ana releases me, I move to them quickly, kneeling down in front of them as they huddle around me. I hold each of them close, Muna the first to climb into my lap and curl up. My heart breaks and melts at the same time as I hold them, check them for any marks, any blood.

A walkie talkie comes alive in one of the soldier's hands. The responder is speaking Arabic very quickly and the soldiers exchange it just as quick. Suddenly, the door opens and all the guns in the room take aim, just as the solider from the courtyard comes into view.

Thank God he's safe.

He speaks to my savior hastily. My mind is not working in Arabic, so I can't understand what they are saying. Whatever the exchange, the man who shielded me turns to Tom and me. "They will stay with you. Do not leave until it is clear."

Seemingly torn by his duty to defend and protect and staying here, he looks at me once more then leaves, the courtyard soldier tailing him.

Minute after minute passes with silence. The gunfire has stopped and there is the sound of heavy footsteps on broken glass outside of the door, along with the static of walkie talkies. The soldiers protecting us receive a commanding voice on their walkie talkie, letting us out into the hall. As they usher us out, the girls encircle me, holding onto any piece of fabric, arm, or leg they can. Tom walks ahead of us and Ana turns to go toward the classrooms.

"Ana?" I question her leaving my side even for a second.

"I need to check on my girls. Amanda has them," she says as one of the soldiers follows her down the hall.

I stand with Tom, the soldier, and the girls in the hall, taking in the broken glass covering the length of the hallway. The light fixtures blown out, the windows gone, and streaks of blood along the wall. Seeing the blood, I look away, unable to prevent the surge of fear.

"I can't have them here. I need to get them to the classroom," I say to Tom, both trying to leave the scene for my sake and my girls.

Tom is visibly shaken as he runs his hands through his hair and looks around at the shattered portion of the center. "Okay, we will take you."

The soldier walks behind Tom, my girls, and me, and I carry Muna on my hip. Tom speaks to the soldier in Arabic, asking him a question about the director of Caritas. The soldier talks over the device and quickly gets a response.

"She is fine," he says in English with a thick accent. As we walk down the clinic section of the center, the movement of staff and those who were being seen is slow, but awakening from the strike with cries, sobs, and tears of shock and fear and despair. Despair ... they couldn't get away from it. That is what must be going through the refugees' minds right now. They can't get away from the despair even here surrounded by those who care about them.

Tom's cell phone rings and he quickly picks up. "Yes."

As I watch him speak, he looks at me. "Yes, she is fine. Okay, I will."

He hangs up as we keep walking and I'm curious about who he was speaking to. "Who was that?"

He puts his arm on my back and leads me along. "It was nothing. Don't worry."

Where the lights were blown in the front portion of the center, they are working back here along the corridor. I nod and hold Muna closer as she rests her head on my shoulder.

The weight of her head gives rise to the soreness of being pushed to the ground by my rescuer. "The man that shielded me. Is he a soldier?"

Tom is taking in our surroundings, assessing everything and everyone around us. "Yes, among other things."

"What other things?"

I see one of my girl's mother crying as she comes running down the corridor, looking around with fright until she sees me and releases her cry. "Nooda!"

The little girl lets go of Tom's hand and cries desperately until she reaches her mother and is swept up in her arms. As Tom and I get closer to them, the mother comes up to me.

"Shukran. Hafazat abnatay. Shukran." Her weakened voice trembles as she takes my free hand and holds it tightly between hers. *Thank you for saving my daughter,* is what she keeps saying. The glimmer of light cast in her tears, knowing her daughter is alive, when moments ago her fear was she may be dead in the courtyard.

I try to pull my hand away as I nod, not wanting to speak, knowing my voice will give way and release the cry I'm desperately holding in. Tom must see me struggling inside as I continue to nod and try to smile while holding Muna.

"Bikill Sroor," he says to the woman, who clings to her daughter and runs in the opposite direction.

Tom puts his arm on my shoulder again as he moves us along faster, the soldier still to the rear of us. His walkie talkie dispatches the sound of soldiers speaking quickly in Arabic.

He speaks to the soldier behind us as we enter the wing containing all of the classrooms. Tom turns back to me. "I have to go check on everyone. He will stand guard at the classrooms. He is calling for another to come down to your wing as well. You will only need to stay until the children are picked up."

"Then I can go home?"

He nods as he starts to walk away. "Yes."

"Wait. You didn't answer me. What other things is this soldier?" I needed Tom to confirm what I felt deep within; I have just been saved by the man I've met before, far away from here, back in the States.

Tom and the soldier standing guard by our sides exchange a knowing glance, then he looks back at me. "He is the silent benefactor of this program and the Prince of Jordan."

The soldier speaks quickly in his device, responding to the voice on the other end, then turns back to us. "The authorities have arrived. They need you."

As Tom walks away, he calls back to me, "We will send the parents back to pick up the girls. Don't leave the classrooms until I or one of the authorities has come to get you. Do you understand?" His serious tone strikes a nerve of fear in me again as reality sets in. I had been rescued from death by the fucking Prince of Jordan, a man who has touched my soul on more than just this occasion.

The comfort of my small hallway of classrooms is filled with the small cries as I pass each door to mine. Once I'm in my room and Ana and the other girls come into sight, my girls immediately go to them and hold each other.

As each of our girls are picked up, the same scene unfolds: a mother, father, or aunt with fear in their eyes turns the corner and comes into the classroom. The fear only disappearing from them when they have spotted their little girl alive, then the wails and cries come, bringing up all of the anxiety I had just controlled. It happens over and over again until the last one is picked up, my sleeping Muna, snuggled in my arms. I can't imagine being the one to tell any of them I failed in protecting the life of their daughter and she has died.

I hand Muna off to her crying aunt, only to stir Muna from her sleep and renew her own frightened emotions. I think if I had lost one of them, I wouldn't be able to carry on here.

Ana and I don't speak after the girls are gone. We just sit at our chairs and wait for someone to take us home. The home I want most of all right now is the small, cheap apartment I share with my best friend Allison back in D.C. The more I think on it, though, the more I think of him, the soldier, the prince, the benefactor, the man at the loft. *He is the fucking Prince of Jordan.*

I hear Tom's voice before he appears at the door as he speaks with a few of the other teachers. His face is still as morose as it was earlier. "Okay, let's get you home."

I look at the empty streets on either side of us as I ride in the backseat of the black-on-black SUV. The panic of another attack has turned the busy streets of Amman into a ghost town. I glance around at the buildings. All are standing and are untouched, so the explosion must not have been this direction. Where, though?

Getting closer to the Ba'ashirs' home, worry for Ghalib, Ameena, Laila, and Rushdi revives the dread from earlier. What if they were in the buildings bombed? Why did I not fucking think of them earlier? Pulling up to the house, I thank the driver in Arabic and rush to the front door. I knock quickly, still feeling the creeping panic at my back, worrying an attack may come again right here, right now at my back.

Ismad opens the door quickly and lets me in, closing and locking it behind me. "Oh thanks to Allah, you are safe, Ella. Hoda!"

As if they were waiting anxiously for me, Hoda, Ameena, and Ghalib appear at the top of the steps, while Uncle Naz, Jasara, Laila, and Rushdi stand at the open doorway of their small living space.

All of a sudden, my body begins to shake like I am freezing, but I am not in the desert heat. I am fucking scared as shit and I can't move other than shake and chatter my teeth uncontrollably. I notice Jasara and Laila walk toward me as Rushdi stays close to Naz. Without a word they come to me, Jasara the first to take me in her embrace, the warmest I have ever experienced. I don't think my own mother has hugged me like she is.

That night I cried so hard and they each took turns holding me. Jasera cried with me, telling me in Arabic she wished she had stayed at the center with me, but they wouldn't let her. I hugged Ameena, Laila, Ghalib, and Rushdi, relieved they were safe. Ismad told us the explosion happened east of the center, but there were multiple attacks by shooters in the area, including the center's attack immediately following the explosion.

Hoda and Jasara make dinner like every other night, while I lie in my room. The sound of Ismad's small radio playing the news in Arabic resonates through the upstairs throughout the evening as him and Nazeer listen to the updates on what happened. I don't attempt deciphering what is being said.

Don't want to know right now. I just want to shut off.

I don't come out of my room once the men have eaten and it's the women's turn. Hoda brings me Shrak and a glass of water, sets it on the small table next to my bed, then leaves quietly. She leaves the door cracked and I can only think it is for her own benefit to hear me if I cry out.

I hear the women talking in the kitchen. My name is spoken a few times, but I can't hear the rest. I don't want to, I suppose. The only thing I want is sleep to find me, but it doesn't as I roll over and stare at the uneaten food sitting on the small table next to my bed.

I close my eyes and wonder what my chances are of being sent back home to D.C. over this. I should be begging, pleading to go back, but all I can think about right now are my girls and the prince saving me, those unknown words he spoke as he captured me and held me to him.

"*Eh enta.*"

Chapter 8

Rajaa

Standing on the balcony off my room, looking out into the night, I think of her, the woman with the blue veil and the fallen hair blowing in the wind in the courtyard at the center, then the woman huddled on the floor with screaming girls, frightened out of their minds, surrounding her. When she rose, her veil fell, revealing her fear and eyes I knew had looked upon them before upon, a girl lost in her circumstance.

It was her.

Ella is what Tom called out just before the gunfire. I ran to her without thinking. I didn't need to think, I just needed to protect her. Tom and the soldiers with us in the office were running toward me as I shielded her. One of my men tried to pull me away from her, but I told them to take the girls. I watched through the deluge of bullets as they found shelter in a nearby room. Once the avalanche of broken glass from the bullets subsided, I pulled her up and raised her over my shoulder, knowing I didn't have much time before another assault of bullets might target us.

"Eh enta."

It's you were the only words I said, the only thought I held in my head. The only words that left my lips as I studied every angle of her tear-streaked face, making sure I wasn't imagining the likeness of the lost girl from D.C at the party and the one I should have followed down the elevator at Stern's office. How can it be this same girl is here in Jordan at this center? Was she some kind of mirage then? A fabrication of the likeness of this woman? No, the likeness of her haunting eyes was the same as those I held in my gaze for as long as I could in the loft that night in Washington and for a fragment in time before the elevator closed. She was probably there speaking to Stern about the program.

The connections I'm making with this woman are screwing with my head as I lean on the railing. I look down at my hands, remembering the feel of her weight in them when I lifted her to my shoulder, keeping her silent with my hand over her mouth when I was face to face with her, then the obsessive desire to wipe the streaks of dirt and tears from her cheeks. It was her. There is no mistake. She was the one possessing my every thought that night, the next day in the elevator, and today.

Pulling my phone from my pocket, I dial Tom Stern. He picks up quickly. "Prince Rajaa."

"Are you home safe?"

"Yes."

"The woman I shielded, is she safe?"

"Ella. Yes. She is with her host family."

Uncertain of him knowing her condition, I ask, "You are sure she wasn't injured?"

"She was shaken, but not hurt."

"What do you plan to do?" I fully expect him to tell me he has decided they are returning home to the States.

He breathes out deeply. "Tomorrow, I am going to the center to start cleanup. A few of the men from the staff and a handful of Syrian men plan to return to help."

"I will be there." There is no hesitation in my response.

"Rajaa, I'm not sure that is a good idea. I have told the volunteers and staff to stay home just in case something else happens."

"Tom, this isn't up for negotiation. You are going to be there, then I will be there. You have come to my country expecting safety as you support the refugees at the center. When I agreed to support this program, I agreed to keep you safe, and I am not the type of man to walk away from my responsibilities. I will be there tomorrow with more soldiers and a crew to begin cleanup. I will spare no expense to get the center up and running."

"Okay."

I hang up the phone just as my name is called. "Rajaa!"

Zaid didn't come home until late the day after the party at Sam's. Even upon his return, I didn't see him. The combination of Arak and the drug, Captain, made for the worst fucking hangover I have ever had. I don't remember getting to my bed after leaving Sami's house with our guards. I woke in my bed, so I assume one of the guards got me there. I have never used in my life, and after witnessing the shit Zaid and Tariq were doing, how they drugged me with shit they give extremists before war attacks, I was ready to go straight to my mother and father with what I knew.

But then I thought, what the fuck did I really know? Zaid was smart, and even though he was being a dumb fuck, he was methodically smart.

He didn't come home until late on Sunday, telling my father he was staying with Anwar. I know Anwar and he would cover for him, especially with all the shit Zaid probably has on him; the prostitutes they used to hire, shit he is probably partying with Zaid and Tariq, lying to his wife when he goes out. I'm sure Zaid told him those nights would be divulged to his very traditional wife if he didn't cover. Samir, housing his fucking drug-dealing Sheikh, was another cover. Who the fuck knows what else Tariq is dealing. But I do know if I try to out them, there will be more lies backing my brother's story than mine having built walls of protection for himself.

So, I will hold what I know until I can make my direct approach on Zaid and Tariq. While both of their covert innuendos about a pact meant to give rise to both Syria and Jordan in the Middle East was vague, I knew the key element of their plan would not be good for either side involved. My fear is Tariq is the puppet master and my brother the puppet in this scheme, and time is running out to discover their plan. Not to mention Tariq is my brother's fucking drug dealer.

"What the fuck do you think you were doing there?" Zaid's eyes are wide, fueled by ripened anger as he strides toward me.

"I had a meeting with Tom."

He mimics me condescendingly, "I had a meeting with Tom. Fuck! We talked about this! You agreed you would not risk going down there unless it was necessary!"

Does he not remember my last conversation about this! "No, I told you I was going to be more involved, you just didn't want to hear it! Lives would have been lost if I wasn't down there today!"

"Yes, Tom told me you threw your fucking life on the line for a bunch of children and that American teacher compelling you to be more involved. Are those the lives you were so ready to lose your own for?"

"I wasn't going to lose my life, Zaid! I have been on missions with the King. You seem to forget I can handle myself!"

"Three fucking missions as a first Lieutenant and you think you are a war hero! I have been on two dozen missions and I don't throw my life on the line for anyone!" he growls.

"Those lives are worth their weight in gold and I can't understand how we carry the same blood and you still don't get that!"

"We only share half of our blood and the better half is our father's, Raj." The strike at my mother, his Queen, makes my chest tighten with anger.

He continues on, "Some lives will be casualties of war. Princes, kings, royalty, those are the lives worth their weight in gold, Raj, not Syrian children and a Westerner!"

He shakes his head in disgust at me, like his logic is resolute and mine is insanity. "You think those children, those little girls that will grow up and become our whores, will remember you? You think the American will remember you? They will save you when your life is on the line? They won't give a shit about you and what you have done for them today!"

He raises his hands up like he is balancing two objects. "On one hand you have Syrian peasants and on the other Americans pretending to care about our crisis for a free summer trip to an exotic land. Maybe see the desert, the Dead Sea, the sites, get under the skin of some naive prince?"

Zaid laughs as he drops his hands and walks to the other side of the balcony, only to turn on his heels maddeningly and come back to me, fully fueled. "With this attack, do you really think those volunteers you paid to come here are going to stand by your side and continue to help those Syrian vultures? Do you think Mr. Stern will stay here and support your dream?"

"Those Americans, Tom, they are helping us with this crisis because they believe in it! If you could only see what they do, you would realize how wrong you are."

"What I realize is this program, this center father agreed upon, is a liability to us. Tariq believes he has misjudged its use as well after today."

"I don't give a shit what Tariq believes! Soldiers will continue to be present at the center around the fucking clock giving them the security they need, they will return, and I will be there to stand by them, show them Jordan's leaders aren't going to hide because of this. Clean up on the center starts immediately."

His eyebrows raise as his eyes widen. "Do you realize while you were playing hero, I was walking through the remnants of a shop that had been bombed? I dispatched soldiers to multiple areas of gunfire and explosions, while I dug through body parts along with investigators, looking for any evidence of these fucking extremists. Then I find out you are at the center in the middle of an attack! I knew this program of yours was a bad idea from the beginning! No, you will not return to the Makan Lil Amal! From here out, you will work with me on programs to build our nation, help OUR people, not tear it down by giving away our resources to immigrants!"

As he walks away from me, I defy him. "The King will decide if I return, not you and not your silent fucking benefactor!"

He stops walking and turns around. "What the fuck did you say?"

My brother's eyes have turned feral from my conditions and I don't see any remnant of the brother I have known all my life. "What happened to you, Zaid? What happened to the honorable, responsible, strong, and smart brother I knew?"

He has changed so much in the last two summers. Fucking drugs, sex, alcohol, addictions multiplying one by one. Slowly he stalks back to me, his head lowered, set on shutting me the fuck up. "Your brother has spent his days and nights growing up in this crisis, the one in our world here in Jordan, while you have been pampered in the States! The world you think we live in here, the one you have missed while away, the one your mother has filled your mind with, is not the one we live in! She discovered this when she came too close to the flame recently. Now there is a fucking bounty on her head! The way our father the King and your mother the Queen have been ruling has done nothing to protect our country from attacks that are only worsening. We are in the fucking middle of all of it! An island of order in the middle of this fucking sea of chaos, our allies thousands of miles away, across oceans! The storm is all around us and when it comes here, who will protect us from it? The allies on the corners of this earth in their fucking 'safe zones'? Your mother, the Queen? Our father, the declining King? No, I will! I will secure our resources, I will create bonds, relations, networks, not wait on fucking resolutions to be approved by diplomats!"

I consider his way of protecting us from the coming storm and how he and Tariq had kept it hidden. "So, going to parties, potentially extorting from Sheikhs, getting your fucking drug fix, fucking up your brother with laced Arak and orgies? Is that your brilliant strategy? Tell me, is that part of yours and Tariq's plan to change the Middle East?"

His chuckle is low and menacing. "Don't be so fucking righteous, Raj. You didn't seem to mind bought whores in summers' past and don't tell me you haven't gotten stoned at that fucking school of yours! All those kids are getting loaded!"

I run my hands over my face, then open my arms to him. "No, I haven't, you fucking asshole."

He paces in front of me nervously as he forces his belief. "It was just a small amount of Captain."

"Captagon, a highly addictive drug that can fuck you up. Makes you do and see shit."

"We don't take enough, Rajaa. It isn't my fault if you are a lightweight."

Son of a bitch. I want to deck him so badly right now.

He stops in front of me and holds his hands seeming to pray in front of his face. "You know what? Stay with your philanthropic endeavors, brother. You are too fragile to do what I have to do day by day. Too weak to handle anything I may show you. While I aim to be the strong arm of our monarchy, you can be the soft hand of martyrdom. My soldiers, the ones I have dispatched for your precious center, will keep your program safe, but make no mistake, Rajaa, do not get too close to the open flame of this kindling fire. Your mother was smart to back away when she did. You would be smart to do the same."

He takes a step back and looks at me smugly. "You have forgotten our ways here; too much of the West has consumed you. Tariq warned me about this. Said you weren't ready. For your sake, I hope you smarten up, or you will be a prince with a thousand enemies, Raj."

A haunting thought suddenly rises within me. What if my mother's bounty had been set into motion by the workings of Tariq and Zaid's plan? Had they been working together this long while I was away at school? Was she getting too close to the coming storm? Disrupting the kindling fire Zaid and Tariq may be fanning with their plans?

Zaid glares at me. "That stunt, saving the American woman Ella Wallace, is a risk that can get you burned."

It isn't a surprise he collected her name, but it is disconcerting he has taken the time to connect her and I to each other.

"Running out of Tariq's like some fucking imbecile. It was an insult, Raj! That is a risk that can get you and I both burned and I will not get burned, brother! Mark my word, if you try and pull me down with you, I will step away and leave you."

His callous statement, leaving me to the wolves if attacked, strips away a layer of hope I held for any lingering sanity in his fucking head. His blackened eyes are fixed on me as he tells me evenly, "I may not be able to send in our soldiers to save you the next time you do something foolish for your precious center."

As Zaid backs away, his tone becomes eerily stoic and commonplace. "Our father and your mother have requested both of us at dinner. I would assume they want to speak about the attack on your center since you didn't report to them once you returned home."

I correct his innuendo of my being lax in reporting to the King. "Father was resting. I didn't want to disturb him."

He shakes his head. "His son's safety would never be a disturbance, Raj, especially with his life being risked irresponsibly. He would want to know about his safe return, just as you would want to keep both our King and Queen safe from any harm that could come to them if they got too close to a kindling flame."

My brother implicating my father and mother in this threatening game he has pulled me into has me right where he wants me: trapped and bound to say nothing about what I know for their sake.

"See you at dinner," Zaid says, turning and walking out of my room.

I am the last to arrive as I walk into the dining room. My brother is sitting to the right of my father, while my mother sits to his left and my sister next to my brother. Tamanna is almost fifteen and resembles the beauty, patience, and demeanor of my mother. She inherited her intelligence from them both. "Rajaa. Thanks to Allah you are safe!"

She wraps her arms around my waist and rests her head on my chest. I pat her head and hold her close. "Of course I'm safe."

I hold her at arm's length and seek out her downcast, tear-filled eyes. "I am fine, Tamanna."

As I sit next to my mother, I notice my father is sitting in his wheelchair instead of a dining chair tonight. I try not to appear concerned but fail, as my mother has already noticed. "It is more stable for him. Today was ... a challenge."

I sense the frustration in her voice, but appreciate her choosing words carefully in explaining the challenges. I know one of the challenges was my being caught in the crossfire at the center.

The dining room is not ornamental or magnificent in a kingly way, but simple and warm as my mother and father intended when they built it together after marrying. Even as the servants deliver the food, it is traditional Jordanian cuisine. Nothing exotic, everything authentic to our culture. I could never tire of the comfort this food brings.

As the servants leave, we thank them then my father says shakily, "By the name of Allah. We thank you for our food, our family, and the safety of our sons today."

We all repeat in chorus before we begin eating, "By the name of Allah,"

"My apologies for not seeing you earlier, Rajaa. I ... wasn't myself."

I glance at Zaid as I respond to my father's apology, driving home my reason for not disturbing him. "It is fine, Baba. You needed rest."

"No, it isn't fine. I needed to know what was happening in my country under my rule, not sleeping. I can sleep when I am dead." The constant yet slight movement of his head is visible now that I look at him, hammering further how fleeting life is. My father's twitch has gotten worse in the weeks I have been home.

Zaid clear his throat and wipes his mouth. "Well, as you know from my report all is secure for now. We have not found the shooters, but with further investigation the remains of the suicide bombing sites will reveal what we suspect: extremists, surely from our neighbor, Syria."

My father breathes in deeply before focusing on me. "What happened down there?"

I look across the table at Zaid as I speak. "I was making sure security was working with them and discussing my continued involvement while I am here for the summer when the explosion happened. I heard the screams of children in the hall outside of Mr. Stern's office."

"And the compelling American teacher," Zaid adds.

Ignoring my brother, I continue to explain, "The windows, I knew if I didn't cover them, they might try to rise and run. I reacted as a soldier protecting the helpless. "

All of a sudden Zaid drops his arm to the table out of frustration. "Yes, they are helpless, but a prince shouldn't be saving lives, putting his own at risk when there were experienced soldiers on hand. You did not have to throw your life on the line for them!"

"Zaid!" My father's voice may have been weak moments ago, but now it has found renewed energy. "You were not there! Do not speak of what you do not know!"

Bowing his head, Zaid relinquishes his apology through his clenched jaw of embarrassment. "Ana asfa."

I play my next hand very carefully, knowing my father will be the deciding factor if I return to the center. "You are both right."

Zaid's attention is piqued by my agreeable remark. I patiently take a bite of my food and glance from my father to Zaid as I chew slowly. Swallowing both my food and pride, I explain, "Our soldiers, the soldiers Zaid has trained, were more than capable of protecting the volunteers, staff, the refugees, and their prince. While there is extensive damage to the front of the center, no one was injured, and everyone walked away safely with the defense we had in place."

I nod to Zaid across the table. "Thanks to Allah and Zaid, the center will not waiver in its mission to help the refugees and keep Makan Lil Amal safe for the volunteers and staff, and me."

Zaid sits back, takes his glass of water in hand, and drinks as he watches my move take form.

Wearily, my mother looks from my father back to me. "Rajaa, after today, you still plan to return? You have seen how I have had to back away from my support and aid for refugee programs among others. I am not sure your presence there is wise."

Zaid clears his throat. "I couldn't agree with you more, my Queen. His presence would be irresponsible and naive, just as it was in your case not too long ago."

His intentional jab strikes home in both my mother and me, silencing any further comments from her and getting deep under my skin.

Looking onto my father for his final word, I ask, "Baba? While I still have faith the reward outweighs the risk, I will do as you say. Will you allow me to return to the center?"

Leaving the decision up to my father is a risk of never setting foot in Makan Lil Amal again. Never seeing Ella again.

With shaking hands, my father wipes his mouth as he works the food in his mouth; making it small enough to swallow is agonizing, so I look down at my plate, unable to watch him any longer.

"You should be at the center, Rajaa." His shaky words are surreal. I expected him to reject my being there.

"What?" Zaid's says, surprised.

My father's strong voice returns as he rejects Zaid's question. "It will show the continued unification of Jordan and the Syrian refugees as well as the Royal support after a barbaric bombing and attack on a refugee camp and Makan Lil Amal!"

My father peers at my mother. "I need to make a speech to the people of Jordan."

My mother cover his hand with hers, knowing how he dreads being in front of them in his lesser condition. Zaid speaks up, "I can speak on your behalf, Baba. Show the strength of our lineage and how we will not waiver in the eyes of these Islamic state fighters."

"No, they need to hear from their King," my father says.

The comment seems to offend my brother.

"However, I do think you should go your brother to the center, Zaid."

My brother glances from me to my father, surprised by his statement. "Go to the center? No."

His flat defiance has my father slamming his fist on the table. "No! You say no to your King's request?"

"Ammaar," my mother warns him quietly.

I am surprised at my father's suggestion as well. I didn't calculate getting what I asked for to include my brother. "Baba, it isn't necessary."

My father turns on me now. "These militants need to see we will not cower because of this attack. Our unified efforts will make our cause, our mission to protect Jordan, and those seeking asylum within its borders more powerful!"

The twinkle of a strong leader with vision in his eyes strikes a chord as I remember how active he had been with his people, for his people, when I was younger. He coughs suddenly and his expression loses its intensity. "I do not have long on this earth with my family."

"Ammaar, please don't," my mom says softly.

He closes his eyes briefly as he responds to her. "No! They all need to hear this."

When he opens them again, he looks between my brother and me in tandem. "Two princes ... one will become king after me. I want to see my sons form an unstoppable alliance."

My sister suddenly rises and leaves, small sobs follow behind her.

"Tamanna," my mother calls to her.

My father lowers his gaze and claps my mother's hand tighter, keeping her from going after her. "Let her go, it is fine," he says tenderly. "She is delicate, but she will be as strong as her mother someday." He weakly smiles as he looks up at my mother.

Zaid drinks from his glass, then wipes his mouth with his napkin. "We will be an unstoppable alliance, Father. Each of us have our strengths, and while we work separately, we will always come together, because blood is everything. Family is everything. Right, Rajaa?"

Deciphering his intention is deeper than the words he is speaking and I can't decode his distorted logic, but I do know I will not let him bring this family down. "Yes, it is."

My father starts to push away from the table. "Now if you will excuse me, I have to prepare a speech for our people. Zaid, could you prepare the staff to receive the media?"

"Yes, Father." Zaid rises as my father wheels back from the table, aiming to assist him as I'm sure he had to do regularly while I have been away.

"Rajaa, will you help me to my room?" My brother stops mid-stride, replaced by my father's request for my assistance.

I push back from the table and rest my napkin on my chair, exchanging a glance with my brother before tending to my father.

"I will come to you soon, my love," my mother says to my father before I push him away. "I am going to look after Tamanna."

My father nods. "Tbea Zahrat Baladi."

My mother looks on him lovingly as he calls her his little flower. It is an intensity I could only compare to what I experienced as I touched Ella's face after the attack.

When we are out of earshot, my father speaks evenly. "I have spoken with the Amir Husaam about Daya. Have you seen her since returning?"

I think back on two nights ago at Tariq's and how the lesser of two evils would have been to see Daya rather than be a part of the indulgence I should have rejected from the beginning. "No, abi. I haven't."

"He and I plan to talk about the future soon. Yours and Daya's. You are graduating in the fall and plan to return home. It is time for you to ask for his daughter."

I grip the handles of the wheelchair tighter. Marrying Daya is not what I want. I don't love her, don't even know her, and while my father has never pressed me directly on the matter, I am caught now, expectant of an answer. "I'm not sure I am ready, Baba."

"I remember the feeling both with Yaasmeen and your mother when I called on their hands in marriage." My father had loved my mother madly, but he never spoke of Yaasmeen and their love.

"You loved them both?"

"I loved them differently. Yaasmeen? Our union was for our territories, my father's and her's. While it didn't start as love, it became so over time. Just as it will for you."

"And if it doesn't? I will be in a loveless marriage."

My father angles back to look at me. "It will. You will come to love her."

I know that I won't. I challenge him, "And my mother?"

Your mother, she is my true love," he says tenderly. "Through all of this illness, she has been my shining star, my light in the darkness. My little flower. Tbea zahrat baladi."

While he talks to me about true love and my mother, he is pushing for a bond with a woman I don't even know. As we come to his doorway, I move away from his chair and come around to face him. "You loved her. It wasn't about duty."

He nods shakily. "Yes, but in these times ... we need alliance more than anything. You and Daya can be the bearers of it."

Wanting this conversation to end, I ask my father, "Can you get into your room okay? Do you need help?"

He furrows his brow and puffs out his lip, realizing I am removing myself from this talk. "No, I'm fine. We will talk about this again later."

I nod, then start to walk away when my father calls after me, "I am proud of you, Rajaa."

I turn back to face him.

"What you did for those children, the teacher, I would have done the same." His pride is evident as he raises his chin to me. "You are a passionate leader."

"Thank you, Baba."

Walking back through the house to my room, I notice my mother holding my sister in her arms. Her ability to be both tender and strong has always amazed me. She kisses Tamanna atop her forehead and says good night in Arabic before releasing her. Tamanna sees me and leaves my mother's arms to wrap hers around my waist.

"I'm glad you are safe, Raj."

I rock her side to side and squeeze her tightly. "Don't worry, Tamanna."

My little sister says goodnight and leaves my mother and me. She is smiling and I'm curious of her thoughts. "What?"

Close enough to her now, she places both of her gentle hands on my shoulders and looks up at me. "You would have returned to the center tomorrow with or without your father's permission."

While I had intention to follow my father's decision, if he was to say no, I would have returned anyway. I had more than one reason to return to the center now. More than one purpose. And while one was a long time in the making, the other was just discovered. I nod and look down. "Yes I would have."

She smiles wider. "Today, I think you left your heart there."

Ella.

Her ability to know my heart so well takes me off-guard.

"I did."

My mother lowers her hands and nods with determination and vigor. "Then you should return to your heart."

Though my secret is safe, I realize my mother is speaking to me as equally about Ella as she is about the center. It makes me smile as I turn away from her.

"The American teacher..."

I turn back to her, surprised at her preternatural expression as she continues. "The one you shielded. She is the one Zaid has spoken to us about before. The one he said compelled you."

I place my hands in my pant pockets, debating my disclosure. Fuck it. "Yes, she is."

She nods and lowers her gaze as she folds her arms over her chest. I sense her calculating my intentions behind her light-brown eyes. "You have always known me to be an open-minded person, Rajaa. But while I am open-minded, I am also faithful to our beliefs and traditions."

First my father, now her. "Mama, I protected the woman, plain and simple. I would have done the same for any other person in that hallway today."

She nods evenly. "I believe you."

"Zaid has made this out to be a bigger deal than it is."

She places her hands on my shoulders again. "Rajaa, I understand. It's just I know your heart, and while your heart should always lead you, sometimes it is wiser not to venture too far from the path that has been paved for you. You are a prince promised to a princess."

I have already heard my father's speech on this. I don't need to hear hers. I pull away from her hands resting on my shoulders. "Yes, yes, I know, Mama. Both you and Baba have made it very clear. For love or not, I am going to marry Daya!"

I realize my harsh response and shake my head. "Shukran, I'm just tired."

She folds her arms over her chest and nods, searching my eyes still for something more. "Yes, of course. Please rest."

As I kiss her cheeks and leave her standing there, I sense that she is not going to easily let go of her concern for my presence at the center, nor the reason for my heart settling there.

Chapter 9

Ella

The morning after the attacks, Ameena and I sit on my bed as Laila stands at the open doorway of my room. I don't say anything about the prince shielding me from the rain of bullets at the center. The whole event is still intimate to me, something I want to keep inside. I ask Ameena if her family has been through an attack before. She looks at me timidly and nods.

"It has never happened here, but I am afraid it is coming," she says. Laila says something in Arabic I don't catch completely, then suddenly steps into my room and sits on the corner of my bed opposite Ameena. "My home is gone. My father gone. Dead from the men that came. Uncle Naz, he took us, drove us to border. Not leave Grandpa. He left us and we run to the soldiers." I'm shocked by Laila's account and also her speaking in English so well, having only used it minimally with me.

"We go to the camp. Zaatari. Eat small food and water. Have bed, then men took from us. We have no man to protect. So they take. They try to take me. Try to touch me. Mama fights, but they hit her again and again. Then they touch her. I hold Rushdi and cover his eyes, and close mine so tight until I hear them leave. I hold Mama until she stops crying, then we run. We come to camp in the city, here in Amman. Again we have bed, small food, small water. It goes away soon when there are too many people. Always too many."

The entire time she recounts their journey, she is void of emotion, no expression of pain or terror, emptied, gutted from everything she encountered. "We find Makan Lil Amal and they take us here to Ba'ashirs."

The first glimmer of light shows in her eyes as she continued to speak, looking over at Ameena. "They give us room, food, safe, family, love."

Her smile lessened. "This is safe. We are safe here."

Laila rises and leaves the room quietly without another word. Ameena quickly changes the subject. "Some were saying Prince Rajaa was at the center."

"Rajaa," I repeat the name and she nods.

"Yes, they say he shielded a teacher from being injured ... maybe even killed."

My death wasn't a consideration as I hovered and scrambled to protect the girls. Does that make me brave or just fucking stupid? Him knocking me to the ground, shielding me ... that is bravery. Now as I think of looming death in the face of attacks here in Jordan, I feel what I would compare to the refugees, Jasara, Laila, Rushdi, Uncle

Naz, as minuscule. The smallest, almost insignificant fear compared to what they carry with them innately now.

I keep my face even as I nod at her then look away. "I hadn't heard he had been so brave."

Ameena fiddles with a loose thread on my blanket. "I hear one of the teachers protected her girls. That was you." She isn't asking and I wonder who gave her the information.

I nod. "I wasn't going to leave them." I am timid to say why, but I do anyway. "I love them."

Tom calls the first day and asks if I have called my family. I lie and tell him I had. I don't want to hear Jilly crying if she heard about it and if she hadn't, I didn't want to break the news to her over the phone. She would definitely tell Mom and Dad if they didn't know already and I don't know what Dad would do. Commission to have me brought back to the States, most likely. I imagine how Jilly's and my conversation would go. "Hey, it's me, El. There was an attack on my center but I'm okay." That wouldn't fare well and I know she wouldn't be able to keep it from my parents.

No one has left the house for the last three days. Not even Ismad for work. Jasara and Hoda make food all day and store it away in the refrigerator. The amount they have made, I wonder if their own fear is feeding their need to stockpile food just in case more attacks are coming. Ismad and Nazeer listen to the Arabic newscasters on the small radio in the living room as King Ammaar Bin Qadir addresses Jordan about the attacks on the center, camp, and the suicide bombing of a local shop. While his voice is strong, I overhear Hoda speaking about his health being poor.

"'Anna mareed," she says.

Ismad interjects, "He needs to choose which of his sons will succeed him. Choose an heir."

Uncle Naz agrees, saying so in Arabic.

"Princes? He has two sons?" I ask.

Ismad nods. "The older brother should be king without question, but there is talk ... Shaeaa. The news is saying Prince Rajaa could possibly become the heir if his brother Zaid is seen as not suited for the role by his father, the King. Zaid has found himself in trouble before with women."

Hoda turns off the kitchen faucet. "Not good. King should make Zaid king. It is law."

I take in both Ismad and Ameena, wondering if it is true. Ameena adds, "It is law the firstborn son of the King should be crowned the heir to the throne."

Curious about the King's condition, I ask, "What does the King have? What is his sickness?"

Ismad and Ameena share a knowing glance and shrug as Ismad explains, "It has been kept quiet. The King has become less public in recent years. His people say it is from the crisis and war around us ... fear for attacks on the royal family, but I think it is because of his health. The Queen is young in comparison with him. He is twenty-five years older than her. An old man now."

The boys race through the kitchen, chasing each other, and Hoda and Jasara raise their voices at them to stop running in Arabic, then mumble to each other under their breath before exchanging a smile as they work side by side at the counter.

By the third day of being kept in the Ba'ashir home from the outside world, we are all stir crazy to some extent. Hoda, Jasara, and Ismad are at their wits' end with the boys running through the house and in the craze I somehow talk myself into calling Jilly, deciding to tread lightly on the circumstances of my call. I can't believe I remember her cell phone number.

As it rings, I wonder if she is going to ignore it since it will show up as an International call. Just before I give up she answers, "Hello?"

The sound of her voice is like the best sounding music ever. "Jilly?"

"OH MY GOD, ELLA?"

I feel a lump rise in my throat. "Yes, it's me."

"How are you calling me?" she asks breathily, surprised, but still not crying so I guess she doesn't know.

"It is an emergency cell phone from WorldTeach." I realize I probably shouldn't have said *emergency.*

"Emergency? What happened?" she asks sharply.

"No, I'm fine. I just ... I needed to hear your voice and let you know ... everything is good here."

"Ooookay. Are you sure everything is alright?"

"Yeah, yeah. Just hey, don't tell them I called okay?"

"Can you text on this phone?" she asks, ignoring my question.

"Uh, no I don't think so. Hey, don't tell Mom and Dad okay? I don't want them to think anything is wrong. I just wanted to say hi."

"Yeah, I won't."

The pause between us is that quiet sadness that happens before you say goodbye to someone you don't want to hang up with.

"I miss you so much, El." Her voice is low and soft, very much like the day I said goodbye to her in D.C.

I put on a smile and respond with as much pep as I can. "Miss you too. Bye."

She knows nothing about the attack. I wonder if my parents somehow hid it from her or maybe don't even know themselves. It wouldn't be impossible for the news in the States to not know about it.

I roll over on my side and stare at the mosaic picture on the wall. Today will be the volunteers first day back at Makan Lil Amal. The Caritas staff returned yesterday. Knowing they survived a day without any problems puts me at ease about returning. I think of the prince and wonder if he will be there just for a moment, then consider him having a more important duty at his father's side.

I try to close my eyes and fall back to sleep, if only for a couple more hours. Like every night since the attacks, when I close them I see his familiar face and striking golden-brown eyes. Hoda begins to hum a song to Ghalib through the concrete wall separating his room from mine. The words are lost to me but the sound is soothing.

That day at the center, the words the prince spoke when we were face to face after he saved me, they echo just beyond Hoda's humming.

"Eh enta."

I asked Laila what the words meant in English earlier today; I'm trying to work with her more since Ameena has got the hang of it. She said it meant something like "it's you" or "knowing you."

The rest of the day I puzzled over the map of our connection. I remembered annoying Serena say it was a prince's party. There aren't an exuberant amount of princes in the world, but there are quite a few and what would be the chances of Prince Rajaa being the prince at the party. Seeing him at some random Georgetown University posh private party, then again the next day in the elevator, which is still questionable based on my hangover, then saving my ass from waves of bullets on the other side of the world weeks later? How many Middle Eastern princes attend universities in the U.S? In Europe? Many. How many of them have dreamy brown eyes with the most striking golden hue? What are the chances of seeing the same man in D.C. halfway across the world? One in a million?

"A billion?" I mumble to myself as I pull the covers tighter around me. Before I surrender to sleep again, I sigh, knowing I can deny it all I want, lie to myself over and over again, talk my way out of believing the possibility, but it won't change what I know deep in my soul. "It's him."

Hoda is already in the kitchen making breakfast when I come out of my room, fully dressed with my backpack and veil covering my head. She turns to me and nods to the table. "Sit. Eat."

Saying no to Hoda would be more difficult than sitting and eating, so I submit as she brings a small plate of Hummus with my favorite, Shrak. Hoda sits with me as Ismad wakes Ameena and Ghalib. "Ella. You very brave. Ameena tell me. Alfatayaat ... girls. You love. We love."

Hoda's smile warms me and her hand touching mine now, squeezing it, makes my throat tighten with emotion.

I turn my hand over and squeeze her hand tightly, keeping my eyes on hers because if I look away the tears I am holding in right now will fall. "Bahibbik."

I love you.

Ismad walks Ameena and Ghalib to their school, then leads me to the center. I understand his concern for Ameena and Ghalib getting there safely, but I tell him I am fine. "You have work. I don't want to keep you."

He shakes his head as he walks a few steps ahead of me protectively. Normally, women walking behind the man here in the Middle East carries a different meaning, but right now, between Ismad and me, it is for my safety. Jasara kept Rushdi and Laila home today. Ismad told Jasara he would walk them along with me, but she refused, fearful of what awaited her at the center. As I watch her explain to Ismad, the fear in her voice and eyes is acute and ready to reject any suggestion her children will leave her side today. I worry that her and the kids may never return to the center, and while I myself don't really know the outcome of safety at this point, I have a level of trust Jasara has never been offered until we came here. How can it be expected for her to trust so easily, so quickly?

Ismad leads the way past the soldier standing guard at the courtyard gate. The soldier I had feared was killed in the attack. I pause before passing, forcing him to break his statuesque hold and glance down at me.

"Shukran."

Knowing it is more about the attack then his standing guard right now, he doesn't look away quickly like he has done before. Instead, he nods, seeming to know my thanks is more for his protection during the attack.

Ismad opens the door for me to pass just as Tom exits his office, noticing us.

"How are you, my friend? I haven't seen you in a very long time," he says as he shakes Ismad's hand.

"Fine. I wanted to make sure she got here safely this morning." Ismad glances down at me. "I will come back this evening to bring you home."

Tom interrupts, "I can see her home. I have a mandatory meeting planned with the volunteers at the end of the day. We need to discuss what happened and where we go from here."

Ismad seems leery about not being my escort, but Tom reiterates, "She will be taken home either by a soldier or myself, I promise you."

Satisfied with Tom's promise, Ismad leaves and I start to my classroom when Tom stops me. "I received a call late last night about you."

I give him my full attention as he continues, "It was your father. He said he heard what happened through his resources. See, that is the thing, even if it doesn't make the evening news, government officials will always hear about these situations. So, my question to you is, why did you lie to me?"

"Look, I did call my family. I called my sister, Jilly. I told you before, this doesn't involve my mother or father. They didn't understand my coming here and I'm sure all my father would have to say is I told you so. Possibly tell me I have made yet another huge mistake in my life." I start to turn, then decide I'm not done. I want to know what he said to Tom. "What did he want?"

Standing with his hands in his pockets and his glasses resting on the top of his head, he grins slightly and shakes his head. "He wanted to know if we were returning to the States. Said it was too volatile for us to be here and it wasn't worth the risk."

I nod, my expectations met by my father's words.

Tom sighs deeply, then looks down, disappointment on his face. I worry from it, wondering if my father had somehow swayed him to change his mind about us staying. Three days ago I may have hopped the first plane out if it was offered, but now none of the fear matters to me.

He looks up and I hold my breath, preparing for him to say we are leaving. "I told him to excuse me, but he knows nothing about what we are doing here and we are staying to finish out the program."

I raise my chin, proud of Tom standing up to him. "What did he say to that?"

Knowing my father, he had something to say, like "I will have your job" or some bullshit threat.

"He threatened to sue."

"Motherfucker," I hiss, then notice Tom's quick glance at me. "Sorry."

"Yeah, well, it wouldn't be the first time I was threatened. If he did, it wouldn't hold up in court. The waivers you signed protect us and being they were approved by the very government he serves, he won't have a much of a leg to stand on in a suit. Plus by the time it is all said and done you will be back home in the States."

Even though Tom justified our being there, my own release begs to be heard even if not by my father. "What about it being my fucking choice to stay? He has no right to intervene. That is why I didn't call him." I shift the weight of my bag on my shoulder and turn to walk away when Tom calls after me.

"Hey."

I stop walking and look back at him, expecting him to tell me he is just watching out for me or some shit.

"It's good you called your sister. You need someone to know you are okay when these things happen."

I nod and wonder about Tom. "Who did you call?"

"Hmm?"

"Who did you call to tell you were okay?"

He looks away and smiles. "My wife."

I happen to glance at the wall, freshly painted over the blood from days ago. "The blood that was on the wall. Is that person okay?"

He nods. "Yeah, it was the director from Caritas, Alma. She was grazed on the arm by a stray bullet."

"Is she okay?"

"Yes."

I start back down the hall, quickly recognizing the spot I occupied with my girls days ago; huddled on the floor, the prince over me, the exploding and shattering glass, and the ear-piercing sound of screams, yells, and bullets. I quickly glance back to see if Tom has noticed my response to the memory, but he has already gone into his office.

I scan the newly installed window glass. It's clean, spotless, no signs of broken glass missed when they cleaned up. As I walk on, I find myself trying to find a divot in a wall or something to indicate this place was ambushed days ago, but I can't. While the fear from the memory has already lessened, the face of the man that saved me, Prince Rajaa and his entrapping eyes, are a memory I never want to fade.

Ana is sitting at her chair eating when I enter the classroom. As soon as she sees me, she crosses the room to hug me. "You okay?"

"Yeah. You?"

She crosses her arms over her chest and tilts her head. "Yeah, just a little on edge." She scoffs, "It might be the strong-ass Turkish coffee."

I grin. "Did you call your family?"

She nods. "Yeah, called my mom. I didn't tell her much. She didn't seem to know about it and was surprised to hear from me. You know, phones for emergencies. Did you call?"

I walk over to my desk and put my backpack on the side. "Yeah, I called my sister. Same, she was surprised and didn't say anything about the attack."

"I'm kind of glad. I don't want Ma to worry. She has her hands full with my brother and sister-in-law."

Leaning against my desk, Ana walks back toward hers and picks up her coffee cup. "Do you still feel the same?"

Her question isn't clear. "About what?"

Ana leans against her desk, mirroring me. "About being here?"

I look down at the small rugs lined in front of me, my girls' rugs. A gush of a thousand memories rush through my head. Memories of intimidation, being in a foreign place learning a foreign language. Memories of anxiousness meeting my host family for the first time, my beautiful little girls in this classroom the first day. Memories of going to the Roman Amphitheater, then Hashem Restaurant with the other volunteers. Talking with Ameena and Laila, teaching them English, and them teaching me Arabic. Hoda and Jasara, my Arab mothers always guiding, always cooking, always making sure everyone is cared for. The double kiss on the cheeks Hoda gave me this morning before I left is the culmination of the love I have grown to have for this family in the short time I have been here.

How can the love of these people, my girls, the Ba'ashirs, the Ahmadis, be so rich yet so young in time, when the love of my own family is so broken and has existed my whole life? The intense memory of my heart pounding quickly replaces any ill thought, as I recapture the moment Prince Rajaa covered my mouth with his hand and looked into my eyes with his golden embers. The feeling of his hands on me, the feeling of his words whispered to me. *"Eh enta."*

I blink awake from my vivid reconnect and focus on Ana waiting for my answer. "Yes, I do."

Chapter 10

Rajaa

Stepping out of the shower, I notice my brother leaning against the open doorway to my bedroom. "Where are you going?"

Zaid has no social graces when it comes to privacy, something I have always known. I turn my back to him as I dry my back then wrap the towel around my waist. "I'm going to center. You know this." I had already made it clear, yet he finds it necessary to hound me about it.

He moves into the bathroom as I step in front of the mirror to shave. "Still set on putting yourself at risk, eh?"

With shaving cream on my face, I look over at him pointedly before I make the first pass. My remark is intended to piss him off. "Yes, I am."

His smirk quickly dissolves. "Better you than me."

I focus back on my image in the mirror with little reaction to his biting comment. "So you aren't coming to the center as father requested?"

He tilts his head back, popping his neck from side to side. "No, I have an important meeting. After the King's speech, many of my advisors, the Cabinet, and Prime Minister want to discuss the climate of things over coffee at the palace."

He forgot to mention is most prized advisor, Tariq bin Qasim.

"We have an event tonight at Raghadan Palace," he says evenly, distracting me from my train of thought. No one had mentioned it to me.

"What is it for?"

"Dinner guests." His smirk has me uneasy.

"Why would we have dinner guests at Raghadan Palace? The house would suffice, wouldn't it?"

He leans forward, looking at me through the mirror now. "Because they are special dinner guests. Our father has requested we both be in attendance. Our sister and your mother will be there, the Prime Minister ... and others. It will be a royal family affair. We will leave here at seven. Don't keep us waiting because of your duties at the center."

With nothing more to say, he disappears into my room, shutting the door behind him.

The SUV stops in the back alley between the center and an adjoining building so I can enter out of sight from any onlookers from the street. A truck identical to mine is in front and behind me, the decoys in place. Once I am dropped, all three of them will leave the other end of the alley, taking three different directions hoping to distract anyone watching.

The whole action is very quick and precise. Two heavily armed soldiers move with me from the truck to the back door of the center. Once I'm inside, they stand guard on the other side of the door, securing a point of entry. Just inside the door, a guard is waiting for me, his gun holstered.

"Good morning, Your High..."

I stop him before he finishes as we walk side by side down the hall. "Good morning. How many soldiers do we have stationed at each point of entry?"

"Three."

"Good." As he continues to walk by my side, I frown. "Where are you supposed to be?"

He looks at me oddly. "With you, Your High...."

I stop walking. "Who ordered that?" I had not ordered personal protection while I was here in the center.

"Prince Zaid ordered it this morning."

Motherfucker. I walk on with the soldier by my side. "How many soldiers are stationed at the classrooms?"

"Three, just as Prince Zaid commanded," the soldier answers quickly.

My stride becomes wider, angrier. "Prince Zaid has no command here. I am in charge of this program and all workings in this center, not him. Do I make myself clear soldier?"

"Yes, Your Highness."

I stop in front of him, not able to stand the use of the title again. "Prince Rajaa will suffice, please."

"Yes, Prince Rajaa."

I didn't want to walk around all fucking day with every soldier calling me Your Highness. My being here is not for any title. It is for the people under this roof. My mind immediately focuses on Ella Wallace being a purpose. "Find Ms. Wallace's classroom and station yourself there."

"Yes, Prince Rajaa," he says, then swiftly leaves my side toward the classrooms.

Mr. Stern's door is open when I walk up to it. His back is turned to me as he holds his cell phone to his ear. "Yes, thank you."

As he hangs up, he continues to look out the window into to the courtyard. I knock on the open door, catching his attention. "Oh, Rajaa, I didn't hear you come in."

His lacking my formal title is comforting. "I wasn't expecting you this early. Would you like some coffee?"

While I should be thinking only of my dedication to the program and the safety for everyone it involves, I can't help my sole focus being on Ella Wallace.

"No, thank you. Have the volunteers arrived?" I ask as I sit in the chair across from Tom.

He nods. "A few have."

I want to ask if Ella is here, but refrain. "Good. Did the staff have any concerns or problems yesterday?"

Tom shakes his head. "No, everyone was fine. Even though it was the first day back, the staff seemed at ease. The added security and the pristine cleanup your people did had everything to do with it, Rajaa. Many of them asked if you were here so they could personally thank you."

"While I appreciate their desire to thank me, it is not necessary. I should be thanking them, and I will. Every one of them, today. I'm sorry I couldn't stay yesterday to see them off."

He furrows his brow. "Rajaa, you have been here faithfully for the past three days making sure everything was returned to its original appearance. They understand you have duties other than the center."

I consider his comment and realize he hasn't factored in Ella Wallace. His knowledge of her being a factor should remain unknown. "Being here is my main focus until I return to school in the fall."

I ask Tom to give me a tour, telling him I don't want to wait another minute to thank all of the staff and volunteers for their service here. "Where would you like to start?"

While my immediate thought hangs on Ella and my need to see her, talk to her, I ask if we can tour the medical clinic. "We can work our way around from there."

Tom rises. "Okay, where is your escort?"

I remember the soldier from earlier saying my brother had demanded my protection. "I don't need an escort," I state flatly. "You are my escort."

His smile weakens. "Rajaa, your brother said he expected you to be guarded the entire time you are here. He called just before you got here."

Zaid needs to stop meddling. He wanted nothing to do with this program and now he is pushing orders and calling Tom making sure I have a babysitter. Bullshit.

I rise from my chair and move behind it, mostly from irritation of my brother throwing around his command over me. "My brother's expectations and commands stop at the doors of Makan Lil Amal. If anyone is going to dictate commands it will be me."

Tom nods. "I understand."

I wonder what kind of threats my brother contrived to build a visible concern in Tom. "My only commands are for the safety of everyone in this center and I will handle my brother on this matter. You don't need to worry about his warnings. My brother thrives on intimidation, something I have always despised about him."

Tom shakes his head, appearing to dismiss my excuse. "It is fine, Rajaa. He is concerned for your safety. To be honest, I am as well."

I take my sports coat off and hang it on the back of the chair, revealing my holster. Tom notices my carrying right away, then watches as I unfasten the holster and remove it, laying it on the chair. "While my brother may think I do not know how to take care of myself or those around me, I know you are aware of what I can do and I don't need a gun to do it."

Referring to the attack is more than enough of an answer for Tom as his apprehension relents.

"Do you have a place I can store this?" I ask.

Tom unlocks a draw in his desk and I hand him the gun and holster.

The number of refugees at the center is stunted from the attacks and the bombing, making me hate what the militants have done to their resolve. Sending the refugees into hiding, since they couldn't kill them, to make a point that anyone giving them asylum will suffer. The refugees who have come to the center today have a distinct look in their eye; rebellion. Defiance against those who have stripped away everything they had before Makan Lil Amal. This was their way of saying they couldn't take this center.

Many of the refugees recognize me, but stay away, like they are frightened to look at me. I walk up to them and hold their hands, and touch their children's heads and faces. As I hold one infant's small hand, the mother tells me in Arabic she is sorry her soiled baby's fingers were getting my hand dirty. Her husband bows to me and apologizes again and again, saying they were ashamed of themselves to be in front of me in such a state. I speak freely to them in Arabic, telling them no amount of dirt could ever cover what I see in their eyes.

What I am seeing is something that can't be read about, interpreted from a report, or transmitted over a television screen. I am seeing the casualties of war, the remnants of revolution stripped down to the rawest purpose for existence, to survive for one more day, one more hour.

I damn myself for pretending I have a handle on what is happening here. I have no handle on their well-being, only the conduit to provide it, which makes me almost worthless as a human if I am not here with them to feel it, to live it, to truly understand what they have suffered. I damn my brother's ignorance even more for referring to them as less than human, because they are more human, closer to the soul they were given by Allah, than the rest of us.

With the sleeves of my shirt rolled up, I wash my hands in the facilities outside of the clinic. Tom watches me, seeing the aggression in the way I wash my hands and quickly dry them with the napkins from the dispenser. As I turn to Tom, I can see he is concerned. "Do you want to take a break? Eat lunch? I can have the staff bring you..."

I throw the napkins in the trash can. "No, I'm fine. I need to see this. If only my entire family could see this, Zaid, the King, the Queen. Maybe they would understand what I hope this center will do for these people."

I want to say so much, but I don't know where to start. I can only think in one direction and that is what isn't being done. What isn't being achieved here. "More needs to be done," I blurt out, leaning against the hallway wall. Some of the children are standing at the window in the clinic gazing at me.

Tom nods. "We are doing so much. So many families having been turned away from camps, living on the streets, starving, sick, dying; we are helping them. Yes, there are thousands upon thousands entering your border and more to come that haven't found our doors, but the lives you are changing now is the heart of your purpose. A purpose that will spread once your family, the Prime Minister, the Cabinet see what your vision can do."

Having Tom emphasize his faithfulness in what we are doing here is what I need to pull me from my temporary sink to despair. I push off of the wall. "I'm sorry. Being with them..."

"It pulls you in. Pulls you down at times." Tom speaks freely now, from his own experience. "You did good. Telling that woman her baby was beautiful, touching the children's faces. That wasn't done because of your position as Prince or for show. That was done from you, Rajaa, the man. You connecting with them and sometimes it is hard to snap out of the low you feel once you leave them."

"You feel this too, I guess."

"Yes, I feel it every day. But then I see the smiles, the laughing. I talk to them about their lives here and the low turns into a euphoria that is indescribable, Rajaa." Tom smiles as he looks through the windows of the clinic at the gazing children waiting to be seen. "They have taught me how to really appreciate life, love, and purpose."

He laughs out loud, making me wonder what is so funny. "I have told them in Arabic I could never repay them for what they have given me. They laugh at me like I am a crazy American."

I smile, imagining the interaction as Tom continues. "You will feel it too."

After visiting the counseling section of the center, I had finally begun to rise from the low, seeing the tears of joy as they received registration for food, clean clothes, and a meager allowance to help with living. Standing outside of the wing, I speak freely.

"What they are given, it isn't enough to survive."

"No, it isn't."

"They can't legally work since they are not citizens," I state mostly for myself.

"Correct."

"If they register with the United Nations High Commissioner for Refugees, they fear retaliation from the Syrian government upon return."

"Yes, if returning is made possible."

What we were giving them was only enough to sustain them for a short time. "Are they finding work?"

"Yes, illegally. Sometimes not getting paid at all. Some of our families, the staff, those that host our volunteers, have subleased portions of their homes to help."

Him mentioning volunteers brings Ella to the forefront of my mind and as we leave the counseling wing, I think of her host family. "Who are they?"

Tom looks at me questioningly.

"The host families. I want a list of their names and where they live. They are doing a service beyond what has been asked and I would like to thank them."

"Of course. I will email you the list."

Rounding the corner, the sound of children singing the Arabic alphabet filters through one of the rooms. The door is shut, but I peer into the small cut-out window on the door. The boys are sitting on their small rugs, staring up at their teacher as he points to the Arabic letters on drawing board. By the looks of them, they are maybe six years old.

"Do you want to go in?" Tom asks.

I continued to watch them without them noticing. "No, it is fine. I will watch from here."

As I move from window to window I see the boys doing math, reading, singing, creating art, smiling. These children don't resemble the ones I saw in the clinic gazing at me through the glass. "These can't be the same children passing through the clinic," I whisper as I watch one class of boys laughing as their teacher reads to them in Arabic, then translate to English.

"It is hard to believe, but these volunteers, they have come here eager to make a difference in these children's lives. They have come to love them, even lay their lives on the line for them at times."

His reference is for Ella. "You mean, like Ms. Wallace."

He doesn't respond right away, so I turn to him. "Yes, Ms. Wallace has bonded to her girls so intentionally. Her passion is truly inspiring."

"Yes, it is." I abandon my hesitation to ask about her. "Where is her classroom?"

As we cross over to the girls' hallway, giggling and soft-voiced singing escape into the hallways through closed doors. I see the soldier from earlier stationed in front of a closed door. Tom notices too and walks over to him. "Is there a reason you are stationed here?"

Not wanting the soldier to out me, I dismiss him. "Please guard the boy's hall."

The soldier nods and moves past us, leaving space for me to look into the small window on the door. She is sitting on the floor leading an American rhyme, "Twinkle, twinkle, little star. How I wonder what you are..."

Her voice is a beacon for both the girls and me as I listen to her sing and watch her engage the girls with music.

I stand at the door and look through the cut-out, watching her sit in front of her girls.

My girls is what she called them when I shielded her. Not as a possession but rather possessing love for them.

Her arms are raised high, swaying from side to side as she sings. There is a partition behind them, dividing her area from another teacher just like the other classrooms. While today wasn't a fair assessment of the population, this is a sign they are already running low on classroom space, something I would need to address. Right now, my attention is solely for Ella as she slows her singing so the girls so they can keep up.

I sense Tom moving on from the door, but I stay watching. "I would like to go in."

"I didn't think you wanted to disturb them." He sounds surprised by my request.

"I will sit in the back and watch." My statement is not a request, but an expectation as I open the door for Tom to pass before me.

Chapter 11

Ella

"Excuse me, Ms. Wallace. You have an observer that would like to join you." Tom's announcement takes me by surprise.

Oh, um, sure."

My heart rises into my throat when I see my observer; my rescuer, Prince Rajaa.

With his eyes penetrating me deeply he asks, "Are you sure it's all right? I don't want to intrude."

Intrude on my class or intrude on my soul even more than he already has with just a look. Feeling heat rise on my neck and face, I stumble over my words. "Yes, it would be fine. I mean, it is fine for you to intrude. I mean, observe me. Us, fine for you to observe us."

Sounding like a babbling fool, I wave him into the room. "Please come in."

Shit, just great. I'm waving in a prince like he is fucking on-coming traffic.

Tom whispers something to him then closes the door, leaving the prince to walk to the back of my side of the classroom. He is wearing khaki pants with a white and navy-checked long-sleeve shirt rolled up to his elbows. I skim over his deep-golden forearms, just as he glances back at me. Dodging his gaze perfectly, I ready the girls to start again. "Okay, girls, one more time."

Like myself, the girls have completely lost focus, but for different reasons. Two of them have about faced, watching the prince as he sits down on one of the small empty rugs behind them.

"Girls. One, two..." I call to them to bring attention back.

"Eyes on you," the girls call back, finishing our quick rhyme for attention.

Even with the prince's heavy gaze on my every move, I manage finishing the song just as Ana opens the partition separating our classes. Ana's girls and mine quickly exchanged excited glances with the prince's presence. They all are hesitant to move even as the prince starts to rise to his feet. "Please eat. Don't let me keep you. Arjook tfaddal."

"Girls, time to line up," Ana says just as the prince approaches her.

"Thank you for volunteering here in Jordan. You are doing such amazing work for these girls. None of this could happen without you."

It is humorous to see a bashful Ana. "No, I am excited to do it, your excellence. Oh, or is it Your Highness?" she asks, unsure of how to address him, then looks at me and actually giggles. Like a full-on girly giggle. He's turned her to putty.

"Prince Rajaa will be fine," he says, laughing at her humor. Ana'a faux pas appears to break some invisible barrier between the girls and the prince as they slowly circle around him, no longer shying from his closeness.

Muna remains by my side though, reaching for my hand and interweaving her fingers with mine as she looks on, then smiles up at me, whispering, "It's the prince, Ms. Ella."

"Yes, it is." I smile back at her then watch him as he lowers himself down to their level. He whispers to them in Arabic, making them giggle as they move in closer. He reaches out to one of the girls, taking her hand in his and shaking it. I'm surprised at his contact with her, so warm and nurturing, not at all what I have expected of him with his culture's division between man and woman, male and female.

Like he senses my eyes on him, he turns to me, his smile transforming into one less playful. "I'm sorry, I have distracted them."

And me. You have completely fucking distracted me.

Ana claps her hands softly. "Okay girls, time to eat. Ghada'."

Lingering a bit, the girls slowly line up in front of Ana as she slowly walks backward toward me, pausing to say, "I will take them. It looks like he may want to talk with you."

I peer back at the Prince and notice he is focused on me and patiently waiting in the middle of the room just as she has suspected.

"Thank you," I say softly as Ana takes Muna alongside of her.

"Come with mc, Muna."

Once the girls and Ana have left, I breathe in deep and search for him, still standing in the middle of the room, his hands tucked casually in his pockets. He saved me days ago, this defender and silent benefactor that has paid my way for this program. I can't help scanning his physique. His broad shoulders, how tall he is, how he appears in comparison to the bold man who rescued me. I can't help wanting him to come closer so I can feel the tension of his presence. The look he is giving, the feeling inside, the tightening and twisting in the best ways possible, it all feels so similar to the first night I saw him in D.C.

"Hello, Ella."

"Hi."

Brilliant.

He takes his hand from his pocket as he closes the space between us. "I'm Rajaa."

The fucking oh-so-good tension with his presence I mentioned, yeah I'm feeling it.

His hand is extended, waiting for mine, hovering across my desk. Putting the two concepts of greetings together finally, I lift my hand to meet his, my eyes following. "You are the silent benefactor?"

He holds my hand in his, refusing to release it. "Yes, I am, but I'm not sure how silent I am now with everything that has happened." His words and smile shows his charm and mesmeric feature.

"And Prince of Jordan?"

He tilts his head. "Yes, one of two Princes actually."

I pull my hand from his. "Why are you here?"

"Excuse me?" He laughs at my question. "How many more of these questions do you have lined up for me?"

I busy myself with the scattered colored pencils my girls were using earlier for their art lesson, shoving them in the side drawer. "I'm just having a hard time understanding why the Prince of Jordan and silent benefactor of this center would risk coming here only three days after a fucking attack."

I look up at him, realizing I just cursed at royalty. "Sorry."

I busy myself again. "Hell, I don't even know why a prince would be here the day of an attack or any other day. Seems like you would have other things to tend to. Other duties."

"A Prince of Jordan," he says, seeming to correct my mistake.

Slightly ticked at his finding it necessary to correct me, I move on to stacking the girls' drawings strewn on my desk. "It doesn't seem like the safest place for a royal to be. It might even appear irresponsible."

"Irresponsible? Ms. Wallace, I don't think you know me well enough to pass judgement so quickly." His tone is no longer pleasing and I realize I have hit a nerve.

"On the contrary, I think I know a thing or two about the culture of royalty, be it here or in America, and very rarely do royals find it necessary to be so involved they risk their lives."

He nods and raises his chin arrogantly. "I find that unlikely, as you are just a commoner. And, I have found more reason to be here than originally anticipated."

He looks down at my fiddling hands. "And, if you are going to shoot your mouth off, make sure you have your facts straight. I have been here for the last three days, making sure the center was secured for your return."

I bite my lip, keeping from telling him to fuck off with his arrogance. "Oh."

His gaze dominates me still as I avoid it. "It seems if I had been the lazy type of prince you seem to know so well, you may not be standing here at this very moment."

While his arrogance is not seizing, he is completely right and somewhat sincere, to my surprise. "How responsible would that have been of me, Ella?"

The accent attached to my name starts to melt my resolve, but not before I change the subject. Aimlessly, I stack and restack the same to piles of paper over and over again as I ramble. "I'm sorry there wasn't much for you to observe today. I was just teaching them a song from my childhood. All morning they were quiet, like they were the first few days with me. I have this rule, I need to see each of them smile or laugh or even grin once before the end of the day. The only thing I could think of was to have them teach me a lullaby from their childhood. With most of the girls out today, because of..." I pause before bring finishing my sentence, tapping the stack of papers in hand and glazing over the event. "...what happened, I figure it would get all of them smiling if I shared one of mine."

Noticing him looking intently down at the piles of papers I have restacked countlessly, I release the stacks and fold my arms over my chest. "It seemed like a good idea and they all smiled."

My eyes connect with his full lips as he says, "There was plenty for me to observe, Ella. And, please, just call me Rajaa."

I slowly shake my head, thinking I shouldn't be studying his lips with the intent of devouring them and I shouldn't be so informal as to address a prince without his title. "It wouldn't be right."

"What wouldn't? To do something I have asked you to do?" His tone tries to dominate me; I really hate that macho attitude shit.

"You are a prince. Having a royal presence among commoners is what you thrive on, isn't it?" I figured my smart-ass remark would shut him up, but instead he folds his arms over his chest and grins at me.

"You really know very little about royalty. It is comical actually, and kind of cute." His laugh is amazing and his accent even more deadly to my resolve, but his mockery pisses me off enough to overcome them and hold a cold, hard stare. His grin quickly disappears as soon as he sees I'm not amused. "If I beg you to call me Raj, will you?" He holds his hands up in surrender. "Not a royal request in the slightest."

"Oh, so now it's Raj."

His bashful grin reveals the smallest dimple on one cheek, before it disappears, becoming something weighty, bold, and completely hot as his eyes travel down my face to my lips. "Yeah, it's Raj."

His seeking my lips pulls me back to the moment he covered my mouth with his hand, his body flush against mine, rough, urgent, immediate, but enticing and seductive as I think of him holding me now. Somehow I manage to stay coherent and tell him what I hoped I would have a chance to. "I need to thank you."

My comment seems to wake him from the magnetic web we are spinning ourselves in. "For?"

"You're right. If you hadn't shielded me like you did, didn't have your soldiers take the girls, we might not have made it."

He lowers his eyes and scratches the back of his neck. Modesty doesn't fit him after our discussion, but my gratitude seems to have softened him. Keeping his hand on the back of his neck, he looks at me through thick, black eyelashes that contrast the light golden flecks dancing in his eyes. "Once I saw it was you ... I couldn't leave you unprotected. Not after finding you again."

"Again?"

It's stupid, but I want his confirmation the mysticism surrounding our chance meetings here days ago and in D.C. are absolute.

He doesn't respond, just watches me as he slowly walks around the desk; my words keep me from losing all sense as he gets closer. "When you saved me, you had your hand over my mouth, keeping me from yelling. When we were in the room, waiting for the attack to stop, you said something to me."

Sailing on the memory, the touch of his hand over my lips and craving it more once it had gone, I don't realize I have rested the tips of my fingers on my lips until they make contact. It has affected him; he focuses on my fingers, watching them run along my lip. Feeling self-conscious, as we both seem to feed on the brush of my fingers across my lip, the imitation of what his touch would feel like again, I tuck my hand under my other arm crossed over my chest.

I see the tension within him as he resists pulling his eyes from my lips, meeting and matching my intoxicated stare, driven by something carnal. "Eh enta."

The tension deep inside quivers from the cadence of the syllables of his native tongue. His voice lowers as he steps closer. "It loosely means to know someone."

With the expectation of him telling me what I feel I already know deep in my soul, I look up at him timidly. "You know me?"

Separated only by inches, the physical doesn't exist. The amber eyes that speared me to that sofa back at the loft are back again with a vengeance and I swear I'm only held upright by them at this very moment.

"I think you know the answer to that, Ella Wallace. Before the day I saved you, before you came here to Jordan. That night, the party, across the room when I memorized every inch of your face within seconds, ingrained in me for eternity. The elevator. I know you, Ella."

A ringing cell phone breaks apart the small world we were building for ourselves. He turns away and puts his cell to his ear. "Yes."

I don't realize the sensation of holding my breath until his golden-brown eyes release me from the exquisite snare they held me in. I knew the guy at the fucking elevator was him.

"No, just tell him to wait there."

I try to avoid eavesdropping on the conversation and search my desk aimlessly for any distraction when I notice my veil laying in a pile on my chair.

Shit!

I snatch it from the desk and quickly cover my head, realizing I have been without my veil in front of a fucking prince.

As soon as he hangs up the phone, he turns back to me. "I'm sorry for the interruption. I..."

He pauses mid-sentence, scanning the top of my head now, noticing the veil. He focuses on it for a long time, then looks away from me, running his hand over his mouth. "I'm sorry for my rudeness."

I realize while his apology might have been for the phone call at first, it has now doubled as an apology for breaking custom, a divide that is deep and one I might have made him forget briefly.

"You haven't been rude."

He walks back toward me, slowly, carefully now. "It's just the veil..."

I badly want to burn the fucking veil now and seriously contemplate taking it off when he explains, "You wore it the day I saw you in the courtyard. The first time I saw you here at the center. I was sitting in Mr. Stern's office and I saw your veil through the window. I think it was the blue color attracting me to it, like your eyes."

He walks around the desk and comes to stand in front of me again. His physical presence gives rise to the tension coiling in my abdomen, pulling and pushing down the tremors he is creating for me with his retelling.

"I didn't know it was you right away until I saw the smallest ribbon of golden hair blowing in the wind, set free from the veil without being tucked back in place. I remember thinking, this woman isn't from here. She is bold and carefree."

His native accent blends perfectly with the English prose he is weaving, pulling me in deeper into what he is saying. He shakes his head slowly, making sure not to loosen me from this link he is creating between us. "I didn't know it was you until you turned just enough for me to see your face. The face that became rooted in me in D.C."

A small smile forms on his lips as he remembers, his brow furrowing with the struggle of what he is going to say. "I told myself that it couldn't be you. The woman I saw that night, then on the elevator was a world away, lost in a place that didn't suit her."

Slowly, Raj raises his hand and reaches for me. While I know I should pull away and preserve the divide between us, I am weak under the spell being invoked by something deeper than Muslim tradition and code.

His touch is gentle, like the lightest feather pushing the veil away from me, down off my head to rest around my neck. "The veil is a symbol for a woman to maintain modesty among men."

The sound of him speaking is a sensuous song, while his heavy gaze, taking in every inch of my hair, my face, my lips, is an alluring dance he is tempting me to take with him. His eyes travel down the length of my hair, beyond the veil around my neck, to my body, fervidly sending shockwaves with just the lightest touch of the back of his hand against my bare arm.

"Your boldness, across a room at a party, a glimpse of you in an elevator, in a courtyard beneath a veil, in my arms as I save you." He looks down at his hand, like he is committing sin. "Standing inches from you now, why should it be kept hidden?"

He seems to fight with this questions as his eyes slowly return to mine, holding me in this world where only we exist. "It shouldn't be. Ever. Your boldness has possessed me, Ella, and I will never be the same."

His seductive scrutiny weighs on my lips, calling me closer, making my heart thrash with every audible beat as I refute the haunting notion of our chance meeting not once, not twice, but three on different ends of the world was somehow fated in an unforeseen pact between destiny and the universe. An Arab prince and an American outsider, min barra, to cross the stars, defy the rules, the codes of law dividing us, no matter the cost, no matter the risk. Still, his golden embers burn into my soul, daring me to surrender to this sublimely magnificent and cruel covenant.

The harsh knock on the door break us apart, Raj backing away just as Tom comes into the classroom. He looks between us around the room, inspecting our being alone

"Your brother is here, Rajaa. He would like to speak to you in my office."

He turns his watchfulness back to me. "Ms. Wallace, you should go to lunch with the girls."

Interrupted from our moment, I stumble over my words. "I was just coming. I'm sorry."

I attempt to detour Tom's analysis of what we were doing along in here as I look back at Raj. "Thank you again for creating the program bringing me here. I would have never been able to come if you hadn't been so passionate about the center."

Rajaa's hands are casually tucked in his pockets, never revealing any sign of stress or tension with Tom's scrutinizing stare, unlike myself. "Of course, Ms. Wallace. Thank you for being here for the girls. Let me escort you to the cafeteria."

Tom's watchfulness becomes hawk-like as he makes a comment to deter him. "Rajaa, it isn't necessary. Your brother is waiting."

Rajaa stops short of Tom. His tone is dominating and solid as he tells Tom, "My brother can wait as I walk Ms. Wallace. It is on the way to your office, if I'm not mistaken."

Tom seems to shrink at Rajaa's demand to walk me. "Yes, you are correct."

The three of us silently walk toward the front of the center, Tom on one side of me and Raj on the other.

"Mr Stern." One of the medical staff peeks through a doorway we have just past. "Could I borrow you for a moment?"

Tom seems to contemplate leaving us as the man regards the prince. "Hello, Your Highness."

He begins to bow, when Raj interrupts him, taking a small step toward him. "Please, just Prince Rajaa."

The man nods. "Yes, of course. Prince Rajaa."

"Tom, please see to what Mr. Gillis is in need of." Raj comes back to me. "I will make sure Ms. Wallace gets to the cafeteria and I find my brother."

As we walk through the medical clinic corridor, his phone rings again. He declines the call and starts typing on the keypad. "I'm sorry. My brother, Zaid, has no patience." The tension in his tone is palpable.

I notice how Raj knew the man's name. "You know some of the staff, I see."

He nods as he types. "Yes. Mr. Gillis is a good man. He has worked with Caritas for three years here, when the center was much smaller and my family was less involved."

He puts his phone back in his pocket and focuses on me. "I plan to be here more, under the recent circumstances."

The way he says circumstances has me questioning if it's the attack or me that has changed his plans. Coming to the cafeteria doors, he reaches to open it for me just as his name is called. "Rajaa."

We both turn to look down the hall at the caller. He resembles Raj and I assume it is his impatient brother. The way his eyes are only focused on Raj leads me to believe this conversation is more urgent then he let on.

"I should go. Thank you for escorting me." I keep my comments short as I reach for the door and attempt to sneak away and out of the discussion between them, but I'm called on.

"Is this *the* Ella Wallace?" I turn toward Prince Zaid, surprised he knows not only my name, but his question seems to hold a deeper knowledge of who I am. I sense Raj tense as his brother approaches us quickly now.

"Yes, this is Ms. Wallace, but she needs to collect her students, Zaid."

Zaid ignores Raj's attempt at dismissing me as he focuses on me. His eyes are much darker than Raj's, almost black, as the pupils are lost within them. His touch is heavy as he places his hands on my shoulders. "Ella Wallace. It is a pleasure to meet you. I have heard so much about your act of bravery and selflessness."

I'm unsure how to answer, so I settle with a small, "Thank you, Your High..."

"Prince Zaid," he corrects me, then continues on with finishing his intended thought. "My brother, Prince Rajaa, has a similar character of selflessness, don't you, brother?"

Raj forces a smile and nods. "Yes, well, Ms. Wallace needs to collect her girls. They have much to learn."

Prince Zaid smile suddenly tightens into a smug smirk. "Of course."

He looks down on me, standing equally as tall as Raj. "I am sorry to keep you. I'm sure those girls have so much they can learn from someone like you. It is a good thing you were saved by my brother. Tell me, what did it feel like to be saved by a prince, Ms. Wallace?"

I don't like the direction of his comments, or his question, and sense his anger toward his brother has expanded to me for whatever reason. "The same way it would have felt to be saved by anyone else I suppose, prince or not."

My comment seems to have Prince Zaid's undivided attention as the smirk on his mouth disappears. "Is that so? The same as anyone else?"

He folds his arms over his chest, more offended than intrigued. Part of me wishes I would have kept my fucking mouth shut. *Always my mouth getting me in trouble.* But the other part of me wasn't going to let him intimidated me because of his status.

Shit. If this gets back to Tom, I'm going to hear it.

"I think your girls need you, Ms. Wallace," Raj interrupts our exchange again. I look up at him and see the unease in his eyes. "Have a good day, Ella."

"Thank you." I nod and pass through the door he has opened for me.

As I walk toward Ana, the adrenaline from the unexpected confrontation with a Prince of Jordan has my stomach fluttering. When I get to the table, I sit and smile at the girls, attempting to hide my concern for the small pissing match I have started with Prince Zaid.

Ana is watching me as she eats her Hummus and Shrak. She left two dolma for me, having eaten two herself, just as she always does. "What's going on?"

She is looking beyond me at the door, keeping the temptation to glance back at bay, knowing the two brothers may still be there.

"What?" I ask, playing dumb.

She leans in and lowers her voice. "Prince Rajaa observing you, then escorting you to the cafeteria some fifteen minutes later." She pauses to wait for a response. When I don't give her one, tearing off a piece of Shrak and dipping it in the creamy hummus, she probes further, "What is that about?"

I pick at the grape leaves of the dolma as I fabricate a reason. "He wanted to thank me for letting him observe. He had a few questions, I thanked him for granting funding to get us here, and the opportunity to volunteer."

My hope that my added explanation has satisfied her fails when she asks for more. "And?"

Noticing the cafeteria staff cleaning around our tables, I realize we have stayed past our lunch time. I look at Ana quickly. "And I thanked him for saving me."

I snatch the rest of the Shrak, wrapping it in a paper towel along with the leftover dolma.

"Saving you?"

I rise as her question lingers between us.

"Wait, he is the one that saved you during the attack?" Her voice rises louder and I hush her to be quiet.

"Yes."

Ana seems astonished by the leak of information. She sneers, "Well, I guess it isn't every day you are rescued by a prince."

"Time to go! Yalla Yalla!" I sing in a soft voice to get the girls' attention. I rise and back away from the table ask the girls file in toward me. As I lead them out into the courtyard, I notice two soldiers standing with the one I thanked this morning. The added security made me feel safe to bring them out, and was the only reason I agreed with Ana this morning on letting them play. The sun is overhead and the heat is at its peak.

Adjusting my veil, I remember the way Raj's hands pulled it away, how it sent waves of desire through me, a feeling I haven't been able to appreciate in a very long time. The desire, his words, his touch stayed just at the forefront of my mind for the rest of the day. My focus on my girls was still there. I did find myself drifting away to the world Raj had created once or twice, but their energy kept me in the moment with them.

Ana and I walk into the volunteer meeting Tom had called. While I smile and hug a few of the other volunteers I have become close with, I am more focused on seeing if Raj is here. Surveying the room between hugs, hellos, and smiles, I don't see him.

Tom starts the meeting quickly, saying he doesn't want to keep us too late. "Prince Rajaa could not stay as he had expected. He has been called away to an engagement for the royal family. He did want me to convey his heart-felt appreciation to those he wasn't able to see today. I'm sure he will visit with each of you soon."

As Tom discusses the day and how the plan of protocol will continue as it is for the remainder of our time here, he comments on the media leak creating an added concern. He tells us there is not a need to worry, as the soldiers will keep them out of the center, but he will need us to refrain from talking to the media until they back off.

While I should be listening to all the questions from the volunteers and the dialogue Tom is having with us, I find myself wondering what could have pulled Raj away from staying for the meeting, something I assumed was important to him. I mean, a royal engagement, really? I am familiar with engagements, royal or not. In America, an engagement either means the literal term or a party and I'm certain it means the same here, just segregated to royalty where ours are segregated to the most influential. Could this party have meant more to him than the support of this program? Or was this entire program his parents' idea, to improve their royal image?

Suddenly, his chivalry, his seductive notions seeming sincere in the classrooms, sweeping me away into an intimate place only for us and building a fantasy within me of how fate has linked us, pulling my sex-deprived ass right in, doesn't seem as untainted as it does now. Could this royal prince be a royal ass, like his brother Zaid? Could he be a fucking Logan Bristol? I should know better, coming from a family thriving on strategic moves within the confines of our status of American royalty. This whole program could have been a strategic move for Raj, nothing more. I could be a strategic move.

Feeling my blood boil the more I think on it, I don't realize everyone is rising to leave.

"Is that it?" I ask Ana.

She puts her bag on her shoulder and looks at me oddly. "Yeah. Hey, are you okay? You have been distracted all day."

My defenses already on the rise, I snap at her, "No, I haven't."

She raises her eyebrows at me, identifying with the tone quickly. "Okay, something has crawled up your ass. I'm out of here. See you tomorrow." Ana was definitely a no-nonsense type of girl, and my jumping her wasn't cool at all. "I'm sorry," I call after her as she walks away. She waves her hand at me, a small indication of her way of forgiving and forgetting.

Tom assigned us each drivers to take us home. "It's late and I want you all to get home safe. Prince Rajaa provided us with drivers."

Of course he did. It looks good for the press waiting out front for us as we drive away in royal cars.

"Thank you for serving," I mutter under my breath. His appreciation to Ana and me earlier was just words, a cordial sentiment asshats say to the people serving for them.

As I exit the center, only a handful of newscasters remain. I'm sure they have moved on to the royal engagement the prince is attending tonight. I toss my bag into the SUV waiting for me before climbing in.

Chapter 12
Rajaa

Once Ella was through the cafeteria door, I close it and wait for her to put distance between us. Her sharp response to my brother was not received well and I needed her to leave quickly to save her from his wrath.

"What are you doing here, Zaid?" My voice reflects my irritation with his presence.

He watches Ella as she sits down; a thousand curses fill his eyes, ready to spear her. "You may want to talk to her about watching her place around men, brother. Well, since you are so comfortable with her it may not be the best idea. Maybe I should teach her a lesson or two."

I ignore his provocation and ask for his response. "Zaid?"

"We have to meet with father before tonight. I have come to get you."

"A meeting? Why do we need a meeting before a family celebration?"

This meeting sounds bogus, like a ploy to pull me from the center.

"Because the list of guests has grown and it now involves Prime Minister Shafar Badran and a few of the Cabinet members, along with others."

"How can a fucking party turn into a state of affairs?"

He breathes in deeply, seeming put off by my frustration as he turns away from me and waves me on. "When it involves the Amir of Kuwait. Now, come. We have to meet Father back at the house soon, and you have already made me wait long enough while you were sniffing around Ms. Wallace, drawing fucking attention to this place with your presence."

I rush to him and match his stride as two soldiers fall in beside us. "The Amir?"

Zaid keeps walking. "This party is for Princess Haleema's sixteenth birthday. Your mother decided to host it at Raghadan Palace weeks ago."

Princess Haleema is the daughter of my father's sister, Princess Izza al Jabara. She is married to a Kuwaiti Sheikh Haneef Abdou, who in turn has strong association with the Amir of Kuwait, and Daya's father.

My brother continues, "Since we are honoring a princess of Kuwaiti blood, I suggested we invite the Amir and his family."

"Yes, I'm sure you did." I'm positive Daya would be there because of his suggestion.

Zaid overlooks my comment as he continues, "Tonight may be the night our father and the Amir agree upon ties more binding, including your marriage to Daya. You should bring up the discussion topic."

As we exit the back door of the center, I follow Zaid into the backseat of the truck. Once the door is shut, we are moving fast down the narrow alley. "Will this sit down include a discussion about your alliance with Tariq?"

My angled question has Zaid look at me warily at first. I know it is because of the Kuwati and Syrian relations being severed.

"A discussed another time, later, once Kuwait's and Jordan's future has been well established. Oh, and we will talk about your center!"

His last comment ending on a rather high note, like he has a surprise to tell me.

"What about the center?"

He scoffs and pulls out his phone, opens the screen, and shows me a picture of the front of the center on the Jordan Times news feed. "Your program has drawn attention yet again." His sarcastic tone quickly rises to anger as he growls, "I have soldiers blocking the courtyard of your precious center holding off the fucking paparazzi because they found out you were there. Soldiers shouldn't be policing these hounds and if your ass wasn't there..."

He cuts himself short mid-sentence, realizing his anger is getting the better of him. He leans his head back against the headrest, closes his eyes for a moment.

I take my chance defending the good that can come from this. "Let the media see what this center will do for the refugees and Jordan. Our father said it himself. We need to show those fucking attackers we will not hide from them. We will protect those we have welcomed into our country."

I pull out my phone to dial Tom. Zaid notices. "Who are you calling?"

"Tom. I need to tell him why I left without telling him. I'm supposed to attend a meeting with the volunteers."

Zaid reaches for my phone and takes it from my hand. "I have already talked to Tom, while you were flirting with Ms. Wallace."

His tone of disgust when he says her name pisses me off. "What did you tell him?"

Zaid tosses my phone on my lap. "I told him to brief the volunteers on why you will not be attending their meeting tonight and how gracious you are for their service. I have also told him he needs to make sure the staff and volunteers keep their fucking mouths shut around the media! The leak came from one of them and I told him the funding for this program can go away as quickly as it came if anything else is leaked. This bullshit is what got the Queen into her predicament months ago, and now here you go following in Mama's foot steps!"

I want to pummel him in the fucking face for speaking about her, but I yell at the driver instead. "Stop the truck!"

"What the fuck are you doing, Raj?" Zaid sounds nervous for the first time in his life. "Don't! keep going!"

My blood is boiling and it is close to spilling over unless I get out of this truck now.

"I said stop the fucking truck!"

Both the driver and passenger security details exchange a quick look, then pull over quickly. Without warning, I turn to my brother and even my glare with his. "This program will not go away. This bullshit will be what saves the Middle East from itself, and if you ever speak for me again to anyone, I will beat the shit out of you."

I open the door before security can get out of the car to shield me. I'm an open target as I walk to the truck behind us, but I don't care. I'm so fucking angry, I could spit fire. Speaking for me, pulling me from the center, talking to Ella the way he did. What would he do next? Propose to Daya for me?

The guard barely has time to get out of the front seat, as I come up to the side of the truck and open the rear door to get in. As soon as I slam the door shut, the caravan of trucks is gunning it as we weave through the streets of Amman toward home.

I hold the tumbler and swirl the golden liquid with the smallest turn of my wrist. The wedge between my brother and me is driving deeper, making the space between us wider. While my father has hoped I can bring him to understanding, I have lost almost all of mine.

I drink down the last quarter of whisky in one gulp. I'm glad I brought this along when I came home. I'm not a drinker, but I fear tonight I will need it. The short meeting at home before arriving here at Raghadan Palace was monopolized by Zaid, discussing the future of Kuwait and Jordan, how the Prime Minister's attendance would show the Amir our solidarity in wanting this bond to no longer be talk, but action. The proposal between Daya and me would come soon, and the possibility of announcing a crown prince, heir to the throne, sooner to relieve any pressure on our father. He even had the balls to bring up the center, Makan Lil 'Amal, and how he has had a change of heart about its purpose and how I have been the cause of it.

He had mapped and contrived his discussion points artfully, bringing me into it. He never once mentioned his ally, the Syrian Sheikh he has been working with covertly. Of course he wouldn't, not with the known climate between Kuwait and Syria.

"Looking for a quiet place, I see."

My father is standing in the doorway behind me, using his cane for support. He knows me well. I place my empty glass down on the side table near the window and go to my father. "Yes, have they arrived?"

"They are beginning to," he says as I walk toward him.

Tonight my father appears strong, even if he isn't. He has not walked with my grandfather's cane in weeks, but tonight he is meeting with leaders, will be photographed at a very public event. He must appear strong, well, for the people. I place my hand on his shoulder. "How are you feeling, Baba?"

Matching my height almost exactly, he raises his chin with pride. "I am feeling well. It is you I am not sure of." He continues toward me and I meet him halfway.

"What? I'm well, Baba." I make sure my air of confidence is on point as we turn and walk out of the office.

"In the meeting before arriving here, you did not say much. It isn't like you."

I make an excuse as I avoid looking at him directly. "Just observing."

"Yes, well, your brother had plenty to say."

I remember the relief my father and mother both displayed as Zaid maneuvered his talking points, reflecting my own visions as his own about the center, highlighting the transformation it will bring.

"I did not think it was possible, Rajaa. Just the smallest amount of time at the center and he is already changing his views of the refugees." He smiles contentedly.

I nod. "Yes, it would appear so."

"It is because of you," he says faithfully.

He should not have such faith in me since I have done nothing. "It isn't because of me."

"Baba," Tamanna voice follows behind us. She is dressed in a beautiful teal dress, the sheerest matching shawl covering her shoulders. "Come back to the party," she pleas.

She looks at me now accusingly. "Why are you hiding up here?"

I laugh at her observation, even though it couldn't be truer. I was hiding, mostly from Daya, who I know will arrive any moment, if she hasn't already.

I see my mother come around the corner, her expression firm, then my father. "The Amir just arrived. I need you to come down with me. He says he needs to have words with you both."

"Where's Zaid?" my father asks.

She shakes her head, "I'm not sure. I saw him earlier speaking with Daya and some of the cousins, but then I lost sight of him."

"I saw him speaking with a man in the courtyard," Tamanna adds as she walks away from us. She waves to me and smiles. "Come say hello to everyone, Raj. I will show you where Daya is."

"Tamanna, go back to the party; your brother and I have to speak privately with the Amir."

She pouts as my father turns her request down. Appearing flustered, my mother sharply demands, "Tamanna, listen to your father. Go."

She is holding my father around the shoulders, walking with him slowly with me on the other side. Her apprehension and serious focus on getting my father down there has me worried about what we are walking into. "Mama, what did he say it was about?"

She shakes her head. "I don't know. He seemed disturbed and he said it was urgent."

My father pushes my hand away and stops walking. "Here, you go down with the guests. Rajaa will accompany me. Go, zahrat baladi. Go, my flower." He squeezes her hand then releases her.

"I will look for Zaid," she says as she walks swiftly down the hall. I remain alongside of my father.

The remainder of the walk and short elevator ride down seemed saturated with a disrupting anxiety set apart from any other. What could this be about? Is he upset about my not proposing yet? Could it be as simple as that? If that was the case, I was armed with a loose tongue due to the whisky and I might just be brave enough to tell him the bond of Jordan and Kuwait would not be weighing on a marriage between Daya and me.

The sound of music and laughter fill the main hall as the elevator opens to the second level of the palace. My father and I get no more than a few steps out of the elevator when Amir Hussam and two of his guards approach us.

My father tries to appear jovial even though he is concerned about the Amir's temper. "Hussam, my friend. I'm told you needed to see me urgently. What is it, my old friend? Is everything all right?"

The Amir's smile is tight lipped as he approaches my father, taking him by the shoulders with open arms as they exchange the traditional kiss on the cheek once, then twice.

"Ammaar.I am well old friend."

The way the Amir caters to him gently in both handling and voice, it is evident he knows his frailty. The Amir moves to me, his arms open and his smile mild, but genuine. "Rajaa, it is good to see you."

He takes my shoulders as he did my father, and I his, accepting the traditional greeting. "Amir, it is wonderful to see you again."

Being in the Amir's presence has always been a pleasant one, but the tension tonight among us is tangible. Unable to withhold the concern, my father asks again anxiously, "What is it, Hussam? Whatever it is, my friend, I know it can be resolved."

The Amir looks around us. "Is there a place we can speak privately?"

Once we have relocated to a more private room, my father moves around the table to sit opposite the Amir. I join my father's side.

Hussam raises his chin and looks between my father and me. "There is something I fear may prevent a deeper bond from happening between our nations, Ammaar."

I'm surprised by Hussam's revelation, as is my father, sitting frozen, unable to fathom what could have possibly affected the Amir's adamant desire for unification.

My father's hand begins to tremble on the table, unable to withhold the symptom stirred by the tension in the room. "I don't understand. What could possibly prevent it?"

He levels his eyes with my father. "It is your son, Ammaar."

My father looks to me accusingly and I immediately consider what the Amir has somehow discovered as my sin. Could he know that I do not want to marry Daya?

"Not Rajaa." His admittance is a relief. "It's Zaid. I have been made aware a Syrian guest, Sheikh Tariq bin Khaddam, has been given temporary asylum here in Jordan. Your son Zaid is said to be keeping company with him, partying frequently, among other things."

Too familiar with this story, I glance at my father as it unravels before him, something I fear will destroy him. My father listens to the Amir continue to unhinge Tariq's and my brother's involvement. "My sources say he is funding the revolution by moving the drug through the Arab states and supplying it to the Islamic state fighters."

I feel my stomach sink and my heart races hearing the allegations from the Amir as I had imagined in theory.

My father clears his throat in the uncomfortable silence of his shock. "I have not heard this. My Prime Minister, the Cabinet, our people, would know of this if it were true."

My father's effort to save my brother is embarrassing and pitiful. Nothing can save him now. He has been caught in his fucking web of lies.

The Amir folds his hands on the table. "My concern extends to them as well, Ammaar."

"What are you saying? That my executive office is aware of this asylum my son has enforced behind my back? That this Sheikh is using both him and my country as their hideout?" My father's voice quivers as it rises.

The Amir places his hands in the air just above the table. "I would not bring this to you unless I feared for your family's and country's safety."

He looks between my father and me. "You both know the severed relations we have with Syria. President Faraj Al-Dawood is a butcher, a murderous bastard, and a terrorist himself to his own people. Now, the revolution against him has fed a more deadly virus. An illness is spreading, coming to our nations, and people like this Sheikh are the transporters of it. I can't have my family be a part of it. I will not support it by agreeing to Daya and Rajaa's marriage, and if Zaid is to be the heir to the throne, I cannot in good faith link Kuwait to Jordan in any way. I'm very sorry to bring this news to you on such an occasion, Ammaar."

He looks from my father to me. "I'm very sorry, Rajaa. I know you wished to ask for Daya's hand, and I have wanted nothing else for her, but with Zaid's apparent involvement in this, I can't allow it."

Amir Hussam rises and bows his head to both of us before leaving the room. The stillness my father expresses is frightening. "Baba."

He raises his hand to me. "Don't."

His breathing is uneven as he rises with the aid of his cane. Suddenly, the door swings open, Zaid standing in the open doorway. "I'm sorry, Baba. I was tending to the guests."

I notice his rumpled shirt and the top button of his pants undone as I walk straight to him. Realizing the atmosphere in the room, he senses something has happened in his absence. I stop in front of him. "Zip up your fucking pants and sit down."

"No! Don't sit down!" My father's directive is fueled with pure disgust as he comes at Zaid, his cane dragging beside him. "You have disgraced our family, Zaid!"

Zaid looks between my father and me, appearing to be surprised. "What? I have done no such thing!"

My father stumbles just as he gets to my side. I quickly reach for him, as does my brother. He swats my brother's hand away with his cane, accepting mine. "Don't touch me! Do you know what you have done?"

Zaid pulls away, avoiding the swing of his cane. "The Amir? What did he tell you? Whatever he has said, I can explain!"

"There is nothing to explain! He has explained it all!" my father argues as I pull up a chair for him.

"Please, Baba, sit."

He swats my hand away as Zaid pleads with my father, lowering himself to stare into his eyes. "Please, Baba, tell me what he said to you. Whatever it is, I'm sure I can explain! Please, Baba!"

"No!" My father begins to cough. "You mean to tell me you can explain why you have given refuge to a drug lord, a Sheikh from Syria!"

"Baba, no, no, it is not what you think," Zaid continues to plead with a softened voice, begging for understanding.

My father breathes in laboriously. "Drugs, Zaid! The Prince of Jordan dealing in drugs and the revolution!"

"Baba, please, just give me a moment to talk!"

"No! You do not get to speak! You don't deserve to be in my sight! Your brother's marriage to Daya is no more because of your dealings with Tariq bin Khaddam!"

The door opens and my mother enters, her eyes filled with horror as she walks into the fire my father is setting ablaze. I try to place my arm on his back to help him keep the balance that is failing him.

"Baba, please. Listen to me," Zaid begs, his voice breaking with every word.

My mother rushes to my father's side. "What has happened?"

"The Amir has refused Daya and Rajaa's union!" my father bellows as he lunges for Zaid, clutching his shirt by the fistful. "You have destroyed everything!"

"No, Ammaar, stop!" My mother's cry goes unheard as my father growls and seethes.

"You will not be king. You do not deserve to rule our nation!"

"No, Baba, please hear me! I have done it all for our family!" Zaid's pleas are cries of petition. "It is all for us! To protect us!"

As my mother and I both try to pull my father from Zaid, I see my brother's eyes widen. "Baba!" Suddenly, my father's livened body turns spiritless, limp in my arms as he clings to my brother's shirt. Zaid wraps his arms around my father as my mother screams.

"Ammaar! No! Saaedni arjook!"

I can't mask my own fear as I wail for help with my mother. "We need help!"

As Zaid and I lower my father to the ground, my mother collapses on him. "No, Ammaar! Don't leave me!" I pry her from my father and hold her to me as Zaid slips away from us, into the hall as the guards circle around my father laboring for every breath.

Chapter 13

Rajaa

Days later ...

"I am fine, please stop coddling me, Laiyalla!" My father's demanding yet shaky voice is back. I stand at the window listening to my father beg my mother to stop doting over him, and can't help but reflect on the day of his episode.

Once the paramedics started working on him, they quickly determined he was having a stroke. The staff of doctors working on my father at the hospital explained the quick response and medication in the ambulance were key to preventing any irreversible damage.

The staff told us to go home, rest, but we weren't leaving. Part of me was there for my father, and another for the hope my brother would show his face, to see how our father was. As the sun rose the next morning, they released my father from ICU to a private room, and Zaid was still nowhere to be found. I called my cousin Anwar; he knew nothing of his whereabouts. I asked him for Samir's number, the one giving safe haven to Tariq. He gave it willingly and I called him. Going straight to voicemail, I kept the message vague, telling him to have Zaid call me as soon as possible.

Once they let us in to see my father, both my sister and mother went to my father and wrapped themselves around him as he lay on the bed. I stood tall behind them and rested my hand on the top of the arm holding my mother to his heart. He looked up at me, the exchange lacking words but not emotion.

"Zaid?" His voice was weak as he asked for my brother. Even as he healed from a stroke, stricken on top of his already failing health, he asked for the one who put him there.

Shaking my head, I stare out the window at Zaid as he paces along the cobblestones of the courtyard, talking on his cell. My brother never came to the hospital, but was waiting for us at home after my father's release. He sat at the bottom of the stairs in the foyer, his eyes red from what one could assume tears, but I assumed drugs. My mother couldn't contain her rage. "Here, now? Why? Why didn't you come to the hospital?"

Speechless, he shook his head and held his hands over his mouth as if to conceal the emotions, the guilt, the disgrace he has brought upon us.

My father walked toward him; I feared his reaction and took hold of his arm. My mother stepped in front of him, and with warning in her voice said his name. "Ammaar."

He glanced from her to me and spoke evenly, "It is okay."

My father stood over my brother and extended his hand, an extension of grace I never expected my father to give to Zaid. My brother fought the compassion my father offered, lamenting through his tears, "I don't deserve your mercy, Baba."

My father lowered his hand to my brother's, covering it, squeezing tightly. "But still it is mercy I give you. You are my son; receive it and become it."

Receive it and become it.

My father's words were a message for Zaid. His leniency to my brother was an extension of his humanity, his tolerance. A tolerance I couldn't fathom giving to Zaid myself. I struggle with it now as I look down on him from the window.

The days following, my brother and father were inseparable, working to relinquish ties Zaid had to Tariq, as well as the addictions that have driven him to his lowest. I watched as Zaid appeared to transform into the son he once was, the brother he used to be. I see my father's hope that this transformation will bring his Zaid back to a righteousness that I fear is lost. The first meeting my father requested was with the Prime Minister and Cabinet. It is set for today in the dining hall.

The gentle hand of my mother comes to rest on my shoulders, pulling my attention from the window to her. "You have been by your father's side night and day, Rajaa. You need to rest."

"I'm fine. I slept last night."

She shakes her head. "No, I'm talking about a break away from here."

I'm not understanding what she means. "For me to go away?" I scoff, "I can't do that. Not with everything as it is."

She folds her arms over her chest as she looks up at me, a gentle smile to match her delicate reminiscence. "In high school, whenever you needed time to think, you, Anwar, and your brother would go to Wadi Rum. Do you remember?"

I bow my head, remembering the place that let me breathe freely. Suddenly, Ella Wallace slips into my vision of Wadi Rum. "Yes, I remember, but I haven't been to the center in days. I need to be there."

I need to see her again.

She nods and keeps her eyes level with mine. "Ah, yes, where your heart remains."

She stares as me a little too long and I wonder if she is thinking about our conversation nights ago about my heart, my passion, being kept within the center. Something comes to mind, a possible way for me to see her again, while getting away to the place where I feel free. "I will consider getting away. Shukran, Mama."

"Please don't let your father's health keep you here. He is well taken care of."

I look back at Tamanna tucking my father's blanket in around him as he reads the newspaper. I don't think he heard my mother's comment until he says, "Yes, I am being swaddled like a baby, unfortunately. I do not need all of this attention!"

His sharp response is playful and directed at my mother. Zaid appears at the door, knocking softly. Since my return home, Zaid's appearance is crisp and tailored for the first time, opposite of the image he had assumed days ago. As for my father, aiding my brother to get back on his feet, back on track, suits him and has given him a strength I haven't seen in a very long time. As my brother speaks to my father, the old Zaid, the one always carrying himself as honorable, untainted, pristine, and sober, appears, determined for redemption. I want to give him the benefit of the doubt, I want to believe he is seeking redemption, he is the brother I grew up with, but I am hesitant.

Chapter 14
Ella

I watch my girls divide as half jump rope and half play hopscotch. It is definitely their favorite American game. Jumping rope is catching on now that I've shown them how to do Double Dutch. Muna is the quickest on the ropes because of how small she is.

The sky is overcast with more clouds than usual; they somehow have caught an infinitesimal amount of moisture in the air. Hoda says we might get rain, which I haven't seen in the time I have been here. As I watch the girls now, I hope it doesn't rain, so they can have more time to simply enjoy being children.

The girls try to get me to join them. "Come play, Ms. Ella. Show us you Double Dutch," Muna calls to me.

"In a little bit."

She looks at me strangely. "Bit?"

Shit. I haven't taught them the double meaning of the word "bit" yet. "Um, in a few minutes."

She sulks back and starts playing again, and I feel worse than I already do. It has been days since I saw Raj, and while I wish I could say it isn't because of him not being here, it is. I think what is making me feel worse is how bitchy I was about him leaving and not returning for our meeting and then discovering from Ameena and the rest of the family that the King had fallen ill during the family celebration of Raj's cousin.

I want to see him again, and to know he was dealing with a painful event for his family, I feel like the biggest asshole in the universe. Even though logic tells me he is caring for his father, his family, I am still wishing to see him right now ... The worst fucking asshole ever, I know.

I feel a presence come up behind me. Thinking it's Tom, I don't respond to his approach.

"I have missed you."

Raj?

Unable to keep myself from meeting his eyes to make sure he is really here, I turn to face him. "What are you doing here?"

He doesn't look at me, instead focusing on the girls playing. "The little one, she is really good at jump roping."

Still stuck on him being here at the center, I neglect his comment. "Shouldn't you be at home?"

Raj glances at me, then back at the girls, grinning. "You may not want to stare long, Ella, we are in public among watchful eyes. You are a single woman and I a single man. It will look inappropriate."

I snap my head back to the girls, realizing he's right. Anyone watching us from the center, the guards at the courtyard gate, would think poorly of our casual chatting.

I fold my arms tightly over my chest and make sure my hair is tucked beneath my veil. Somehow I feel my confession to him is necessary and can't wait any longer. "I have to apologize to you."

"Why?"

"The night of the meeting, you weren't there and I figured it was because the program didn't mean everything I thought it had. I was disappointed, thinking a royal engagement was more important to your reputation than ... than the center."

More important than what you said to me.

"Then, I found out what happened to your father, and it being a family celebration, and I felt like a total bitch."

I don't realize I have offended until the weight of his stare is on me. "Sorry. I'm just really sorry for your father's stroke and judging you like I did. I don't know enough about you to judge you."

His silence is concerning as I blindly watch the girls play, occupying the uncomfortable silence while I wait for his response.

"My father is healing, and while I would like to say he needs me right now, he would rather be back on his feet and tending to himself, not being spoiled by my mother and sister." The smile in his voice delays my fear of him despising me for my misjudging.

"As for the other, you are forgiven and I plan for us to know a lot more about each other in the future, Ella."

I can't keep from staring at him now and he can't either, his eyes finding mine just for a moment. "I couldn't stay away any longer. I had to see you again."

Realizing the length of time we have stared, too long, we both look away back to the girls as he starts toward them. I'm not sure what he is doing, but as he gets closer, the girls all stop jumping rope and hop-scotching.

He smiles. "La tatawaqqaf ... Don't stop. Play, girls."

He picks the rope up from the ground and holds the ends between his hands, then winks at me charmingly before he starts jumping.

Pinching my lips tightly together, I try to hide the smile wanting to break free as he plays with the girls. "See, the prince can jump rope!"

The girls giggle and clap their hands as he continues to jump. He picks up the other rope the girls were using to jump Double Dutch, then looks at me, holding both of them up, before glancing over at Nooda. He speaks to her quietly in Arabic. She catches my eye and giggles. He looks at me too, then back at Nooda as she says, "Double Dutch," with a heavy accent.

Raj turns back to me playfully. "Double Dutch, huh. Okay."

He hands the end of the two ropes to Nooda, then he holds the other two ends of the rope to me. "Ms. Wallace."

Is he seriously going to jump rope? "Do you know how to jump?"

I take the rope from him as he lowers himself to Muna's level. "She will show me. Muna, 'farjeeni min fadlik."

At his asking her graciously to show him, she quickly nods.

"Shukran," he says as he steps aside.

Nooda and I start turning the rope as the rest of the girls circle around. As I turn it, I watch Raj study Muna's quick feet as she jumps in. Suddenly, he moves in and starts jumping. Face to face, I can't help grinning at how he is moving. "I'm impressed."

I think he winks at me, then turns to face Muna, still jumping, giving me a view of his perfect ass. I shouldn't be staring at it. Instead I focus on his broad shoulders, which I shouldn't be doing either. The girls are clapping faster as we turn the rope quicker and quicker. Suddenly, the rope catches on the shoulders of Raj's tall frame, collapsing the rope on them, and the girls laugh. Raj picks up Muna in his arms and cheers with her as the girls circle around them both.

The rest of the day I am on a high after the short time with Raj. I never imagined myself to be that girl, the one who went gaga over a guy, feeling down when he is not around, feeling energized when he is. I kind of feel like a schoolgirl as I sit here reliving the excitement, the energy his presence gives me while I string beads with my girls.

One by one their families come to pick them up. Ana's girls are have already gone and so has Ana. Muna is the last to leave, and as I clean up the beads and string, placing them in the small file cabinet, I hear the door latch shut from behind me. Startled, I bolt upright and turn to see Raj standing in front of the now closed door. My heart is jumping out of my chest as I catch my breath.

"Shit, you scared me."

He raises his eyebrows as he walks toward me, his hands tucked casually in his pockets. "Ella, please don't curse." He seems injured in some way by my using the word "shit" in his presence.

"Well, don't sneak up on me and you won't hear me say things like that," I say, smiling demurely.

The grin he provides is not lacking the dimple this time and I'm proud of bringing it out in him. "For some reason, I doubt that would stop you from using profanity."

As he continues toward me, I lean against the chair in front of me. "You're probably right."

He looks at the ground as he speaks carefully. "So, there is this place, Wadi Rum."

I'd read about it before arriving here. "The Valley of the Moon. I have wanted to go there but I'm not sure we will have a chance. There and Petra were on my bucket list."

He squints, seeming confused. "Bucket list?"

"Oh, like a list of things I really want to do."

He nods, stopping in front of me. "Well, we are doing both this weekend."

I'm taken aback with him telling me "we" are doing something together. "What?"

With an air about him, he asks, "Did you not hear me the first time?" His smile is playful. "I can repeat it if you like."

I try to clarify without sounding too obvious, just in case I am completely off, "You and me?"

He leans toward me a little, like he is telling me a secret. "And the volunteers."

"Oh, yeah, right." The letdown of him and me going alone is a fantasy I should know will never come true here on this side of the world.

Like he has read my mind, he speaks tenderly, his voice seducing me slowly, "If having you with me in Wadi Rum for the weekend means renting out the entire campsite and accommodating for every volunteer with WorldTeach to experience this, then so be it."

I'm blown away by the lengths he has gone to coordinate a loophole for us to spend time together. I should be enamored now that I know he and I want the same thing, but instead I think of the place we stand in, the people I serve, and how, while I am out touring Petra, sleeping under the desert for fun, a getaway, they will still be here with no break or getaway in their future.

"What is it?" Raj's concern is alerting. "Do you not want to go?"

"No, that isn't it at all."

"What is it then?" he asks, concerned now.

"I just feel like I am leaving all of this behind, turning my back on the reason I am here."

He tilts his head, then raises his chin. "You feel like you are leaving them. Your girls."

"Not just that. The Ba'ashirs, the Ahmadis, they have been so good to me. Living with them has shown me a world I had not known before. One with the simplicity of just being with each other is richer than I could have imagined in my own home. And to know they may never experience the Roman Amphitheater, the Lost City of Petra, or Wadi Rum, it makes me feel like I am abandoning what they have taught me."

He stares at me, seeming to analyze what I have said, and I feel self-conscious. "I know it's silly to feel so heartfelt about this, but..."

Before I can finish, he speaks over me, "You are passionate. That is not silly in the least. We don't have enough of that passion in the world, Ella. I understand." His smile is tender as he continues to look down at me. "And now I feel like the selfish one."

"Why is that?"

His eyes drift to my lips. "Because even though I respect your feelings, I want to take you away from here, show you the place that sets me free, the way you do."

I'm without words, without breath, without the ability to swallow.

He moves a step closer, not yet breaking the hold his golden eyes have me in. "Please say you will go."

I nod slowly before the words glide easily from my lips. "I will go."

His body seems to relax with my answer as he looks down at his hands, running them over each other fervently. Was he afraid I might say no?

He backs away a step, seeming to give me room to breathe, but I don't need it. I need him close again. "The Ba'ashirs, the family you live with, do you walk there from here?"

Reminding me I need to get going, I grab my bag and place my veil over my hair, tucking it as I talk. "Yes, it isn't far."

"I will take you." His words are commanding, and while I am finding I adore everything about this man, the demanding tone doesn't settle well.

"Um, no I can get there on my own."

I start around him, but he backs up and places his hand on my arm. His touch isn't harsh, rather gentle; the force of the contact, skin to skin, sends shivers through me. "I don't feel comfortable letting you walk alone. I will take you."

His knee-weakening touch, his thumb running along my forearm, sends my mind spinning. Even though letting myself go under his touch feels so good, I hold my position, my sarcastic ass taking over. "You know, I have functioned on my own without an escort for the last, oh I don't know, almost two months. It's light out. I can handle walking home on my own."

His jaw tenses. "I don't like this at all."

I smirk, seeing he doesn't like not getting what he wants. "I can tell, but I promise I will be fine."

I start toward the door again, and he moves ahead of me, opening it for me to pass. I turn off the lights and walk passed him. "Thank you."

"You have a phone?" He sounds on edge.

"Yes, for emergencies," I say, considering he may be moving to ask me to call him.

"Good."

As we get to the front entrance by the courtyard, I stop and turn to him, wondering where he is going. "Don't you exit through the back alley?"

He holds the door open for me, realizing I have found him out, him coming to the front was just for me. "Yes, right. Once I see you have gotten off okay. The soldier could see you home if you don't want me to."

I nod, as he tries to reason into having me escorted home. "Really, I'm fine. I will see you tomorrow."

On my way home, I glance off to the side of me every few blocks, feeling someone watching me. As I cross the street I see the iconic royal SUV that drove me home the night after the attack, one of the royal trucks. I pretend I don't see it as I pull my veil farther down, hiding my roused smirk. He couldn't bring himself to let me walk home alone. While part of me doesn't understand his demand, his innate cultural obligation to be vigilant over me for me, the rest of me thrives on knowing he can't stand my not being watched by him.

With the Ba'ashirs house only a few yards away, I slow my pace, coming to a stop. I don't move, knowing if Raj has followed me this far and I stand still, he will be overwhelmingly curious why I am standing here, not moving on. The truck rolls up next to me, the rear window coming even with me. I turn to the window and gaze up at it, then lower my eyes, waiting for him, daring him to roll down the window.

I'm surprised when the dark-tinted window lowers halfway, his full lips smirking at me.

I keep my eyes down as I speak. "As you can see, I am safe."

"Yes, I can." I glance up just as he says, "Goodnight, Ella."

He closes his window and drives off.

Saturday morning couldn't come fast enough and sleep the night before was a struggle. I intended to dream of riding camels across Wadi Rum, walking among the ruins of a lost city, eating food, living for just two days the bedouin way; nomadic, free, just as Raj had hoped for us. Instead, I dreamt of him and I intertwined, pushing, pulling, tugging, thrusting, sucking, rising and falling together in fervid, flesh-driven fantasies fulfilled in the mirage of orgasmic solitude. I woke flushed and pulsating from the sensual figment, wanting it desperately to not end. I tried to go back to sleep, prolong the sensation, relive it even if it would only exist in my head.

Hoda and Ameena woke with me, seeing me off with a full stomach of Manakeesh. Ismad said he would walk me the night before, but I asked him to please sleep in, explaining I know how hard he works and I respect him for it. My lengthy explanation seemed get through to his insistence, which surprised me and made me feel good, saving me from feeling guilty about him waking on his day off to take me to a weekend of touring. I couldn't bear it and I'm glad he understood. The number of cars passing is near to none this early on a Saturday morning, so hearing the sound of an engine slowly approaching me is transparent.

"Good morning, Ella."

The sound of Raj's deep voice with the curl of his accented English isn't just a welcomed surprise but a reminder of the sordid sleep I had with the ghost of him.

I stop walking as the car matches my pause. "Are you stalking me?"

He scoffs, then clears his throat. "Stalking, no. Just making sure you are safe by following you."

I nod slowly, looking ahead. "So, safety stalking."

Wanting to see his reaction, I cannot keep from peering over at him. He has lowered his sunglasses to the bridge of his nose to observe me, but keeping code he puts the glasses back in place and looks ahead, avoiding my quick glance. His smile gives away his sentiment. "Yes, safety stalking."

I stare down the street ahead of us. "It is about two more miles of this, or you can just trust I can take care of myself."

His smile fades a little. "I know you can take care of yourself, Ella, and yes it might look suspicious if we drive up slowly to the center keeping pace with you. Mr. Stern might have greater suspicion than if we were to tell him I saw you walking and offered you a ride."

Keeping his glasses on, he looks over at me. "Sitting in the front seat with my driver, of course. It wouldn't be right for you to sit alone with me." His grin slowly creeps back in, sending my mind back to the carnal crevices it lived in as I slept last night.

I wonder what he dreamt about last night?

We pull up to the front of the center, a large tour bus parked at the front gate waiting to load. Our SUV pulls behind another black-on-black SUV behind the bus. Five body guards in suits and darkened sunglasses get out of the SUV in front of us, as does our driver.

I get out, wondering what the volunteers, Ana, and Tom will think seeing me get out of the front seat of the prince's convoy. Ana is staring at me open-mouthed as I wait for the driver to hand me my bag out of the back of the truck. Raj comes to stand by my side, making me feel even more self-conscious as he waits for his own bag.

As the driver hands me mine, Raj speaks to me. "Ella, if you are this tense all weekend, they might think we are having more than pleasant conversation. Please, relax."

I nod slowly and put my bag on my shoulder, Raj taking his and walking around me toward Tom. *Yeah, okay, I can do that. I think.*

As I walk behind him, my eyes gravitate to the way his faded jeans hug his ass perfectly. Shit, this is going to be really difficult. I scan away from his ass as we walk up to Tom and the volunteers. Tom looks from me to Raj, then back to me again. "Everything okay?"

I try to brush off his investigative tone, casually saying, "Yeah, everything's good."

Raj quickly takes up after me, "My driver saw Ella walking and we offered her a ride the rest of the way." He glances at the group behind Tom. "Who's ready to get away to Wadi Rum?"

His powerful rally is meant to excite and it provokes an equally compelling response as the volunteers' voice their clashing support.

Raj explains the weekend will consist of first a stop at the Lost City of Petra this morning into the late afternoon, then a drive south past Wadi Rum to the Captain's Desert Camp where we will be staying, living in the bedouin manner, under the moon in the desert. Sunday we would travel camel back into the Wadi Rum desert from the south traveling north, then returning to a lunch before departing for Jordan.

The way he describes the trip, I can tell he organized it all himself. "Before we leave, I want to thank Tom for allowing me to take you away with me for a few days. For me it is an honor to show you a part of my country that is close to my heart." He turns to Tom and holds his hands together, bowing slightly to him. "Thank you, Mr. Stern."

Tom imitates his sign of respect, slightly bowing.

Ana slips in line behind me as we get on the bus, Tom and Raj lingering behind discussing the itinerary. "Um, so you get rides from the Prince of Jordan now?"

Her comment is intended in the non-literal sense as she slips in a wink. I roll my eyes and shake my head. If only it were true. "Like he said, his driver saw me. It was the right thing to do."

As I step onto the bus, she slyly responds, following closely behind whispering, "Yeah, keep telling yourself that, but I'm not buying it."

The bus is big and I take up one double seat, tossing my bag down on the seat next to me. Ana sits behind me and leans over the seat, spying to see if anyone is listening. "Look, I think it is cool as shit to have a prince all over your ass, but if I notice it, I'm sure as hell Tom notices and every other nosy fucker on this bus."

She was right, while everyone said they watched out for each other, and they did, they also liked to nose around. "He is a prince, royalty, Muslim, code, remember. You are none of those things."

As everyone files in, I watch them, making sure her comments aren't overheard with the slightest expressions from them. "Yeah, okay, I got it."

She puts her hand on my shoulder, making me focus on her. "You got it?" Her question is meant to confirm in the truest form. "I don't need my girl getting in over her head."

I nod, keeping my eyes solid on her. "Yeah, I'm good. I won't."

Ana looks away and I follow her gaze. Tom is followed by Raj. and when Tom sits on the second bench back, Raj keeps coming toward me, sitting directly across from me, placing his bag on the seat next to him and putting ear buds into his ears.

I face him in all of his boldness, making no attempt at hiding his heavy stare as he leans his head against the window behind him. As Ana slowly lowers herself back into her own seat, I hear her mumble, "Yeah, you got this, all right."

His heavy gaze not leaving me any time soon, I turn my body to face the front of the bus, tilting my head to peer out the window, imagining what parts of me he is staring at now.

The drive to Petra is expected to take three hours and the trip there is all highway, which makes for the perfect backdrop for nodding off. With the welcomed restless sleep last night, I willingly let it consume me on the way there. I'm not too sure how long I'm under when I stir awake, opening my eyes to find Raj leaning his head against the seat across from me, gazing at me. He isn't smiling, his jaw set, his eyes deeply engrossed in what he is thinking about.

What is he thinking about? I could guess, but it would just be self-inflicted torture.

Seemingly pulled from his meditation of me having been caught in the act of staring at me sleep, he chastely looks down at his phone. I sit up and hastily tuck my hair behind my ears, masking my hands checking the sides of my mouth for possible trails of sleep drool; it has happened before. I'm clear though and I sit back and stare at the seat in front of me until I can't resist looking back over at him.

He is still focusing on his phone, but I notice him glimpse up at me as his grin widens and the infamous thought-provoking dimple surfaces on his right cheek. He licks his lips in the most sensual fucking way and rests his head back against the window behind him. Before I give away the slightest flush of my cheeks from what he does to me, what the lick of his lips is making me think, I shift toward my window, imploring for the gods of wanton lust to deliver me from evil. Amen.

Chapter 15

Ella

Once the bus parks, I push my backpack under the seat in front of me. As everyone stands to stretch, I make sure to take my veil from my seat as I rise to exit my seat. Raj steps toward me, letting me pass in front of him as he moves in behind me. He is standing so close and I'm not expecting it when he reaches for my hand, taking the veil in his. He slowly tugs on it, drawing it through my fingers as he whispers, his voice low and rough in a really amazing way, "Don't wear it today. I want to see you, Ella, bold and free. Be free with me."

I don't realize I'm leaning into him until my back meets his chest, quickly sending me forward a step. I let the veil slip through my fingers completely with his pull as he lays it on the seat I had occupied. My release is my accepting his invitation to collide and fall with him.

Raj got each of us a pony to take each of us on the tour. Tom was given passage on a cart. Some of the volunteers hissed playfully as Tom waved back at us and rode ahead. As Raj rode up on a pony behind me, coming to my side, it became evident as to why he had sent Tom on his way ahead of us.

I playfully asked, "Hey, why does he get a cart?"

Raj leaned toward me and lowered his voice. "Would it be wrong to say to get him out of the way so I can be by you?"

His gaze wouldn't release me until I responded. I glanced down at the guard by his side, watchful of the few tourists who have started the trek in with us. "No, but what about everyone else watching you?" Even though we were in public surrounded by our group, and the number of tourists here was surprisingly light, I worried. He shrugged and looked around us curiously, seeming to notice the sparsity of onlookers.

"The handful of people around us are tourists, not likely to know me, and for the few that do recognize me, they aren't watching me watch you. They are just watching me."

He grinned mischievously with arrogance, then looked on at the land around us. "Tourism and travel to Petra has not been what it used to because of the unrest here in the Arab states." He sounds frustrated by the climate all of a sudden and I want to push it out of his mind, bring back his smile, the joy he expressed when he spoke of Petra.

"Well, I can't wait to see all of its beauty."

My enthusiasm lit him up again, as I had hoped.

Raj hired multiple tour guides to take us on the journey through the Sig, the passage leading to the Khazneh, the

Treasurym, which is the most photographed and most well-known site in Petra. The tour guides gave us the history and myth of Petra as they guided our group of ponies to the Roman theater, walking among the empty tomb cut-outs bordering the thousands of seats in the arena. The body-guards kept some distance giving us room to explore, but were always within seconds of Raj. We rose up the carved steps on horseback and descended on foot, traveled to the Urn temple, one of the sites we could discover from within. As I stepped, I imagined the kings, pharaohs, travelers, tomb raiders, and bedouin tribes walking on the softened sand beneath my feet. I'm sure my mouth gaped as I looked up at the ceiling of the temple, unable to imagine human hands carving out the hardened sand to form this structure ... all of these passages, tombs, and dwellings lining the valley we walked.

I'm positive Raj didn't miss a single one of my expressions from Petra. He never lost sight of me and was always separated from me by a volunteer, mostly Ana. Even with Tom's presence, Raj didn't hide his attention on me or his proximity.

The sun was high and the heat just becoming unbearable when we made our way back to the bus.

"So, what do you think of Petra?" Raj asks the group as we walk, renewing their frenzy of what they appreciated about it. The myth, the archeological investigation, the history, and the mystery that still shrouds its existence and what it still holds secret from civilization were all the chatter and while all of it fascinated me, I wanted to know more about the bedouin people, the ones who occupied the carved caves. Where had they gone?

"The people that lived here, where did they go?"

"The bedouin are nomads, inhabitants of the desert. They do not stay in one place, and when Petra became a tourist attraction, they left." His explanation has him scanning every face, then resting on me. "There are few authentic bedouin people remaining, but you will be happy to know where we are staying will fulfill your inner bedouin."

David's question breaks my concentration on Raj's seemingly seductive call to my inner bedouin.

"How far is it from here?"

He looks at Tim then at everyone else. "Not far. Tonight we will celebrate as the bedouin with zarb, a traditional feast, music, dance, and night under the moon and stars you will never forget. Tomorrow we will have activities in the Wadi Rum."

On the bus ride from Petra to Wadi Rum, Raj had planned a catered lunch en route. I expected something light, but when one of the drivers came through the bus distributing small boxes still warm to the touch as I held it on my lap, I was curious about the contents.

Two words: stuffed falafel.

The portion isn't skimpy, with a full box of eight stuffed falafel balls calling my name. I didn't realize how hungry I was until I had already consumed half of them and was anticipating the rest eagerly. By mid-bite of my last falafel ball, I notice Raj watching me, grinning as he takes a bite. I'm embarrassed both for eating like I am and not knowing how long he has been watching me eat like this. I must look like a fucking pig. Cordially, he lifts his bottle of water to me and I take hold of mine and do the same.

After he drinks he leans toward me. "Do you like them?"

I look at him like he is crazy, then down at my plate, only half a ball remaining. "Uh, yeah." I wipe my mouth with my napkin as he returns to his own food, his grin undisguised.

"I made sure to get them from the best place for stuffed falafel in Jordan. Hashem's."

Holy shit! He got my favorite! "I've been there!"

He nods. "Yes, I know."

I tilt my head and laugh a little. *He got my favorite.* "You know?"

He nods. "I asked the volunteer that talks a lot. What is his name again?"

"David."

Having taken a bite of falafel, he swallows it then leans toward me, looking for prying ears as he whispers, "He told me you couldn't stop eating them. He said you even took some home."

Thanks, David. I feel my cheeks redden a little as I try to make excuses for my overindulgence. "I didn't eat any more than them. And, I took some home for the Ba'ashirs and Ahmadis. The waiter, he insisted."

I know my explanation falls on deaf ears as he continues to grin and eat his falafel. After a few moments of silence between us, and a chance to consider the lengths he went to talking to David about how much I enjoyed Hashem's stuffed falafels, I whisper, "Is this like the safety stalker thing."

He looks at me sideways.

"You know, like following me home, finding out where I eat, what I like?"

He raises one eyebrow and the dimple on his cheek becomes visible. "It is purely for your safety, Ella. I could not have you eating a poorly made falafel."

His grin widens as he pops the remaining bit of a falafel into his mouth and sits back, obviously fucking proud of himself. He is totally screwing with me now. I roll my eyes and sit back in my seat, disguising my own smile by indulging in my last bite.

Once past the visitor's center to Wadi Rum, we pass camp sign after camp sign, directing us to their sites. The deeper we get into the Wadi Rum, the more curious I become about this campsite. Our bus stops at what seems like the end of the road. I look out my window and the windows adjacent to me. The two SUVs following us have stopped behind us, the sun-glassed bodyguards waiting for directives of where we go next, I suspect.

Raj rises and steps out from his seat, calling one of his security men to him. He speaks quickly in Arabic then turns to the rest of us. "I have trucks waiting to take us the rest of the way into the desert."

When he said trucks, I assumed they were the SUVs he has used at the center and the one I had ridden in before. I was mistaken. The trucks are pickup trucks. Old, dusty, paint-chipped, rusted pickup trucks with tent tops rigged on the back for coverage from the sun. The men sitting in the bed and leaning along the side of the truck are covered with head wear, much like a hijab, but Raj's says it is called djellabiyya and a smagg, a long red and white head covering.

As we walk up to them, they quickly come to us and take our bags from our shoulders. Raj speaks to them in a dialect not like the one my ear is trained to. "What are they speaking?"

Raj laughs with one of the men as they finish speaking. "It is called Badawi, the bedouin dialect."

Our bags are loaded in the fourth truck in line while the rest of us are helped into the beds of the other three. Raj's well-maneuvered plan to sit next to me works, putting me arm to arm in tight quarters as we all squeeze into the bed of the trucks. To make more room, Raj places his arm behind me, as do some of the other volunteers. The other's closeness don't seem to draw attention like Raj's and mine as Tom watches us. I pretend I don't see him, let his inspection blow over, far away as I melt against Raj's thumb running along my back, hidden from prying eyes.

I notice the royal security in two SUVs latch onto our caravan. I figured they would have turned around, but I guess royalty needs security even in the desert. I lean over to Raj and cup my hand to keep my words isolated to him. "Is it safe out here for you?"

He looks down at me, then back at the security we have gained. "It is just a precaution."

The caravan begins to slow as we approach a grand expanse of canyons. The closer we get, the more enormous the stature of the horseshoe-like shape it creates. Beneath the cove of ridges, multiple tents surround an open center, with a line of pillars adorning the passage into our camp. We are about a hundred feet or so from the entrance as we unload from the trucks.

While the men unload our bags and the eight bodyguards begin transporting them to the camp, Raj explains, "This campsite is one of the few run completely by bedouin. The family is very close to my family's hearts. Our family trips to Wadi Rum in the past have always been here and I wanted to make sure you received the same treatment as my own family. The entire camp is ours tonight and tomorrow. The staff will get you situated in your own private tents and we will meet for dinner after you have settled."

Raj is gleaming as he welcomes us to our very own bedouin camp experience.

"He reserved the entire camp for us?" Ana questions me under her breath.

I watch Raj graciously reciprocate the thanks he is receiving from some of the volunteers. "Yeah, he did."

Ana moves on after the other volunteers as I hang back, waiting to have my own moment to thank him. Suddenly, he stares off in the distance, his brow furrowed. I follow the line his eyes have taken. Another black SUV is approaching quickly, the red glow of the sunset behind it.

It slows to a stop, feet away from the trucks and bedouin men that brought us here. The rear door to the SUV opens and Zaid steps out onto the sand, wearing khaki linen pants along with a linen long-sleeve shirt rolled at up to his elbows. He greets the men casually, going to them first, embracing and exchanging words and laughter as Raj and I look on.

"What the fuck is he doing here?" Raj says under his breath roughly.

"You weren't expecting him, I take it?" I ask hesitantly.

"No."

Tom walks past Raj and me to meet Zaid. "Prince Zaid. I didn't know you were meeting us here! What a surprise!"

He pulls Tom in for a hug, one he wasn't expecting as he awkwardly hugs him back. Zaid pulls back from him. "I didn't know you were coming out here until this morning."

I notice him staring at Raj now. "It seems my brother forgot to tell me. I had to hear the news from the Queen."

He makes sure to exchange a glance with me before saying to Tom, "The point is, I have been looking for a chance to get away and visit more with the volunteers. Get to know them. This is going to be a great evening to do it, under the moon and stars of the Wadi Rum!"

I observe Raj; his expression is hardened and stoic, not the man I am accustomed to. "Ella, I will see you at the camp. I need to speak to my brother."

As Raj starts toward Zaid and Tom, I slowly move on toward the entrance of the camp.

Chapter 16

Rajaa

As I walk toward my brother, Tom already heading up to the camp site behind Ella, I notice Zaid watching her. I have never needed to be a jealous man. Never cared enough for a woman to be jealous or territorial, but the way he is looking at her, like she is prey, I want to rip his fucking eyes out with my bare hands.

I block the scope he has on her as I stand in front of him. "What are you doing here?"

Zaid pulls back from me. "What kind of greeting is that?"

Roughly he pulls me into a manly hug, slapping me on the back. "There! That is a brotherly greeting!"

The smell of alcohol on his breath, on his clothes … he likely spilled it on himself as he drank on his way out here. Knowing he won't release me until I hug him back, I slap his back and speak into his ear, "You have been drinking."

He laughs loosely as he pulls away. "Just a little. Remember how we used to sit by the fire and drink out here?"

"Yes, I do." While those were fond memories in the past, I try to hide my frustration with his presence here now. "After what happened, you should not be drinking." I start toward the entrance and Zaid comes to my side. The staff is already leading the guests to their tents. I notice Tom and Ella speaking with the staff, Ella looking back at me, worry in her eyes.

"I have to say, she is a beautiful woman. Natural beauty."

His words burn me up as he talks about her.

"I see she isn't wearing her veil."

"None of them are, Zaid," I comment, put out by his attempt to attack her.

"Yes, I know, but none of them are as compelling as she."

Fucking asshole. "That's enough."

"The way her body sways when she walks. I can see what compels you."

I whip around and close in on him, toe to toe. "I said enough. Don't fucking talk about her, look at her, or speak to her, Zaid, or so help me."

My flesh feels like it's on fire, ready to explode as I glare into my brother's blackened eyes. He stumbles back and looks me up and down. "You need help, Rajaa. So violent all of a sudden. Does she make you act this way? All crazy and shit?"

He laughs, snorting once, and speaks under his breath, "Fucking women." He breathes in deeply all of sudden, closes his eyes, and stretches his arms up to the sky, releasing a cleansing sigh. "Ahhhhhhh, I have missed Wadi Rum."

He sways from side to side, the high from the alcohol a contributor. I look at the two guards who brought him here. They turn away, sensing the disgust I have for my brother and how quickly he has returned to old ways. I glare at him. "Look at you, fucking drunk!"

As he blinks his eyes open, they quickly turn narrow, darker, more evil as his voice rumbles, "No, I'm not fucking drunk!"

Abruptly his maniacal expression shifts instantly to a beaming smile as he casually and peacefully responds, "Just a few drinks on the ride here. Nothing more."

The quick shift in his polarity is too familiar and I can't help wondering, if one addiction has returned, how close behind are the others? I shake my head, thinking of when and how they will return. "What is next, Zaid?"

He settles his smile into a sinister grin. "Next? We feast!" Him compressing my concerns into what's next in the events here at the camp is expected as he cackles and walks around me toward the entrance.

Chapter 17

Ella

Standing at the entrance of the camp, I look back at Raj and Zaid down by the trucks that brought us here. They're arguing and I'm sure it's about him showing up. Tom is shaking hands with the bedouin staff. "Ella, come here."

I move closer to the staff and bow my head out of respect. One of the men takes my bag from me.

"Shukran."

The man smiles and bows his head, then starts walking away with my bag, beckoning me to follow. One of the other staff and a few bodyguards take Tom and a few of the volunteers down an opposite walkway toward another set of white tents, I assume our accommodations for the night. I see Ana ahead with a few of the volunteers who are sleeping on the same side of camp as me.

The canvas path we walk along is lined on either side with candlelit vases every few steps. There is a large tent to my left, under the widest part of the mountainous horseshoe. Another large tent mirrors it on the right. The tarp has been rolled up on one side as we pass, revealing seating all along the back side adorned with deep burgundy and navy cushions for comfort. A large rug covers the sand floor and at the center, a tall elegant hookah surrounded by short metal tables and pillows for sitting. In the center of the camp, four palm trees rise high above, swinging and shifting in the desert air. Below them is a small fire pit, being kindled by a few of the bedouin men who drove us here. Farther into the belly of the camp are large circular sitting areas, large pillows being laid by the staff as my guide leads me to our overnight tents.

The few volunteers on our side of the camp have found their tents for the night, their tarp entrances tied back. Ana collapses on her bed just as I pass hers.

My attendant stops at a tent and pulls back the tarp for me to pass. As soon as I enter, I no longer feel like I am in camp, but a luxurious hotel room. The tent's walls are lined with shades of red and gold sheer cloth. Kerosene lamps embellish the four corners of the chamber, setting a mystical and romantic feel in the space. The bed is in the center of the room, white linens accented with bright red and gold pillows in the center. A set of towels twisted into the shape of a heart sits on the bed, while billowing sheer netting is at the peak of the tent's roof, to be released over my bed when I sleep tonight. My server has set my bag on the armchair across from my bed, next to a small metal table, much like the ones at the hookah tent. He is rolling back the tarp entrance of my tent, just as Ana peaks her head in. "Wow! Um, your tent seems giant compared to mine."

The attendant bows and smiles and I do the same before he exits the tent. "I don't think it's any bigger than the others."

She looks around then sits on my bed. "Yeah, maybe just different colors or something. Hey did you see the hookah tent?" Her eyebrows dance as she cunningly smiles.

I shake my head and laugh at her under my breath. "Yeah, I saw it."

"I saw the prince's brother came." She is leaning back on her elbows as she comments.

My mind already busy about his showing up and Raj's reaction to it, I get up and begin laying my things out on the bed. "Yeah."

I don't offer anything else, even though I know she is searching for information.

"Well, I'm going to find the ladies room and unpack. I'll see you later."

"Okay."

After she's left, I place my clothes in the set of drawers next to the bed and sit on the bed. I'm about to lay back just for a moment when Raj's voice interrupts me. "So, is everything to your satisfaction?"

His presence at my tent entrance seems to relieve the tension of his absence with Zaid. I raise my brows at his insane question of how this tent could possibly be unsatisfying. "Uh, yeah. This room is bad ass!"

He appears disappointed by my word choice so I quickly change it. "I mean, it's amazing. Completely satisfying and breath-taking. I wasn't expecting all of this."

Again, I take in the ornamentation, the lavish, bold-colored sheers lining the tent. "It's hard to believe we are in the middle of the desert. I feel like I am at a five-star hotel."

He smiles. "May I enter?"

I grin at his politeness. "You may, Your Highness."

He smiles at my use of his title. "Ha, ha."

He looks around at the room, like he is examining for anything out of place. "Are you sure you like it? I asked the owner to choose the most ornate one for you."

I can't speak for moment as he continues around the room, inspecting, touching, then glancing back at me with a grin I swear will set my panties ablaze any second. "You what?"

He continues around the room, coming to stand in front of me. "I wanted you to have the most lavish tent on the site."

So that's why Ana thought her tent looked different.

He leans toward me, feeling my attention is lost to him. "Ella, do you like it?"

I'm still stuck on him wanting me to stay in the most lavish tent on site. "Yes, I love it," I say, smiling widely.

He seems to relax with my answer. "Good. Well, I will let you settle. Dinner will be served shortly and the music and dance will follow."

He starts to walk away, but I stop him. "Wait, why is Zaid here?"

My question quickly spoils his smile as he faces me, occupied with what he is going to tell me. "He says he has come to visit with the volunteers. Get to know them."

"He hasn't spent much time at the center. Maybe it's true." I try to be optimistic about Zaid's intent, even though the expression he gave me earlier doesn't feel like the type used to welcome guests

Raj tucks his hands in his jeans and shakes his head, avoiding my eyes as he stares into the light of the kerosene lamp next to my bed. "When I met him at the trucks, he reeked of alcohol. He shouldn't be here." He breaks his meditative stare into the lamp's flame, then looks at me urgently. "If he speaks to you, come and find me."

His explicit response worries me. "Why? Because of what he said to me the other day at the center? Raj, he doesn't bother me. I can handle myself."

He doesn't smile, doesn't look away, doesn't negotiate as his golden eyes command of me. "Just do as I say."

Staring at him, I try to get beyond the hard surface he has shown me, but what is between him and his brother is too deep to break through.

"Ella."

His saying my name is a warning for me to heed his instruction and while it seems a little much for me to be fearful enough of Zaid to come running to Raj, I'm willing to agree to it if it gets him to stop worrying. "Okay, I will."

The only signal my answer has been received is a firm nod before he leaves the tent he handpicked for me.

The restrooms and showers are behind the tents, and after I have washed and dressed in a clean sweater and jeans, I head back to my tent. The sun has fallen behind the ridge line cradling us and the stars and moon have found their place in the sky for the night even with the sun still waning. The desert chill I was told about is real, as I feel it seep through my sleeves, sending the smallest shiver up my arms. I walk through the maze of tents toward the sound of woodwind instruments, drums, and the crooning voices of the bedouin singers.

The fire in both the large sitting area and the smaller one near the entrance are ablaze, seeming to dance with the strum and drumbeat of the music. A few of the staff are fluffing pillows and rise to smile when I walk by. I return their smiles and continue down the incandescent lit path toward the large tent on the opposite side of the camp.

I enter the tarp where it has been tied back, instantly feeling the warmth of the space after entering. Like my tent and the hookah tent across the way, the sand floor is covered with a similarly bold-colored rug with pillows lining the walls of the tent.

The musicians are playing at the far end of the tent and Zaid is camped out in the middle of a group of volunteers, chatting and laughing as he speaks to them. They all laugh loudly as I watch him. "I tell you, the size of the lizard was four feet long!"

With his hands stretched out long ways, the volunteers continue to laugh. "My brother and I ran out of that cave as fast as we could, yelling for our father. Pleading with him to not leave us!" Zaid is laughing just as hard as he explains his and Raj's apparent escape from a giant lizard as kids. I smile from the contagion of watching them all laugh, just as Zaid looks over in my direction. He nods and waves at me before returning to his talks with the volunteers. I remember Raj's warning and think it crazy as I watch Zaid interact with our group. He seems like he is having a good time telling old camp stories.

Ana is occupied on the other side of the tent talking with Tom when I catch her eye and head over to them. "Isn't this music amazing!" Ana says, leaning over to me.

"Wait until dinner is over, they really get going!" Raj says as he comes up behind me.

His hair is still damp from having just showered and I find myself staring at him, imagining the act of him bathing, when I bring my focus to the line of servers delivering the many dishes of food.

"You missed the best part, Ella. The earth oven!" Ana smiles excitedly as she moves to sit down, pulling me with her. "They buried the lamb into this oven below ground then cover it to cook for two hours!"

A few of the other staff begin moving about us as we all settle on both sides of the line of food placed in the middle: ribs of lamb, homemade kebabs, and the infamous lamb's meat Ana described buried in the oven below ground. Skewered chicken finishes out the line of meat as the small metal tables I saw earlier are put to use. Attendants deliver portions of bedouin rice, corn, and Fatir, the bedouin bread. As if that isn't enough, the first round of servers return with small bowls filled with pickles, fried eggplant with cabbage, and a side of thick tahini.

Raj sits across from me and started listing off all of the food, explaining what they are made of and how spicy they are. "The matbucha is spicy, that is the way it is meant to be so be careful." His smile settles on me when he is done presenting the menu. "Please, eat."

Zaid calls from the other end of the invisible table, "Yes, falinakul!" He holds up a glass occupied by a milky content, celebrating the start of the meal. I notice Raj glance over at him, then visibly breathe in deep, agitated by Zaid's obnoxious yell. The volunteers around him seem to like it, but I can see it is upsetting to Raj. As everyone starts chatting and reaching for food, I lean forward, catching Raj's eyes. I pretend like I am searching for the perfect piece of skewered chicken, but my intent is to draw him away from the anger he seems to have where his brother is involved.

Once I have caught his eye, the grin that melts me returns. "What is this again?" I ask as I point to the red tomatoey sauce in one of the small bowls.

"Matbucha." His accent sounds thicker all of a sudden, sending my senses soaring as I listen intently to him intermingle English. "It is a sauce for dipping and also for the meat. I prefer it with the meat. It is very hot." The way he curls his accent around certain words, "dipping" and "hot," I can't help but lean closer as I take a spoonful to add to my plate.

"Be careful, I'm not kidding when I say it's hot," he laughs, surprised at the portion I have taken.

I tilt my head and peer up at him as I sit back. "I like it hot."

His smile suddenly loses its humor, becoming a seductive smirk. "I do too."

The rest of the dinner, I hold his attention, exchanging glances as we eat and pretend to listen to the conversations around us. We look away at different times throughout the dinner, but always, one of us is watching the other when we return to each other.

I sweep the last dollop of Matbucha with my bedouin bread, Raj carefully watching me place it in my mouth. He leans toward me and takes one more piece of lamb. My eyes only on him, he says to me, "You surprise me. Most can't stand the heat." His eyes glance up at me through his dark heavy lashes. "I'm sure you are full of surprises."

My chest rises and falls with the quickening beat of my heart, our conversation taking on a seduction hidden from everyone around us. "Yes, I am."

Suddenly Ana leans over, nudging me. "You are what?" She places another small piece of chicken in her mouth as she looks between Raj and me.

"She was just telling me she is enjoying her time here at the camp. She finds it captivating. Isn't that what you said, Ella?" Raj's ability to pick up quickly on Ana's question and even quicker ability to pose a question to further intoxicate me, has my mind whirling.

I glance at Ana. "Yes, I did."

The three glasses of mint lemonade sends me to the ladies room just as the Turkish coffee and Baklava are delivered. Raj watches me leave the tent, not letting me escape his heated amber eyes. On my way back, I notice Zaid standing on the path looking up at the stars, an empty glass in his hands.

As I approach him, I tell myself to keep it simple, avoid him, remembering what Raj had said. "Hello."

As I move passed him, he catches me off guard with a question. "What do you think you are doing, Ella?"

I stop and turn back to him, somewhat confused by his question. Did he mean in the literal sense? "Using the restroom."

His chuckle is low as he shakes his finger and me, angling his dark eyes to reflect the grand, kindling bonfire in the center of the camp. "Ahhh, I think you know I mean my brother and you."

"Excuse me?" My throat tightens considering what he might think is going on between us.

He flails his free hand at me menacingly. "You and my brother. Tell me, has he fucked you yet?"

I can't breathe all of a sudden as his words batter me with his biting notion.

I find my voice somehow. "I don't know what the fuck you are talking about."

"No? Oh, well then let me explain it to the naive American girl. My brother is a prince, intended for a princess. A clean Muslim princess, not a foreign whore that has slept her way through college."

Motherfucker! "You don't know shit about me."

He slinks toward me, lowering himself to meet my height. His presence is as overwhelming at the smell of heavy liquor on his breath. The way he looks down at my body turns my stomach. "I admit, you are beautiful, but you are used, a piece of ass he will fuck, then leave. He has done it before, many times."

He has done it before?

His cunning words work into my mind, making sense when I should be denying them because he is fucking drunk. "Before he leaves this summer, he will propose, and anything he does with you will just be a fling. A seductive game."

A fucking princess? A proposal? Why did he lead me on?

I dig my fingernails into my palms as Zaid backs away. He studies me curiously all of a sudden, licking his lips and turning my stomach. "He is good at it, yes? The way he speaks to you, the trip here to the desert, the getaway. Making you think you are the only one. It is all part of the seduction. The one you have fallen so easily for. The one that will end the moment he proposes to Princess Daya."

"It's you, Ella. 'Eh enta."

Fucking "it's you," bullshit!

Zaid's sinister smile rises wider. "Don't say I didn't warn you, Ms. Wallace."

As I watch Zaid walk back to the tent, sauntering drunkenly, I stand there questioning everything that has happened between Raj and me: the night at the loft, the elevator, the day he saved me, the apparent fate of it all, his interest in me, saying I have possessed him. How can it all be a game? Can they all be lies, the universe and fucking fate revoking the pact I made up in my head?

"Fucking asshole!"

The words roll from my mouth just as I see some of the volunteers spilling from the tent. Holding my breath and tears at bay, I turn around and walk toward the cluster of tents housing us tonight. I can't see him, can't look at him. If I do, I might deck him.

As I stalk back, the bedouin musicians have started to play at the large arena circling the bonfire, strumming and thumping their instruments to inspire a crowd. I keep my head down, breathing erratically and fighting back the tears I refuse to shed. The candlelit path blurs as I remember my place: a stupid American girl who fell for a game-playing prince.

Chapter 18

Rajaa

Some of the volunteers are taking their baklava and Turkish coffee out by the bonfire. The musicians have already started singing and playing, but Ella still hasn't returned.

"Rajaa, are you coming?" Tom asks as he rises from his cushioned seat.

I hesitate, looking to the entrance of the tent, Ana disappearing beyond it. Maybe she is out there waiting. "Yes." I take a baklava with me as I rise. As soon as I pass through the tarp, I search for her, scanning the open circle of the camp, the lit paths and bonfires giving me sight. Zaid is stumbling toward us, his empty glass tipped to the ground. Backtracking from where he came, I see Ella rushing away, back toward the tents. He has said something to her, something that would send her back to the tents without coming back to tell me.

I stride toward him down the candlelit path, not stopping until I am nose to nose with him. "What did you say to her?"

He stumbles back from me, feeling both the punch of my words and presence. He scoffs and stares back at me with his jet-black eyes. "I told her what you didn't, I assume. That you are intended, promised to another."

I look around us, noticing all of the volunteers gathering at the bonfire, near the music. If we weren't in their sight, I would fucking pin him to the ground.

He raises his eyebrows at me. "You better watch yourself, brother. You have a princess back home waiting for you to propose."

Princess? "What the fuck are you talking about? That is over, not going to happen now that you have destroyed the Amir's trust in our family. Do I even need to remind you of the mess you created?" I hiss as I lean into him, concealing my words from anyone in earshot.

Zaid rolls his eyes and nudges me off of him. "Ah, that is right. You don't know about Father's and my meeting with the Amir this morning. My plea, my confession, and my path to redemption. God bless Allah." He puts his hand on his forehead, exaggerating his non-existent forgetfulness. "That's right, you were visiting the sites with your fucking American entourage!"

I move toward him, his voice getting too loud. "Lower your voice, Zaid."

He ignores my request. "Seems the Amir is considering your and Daya's union again after our talks. Duty is greater than love in these arrangements. Isn't that wonderful news?"

Zaid's smile is maniacal, plagued with drunken insanity, and has now fed Ella lies. "You are delusional. Daya and I will never marry, even if there is the smallest truth of what you are saying. You will be king, why don't you fucking marry her!"

He laughs, "Daya marry me? No, you and her were meant to be! The Amir will only have you for his princess. Plus, I can't fuck one woman forever." He studies me deeply, looking into my eyes. "What? You think you will marry her?" He points back toward the tents. "This American outsider, min barra, you don't know her, who she is, who her family is. You would be disgracing your family by pursuing her. You and her can never be and I have made her completely aware of that."

Needing to put distance between my brother and me before I take him down, I place my palm on his chest and lean close to him, a mere breath separating us. "You should leave. Now."

Zaid grins and glances at the volunteers settling in around the musicians, the drum beat of the tarbuka driving the dancers, shadows against the bonfire. The glow of the fire casts swirling dark shadows over Zaid's sinister face. As he backs away he narrows his eyes on me. "I am already gone." He tosses his glass onto the sand as he stalks toward the entrance of the camp, the two guards who brought him following behind him. I make each stride count as I take the path to find Ella.

The son of a bitch is lying. It can't be true. I know he has told her lies, made her feel like she is nothing, just like he has done with any woman he has come in contact with. Any *human* he comes in contact with! How could I have missed him leaving the tent? He must have walked out while I was talking with Tom, waiting for Ella to return from the restroom. While I was waiting for her to return, he was fucking persecuting her! Feeding her lies about me, about her, about an us that can't be.

I can't get to her tent fast enough as I march to the rousing drumbeat.

Chapter 19

Ella

"Son of a bitch," I mumble under my breath as I pace the floor of the confined space of the tent. I replay Zaid words in my head and damn myself for falling too easily. How could I have been so fucking naive. "A fucking princess, marriage." I breathe out a whimper with the words, feeling the tears and emotions come over me again. I fucking hate myself right now and all I can do is cry here in this tent, the one this piece-of-shit liar wanted specifically for me!

I shake my head, hearing Zaid's words repeat again and again. *A proposal this summer to a pure Muslim woman. Not a cheap, used piece of ass.* While Zaid's words were saturated in drunkenness, he had sobered me, reminding me of what is logical, what is true: he is royalty and I am insignificant.

I grab a pillow that has fallen from the bed and toss it against one of the walls of the tent. I am smarter than this, damn it! I had told myself that very thing when he came to my classroom at the center! I step out of my jeans, kicking them into the corner. The way he spoke to me, looked at me, captured me in his eyes again. All while he was fucking promised to a princess! "Motherfucker!"

I stalk over to my bag on the side chair and rummage for my night clothes, when his deep, urgent voice breaks the rhythmic drumming and crooning of the men singing in the distance. "Ella."

I turn to the enclosure his voice is coming from. "Get the fuck away, Raj!"

I move to the bed and grab another pillow, throwing it in the direction of his voice, barely brushing the tarp out of place.

He growls through the closed tarp, "You need to keep your voice down!"

I march toward the tarp, directly in front of where he stands. "Don't you fucking tell me what to do! I'm not a Muslim princess you can boss around. I'm a cheap, used piece of ass you were fucking playing with! It was all a game for you, just to fuck me, right?"

All of a sudden the tarp whips open as Raj stalks straight toward me, his eyes narrowed on me. "What the fuck did you just say?"

His towering presence, his menacing anger-filled eyes, are overwhelming as all hell, until he scans me, noticing I am only in a sweater, my jeans tossed aside. Feeling vulnerable under his inspecting eyes, I remind myself he is the fucker at fault here as I fire back, "I said games, asshole! You wanted a fling before you proposed to your princess!"

He raises his hands to his head as he turns away, breathing quicker as his anger rises. He comes toward me again and I back away, needing space from him. "Is that what my fucking brother told you? That I just wanted to fuck you and leave you? A fucking fling?"

I move back in time with his approach. "Yeah."

"Yeah? And you believe him?" he demands as he stares hard at me. "Believe I am playing a game with you?"

He places his hands on his hips and looks at me, confused, which only gets under my fucking skin more. I don't want to believe it. I want to believe him as he stands before me right now, but everything Zaid said has completely shifted my thinking.

"I don't know what to believe! How else can you explain away all of this, Raj? You have a princess waiting for your hand in marriage. He says you have done this before ... this fucking seductive game you play with women. I'm a quick fix you can walk away from after you are done with me, right?" My own words cut me, making me stop before I sob like a baby in front of him.

My words have caught fire in his eyes. He squints at me like I have speared him with a dagger, with my words. "Listen to me. I couldn't walk away from you if I tried! You have no idea what you do to me, Ella! And, I am not fucking proposing to Princess Daya, ever!"

I fold my arms over my chest matter-of-factly and grin through the tears coming without my control. Goddamn them! "Well, you should. She is royalty! It is planned, a custom, tradition. I am none of that. I am just a naive little American that got carried away! A fucking outsider!"

He shakes his head. "I don't want her!"

I move in on him and run my hands up his chest, not realizing I am screwing with my own desires as I try to screw with him. "No? You would take this washed-up little American whore over a pure, royal Muslim woman?"

He growls and snatches my arms up with his hands, gripping me thoroughly. "No! I want the woman I saw from across the room in D.C. The woman I should have followed down the elevator. The woman tending to children in a courtyard, her hair loosened from the fucking veil she is too bold to wear."

I close my eyes and writhe, set on breaking free from the words he is drawing me in with, but fighting his strong hold is trivial; it has to be with words. "That woman is off limits. A harlot, tramp, a fling for a prince's last hurrah before he gets hitched."

Raj takes hold of my face with his hand, keeping me from looking away from him as he narrows his eyes on me. "You are not any of those things and you could never be a fling to me, Ella."

Feeling my heart being gutted with every moment I am held captive by him, I try to look away, but it only pisses him off, making his hold on me more absolute. "Look at me, Ella." His rough tone escalates with my resistance, as I refuse to meet his eyes, keeping them downcast, knowing all bets will be off and he will have me captured if I look up at him.

"I can't."

Suddenly, he releases me, slides his hands down around the back of my thighs, lifting me up to eye level, then turns us around as he sits on the bed with me straddling his legs. As he wraps his arms around my back and pulls me into him, every inch of him is against every inch of me, seizing every battle I have attempted to push him away.

"Yes you can, and you will look at me when I tell you this." He cups the back of my neck with one hand as his other keeps me to him over the middle of my back. I am a mere breath away from him as he says, "Eh enta, Ella."

I try to turn away, pull back, avoid the words that have a hold over me, but he pulls me down into him with the strong hold of his hand on my neck and back, the motion rocking me against him adding risk to the deeper surrender I want to submit to.

"Don't fucking fight me, Ella." His guttural and breathless words tell me I am not alone in the wanted surrender, making it harder to fight against what is true and what is false about this man. "I know you and you know me. You can't deny this."

I look into his eyes as they search mine, his voice softer now that I am rendered helpless in his embrace. "No, you aren't Muslim. No, you aren't fucking royalty, and no, you are not pure. I know all this about you and none of it matters! What matters is what I see in you. Your heart, your soul when I look into your eyes."

His hold doesn't loosen as he concentrates on every word he is saying. "You are the woman that penetrated my soul in D.C, with just your presence in a crowded room. The woman that would put her life before the lives of ten little girls. The woman I would protect and defend, never let perish. And the woman that believes in something greater than herself, because she wouldn't have risked traveling across the world in search of it if she didn't have extraordinary faith."

His rough, solid touch, his body flush against mine, my hands trembling above his heart, our breath mingling, his golden embers burning deep into my soul, and his words striking right to the core of me is too much to resist and I can't hold back much longer.

"I want all of you, Ella." As he lowers his eyes to my lips he whispers, "I don't want to fuck you. I want to make love to you."

My eyes locked on his, I feel the touch of his hands as he slips them under the back of my sweater, skin to skin, making my eyes close as I bend and sway into his touch, pulling me deeper onto him, to him, his erection rubbing against me. "Do you want to know how you make me feel?"

The strap of my bra breaks free as his hands continue up, pulling my sweater over my head. He lets it fall where it may as his hands return to me, resting on my hips. Nakedness has never bothered me in the past, but having been covered almost completely for two months, the eroticism of nudity in front of Raj has me guarded and I raise my arms to cover my bare breasts. Still, my eyes don't leave him for a second as he watches me.

"Yes, I want to know."

He takes hold of the collar of his cashmere sweater and pulls it over his head before taking my wrists in his hands and pulling them away to rest on his golden-toned shoulders, exposing me to him completely. His hands move down my back to my ass, then shift me onto his hardness, meeting my center and making it impossible to hide the whimper it produces, escaping through my parted lips. His hand moves fast up my back, pressing me close as his mouth finds the most tender part of my throat and covers it with his lips.

My breath comes faster as he grips my shoulders and rocks his sizable bulge beneath me again. His own moan hums against my skin as he tilts me back and takes my nipple in his mouth, drawing it in as I arch my back and feel the titillating grind of material against flesh dividing us from the full pleasure we seek.

"Ella?"

Raj releases my hard nipple and pulls me into him as I glance over at the tent entrance, the tarp untouched. Shit, it's Ana! I breathe in, hoping my words come out unsexed. "Yes?"

"Hey, are you okay? You never came back."

I feel Raj's hand slide down the front of me, feathering the nipple he had claimed. Oh God, that feels so good.

"Yeah, I'm fine. I'm just tired. Long day." I know my voice is quaking, but damn it I can't help it. I watch how he circles one nipple then moves to the one he hasn't taken. He looks at the entrance, then back at me seductively, a grin playing on his lips as he dips his head to capture my other nipple in his mouth. I hold in the moan that wants to escape, the dampness between my legs quickening as he shifts me to take in as much of me as he can.

"Do you need anything?"

I need him, right fucking now.

As his tongue teases the tip of my hardened bud, his eyes spear me, making me moan. "Mmm, no."

He grins as he wraps his mouth around my nipple again, proud of how he is teasing me.

I harden my sultry response, hoping Ana doesn't notice. "No, I will see you in the morning."

I run my hands through his hair as he places the softest breath against my breasts, his tongue flicking out to tantalize me as he ravishes my nipples one at a time. He works his way up, the kisses he places significant of his path; my chest, the nape of my neck. I glance at the tarp, hoping Ana doesn't open the damn tent.

The tip of Raj's finger rests on my bottom lip, bringing my attention back to him.

His finger runs along my chin as his eyes remain focused on mine, his touch running along my chest, over my navel, then lingering at the lining of my panties.

"Okay, sleep well, El." Ana's final words couldn't come soon enough.

"K." I know my breath is coming too fast to get any more than that out without sounding like I have run a fucking marathon.

Raj's eyes fall to my lips, then claim them with the fullness of his. The warm maddening roughness of his tongue connecting with mine is fucking perfect. His fingers don't waste any time as they plunge beneath my panties, slide along my moistened skin, and slip within me, making me gasp and moan into the kiss he has me in.

With one hand holding the nape of my neck and the other moving in and out, his thumb running circles slowly against my clit, he pulls back to watch what he is doing to me. His eyes are sleepily watching me; he has me moving against the rhythm his fingers, the rhythm of the tremors I am cycling through slowly building as my breath catches with every press of his thumb on my sex.

His breath is coming just as quick and ragged as mine, as if he is climbing this peak of intimacy with me. The drumming and strumming of music echoes louder now, and I hope it masks the sound coming from my tent. Raj runs his thumb over just the right spot as he plunges two fingers rather than one now.

"You are so beautiful when you are about to come." His deep voice dominates me, quickens the pulsing, the building, the rising he is giving me. Unable to keep my eyes open, I close them and let the sensations engulf me, my head falling back as I ride to the tipping point. The graze of his thumb at just the right moment sends every nerve ending straight to my clit and has me gasping and moaning, wrapping my arms around Raj's neck as the summit of my ride pulses again and again, melting me into this endless ecstasy.

Quickly, Raj rises with me, flipping me onto my back then standing over me as he unbuttons his pants, letting them fall to the ground. As I slowly scan the sinews of his chest, his well-defined abdomen, and impeccable V dipping beneath his boxer briefs, my eyes make their way to meet his. Now that I have gotten a taste of Raj, I want more.

Slowly he leans toward me, clutching my panties at my hips, then sliding them down the length of my legs, his eyes following the trail of skin it leaves behind. Dropping my panties to the ground, he climbs onto the bed, parting my knees with the bulk of his legs as he towers over me. Watching this exotic Adonis stalk toward me, my craving for him grows desperate. He claims my breasts again as he runs the length of his bulging and captive dick against my bare, tender skin, making my sex ache for the length of him to fill me.

I run my hands through his hair as he peppers kisses down my neck. "I can't get enough of you."

He pulls on the redness of my breast with the tip of his teeth, then circles it with his tongue, lapping it, teasing it. "I will never get enough of you."

He continues his journey down farther, kissing then licking his way down past my navel to the tender skin of my groin. "Never will leave your body or mind."

His mouth dips between my legs and the warm pad of his tongue runs along my already tender clit.

"Ahh." I can't contain the agony of the ecstasy he is giving me as he strokes me with the expert rhythm of his tongue. The buildup is quicker, having already been sent over the edge, but he pulls back before I come again. He kneels over me, his heady breath full of desire as he kisses me, deep and hard. I run my hands down the length of his stomach and around to his perfect ass. I dip below his boxers, clutching his flesh, pulling him onto me.

Groaning, he pulls away from our kiss and looks into my eyes as he fumbles to free his hard on. I oblige, tugging them down to free his manhood. "When I claim you, Ella, you will be mine forever."

The sincerity of his statement takes my breath away as he stares deep into my soul.

With one hand holding him up for support as he hovers over me, he guides himself to the mouth of my sex while we stare into each other's soul. The heat of his throbbing tip sends a deep ache surging through me. I run my hand against his cheek, studying every inch of his face as he dives deep into me. Our glorifying moan comes in unison as the length of him fills me completely, thoroughly. As he pulls out and fills me again with a deeper thrust, we watch each other, needing to see the effects of our passion. He takes hold of the back of my thigh and lifts it, plunging into me again, hitting the precise spot tempting to send me into a tailspin.

"Oh my God," I whisper against the incredible feeling of pleasure coursing through me.

The sensation has hit him too. His face becomes focused on the thrust and he dives harder and faster into me, hitting the same magnificent spot again and again. "You're mine, Ella. You are mine."

I want to speak, but I'm so taken by the rapture he is sending through me, I can only breathily speak a whisper, "I'm yours, Raj."

As if his hot thickness could become any larger, he runs the length of me faster, striking hard as he looks into my eyes. I'm lethargic with desire as his thrust aims with complete focus on the true spot to send me over the edge. I moan, feeling the precursor of pleasure teasing me.

"Stay with me, Ella. I want to come together." The sound of his aching voice, the carnal plea for me to meet him at the apex, exalts the pleasure higher than before as complete rapture tempts me just on the other side of this pleasure spin.

"I'm ready. Come with me." He slips his hand under my ass and lifts my hips as he hammers thrust after thrust quick and hard, sending me over the edge. "Oh my God, Raj!"

Swiftly, he cups my mouth with his hand before the volume of my cries overshadows the dying drumbeat and singing bedouin men. His deep guttural moan vibrates against my chest as he releases in me, sending me into a chain of wonton spasms I could thrive on for eternity, here in his arms.

Raj stays inside of me, burying kiss after kiss on my dampened skin. Exhaustion of our pursuit has left us breathless, unable to pull apart from our embrace, so we merely look into each other's eyes. Then again, it could be our desire to remain frozen together in this world where nothing else matters.

The sound of Raj's steady heart beating in my ear after making love is surreal. It is also a risk. The silence of the desert, the silence between him and me as we lay here, with only the steady, slow beat of his heart to my ear as I lay naked across his body. We have taken a risk. One with more threat to him than me. Yes, he told me nothing else mattered, but the fact is he has duty, his faith, and his status. Before we made love, he told me I was brave for my risk of coming here to Jordan because I believed in something greater than myself, but he only knows half of my story. Would he still think of me as brave if he knew my search for greater purpose was not the only reason for me being here? Would my escaping the D.C. party because of my overbearing and deceptive family, determined to dictate the direction of my life, change his image of me?

Grandma Wallace's ethereal voice comes into my mind, the lightest whisper in my mind's eye. *Risk. Is it worth the risk to cross the stars and steal the moon for something greater than yourself? Something greater for someone else? For love. I say yes, it is. What is life and love without risk?*

The rise and fall of Raj's chest changes, his heart quickening as he places his mouth on the crest of my head. Slowly he runs his hand up my arm and wraps me tighter in the sleepy hold we had fallen victim to a while ago. "What are you thinking about?"

Too many things. I move to look up at him and settle on the one I hold in my heart. "My grandmother."

He continues to study me curiously, waiting for me to give him more.

"She would tell me risks were worth crossing the stars and stealing the moon for something greater than yourself."

His hand runs along my face as he seeks the meaning. "Crossing fate and seize your destiny?"

I nod, unsure of what his mind is thinking beyond his words. Has he done those things just to be with me?

He rests his palm on the nape of my neck, his thumb running along the edge of my jaw, soothing me. He presses his lips together before seeking mine. I close my eyes, savoring the feel of his kiss, soft and tender. He pulls away just far enough to look into my eyes. "Yes, they are worth it."

"Am I?" I can't help myself. Yeah, it sounds like I am a needy little bitch, but that is not my reason. I am afraid for him, afraid for the risk he has taken.

His brow furrows as he searches my eyes in confusion. "You are worth every temptation, every threat, Ella. The moment I claimed you, I knew what I was doing. Don't you think I know the risks of having you?"

I list them in a low mumble as I lower my eyes, resting my chin on his chest. "Your faith, religion, status, your reputation. It is all at stake. A risk because of me."

He lifts my face back up to his, forcing me to look at him. His voice is as firm as his touch. "I have considered every result, every outcome, and I am willing to cross fate to seize what I want."

He kisses me again, lingering longer near my lips as he speaks, "What I want, what I need, is you."

In the quiet night of the Wadi Rum, under the stars and moon, we make love again, keeping our rapturous world isolated to my tent for the second time while the rest of the camp sleeps.

Chapter 20

Ella

My hand slides against empty sheets as I wake to his missing presence. The sounds of voices and waking guests and the aroma of food being prepared are a distance beyond my tent, the world I wanted to stay in with him. My nakedness, the sublime feeling within me, is the tangible proof we were not a fantasy. He is being smart, discrete, gauging every outcome, that is why he is gone.

I look over at the pillow he had laid upon and run my hand up under it, lifting and pulling it to me, revealing a folded sheet of paper. I take it in my hand, releasing the pillow to open it.

Ella,
You are worth every risk.
Always mine.
R

I fold the note back and hold it to my chest.

Dressed for the day, I walk into the busy tent where all of the volunteers, Tom, the guards, and Raj have convened for breakfast. Raj is smiling as he speaks animatedly with Tom, when he notices me. He only glances at me for a moment, before returning to Tom.

Discretion.

"Well good morning, sleeping beauty!" Ana comes up behind me, placing her hand on my shoulder.

"Hey." I think of her at the entrance to my tent last night as Raj seduced me and find myself avoiding her eyes as she moves past me to sit down on the floor rug and pillows. She pats the area next to her.

"Come sit. We are leaving in thirty."

As I sit next to her, I watch for any sign she heard anything she shouldn't have last night. "Did you sleep well?"

Two bedouin men move behind us with two large dishes, one holding Shrak and the other an assortment of tabbouleh and hummus.

Ana's eyes widen as the men leave them in front of us in the middle of our invisible table. "Oh wow." She reaches for the warm Shrak. "Yeah, you?"

She tears a piece from the mass of Shrak and dips it in the hummus, seeming to be more interested in eating than my sleep.

I sigh, relieved no one is the wiser of Raj and my intimacy, yet the memory of his body and mine together, the mix of severity and tenderness, his passion for me held, the moment we reached the point of orgasm together, I feel myself flush as I recall every sensation again.

Once breakfast is over, we all convene at the entrance of the campsite, Raj standing next to Tom in front of us. "I hope the accommodations were comfortable for you last night." He can't avoid me as he says this, but I make due looking away as I grin, sensing his hidden innuendo. "We have a couple of hours before the return trip to Amman, so please enjoy the activities. We have camel rides through the Wadi Rum, Jeep racing in the sand dunes, one of my favorites." He grins at Tom and pats him on the shoulder. "I know Mr. Stern has enjoyed them on his last trip to Wadi Rum, or you can make yourself comfortable right here within the camp, relaxing before heading home. Please enjoy."

Ana decides to relax at the hookah tent with Laura and a couple of others, while David and a few others, including Tom, divide up between camel rides and Jeep racing in the sand dunes. I choose to ride the camels through the Wadi Rum with three other volunteers I don't know very well. Ana is disappointed, wanting me to chill with her, but all is good once she gets a group going and heads over to the hookah tent. The musicians have already started playing within the tent, a relaxing slow mewing chant, the strum of the woodwinds slipping from the open tarp.

Before heading out to the camels to start our trek, I use the restroom. As I'm coming out, the wind is taken from me as my mouth is covered and I am pulled into an unoccupied tent. Spinning me around to face him, Raj removes his hand on my lips and entraps them with his skillful lips, kissing me deeply. He moans as he slips his tongue into my mouth, his hand around my waist, gripping, holding, wanting me closer. I find the edges of his face in the darkened, vacant tent and run my hands over his unshaven roughness and into his hair. Our lusting embrace loosens once our craving has been satiated, for now. Out of breath from his consumption of me, he whispers breathlessly, "I can't go a second without thinking of you in my arms, Ella."

I kiss him again softly, tenderly, silencing his resounding need for me. As I pull away I look into his concerned eyes. "What is it?"

I fear the worst; someone has come to him about last night. He had disappeared the same time I did. Could Tom have said something to him?

He looks down timidly, then concentrates on his thumb tenderly caressing my cheek. "I have to ask you ... Last night, I didn't use protection."

"I'm on the pill," I whisper, thanking the heavens it isn't something more threatening. He grins with ease, then kisses me again softly. Uncertain if that is his only worry, I ask. "Was that it? Why you were worried?"

His nod is slight, not wanting to look away from me. "I didn't want you to think I was careless. I just, didn't prepare. I didn't expect..." His candid honesty as he stumbles, searching for the right words, is endearing.

I run my fingers from his jawline to his lips, covering them and making him quiet. "I don't think that."

He nods, then sweeps me up into his arms, holding the back of my head and kissing me thoroughly before setting me down and slipping out the back of the tent. It is all so quick, I feel like I'm spinning as I turn to exit the vacant tent, unable to hide the smile on my face.

The ride through the southern corner of the Wadi Rum from the campsite was jaw dropping. Raj had ridden with us. Even though I expected him to go Jeeping, he made an excuse that he didn't want the volunteers on camelback to miss any specific highlights of the trek. For three hours we rode in the low sun of morning, the cool temperatures of the desert night still lingering until the tail end of the trip, when the heat had us removing our layers of warmth. The massive chameleon-toned canyons towered above us, around us as we rode through passages, and even climbed on foot to places Raj said he had gone as a child, then as a teen, and now as a man. The rigid rock transformed as the morning passed, changing from a deepened rose to the vividness of oranges and reds. The light cloudless sky against the vibrant landscape was indescribable unless you have been to the Wadi Rum.

Upon our return, we washed up quickly, packed our bags, and carried our belongings to the front of the camp for the bedouin men to take to the trucks along with the body guards. We were able to eat one last time at the camp with the sun high above us before leaving.

As we rode through the desert in the backs of our trucks, caravanning along the sand dunes and breath-taking ridges, I felt like something was being left behind, not a physical or tangible something, but rather something divine. I glance at Raj sitting across from me in the truck, his hair blowing in the wind as he looks out into the desert, contentment on his face. He must feel me watching and he turns his head to me, taking me in his golden-eyed gaze, just long enough to remind me nothing has been left behind.

I don't realize how exhausted I am until I sit down in the air-conditioned bus on the blissful cushioning of the seats. I take up both seats with my belongings and, like our getaway began on the bus, Raj takes the seats right adjacent to me, making sure he can watch me without being noticed.

The last thing I remember is looking out my window, secured in the comfort of his watchful eyes, when the bus jolts to a halt in front of the center. As we all unload, Raj asks us collectively if we had all had a good time. We exchange a knowing glance as everyone else thanks him for taking us.

I make sure to personally thank him for the sake of curbing any suspicious behavior. "Thank you, Prince Rajaa, for an unforgettable trip. Petra was breathtaking."

He nods at me as he did with the others. "As I'm sure Wadi Rum was equally unforgettable." His comment is made with an attentiveness intended the lingering audience.

"Mindblowing," I add with equal attentiveness, before breaking form and grinning from the mind-blowing endurance we achieved twice.

I release his hand, shift my back on my shoulder, and start home to the Ba'ashirs, an irremovable smile plastered on my face.

"As-salamu alaykum!" I call from the bottom of the stairs. I look into the Ahmadis living space, but it's empty.

"Wa-Alaykum as-salaam!" Hoda's and Jasara's combined voices are musical as the running footsteps of the kids come to the top of the stairs.

"Ella, we have a feast!" Ghalib calls to me.

"A gift!" Rushdi adds.

I climb the stairs, curious about what they are calling a gift and feast, even though it did smell delicious. I set my pack in the doorway of my room before surrendering to their pulling me into the kitchen.

"Oh!" The countertops of the kitchen are filled with silver trays of chicken skewers, ribs of lamb, Tahini, fried eggplant, and bedouin bread, just as it appeared last night. On the table I see more trays and smaller dishes of pickles, baklava, a dish of earth oven lamb's meat, and the red, hot dipping sauce, Matbucha. The smell of Turkish coffee is not to be missed as Hoda brews it at the counter.

"Ella, we have gift from prince!"

Baffled, yet as excited as she is, I laugh. "This is from the prince?"

Ameena and Laila run to me, kissing me on both cheeks as I exchange the greeting with them.

"Yes. They brought just now!" Ameena says to me, her wide brown eyes charged with excitement. Uncle Naz and Ismad enter the kitchen.

"Prince Rajaa sent all of this," Ismad says, opening his arms to all of the trays. I take in everything once again, realizing he had all of the food we dined on brought here to the Ba'ashirs and the Ahmadis.

"The man that brought it said it is given to thank us for service to the center, the people of our country, and taking care of the volunteers," Ameena adds.

"He said he wanted us to feast like the bedouin," Ismad comments as he looks at all of the food and watches Ghalib and Rushdi eat at the table.

Once the boys and men have eaten, Hoda, Jasara, Ameena, Laila, and I sit and eat. Every bite I take tastes just as it did last night; mouthwatering and amazing.

I add the Matbucha to my skewered chicken as Hoda warns me. "Eh, eh, eh. Hot. Harr."

The ends of my mouth curl remembering Raj and my exchange over the infamous hot dipping sauce last night. I nod. "I know. I like it."

Everyone continues to eat and asks me questions both in English and Arabic about my trip to Petra and Wadi Rum. As I tell them every detail of the sites in Petra, the camel ride in the Wadi Rum, the musical talents of the bedouin singers and dancers, I hold the most treasured moments of my journey close to my soul.

Chapter 21

Rajaa

Sitting in the back of the SUV, I lean my head back against the headrest. Watching Ella walk away at the center was the hardest fucking thing and it isn't like I could tell her, show her by taking her hand, telling her I will drive her, not with Tom and the volunteers surrounding us. Our brief exchange before her leaving, her thanking me for the getaway were saturated with overtone of our time in her tent last night making love. Even now, I close my eyes and a see her beneath me, her golden hair laid out on the bed, her breasts rising and falling as I move deep inside of her. I wasn't fucking lying when I told her she could never be a fling. Now that I have claimed her body, mind and soul I will never let her go.

She worries about risk. I could see it in her eyes, feel her thinking it as we lay there after making love. When she told me her grandmother's words, crossing the stars and stealing the moon, it's like her grandmother had written us into the night sky, a constellation meant to stand the test of time and space, years before we had ever met.

While the risks of us were distant thoughts as she laid naked across my body before I made love to her again, because now that I have I won't be able to get enough of her body, it's at the heart of me being back in Amman. Still, the fact remains, I will lay my status, my values, my life on the line for Ella and I will do whatever it takes to be with her.

Now that she is mine, I will never let her go.

Zaid coming to the campsite last night drunk, cornering Ella, and telling me some secret meeting had been attended by my father, him, and the Amir to discuss my marriage to Daya was fucking bullshit. Last night is proof his addictions are back, and I am certain his connection with Tariq never stopped, he is just hiding it. He can't fucking stop, because he has gone insane with wanting to be powerful, lead the Middle East into this transformation he and Tariq have contrived.

I need to talk to my father, find out what is true about Zaid's comments, and figure out how I'm going to keep this proposal between Daya and me from happening. I also need to figure out how to tell my father and mother about my fear of Zaid's state of mind, his networking with Tariq behind the Amir's and their backs.

I look out the window, my elbow on the door as I rest my chin on my closed fist, watchful of Ella in the distance ahead of us. I tell the driver in Arabic to not get too close, that I don't want her to see us. Her veil is back on for the sake of modesty, but when I look at her now, I can't help every nerve ending in my body reacting to her presence, craving the moment to have her in my arms again.

The amount of food left over after last night's feast was generous. I knew we would never consume all of it so I asked the camp staff to take some for themselves after they had packaged helpings for the Ba'ashir and the Ahmadi family. I know Ella's heart and thinking of her feeling guilty for being in Petra and the Wadi Rum really bothered me. I had the food delivered with one of our guards earlier today for them.

Once Ella is at the Ba'ashirs door, I tell the driver to pull away and head toward Samir Fadel's house, Zaid's confidante who had kept Tariq as a guest. My guess is he never left and he is still holed up in his little fucking sex dungeon, popping Captagon and chasing it with Arak, wearing his speedo with my country's flag on his mother-fucking ball sack.

Knowing the royal trucks I assume, the Fadels open the gate for us as soon as we pull up to the front of the property. Samir must think it is my brother, unable to see me in the back with his video surveillance. Once the driver stops at the front steps of the estate, I ascend the steps to the front door. Before I can knock or ring the doorbell, a wide-eyed Sami opens the door, shutting it quickly behind him.

"Rajaa, uh, what can I help you with?" He lacks a smile this time and he seems nervous, like he is hiding a fucking Sheikh in there or something. Motherfucker.

"Yeah, I was wondering if Tariq is here." I laugh a little with a hint of embarrassment. "The night of the party, things ended badly with me leaving and I wanted to apologize."

Sami stares at me blankly, his deep-toned skin ashen from fright. "Uh, I thought Zaid told you, Tariq is gone."

"Already?" I ask, exaggerating the question and furrowing my brow. "Ah, I was hoping to have caught him before he left. Is there a way I can contact him? A phone number?"

Sami's agitation is taking a toll as he keeps glancing back at the closed door and rocking on the heels of his shoes. He is so fucking nervous, the hand he is running through his hair is shaking, not to mention the beads of sweat he is already sprouting. "I would, but he never gave it to me. Your brother always told me when he had planned to come stay here."

Fucking liar.

"Oh, all right. Well, could you do me a favor?"

Samir nods slowly as he looks back at my driver standing in front of the truck watching us. "Yeah, yeah, of course, Rajaa."

I lower my eyes and grin timidly as I fold my hands together. "Could you just keep this visit between you and me? I wanted to speak to Tariq without my brother knowing. I wanted Zaid to be proud that his little brother was trying to make amends on his own. You can understand, right?"

Samir's smile is mediocre, laden with fear of my being here. "Sure, sure. I will, Rajaa."

I nod to him and smile contently. "Thank you, Sami. Tell Rima I said hello."

Sami can't get into the house fast enough, and as I walk back to the truck, I suspect he is talking to Tariq and phoning my brother to tell him about my visit. I expect it, that is why I told him what I did, came here to look for Tariq in the open, so my fucking brother knows I will risk defying him, figuring out what he is doing, to protect my family and my country.

I arrive back to the house at sunset. My father, mother, and sister are eating in the dining hall when I enter.

"Rajaa, we weren't expecting you for dinner. Here, come sit," my father calls out.

I kiss him on either cheek. "I wasn't sure what time we would return."

"Yes, we know you had guests to accommodate. There is plenty of food," my mother says, beckoning the server to bring a plate for me.

"Shukran, Mama."

"How was Petra, Wadi Rum? I'm sure the volunteers were amazed at the history, the sites. It has been years since I visited Petra." My father closes his eyes and looks up to the heavens like he is imagining its grandness before he focuses on my mother. "Zahrat Baladi, we should plan a trip to the camp soon."

I notice my mother give me a quick, wary glance before responding to him with a smile, "Yes, my love."

My father's pet name for my mother, little flower, reminds me of the unique love they have, while my mother's foreboding expression draws my concern.

"Laiyalla, why do you worry? The doctor said I was fine to travel." My father's reprimand is lenient, playful even.

"Do you not want to relax in the desert under the moon and stars?"

I glance over at Tamanna and notice her smiling widely at my father's humor with my mother. I can't help grinning, seeing him be unlike his typical serious self.

My mother smiles as she stares down to her plate, trying to hide the beginning of a laugh.

"What?" my father questions as he takes all three of us in, an impish smile on his own face.

The server delivers my plate just then. "Shukran."

Seeming to avoid my father's question, my mother asks, "How was the camp? Did your guests enjoy themselves?"

I nod as I chew my food, thinking of how thoroughly Ella and I enjoyed our time. I look across the table, her complete attention on my response and the smile she had for my father completely gone. "Your evening?"

It is too obvious she is searching for something. Her knowing I was there with the volunteers, Ella, she is suspicious. Or maybe she is suspicious of Zaid. I keep my delivery even. "Clear. Every star lit up the night sky."

"Were the musicians and dancers there?" Tamanna asks.

I smile at her. "Yes, they were."

Tamanna has always loved the music and dancers. I remember her dancing among them as a toddler when our family would visit the camp. Feeling my mother's eyes still watching me, I turn the tables, wondering what her inquisition is truly about. "What did all of you do last night?"

I seek my mother's eyes, not directing the question solely to her, but expecting the answer from her nonetheless. She focuses on her plate and pushes her food around, then glances at my father. "We had a quiet dinner." She focuses back on me. "Tamanna, your father, and me."

This is definitely about Zaid.

"Zaid?" I ask, looking down at my plate before taking a bite of the Chicken Kabsa.

My father responds, his jovial voice waning with the new subject of my brother, "Dinner with friends."

"He never returned home last night." My mother's comment is greeted with penalty from my father.

"We will not speak behind his back."

I can see the concern for Zaid in his eyes as he stares down at his food, the tremor returning to his hand as he lifts his fork to his mouth. He shouldn't be concerned for him, but it is obvious that he and my mother hold hope in the speedy atonement of Zaid's misdeeds, even though they are watchful of his actions. Their hope would be disputed if they knew Zaid came out to the Wadi Rum drunk and belligerent.

"Father..."

The sound of the front door shutting, followed by quick, heavy footsteps, silences me as Zaid enters the dining hall.

I don't expect him to be as put together as he is. His hair is freshly washed, slicked back, and his attire is on point, just as Zaid had always been known for. He stops at the corner of the table. "I'm sorry I'm so late, I have spent most of the day organizing the banquet."

Banquet?

My father and mother exchange a glance.

"You have?" my mother questions Zaid as he moves to my father, kissing him on either cheek, then to my mother, doing the same. She is as surprised as I am watching him kiss her cheeks for the first time in years. Full of energy and spunk, he steps over to Tamanna and gives her a high five, then kisses the top of her head as he sits down next to her, completely avoiding my presence as he looks at my mother.

"Yes, I left at dawn, couldn't sleep. I have been at the palace all day."

My mother and father share a knowing glance before my father asks, "Where were you last night?"

He laughs and shakes his head, beckoning the server to bring him a plate. "Dinner with friends. I thought I told you."

My mother makes her point, "But you didn't return home."

He peers over at her. "Yes, I did. Did you not hear me come in?"

His direct question has my mother left with a confused yet simple response, "No, I didn't."

"Yes, it was late, but that is because I had to take Samir Fadel home." My brother targets me across the table for the first time since arriving. "You know Samir Fadel, Rajaa. The one that threw the party we attended and the one you have conversed with since. Very good, loyal friend of mine."

He lifts his glass of water to his lips and drinks, burning holes straight through me as he places his glass down.

Stoically, I respond, "Yes, I have seen him recently."

My brother sloppily places a piece of chicken in his mouth and chews it as he speaks, pointing his fork at me. "Yes, that is right. You have, haven't you? Anyway, enough about me. How was your getaway with your American ... volunteers?"

His pause is purposeful, highlighting one in particular, I'm certain. "I'm sure they were so ... eh, what is the word I am looking for..." He searches the table as if it will somehow appear to him, then he focuses back on me once he has found it. "Enamored by the entire adventure."

I return to my food, appearing to ignore his intent on antagonizing me. It is fucking getting to me and I need to end it quick or I might lose my temper.

"This banquet, does it have anything to do with your recent meeting with the Amir, Baba?"

My father swallows his chewed food and stares at me, bewildered that I knew about it.

Zaid speaks up, "Baba, I called him last night and told him. I hope that does not upset you."

"I thought you hadn't heard from him, Rajaa?" my mother probes, her concern transfixed on me now that I appear to be caught in a lie orchestrated by my fucking brother.

"My Queen, please don't blame him, he had guests to tend to. I'm sure he is exhausted from ... entertaining all night. Our conversation must have slipped his mind," Zaid offers my mother, undermining me once again. Son of a bitch.

Unable to contain myself any longer, I drop my fork onto the table, hitting the plate on its way down. "Actually, thank you, Zaid. Yes, too much excitement last night. I remember our conversation now and you did say something about a celebration, oh and the Amir reconsidering a proposal from myself to Daya, which is surprising since only days ago he was very much against a union. Your talk must have been persuasive."

I look back at my father, the false grin plastered on my face. "So what is this banquet for, exactly?"

My father places his napkin on the table, settling back in his chair and folding his shaking hands into his lap. "The celebration was actually Zaid's idea for something entirely different. You and Daya came up briefly, but the Amir would like to see how things ... progress."

I'm lost once again by my brother's ruthless conspiring.

My father nods at Zaid, then returns a look to me. "He had wanted to throw a banquet for the Caritas and the WorldTeach volunteers at the palace, commending them for their service to the refugees and our country."

I stare across the table at my brother, his grin wide and proud as my mother interjects. "I did not know you were going to start planning so soon, Zaid. I am sorry I could not go with you." My mother's apology seems sincere, but I see her inspecting eye nonetheless, looking for any flaw to Zaid's words.

Zaid nods at her as he finishes chewing. "It is fine, my Queen. I am more than happy to have started the arrangements on your behalf. It is the least I can do for the service these people have done for the refugees." His eyes on his plate, he seems to contemplate hard. "I know in the beginning I was a non-believer of Rajaa's program and the center all together."

His eyes slowly rise to meet mine. "Now that I have gotten to see the inner workings of the people ... His interaction with them."

His sinister glare is binding, yet he clearly obscures his reason for my sake. "Rajaa has found something there and I see its value in the big picture."

He breaks our heavy stare and looks back at my mother and father. "I want to be more involved."

Fuck him, he wants to be more involved. Too many words and too many meanings have distorted everything in my mind and I fear we are all more at risk now as Zaid steps up his game. I wipe my mouth and rise from the table. "Mama, Baba, please excuse Zaid and me. We have some items to discuss before it gets any later."

My mother and father nod. "Rajaa, could I also speak to you after you talk with your brother?" my mother questions, bringing me to halt as Zaid continues out of the dining hall.

"Yes."

As I walk out of the hall, I see Zaid exit the house, out into the courtyard. I'm not sure why my mother needs to speak with me, but for now I focus on Zaid.

Entering into the courtyard, I close the door behind me.

"I have to give it to you, Raj, you have balls going over to Sami's house," Zaid says over the sound of the trickling water of the courtyard fountain. He turns to me as I approach. "You underestimate the loyalty I have around me."

I put my hands in my pockets. They are safe there, preventing the chance of strangling him. I shake my head at his naive analysis. "You really think I didn't know Sami would run and tell you? I expected it, Zaid. I just wanted you to see I am not going to be cornered by you and I am going to stop whatever you and Tariq are planning. Your fucking glorious plan to transform the Middle East."

He shrugs and widens his eyes in surprise. "I really have no idea what you are talking about, Rajaa. All I know is that I have video surveillance of you at Sami's talking to him at length. Even voice recording of you asking about the Syrian Sheikh, Tariq bin Qasim." He shakes his head and denounces me with the click of his tongue, like a child getting slapped on the wrist. "If anything were to ...disrupt my plans, this video may fall into the hands of the King, Queen, maybe the Prime Minister and his Cabinet as well. It would appear you might be under the influence of Tariq, now that I resigned all of my contact. It would be a tragedy for the favored son and perfect prince to turn into a power-hungry tyrant. Prince of a thousand enemies ... a true tragedy."

I feel the wrath of the lengths my brother will go to for his purpose to succeed and for my being the scapegoat if it fails. "And this fucking banquet or celebration? It is meant to put you in good light with the King and Queen. You have no real desire to support it."

"No, I don't," he says flatly. "The only value I see is the one you fucked last night."

I close the space between him. "You will not get near her."

"Hmm, we'll see."

Zaid takes a step back from me and runs a free hand over his mouth, grinning loosely. "You know, you say you know her so well. Did you know she is a U.S Congressman's daughter? She is American royalty."

He stares at me now, enjoying the impact this surprise has on me.

My unbelieving silence is his satisfaction as he continues. "The things you can learn when you befriend staff at the center. Tom Stern is a very kind man ... a very malleable individual."

I don't believe him. He is lying. "You are a fucking pathological liar, Zaid."

He walks around me slowly. "Did you know she is putting herself through college? She rejected her family's help, their influence? A defiant little bitch that doesn't respect her father, her mother, won't respect anyone. Like I said, she is a risk and now you have made her a valuable asset to me and our Syrian friend."

As he comes to stand in front of me, he tilts his head and raises his eyebrows as he looks down at the sandstone beneath us. "If something were to happen to her..."

I take hold of his shirt and pull him to me. "I will fucking kill you if anything happens to her."

Zaid pushes me off of him, forcing me to stumble backward a few steps. The fire in our eyes being exchanged could set this whole country ablaze.

"Rajaa?"

My mother's presence at the door is a surprise as she inspects what has happened between Zaid and me. "It is getting late. Can I please speak to you before I retire?"

Trying to blink away the pure anger to calm my breath, I look down and respond, avoiding her probing gaze. "Yes, Mama."

I glare at my brother before turning away and following my mother into the house.

As I follow her into the office, her silence and distance are ominous, resulting from the conversation she walked in on. It is just her and me in the office that is usually occupied by my father. "Where is Baba?"

She folds her arms over her chest as she paces in front of me. Speaking quickly, her voice quivers with anger. "He has gone to bed and I am happy for that, because if he would have witnessed what I just did ... He had a stroke just days ago! Lying to us about talking to Zaid last night, telling him that you will kill him if something happens to her? I assume it is this American girl from the center!"

"Her name is Ella Wallace."

My stating her name is like adding fuel to an already tempered fire. "You would turn against your family for her? Kill your brother? Lie? Have you turned against your values too?"

I can't answer without sending her into another fit of anger, knowing my answer would always contain me choosing Ella, so I stay silent.

"Zaid told us he thought you had changed, but I didn't see it until just now, being caught in a lie! Fighting with your brother! Willing to risk everything you stand for, your status, your reputation, a proposal for this girl?" She searches my eyes for any understanding. "Whatever is going on with you, fix it. End whatever you have started with her. It will corrupt you Rajaa. "

She turns away, leaving me standing there tangled in the web of deceit and lies Zaid is artfully weaving.

Chapter 22

Ella

The hallway to my classroom is quiet with the sounds of teachers working in their classrooms. I wasn't sure if Ana was already here, but seeing the room is dark through the small window, I assume she hasn't made it in yet. It's still early though.

Opening my classroom door and flipping on the light, I don't notice the figure standing behind me until I start toward my desk. I nearly jump out of my shoes. "Holy Shit! Raj, what are you..."

Before I can finish, he takes me by the waist and backs me flush against the wall next to the door. "Shhh," he hushes me with a devilish grin, staring into my eyes then moving quickly to watching my lips as I ask, "What are you doing sitting in the fucking dark?"

He reaches for the door lock, making sure it's secure as he dips his lips down to meet mine softly. "Waiting for you."

His lips consume me, his tongue tangling with mine. The grating moan coming from him is my undoing as I drop my bag to the ground, needing to touch him, hold him again. "I missed you." My breathless words are brief, as my coming up for air is hurriedly taken from me by Raj claiming my lips again and again.

"I thought about you all night," he says against my lips as the kisses soften, becoming tender touches.

Worried Ana is going to knock on the door any second, I place my hands on his chest and kiss him tenderly once more before putting a small distance between us. I'm surprised to see his eyes lacking the golden luster they usually do. Instead, they've darkened underneath. "Your eyes look tired."

My observation sends his gaze down for a moment before it returns to me. Something is wrong. "What is it?"

"I didn't sleep last night. I was thinking about something I need to ask you."

His statement makes my heart drop, not knowing if this could be Raj telling me what we had done was a mistake, or we can't continue our affair, or someone has discovered us.

I watch him closely, waiting for him to deliver his question. "Why didn't you tell me who you your father is?"

"What?" I search his eyes, having expected something completely different from him.

"This morning, I asked Tom to show me your profile. Your father is a Congressman. Why didn't you tell me?" The searching glimmer in his eyes no longer is tender or filled with passion, but urgent and consumed with what he has discovered.

"Yeah, so what if my father is a fucking Congressman? Does that change the way you feel about me?"

"No…"

I don't let him continue. "Look, I made my own fucking decision to come here. If he would have had it his way, I wouldn't be standing here right now. And why the fuck would Tom let you see my file. It was confidential."

He looks everywhere but at me as he runs his hands over his face, frustrated by my explanation. "Tom works for me. He is obligated to show me records. Ella, your being the daughter of a Congressman makes things more complicated."

Is he really fucking doing this because of my father? "So, you and I are complicated because you found out about my father. That is your out?"

He shakes his head at me with confusion. "What? My out?"

I fold my arms over my chest and glare at him. "Your way out of this, us? You know what? I don't want to hear it! Don't do me any fucking favors!"

I start to walk away from him when he pulls me back to the wall, holding me by my arms. His tired eyes have been sparked. "You will listen to me. There is no fucking out! I'm in this with you forever. I told you that! But, you being a fucking Congressman's daughter is something I should have known. It makes everything more dangerous for you."

All of a sudden he is consumed with fear, his eyes losing the luster they held seconds ago. "Raj, what is it? What is more dangerous?"

He must see he has worried me, his eyes searching mine more tenderly. "I'm sorry. I didn't mean to come to you and frighten you. I just ... Now that we are together, I fear something might try and pull us apart. I will do everything in my power to not let happen, Ella."

He runs his thumb against my jaw, resting it on my chin as his lips seek mine deeply once again. The feel of his lips, the way they move against mine. I will never have enough of Raj. His touch stuns my mind and awakens my body, enslaving me in the most blamelessly innocent and magnificently pure way I have ever known. The only way I ever want to know love. Only with him.

But as he pulls away, the concern in his eyes gives me lucidity to ask, "Raj, if there is something you aren't telling me..."

He runs his hands along my arms. "No, no, it is fine. I'm just being overly cautious. Listen, come to my car in the back alley after you finish today."

"Why?"

"I am giving you a ride," he says, his brow furrowed like he is daring me to deny his command.

I try to make light of his demanding words, hoping they will ease his mind. "Oh, you are? What if I choose to walk?"

His grin is only partial as he looks at me through his abnormally thick yet so alluring eyelashes.

"Yes, I am." His arrogance used to be an annoyance, now it is just disarming as hell.

"You know, there should be some kind of law against guys having eyelashes like that." I nod to his eyes, trying to keep my growing smile concealed.

"Hmmm, should there now?" he asks as he leans in, intent on seduction as his hands find my waist again, tucking me closer.

I pull back, taunting him, his grin widening. "And dimples. Dimples so sinful they should be outlawed."

He hovers his lips over mine, a feather's touch with enticing gravity. "Then I am a sinner."

Yes, yes you are in the best possible way.

I swallow hard, holding back my urge to cave and submit to his luscious tease, aiming to turn the tables. "Maybe I shouldn't take rides from sinners."

I can feel the smirk on his lips, my eyes half shut from the sheer pleasure of his breath against me. This volleying of cat and mouse has gotten to him as he succumbs to his desire, kissing me wholly.

As he pulls away and teases me with more, his lips hovering over mine, he whispers, "I will make it worth your time, Ms. Wallace, I promise."

The sound of the door unlocking and the Raj slipping away through it leaves me breathless.

The rest of the day, I am distracted by both the pending ride home and the dangers Raj's mind is afflicted by. So much affliction he has lost sleep. I see Jasara sitting at a table with Rushdi and Laila. I wave from our table and notice they are eating food left from the bedouin feast Raj had delivered to the house. I didn't get a chance to thank him this morning.

Tom meets with the volunteers and staff after the children leave for the day. I don't see Raj among the group that has come together in the cafeteria. "I won't keep you, but I have some exciting news to share. It seems we have an invitation to attend a celebration." His smile is taunting as some of the volunteers call to him.

"Come on!"

"Don't tease us!"

Sticking with his torment, he says, "It really isn't that big of a deal, I suppose. I could always decline." He starts to walk away as the volunteers all call for him to come back. He turns around lazily and smiles. "Okay, okay."

He pulls out a card from his back pant pocket, reads it, squints, then looks up at us, ashamed. "I think I need my glasses." He starts patting his shirt, his pant pockets. "Where are my glasses?"

The volunteers are belligerent at this point, unable to contain their need to know. I even call out, "Just read it!"

He holds his hands up in surrender and squints as he reads the invitation. "You have been cordially invited to a celebration in honor of your servitude and duty to Caritas and WorldTeach by Your Highness the King and Her Majesty the Queen of Jordan."

The volume of the room rises so quickly, I can't hear the rest of the invitation, but I'm not really listening; the excitement in the room is running too high for me to hear anything other than cheering and whistling.

As we all leave the cafeteria, I head in the opposite direction of everyone else toward the rear doors to the alley, when Ana asks, "Ella, where are you going?"

"Oh, I forgot something in the room. I'll see you tomorrow."

"Okay, bye." She smiles and goes out the front doors of the center.

My brisk and concealed walk to the back door gives time for my excitement of meeting the King and Queen of Jordan to wear off and my anxiety of meeting the parents of the man I am having a forbidden affair with to expand exponentially.

As I open the door to the alley, I see the black-on-black SUV parked and running in front of me. With the shock hitting me, I stand still as the driver gets out and opens the door for me. Once my eyes meet Raj's the anxiety falls away enough for my feet to start moving. I get in and the driver closes the door behind me.

Raj is sitting on the far end of the truck, his hand framing the side of his head as he leans against the window sill. "Hi."

"Hi."

The truck drives on as soon as the driver shuts his door. All of a sudden, a wall of darkened glass starts to rise between the front seats and Raj and me. As the glass climbs, Raj watches me with the sexiest fucking allure; I clench my legs from the tension already mounting between them. The glass seals in seconds and we are left alone.

"I made you a promise earlier." His voice is throaty, carnal as his gaze enraptures me as it has many times, but still never enough. I want it to feel this for eternity.

"Yeah, you did."

He makes his move, leaning over the center console, cupping my cheek in his hand, drawing my mouth to his as he teases my lips with his breath.

"Yeah, I did."

His lips find mine, and his mouth, combined with the touch of his fingers grazing my breasts as he undoes my blouse, ignites a spark inside of me, a maddening longing for him to set me free. I take over unbuttoning the rest of my blouse, undoing my bra and letting it fall to the ground as his tongue dances with mine. His hands find the waistband of my pants and tug as I urge both my panties and pants down, breaking our kiss to do so, but never the coveting, purely ravenous watch we have set in place.

Completely naked, I move toward him only for him to stop me. "Wait." His breath is ragged as he scans my body. "I want to see you." His hand reaches for my face, unable to let what he is gazing upon be untouched. The warmth of his hands set fire to every inch of my skin he runs it along the length of my neck, the center of my chest, cupping my breast and running the pad of his thumb along my hardened nipple. I arch my back, leaning into his maneuvers, needing to be felt by him.

He shakes his head as he studies every part of me. "I need you, Ella, more than the blood that courses through my veins."

He takes hold of my waist and brings me to him, my thighs straddling his. As I slide down against him, my tender skin runs against his pants, melting me deeper onto the solidity of his cock.

"I want you inside of me, Raj," I say between peppered kisses of passion as I blindly work on unlatching his belt. Like my demand and touch have called on a primal beast, he takes his hands from me and he breathes fiery breath onto my breasts, tugging at his belt, his button, and zipper, each sound inching me closer to the fulfillment of him inside of me. In one movement, he grips my hip bones and slides me down onto him, taking me to the hilt.

"Oh fuck, Raj!" I call out breathlessly as the satiety of his throbbing dick and the rhythm of the truck in motion heightens the bliss. I can't contain the fervent euphoria as I reach for him, gripping his dark hair, running it through my fingers as his strong hands clutch my hips, bringing me to rise and fall on this salacious and fleshy wave he is commanding.

"Yes, baby, I want you to feel every fucking inch of me. Every single thrust." He pushes deep inside. "Every single shift." He tilts his hips up angling deeper, hitting the spot meant to send me into the erotic spin I am begging for now.

"Yes, Raj."

He pulls back from me, gazing into my eyes as he clenches my hip with one hand and cups my face with the other, the animal in him unleashed as we stare into each other's eyes and ride together, harder, faster, wanting to see the other feel the pleasure we are pursuing.

The throbbing wave hits me just as he leans his head back against the headrest. "Ahhh, I'm going to fucking come!" The painstaking expression I have given him uncoils me quickly. "Oh, Raj! I'm coming! I'm coming!"

As if my words are a command over him, he reaches for me, pulling me into him, clutching his arms around me as his throbbing cycles me through an ebb and flow of sublime ecstasy.

Both of us sway with the motion of the car as we catch our breath, cleansed by our pursuit of rapture.

While our undressing was haphazard, our redressing was slow and nurturing as we found every opportunity to teach other. His warm touch, his kisses on my shoulder as he fastened my bra, running his nose against my throat as he helped me button my shirt. While the foreplay was speedy, the post-sex caresses are conscious and intentional, his touches warm as he fastens my bra and runs his hands along my thighs after helping me shimmy into my panties. He buttons my blouse while I button his shirt, unable to keep our smiles concealed from what we had just done.

"So, did I fulfill my promise?" His question gives rise to the grin deepening his dimple.

I look up at him brazenly, running my tongue over my lips and rubbing them together. "Yes, completely and thoroughly."

He cups my cheek, running his thumb against it. "Every moment with you in this world is immeasurable, Ella."

He kisses me tenderly once more, before we each take turns making sure we are clothed properly. Raj knocks on the mirrored partition separating us from the driver. As the dark-tinted glass slides down, I feel the heat of humility rise on my face as Raj and the driver speak. Raj asks him to circle back to the Ba'ashirs home, reminding me of what he had done for them and the Ahmadis. "Thank you for bringing the bedouin feast for them."

Raj bows his head to me. "They have done so much for the volunteers and the refugees, taking in the Ahmadi family, taking care of you."

I don't know why I'm surprised he knows the last name of the refugee family living with the Ba'ashirs. Raj's dedication to this program and the people involved becomes more apparent as I watch his interaction with the people at the center.

"The program you have funded has given them hope and support. Some of the lives you have changed just by bringing us here ... They were barely surviving and now they have found a safe place at the center. You have brought this to them."

I didn't think I would be able to formulate what I truly think of Raj and what he has done, but I think I have done a good job.

His eyes fall for a moment, his modesty emblematic of the type of man he is, not wanting to steal the focus. "More should be done."

"The King and Queen?" I ask him, wondering if they are holding him back from seeing more ways of helping.

He stares out the window into the streets, a seriousness cast over him. "No, they see my vision. My brother Zaid ... he has a difference of opinion. Other ideas."

It doesn't surprise me Zaid is the chink in the chain. As we enter into the Ba'ashirs neighborhood, I try to lighten the subject sensing this one has brought him down. "Tom told us about the celebration. Did you plan it?"

As he looks back at me, worry in his eyes, he takes my hand in his and intertwines our fingers. "It was Zaid's idea."

"And that is a bad thing?"

Raj looks from our joined hands into my eyes.

Feeling he isn't understanding me, I explain. "Maybe he is trying to do something nice."

Raj raises our linked fingers and rests his lips on mine and closes his eyes. I'm not the praying type, but if I was to, I would think that Raj's posture might signify him asking his God for something important. His eyes open and seek mine in silence. "Are you not looking forward to the celebration?"

His smile is weak, but visible, softening my concern for what is bother him. "If you will be there, I am definitely excited."

He kisses my fingers again, then places his other hand on top of them. His words are a reminder of him and me being in the same room among the Caritas staff, WorldTeach volunteers, and the royalty he calls family. We won't be able to interact, needing to keep discretion at the forefront of our every move, every expression.

As we turn onto to the Ba'ashirs' street, Raj asks, "I will send Badir to take you to and from the center. What time should he arrive?"

I'm confused with what he is telling me. "Like tomorrow?"

He looks at me pointedly. "Tomorrow, the next day, and the next, and so on."

I laugh a little at his explanation and demand. He knows it gets to me. "No, I think I will walk."

The humor I try to display is lost to him as the visible unease of my joke has hardened his face and his resolve. "Ella, please do not fight with me on this. I need you to be safe."

Even though the glint in his eyes and the sound of his voice alert a small amount of panic within me, I try to push it down and reason with him. "Raj, my walking down a street isn't safe all of a sudden?"

I think of what he had said earlier today. "Does this have to do with this morning?"

He turns his whole body and leans across the console, cupping my face with his free hand as he pulls our clutched fingers to his chest. "I just need you to be careful and I don't trust that will happen without security. The conditions are changing in Amman and I don't want anything happening to you." He kisses me gingerly. "Let me do this. Badir is the only one I trust with you."

He has to trust people with me now? "Is this because of my dad, the Congressman bullshit?"

He shakes his head. "No, this is about you, Ella. I would not be able to live with myself if something were to happen to you. Just please do this one thing without an argument! Elayk! Fuck!"

His obsessive and maddening rant in both English and Arabic has me upset and bewildered at the same time. How can he think anything would happen to me? I mean, he is the fucking Prince of Jordan, I'm a nobody here.

I close the gap between us, kissing him gently over and over again, hoping that my alms and words will calm him. "Okay. I won't fight. I'll do it."

My solitary kisses are slowly returned as Raj cups the nape of my neck and locks his ever-rousing lips with mine. Before he overwhelms me, the truck stops, bringing our feverish ride to an end. As I move back from him, he watches me sleepily, like our passion has the same spell-bound effect on him as it has on me. "Will I see you to-morrow?"

He nods slowly. "I will see you at the center."

I look into the rearview mirror, making eye contact with Badir for the first time since getting into the truck. Needless to say, my comfort level with Badir and saluta-tions has changed since Raj's and my ride. "Shukran, Ba-dir."

"Walaw na'am sayyideti."

Him saying "Yes, ma'am" in Arabic brings me a sense of relief that I am not shunned because of what is obvious was happening back here between Raj and me.

I open the door and step out, but before I can close the door Raj asks, "Will seven o'clock be fine?"

I nod. "Yes."

"Ela al-lekaa', Ella."

I had heard the romanticized version of goodbye in one of classes; it means "until next time." I'd wanted a chance to use it and it just so happens to come from the very person I can't wait to see again.

"Ela al-lekaa'."

I close the door to the truck and walk to the front door of the Ba'ashirs, already missing his presence. When I open the door, Ameena and Laila are at the door, pulling me up the stairs giggling. "What is it?"

"You will see," Laila says as Ameena leads us up. "Mama! Hoda, she is here! Open it!"

Once we are at the landing, I see Hoda and Jasara working in the kitchen. Hoda sets down her spatula and turns off the stove as Jasara finishes washing utensils in the sink, both drying their hands on their aprons. Ameena picks up a card from the table, but Ismad takes it from her and shakes his head, smiling as she playfully reaches for it.

"Baba!" she begs him to open it in Arabic.

"Tayyeb, Tayyeb Ameena," he laughs as he raises it from her then swings it around to open the envelope.

I'm not sure what we are all waiting for. "What is it?"

"It is from the King and Queen of Jordan!" Uncle Nazeer says, smiling from the doorway dividing the kitchen from the living room.

I smile a little, having an idea of what it is: the invitation for the celebration.

"It was delivered by one of the King's guards!" Ameena adds, her eyes wider than saucers and a smile to match.

I widen my eyes and meet hers. "Really?"

She nods eagerly as she watches her father hold money in one hand and a card in the other. "What does it say?"

Ismad looks at Hoda, shock filling his face and the smile momentarily gone. "We have been invited to the Palace for a celebration."

"Mazha?" Hoda seems like she is about to cry, pained by what Ismad has just said. She walks toward him, wanting to read for herself. He repeats himself in Arabic to her. Ismad's eyes gleam as his shock dissipates and he hands the invitations to Hoda. As she grips it with both hands, Ismad takes us all in.

"We are invited to a celebration in our honor in three days!" Ismad holds the money in between his two hands. "They have given us money for clothing for the event!"

Hoda covers her mouth with one hand as she passes the invitation to Jasara. "Lana?"

"Naäam!" Hoda holds it to her, putting her arms around her. "Naaam!"

Hoda suddenly begins to cry, then Jasara as she passes the invitation to Nazeer. "Nazeer!"

He looks at the invitation and reads, "Ba'ashirs and Ahmadis." He laughs with surprise and excitement, his eyes widening as he hands it back to Ismad. They exchange a manly hug.

Ismad hands me the invitation, but reading it would be an impossibility. My eyes have blurred and hazed from the tears I am shedding for the Ba'ashirs' and Ahmadis' elation.

Chapter 23

Rajaa

The last two days I hardly visited the center or saw Ella between my coordinating elements of the celebration with the Caritas director and Mr. Stern. With the number of staff, volunteers, and host families as well as the refugee families taken in by the host families, it has become too daunting of a task for my mother, and my brother happily obliged just as he had creating this event. I saw it as an excuse on my mother's part to keep me away from the center.

I'm able to break away twice in the days leading up to the celebration to see Ella in the cafeteria eating with her girls and again as I look in at her through her classroom door window. Both times I wait until she sees me so she knows I have wanted to see her. Badir has made sure to keep a close eye on her and since his loyalty was proven the evening he accompanied me to Sami's looking for Tariq, I can trust he will not let anything happen to her. That is the only element keeping me from watching her every waking moment.

"Where would you like the Cabinet and Prime Minister to sit?" Zaid asks as he studies the floor plan of the palace ballroom he has laid across my father's meeting table in the office, my mother hovering over the print.

"I would think as close to the King as possible. Ammaar, will you help us, my love?"

I sit at the opposite end of the table watching Zaid take extreme interest in the seating arrangements, which is unlike anything my brother has ever done for a banquet or celebration in the past. If he wants to do floral arrangements next, I don't give a shit. As long as I have him in my sights, I know he is not putting Ella in harm's way.

My father comes to the table with the use of his cane today, his hand trembling, shaking the cane as he clutches it. "Yes, my flower."

As my father makes his suggestion and my mother rearranges the seating to his liking, Zaid asks, "What about the Amir and his family? They need to be close to us."

"What about them?" My question has all of their attention, Zaid exchanging a glance of obvious proportions with my mother. "Well, the Amir and his family are dear friends of ours. We are practically family, Raj."

I want to shove the seating chart up his ass and curse him out of the fucking room with his overtone. I think again before saying a word, I would have more to worry about with him gone. I consider that's what my mother and father are thinking too, as they are trying to gain control over both of our whereabouts.

Zaid leaves my heavy gaze as he looks onto my father. "The announcement will come after dinner as you requested, Baba. Will there be any other necessary arrangements for this announcement?"

My father looks at my mother, then between Zaid and me as he answers. "No, I have it under control. I am very excited to announce both of them tomorrow night."

Both of them?

"There are two!" Zaid asks, then glances at me, smiling. Fucking asshole. I can see his mind working. Mine is already there. One will be the announcement of the heir to the throne, Zaid, and the other could only be the union between Kuwait and Jordan through the marriage of its royalty. I can't fucking be in here right now.

I rise from my chair, the sound of wood running against the wooden floor drawing my parents' and brother's eyes on me again. "I need to make a phone call to the center."

I exit out into the courtyard, unable to handle the claustrophobic feeling of the room. Marriage to a fucking princess I don't even know. What? Have my father and the Amir contrived to skip my proposal and seal the ill-fated alliance, disregarding the entities involved in this matrimony?

"Your mother has told me about the American girl at the center."

Surprised by my father's presence and quickness of getting to his point, I turn to his voice, my hands tucked in my pockets.

He moves closer, having my attention. "She tells me you are in love with her."

I don't know why I drop my eyes from him. It isn't from shame. I could never be ashamed of loving Ella. I meet his eyes. "Yes, I am."

He places his cane between us and rests both of his hands on top of the knob, his eyes not leaving mine. Stoically he says, "It doesn't change my mind about my announcement on your behalf tomorrow, Raj."

I have never defied my father, but I am brought the brink. "It does not change my mind either, Baba. I love her and that will never change."

His nods and lowers his eyes, staring at his hands for a long time before looking back up at me. "I knew it wouldn't."

Without another word, he turns and slowly walks back to the house as I consider the measures I am willing to take; rejecting my status, risking my allegiance, and opposing my duty for the woman I have fallen in love with.

Chapter 24

Ella

I slip the handcrafted, midnight-blue halter over my head, the sequins and crystal-like beading glimmering softly in the low light of my bedroom. I'm careful not to mess up my makeup and the up-do Jasara and Hoda have given me. The last three days have flown by between my girls keeping me busy, buzzing about their anticipation to see the palace, the King, and the Queen.

"Ella, we will see Princess Tamanna!" Muna's excitement was my entertainment and privilege. To see her eyes light up and her smile for the last three days was priceless. All of my girls would be able to meet a real-life princess, queen, and king, something they may have never had the opportunity to do in their lifetime if it wasn't for Raj's program. They have been able to see the very man who has brought hope to their eyes jumping rope for their entertainment in the courtyard, for God's sake. Raj had been less visible at the center, but had made sure I saw him when he was there.

Hoda and Jasara had arranged for the girls and me to go dress shopping the day after we received the invitation. Before leaving, Ismad handed her the money sent with the invitation. She took half from his hand and thanked him. For five women, I didn't think it would be enough, but I misjudged Hoda ... Stupid of me, I know. She never ceases to amaze me.

She took us to the woman who had made her wedding dress, Fidda the seamstress, *al kyiyata.* It boggled my mind that such a connection between her and the woman that made her wedding dress was kept sacred. Fidda's store was a short bus ride from the Ba'ashirs' and during the ride I wondered how a little old woman, obviously aged since making Hoda's wedding dress, would be able to create five dresses within three days.

Once there, I understood. She had a whole team of women in the back of her shop working on creating elegant dresses fit for royalty. Her shop had an ample amount of designer-quality creations ready to wear, and as I browsed with Ameena and Laila for their dresses, Hoda tapped me on the shoulder, handing me the two-piece dress I am putting on right now. Fidda said it would look beautiful on my skin, making the color of my eyes pop, and when I tried it on, it fit perfectly. The shoes she chose for me were black, strappy, with a low heel. She said it would be more comfortable, and being that I hadn't worn heels since my debutante days, I figured it best as well.

The boys had an easier time dressing since Ghalib and Rushdi wore similar-size clothing. Ismad had loaned Nazeer a pair of slacks, a button-up shirt, and a sports jacket that fit him nicely, with only a small amount of hemming Hoda took up for him.

I suspected Raj would have Badir come to get me and when Tom told us all of the volunteers would be driven to and from the palace. I was relieved knowing I wasn't getting preferential treatment over the others. Tom also said the host families and refugee families would be transported to and from as well. When I told the family yesterday, the girls squealed, while the smiles on Ismad, Hoda's, Jasara's, and Nazeer's faces had not stopped since reading the invitation.

I slip on the skirt and zip up the back. Feeling the hair on my midsection is strange and I feel self-conscious walking out into the room with Ismad and Nazeer exposed like I am. A knock comes at my door.

"Come in."

As the door opens, I turn to see Jasara, Hoda, Ameena, and Laila entering in their dresses, the girls with a light brushing of makeup and Hoda and Jasara appearing even more like sisters with their hair done and the matching deep burgundy lipstick they have chosen. They all look amazing.

Automatically, I cover my visible midriff, but Hoda pulls my hands away from my body gently, holding my arms straight out as Jasara brings me the midnight-blue iridescent shawl meant to wrap for flair while disguising some of the visible skin. I watch Hoda and Jasara adjust the wrap and tuck it in place as Ismad's voice interrupts, telling us the trucks are here in Arabic.

Hoda calls back to him as she continues to adjust my wrap, then looks up at me and smiles. "Beautiful."

"Shukran, Hoda."

She takes my shoulders and kisses me on each cheek, then leads the way out of my room, calling to us, "Yalla Yalla."

All three trucks are lined up in front of the house. The Ba'ashirs take the first one, while the Ahmadis take the second. I expect the third one is for me and the volunteers I will be riding with. I'm not surprised to see Badir as the driver when he gets out and opens the door for me. "Salaam anees," he says with the smallest smile he can muster.

"Salaam, Badir."

As he helps me in I notice no one else is in the truck. I didn't expect a transport only for me, but I'm sure Raj made sure of it.

As we enter the gates of the palace, my nerves pique just thinking about seeing Raj in this capacity. Meeting his mother the Queen, his father the King. Seeing Zaid again after our encounter at the camp has me on edge as well.

As we pull up to the palace, its grand red-brick exterior is highlighted with lights as people gather at the steps to enter. I suspect it is the receiving line for the king, queen, princes, and princess. Badir opens the door for me and helps me exit. Thanking him, I join the Ba'ashirs and the Ahmadis in line.

It moves quickly, and as we step through the doors of the palace, I glimpse the royal family receiving everyone, focusing on Raj for only a moment, long enough to notice how sophisticated and regal he looks in his suit and royal attire. He is attentive to every single guest, smiling and welcoming them. He dips low for the children, making sure to look into eyes. He glances down the line every once in a while as we move closer, not seeing me yet. Once he sees the Ba'ashirs, his eyes seek me out instantly, distracting him from the line. Once his golden eyes find me, his smile meant for the public he is greeting lessens, becoming the grin he reserves only for me.

Even though he continues with the receiving line, smiling graciously to the Ba'ashirs, thanking them for their service in the program in Arabic, my presence has distracted him. He glances at me between greeting every member of the Ba'ashir and Ahmadi family. Once it is my turn, Raj can't help taking in my appearance, the dress, my face, my hair.

He takes my hand as he has every other woman and holds it in one while placing the other on top. "Thank you for your dedication to your girls, Ella."

I notice the Queen glance over the princess's head at me and wonder if my name has struck a chord in her. I slip my hand from Raj's and lower my eyes. "You're welcome, Prince Rajaa." He does the same, the need for discretion coming back to him as I move to the princess to his left. She is younger than Ameena and Laila. "I am Ella Wallace. It is an honor to meet you."

She extends her hand first, letting me know a handshake will suffice for a more traditional greeting, like a curtsey or the like. "I am Princess Tamanna. It is a pleasure to meet you."

Her soft voice mixed with her well-spoken English is adorable and lightens my nerves, which I totally need before meeting the Queen who is next in line.

Standing before her, she radiates elegance, beauty, and an aura of power I suspect is both status and the fact she is the mother of the man I have fallen for.

As I peer into her eyes, the resemblance to Raj is obvious, her honey-hued eyes lined beautifully with perfectly placed makeup. She extends her hand to me and I do the same. I am about to speak, tell her how honored I am to meet her, when she lessens her smile and says, "Ella Wallace. It is a pleasure to finally put a name with a face."

Her voice is seems tender, but her knowing who I am makes me wary of what she thinks of me. In what capacity has my name come up? Has Raj spoken to her about me? Zaid? "I hope to speak with you tonight, know more about you, Ella."

I can't help being thrown off by her pursuit of me. I lower my eyes and bow to her. "Shukran, Your Highness."

I find my footing through all of my heightened nervousness as I stand before the King now. He takes my hand in his and looks down at me from a height similar to Raj. His hand trembles under mine, but it is only brief as he covers his other hand over mine just as Raj had done. Transparently smiling he says, "Thank you for your service at the center, Ella."

"It is my pleasure, Your Highness."

While I'm still speaking, he releases my hand quickly, moving his eyes from me to the next family, his smile more valid than the one he shared with me. I move forward and am face to face with Zaid. Now I am the one who can barely muster a transparent fucking smile as I look up at him. "It is an honor to meet you again, Prince Zaid."

The disdain in my voice is obvious, but isolated only between him and me. He doesn't seem to notice, his smile wide and his voice as pleasant as can be. "Ella Wallace. I am so happy you are here. It is truly a pleasure to see you again."

I place my hand in his. "Shukran." As his grip tightens like a noose around my hand, the other comes over it firmly, keeping me from moving on even though I try. He leans closer, his false smile still wide. "And tonight will definitely be memorable. Can't you feel it in the air?"

I twist my hand out of his grip and stare into his maddening black eyes. I notice the King glance at me, so I plaster on a smile as I look into Zaid's evil eyes. "I'm sure you have made it so."

He bows his head as he folds his hands together. "Yes, well, it is an important evening."

I move away quickly, following the Ba'ashirs and Ahmadis when I hear my name

"Ella!"

Ana has spotted me and is making her way toward me with David and Laura following behind her. "The volunteers are sitting together."

As she beckons me to come, I glance at the Ba'ashirs, not wanting to leave them so quickly. Hoda smiles and shoos me along. "Go, go."

"Oh my God, El, your dress!" Ana takes my shoulders and turns me around.

"Thank you."

She had on a black satin maxi dress with bell sleeves and the most beautiful sequined tie around her waist, cinching it to her shape. "You look beautiful, Ana."

She smiles somewhat self-consciously "You think?"

"Yes, absolutely!"

Ana leads us to the open doors of what appears to be a grand ballroom where tables have been set, servers are awaiting us, and the sound of woodwind instruments and drums announce the beginning of the celebration. The voices harmonize and resonate through the room as I follow Ana, David, and Laura to the tables.

"You are sitting there, El." She points to a spot on a table we approach. There are cards with our names at each place setting and as I look among the other tables, it's the same. I lower my veil from my head to my shoulders, noticing two large round tables with two guards stationed by them. I assume that is where Raj, his family, and any other royalty will be seated.

Many of the guests have either already taken their seats or are proceeding to them as the volume of the euphony escalates and a large group of brightly dressed women come through the door I had just entered. I take my seat and find where the Ba'ashirs and Ahmadis are sitting. I watch the expressions on their faces as they take in everything around them: the room, the music, the dancers. I take joy in watching them more than taking in the surroundings myself.

I scan the room for my girls. I find it hard to recognize some of them with the elegant dresses they are wearing. A small hand rests on my arm. "Miss, Ella."

I don't recognize this beautiful little girl right away, used to her wearing daily clothes as she clings to me on bad days and stays close on good ones. "Muna?" I turn in my chair and scoop her up in my lap and scan her dress, her curled hair, the tint of stain on her lips. "Is that you? Oh my gosh. You are so beautiful!"

She giggles. "You didn't know me!"

I laugh, conceding to her truth of my not recognizing her. "You are right! I thought you were a princess!" I hug her close as she giggles more.

"A princess! Like Tamanna?"

"Yes, just like Tamanna." I kiss the top of her head and set her down just as her aunt comes to take her hand, leading her back to their table.

The servers make their rounds, offering tea and water as the music continues on and the dancers sway and shimmy, calling on the children to come to the dance floor and dance. Ameena and Laila even get up and dance as I watch Hoda and Jasara rise from their chairs and clap for them in time with the music, Ismad and Nazeer clapping and smiling from their seats.

As I continue to watch, I notice one of the guards leave the isolated round tables. I follow him with my eyes, wondering if he is going to escort the royal family into the ballroom. My eyes move ahead him to the open doorway, where a man and woman stand with a younger woman, possibly my age, by their side. Their elegance and mannerisms show all the signs of royalty and I wonder if they are relatives of the King and Queen. I lean over to Tom, who is sitting on my right. "Who are they?"

He glances back in the direction I am looking, distracted from the dancing. "That is the Amir of Kuwait and his wife."

I watch the guard lead them through the room, all of the guests watching in awe just as I am.

The younger woman appears to be their daughter. The smoothness and charm she exudes is mesmerizing to all, including me. Her skin is flawless, a golden bronze. The pale-pink dress billowing chiffon overlay and crystal beading beneath is the perfect color to highlight her features and petite frame. As the Amir, his wife, and daughter arrive at the table, they turn toward the back of the room. The music and dancers clear the dance floor along with the children having joined them, scurrying back to their chairs. A few of the girls look upon the young woman, in awe of her. Obliging them, she bows to their level and offers her hands to them. The girl's eyes widen as they touch her hands then rush back to their families.

I am so struck by her I lean over to Tom and ask, "She is their daughter. A princess?"

"Yes, Princess Daya of Kuwait."

I feel like I have been stabbed in my chest, my heart bleeding out onto the table.

Tom continues to speak, "There are rumors that Prince Rajaa is to marry her."

Unable to stop staring at her as she rises from the children and stands regally next to her parents waiting to receive the royal family, my heart slowly compresses, the vice tightening as my stomach twists in knots.

I can't deflect that she is gorgeous, perfection in every way; pure, kind, compassionate, and royal ... meant for a prince. *Meant for Raj.*

I tighten the vice even more, envisioning the beautiful children her and Raj will make, needing the torture to quicken and pulverize my heart.

With the Amir and his family still standing, everyone slowly rises to join them in greeting the royal family.

A man's voice speaks over the guests' hushing voices, bringing further silence to the expansive room. "Your Highness King Ammaar Bin Qadir, Her Majesty Queen layaali Al Hashemite, Prince Zaid bin Ammaar, Prince Rajaa bin Ammaar, and Princess Tamanna bin Ammaar. The Royal family of Jordan!"

I'm not sure what formal welcomings of royals looks like in the Middle East, but being the room has more commoners than royalty, the cheers and applause begins and I manage to put my hands together as well as the doors open.

The King is the first to appear, followed by the Queen, Zaid, Tamanna, then Raj. Ignoring all else I watch Raj take in the guests, the smallest touch of a smile on his lips. He doesn't wave like the rest of his family. Instead, he searches the crowded tables, I assume searching for me. As his eyes move toward our side of the room, a sudden fear of him seeing me washes over me and I shift into the space behind a man in front of me, keeping Raj from sight as I continue to clap.

Once I think it is clear I look back up at him, the King and Queen are already greeting the Amir and his family. The Queen embraces Daya, the woman she wants as her future daughter, before taking her seat next to the King. My eyes stay with Raj, needing to see his reaction to Daya the moment he takes her in. Needing to see what it looks like for a prince and princess, promised to each other above and beyond fate and the fucking universe. To lay eyes upon one another. Will there be an instant spark? Will their magical fairy tale unfold right here in front of everyone, while our trivial actuality dissolves, becoming nothing more than an indulgence for a prince?

Raj exchanges kisses on either cheek with the Amir, then moves to his wife to do the same. As he comes to Daya, his eyes meet hers for a moment, his smile not catching as I expected in this fairy tale I created in my head. He takes her hand and kisses it gently, her smile remaining constant as he shows her the utmost respect.

The applause and cheer suddenly escalates, urging on the coupling of their Prince Rajaa and Kuwait's Princess Daya. Even the people of Jordan, Syria believe in this union. As the royal family begins to sit, everyone else follows. I notice Raj pulling out Daya's chair and try to focus on the food the servers are starting to place on our table. The conversation at the table temporarily takes my mind off of Raj as Tom mentions the King making an announcement tonight.

"Jordan has been waiting for the heir to the throne to be crowned. This would be the ideal venue to do it."

I can't stomach much, eating only the Shrak and hummus.

"Is that all you are going to eat?" Ana asks, gesturing to my plate.

"I'm not very hungry."

I watch the dancers swaying and shimmying to the music, a mindless distraction from the temptation of observing Raj and Daya. *Shit, I can't do it.*

I look over at the table and am met with Raj's golden-hued eyes staring back at me. He bows his head and smiles as he rises from his chair and starts walking toward me.

Holy shit. What is he doing?

Raj comes to stand behind Tom and places his hands on his shoulders. "Thank you all for coming tonight," Raj says as he looks at everyone, then rests his gaze on me. "I know dressing and acting a certain way is not enjoyable, but for the event it is necessary."

I consider his words carefully. I think he is telling me he has to act this way with Daya for the event.

"Well, we are excited to be here, Prince Rajaa. Thank you so much," Tom says, looking up at Raj.

Everyone at the table agrees with thanks and I do the same, seeming to keep his attention. "Please understand if I don't seem myself this evening. I don't do well with formal events."

His humble words are another a decipherable apology, sending a calm through me, shattering the princess and prince, happily ever after scenario I created in my head. For the first time since he has come to our table, I smile and breathe deeply as all of the other volunteers at the table laugh at his candor.

In kind, Raj tells us to enjoy the evening and festivities before returning to his table, and I think I just might survive this evening after all.

I'm able to enjoy some of the stuffed falafel and the chicken skewers now that Raj has given me some insight as to why he was being so congenial with Daya. Having been a debutante, I should have remembered things like acting congenial even though you may hate every girl in the fucking room. I suppose my mental block of those rites of passage into elite young womanhood had expired when I threw in the towel.

The music dies away as the King rises from his chair. Standing in the middle of the dance floor, he receives applause and cheers as he leans on his cane for support, taking the microphone in his other hand. The applause dies quickly as he speaks in both Arabic and English for the benefit of the Americans in the room.

"Welcome to all of you and thank you for attending. I know that the notice was short, but I am thankful so many of you could attend. Tonight is a very special night, not only for all of you being here, celebrating the successes of Makan Lil 'Amal Center, but to honor those dedicating their time and support to make it be an effective tool in this fight against a crisis in our lands."

Everyone applauds with this statement, and as it fades away, he begins again, "My son Rajaa, he pushed for this program two years ago." He looks out at each of us, then down at Raj, who has lowered his head to rub the side of his nose. "Two years, my son, and you never gave up hope."

Raj nods at his father's praise of persistence, his eyes still downcast, unwilling to draw attention to himself. I notice Daya look down at him and smile, then at her mother and father, who share the pride of future in-laws. I breathe a cleansing breath and send the thought out of my head as I listen to the King speak.

The King keeps his gaze steady on Raj. "A passion for the people of our country and those we have pulled into our safe embrace. Zaid, the backbone of the Jordanian Armed Forces!"

Everyone applauds again, cheering for Zaid's heavy hand of protection for his country.

The King raises his hand to Zaid, who has in turn raised his chin to his father with self-regard. "You have defended our country by my side many times over the years, and my years are dwindling even though I may not want them to."

The silence in the room becomes solemn with his final statement. He shuffles a few steps with the help of his cane as he looks among the people. "I have served this country, loved this country, all of my life, and tonight is the night I announce the one that will love and lead you into the future!"

The applause is deafening as the king stands before us. He raises his hand for us to stop as he continues, smiling down at the Queen, Princess Tamanna, Zaid, and Raj. "My family."

He returns his gaze to the crowd. "My Jordan. I hereby announce Rajaa bin Ammaar as heir apparent to the throne of our Kingdom, Jordan!"

The entire room erupts with excitement. Rajaa? Zaid is the oldest. I look over at Tom. "I thought Zaid was to be crowned by law."

Tom is as elated as the rest of the room, already rising to his feet. "Inevitably, it is the King's choice."

I rise as well, needing to see Raj's expression. He is still seated and I can't angle around the bodies to see his face.

The King speaks over the crowd, "Rajaa. Come."

I continue to clap as I finally see the top of his head come up from the crowd. His face is as white as a ghost, the shock having quickly settled that he will be King. As he walks up to his father, he looks back at his family, specifically at Zaid, who is applauding with the royal family. While his manners show one thing, I know better than to think he is proud for his brother. He stands stiffly, acknowledging his brother being chosen over him with a strained smile.

The King places his arm on Raj's shoulder as he speaks to him eye to eye in front of all of us. "As you have grown from a boy into a man, you have shown all the qualities of a true leader. I have no doubt you will transform Jordan and the Middle East!"

Everyone sits as the King holds Rajaa in his sights, while the Amir, his wife, and Daya rise and walk toward them.

I feel my heart quicken not just for the simple fact Raj has just received the highest honor of a prince, being crowned heir to the throne, but that the Amir, his wife, and Princess Daya are joining them on the floor.

As the Amir stands on one side of the King with his family, Queen Layaali rises and comes to stand on the other side of the King as he says, "As King you will bring about a unification in the Middle East, one that has been desired for a very long time."

The King glances at the Amir and they exchange a smile.

My heart feels like it has been punctured as I listen to the King tell Raj, "You and your Queen, Daya, will transform the Middle East together."

I want to bolt, save my heart from bleeding out, escape the feeling of it draining as I watch this fucking fairy tale take form before me. The one Raj had made me believe was false all night.

Raj's eyes have glazed over, though mine have awakened to this fucking nightmare. I push away from the table just as the applause erupts and the bodies in the room rise to cheer on the alliance of two countries and marriage of two people as unrequited fate slaps me in the fucking face.

I feel an arm intertwine with mine and pull me close. "Ella, what's wrong?"

Ana.

I lean into her comfort as I let myself melt into the emotion overcoming me. "I have to get some air."

She searches my face and tells me, "It's going to be okay, El."

Through tear-streaked eyes, Ana guides me through the exploding Arabic chants of joy to the doors at the back of the ballroom.

I stare down at the lineup of black SUVs from a second-floor window of the palace. I don't know where she has taken me, but it appears to be an office, one wall lined with books behind an executive desk fit for a King.

The full moon casts a ring around it, like a celestial barrier protecting its subsistence.

Meant to keep me from stealing it.

I run my hand under my eyes, wiping away tears, but they keep coming.

The sound of glass touching glass has me turning to see Ana pouring golden liquid from a crystal decanter. She is generous with it, and when she comes over to me, I take it from her hands and down half before returning her stare.

"I knew something was going on. That night in the desert..." Ana's voice remains low as she analyzes the path of Raj and my love affair.

I nod and numbly offer, "It started way before then. A world away."

"Then you saw him with her, the King announcing their..." She stops herself before she reinvents the development that broke me moments ago. It's too late though.

The pangs of emotion have already settled, and are spilling over. All I need right now is to just be alone.

"Hey, go back to the table. Tom is going to wonder where we are."

She looks at me cautiously. "Are you sure? I can stay with you."

I shake my head and close my eyes, wiping more fallen tears. "No, I want to be alone."

My point is taken as Ana backs away, her arms folded over her chest. "Okay. I'll tell him you just needed some air, too much commotion."

I nod. "Thanks."

As soon as she closes the door, I down the rest of the whisky and walk over to the decanter to drown my sorrow in one more glass before I find Badir and have him take me home.

I hear voices in the hall getting closer, but they are muffled.

All of a sudden, I hear a familiar voice bellow, "Is she in there?"

Raj.

"She doesn't want to see you."

All at once, the door is pushed open. Raj barrels in with Ana moving in front of him, trying to keep him from me. Badir comes in behind them, closing the door to keep the commotion within the room. He looks down at the glass I hold in my hand.

"I need to speak with you, alone." He pushes against Ana's hands as she keeps him from getting any closer to me. He dodges around her and comes at me, but I move around the desk, setting my drink down on the counter and turn to Badir.

"Please take me home, Badir."

He is pursuing me around the desk as Ana comes between us again, stopping his advance.

Raj commands over Ana's head, "No, Badir, you will not!"

Badir stands at the door, not knowing what to do or think of what is happening.

I come around the front of the desk and back up into the middle of the room, Ana keeping the space between Raj and me as his pursuit for me continues.

"Ella, please, you have to believe me. I didn't know he was going to do this!"

I find some sick sense of humor through my tears as I cry through the words. "What? That you would be King or that he would propose for you to Princess Daya, the woman you are supposed to be with?"

He stops pursuing me, hit with the bluntness of my strike.

"Oh, I'm sorry, Your Highness, congratulations are in order." I try to gain control of my shaking voice as I hold in my sorrow and offer my salutes. "Congratulations on being crowned heir and congratu-fucking-lations on your nuptials to Princess Daya!"

He looks between Ana and Badir, letting me chastise him with no defense. I wipe my eyes, pissed at the tears that are falling. "She is beautiful, Raj," I shake my head and stare at him. "Lovely and pure, kind and compassionate. She is everything you should have."

Raj closes his eyes, obviously pained by what I have said. "Ella, stop."

"She will make a wonderful wife to you and mother to your children."

My words have tempered him as he starts toward me, but Ana holds him back with every ounce of strength in her small frame. "Excuse me, Your Highness, but don't fuck with my girl!"

As she stands her ground, I realize what I have to do. End this before it becomes the death of him.

"Okay, just stop!" I yell.

Raj stops pushing and Ana stares at me over her shoulder, her hands still on guard.

I glance between Ana and Badir. "Please leave us alone."

Ana's voice is full of worry with my request. "El, we can leave right now."

I shake my head, knowing that it would do nothing to leave things as they are.

As Ana and Badir walk toward the door, leaving the open space between Raj and me, Ana says, "I will be right outside this door."

I nod and lower my eyes. "Thanks."

He keeps his distance and I'm thankful for that, because hardening my heart to him is difficult enough without him being close. "It was always going to turn out this way, Raj. We just fucking lied to ourselves. The whole time, we created this world that would eventually destroy itself, just like it is doing right now."

His silence is the death of me as I glance at him. He tilts his head up to the ceiling and his mouth slackens, before he settles his dampened golden eyes back on me. "I never lied to myself about you and I never will! I am ready to risk everything, because I fucking love you!" Every word is saturated with unequivocal emotion and the quiver in his voice is gutting me.

I shake my head. "You can't, Raj."

He closes the space between us, his body pushing against mine, walking me backward as I butt up against the desk. "It's too late for that. My life is nothing without you, don't you see that yet?"

His breath mixing with mine is intoxicating, but I fight against my desire. "I see you throwing your life away for something that is just a fucking fling."

I try to move around him, but he wraps his arms around my waist, lifting me on to the desk, running the veil I have let fall to my shoulders through his hands as he pulls it from me. He grips the nape of my neck, holding me to him as he brings his lips to mine. I try to resist, pull away from him, breaking our kiss, but his hold is too strong as he speaks breathlessly to me.

"No, I know you don't believe that."

As he runs the length of my neck with his lips, his hands work quickly, raising my dress around my thighs and sliding me to the edge of the desk to feel his hardness. "I know you believe in chance meetings. A stare from across the room." He kisses me, wrapping his tongue around mine before pulling back to look into my eyes, his fingers finding their way between my thighs. "One soul meeting another. It is so simple, but it means everything."

He releases my neck but I'm the one holding onto him now, my arms wrapped around his shoulders as he maneuvers past my panties and dives deep into me, my gasp full of need as he runs his thumb against my sex. I feel my eyes fall sleepy from his touch, the sensation of his fingers working in and out of me, him stroking my rock-hard nub.

Clutching him to me, I keep my eyes on him for as long as I can as he continues to speak to me, his voice quickening with our growing passion, taking me deep into the place he wants me to fall. "I love you so fucking much, Ella."

All of a sudden he pulls his fingers from me, starving me of his touch as he unfastens his pants, liberating his robust stem. Nimbly, he wraps my legs around his hips, pulls me to him, resting his tip against my tender opening, letting me feel the throbbing warmth of his desire as his slacken stare holds my surrendered gaze.

"I will cross the stars, defy everything that tries to keep me from you. Do you understand me?"

I nod, but that isn't good enough for him. His throaty command and the slightest push against my sex releases the words from my lips. "Tell me you understand."

He pushes his tip into me teasingly, the sensual connection only the beginning as I moan in ecstasy from the quick pulse just the head of him sends coursing through me. Our connection is a deadlock as I look into his soul and tell him, "I understand."

My sensual call gives him command as he grasps my ass and slides deep inside of me. "It is you, Ella. It has always just been you. It will never be anyone else for as long as I live." As he speaks to me he slides out slowly, only to slam into me with sweet vengeance. "'Tell me that I'm not alone in this world, Ella. Tell me that the one I know, 'Eh enta, the one I love, will return it and defy everything that tries to keep us apart."

As he slides from me, then plunges deeper still, I gasp, the coiling tension he is sending to my center relinquishing every ounce of truth held captive in my body, heart, and soul. "I love you, Raj."

Holding my thighs, he drives deep again, and again, and again, my arms wrapped around his neck clutching him to me, sending the sweet gathering pulses higher and higher. "Oh God, I love you, Raj. I love you," I breathe into his ear as we both unravel in each other's arms, holding on as the rapturous swell ripples in me, pulling me out into the deep with my prince.

Chapter 25

Rajaa

Cradled in my arms, I keep her close, my hands still holding her trembling thighs as she hums soft breaths into my ear. I stay inside of her, wanting to remain in this sacred place where we can always be together.

Craving the smell of her skin, I run my nose against her jaw and dip my lips down to touch the pounding pulse on the nape of her neck. The thumbing beat against my lips, so fast; I do that to her. I know her in every way and I can't release her no matter the consequence. If it is death, then so be it, because life without this woman, without touching her soul every single day, will leave me damned.

"I am telling them tonight."

My clouded statement has her pulling back to look into my eyes as she rests her hand on my cheek, waiting for me to explain. I gaze deep into Ella's soul and let my own be my guide. "I will refuse to marry her; if I have to forfeit my crown, so be it. To marry her would be surrendering to a fate I have never wanted. The only woman I want to be with forever is you."

The pop and crackling sound of fireworks being set ablaze and the harsh knock at the door pull me from her. Badir's voice calls through closed doors, "Sahib Al-Somuw, Shakhs Qadim!"

I cup her face in my hands and kiss her tenderly. "Someone is coming."

As I fasten my pants she slides down from the desk and lowers her dress. Nothing is amiss on the desk except the glass of whiskey Ella had been drinking.

Rushing and shuffling around each other aimlessly in circles, I pick up the glass and comment on her habit, "You shouldn't be drinking."

She stops turning and stares at me hard. "You have a decanter of it sitting in the open. Can you fucking blame me?"

Her sharp tongue is infuriating, but I can't blame her after the way this night had gone. I pull her to me and kiss her once more before the knock comes again. "Prince Rajaa," Badir hisses.

I hand Ella the sheer scarf I had rendered her helpless with before opening the door.

Badir is hovering on the other side, anxiously surveying Ella and me. Badir tells me he can take her out the back in Arabic while the family is outside sending off the guests.

"Where is Ana?" Ella asks nervously

"Elha. A distraction," Badir says urgently, telling me she is distracting the person coming.

I turn to Ella and stare into her deep-blue eyes once more. "Badir will take you out of here."

Her brow furrows as she searches my eyes. "What about you?"

I reassure her, "I will be fine. No one saw me leave when the guests started exiting to the courtyard."

She is holding on to my tuxedo jacket like I am her life line. "I love you, Raj." Her voice catches so innocently as she says my name, reminding me once again that Ella is pure love above everything else in this world set on tainting us.

"I love you too."

I kiss her once again before Badir pulls her from me, taking her through the hall and down the back stairs.

I quickly look over the room, searching for anything out of place, then glance down at myself and my rumpled shirt. Quickly, I set the glass down and tuck in my shirt, straightening my bowtie the best I can when a knock comes at the door. "Rajaa."

It is my father. I take the drink from the desk and dash to the window. "Yes, I'm here."

My father opens the door, his cane leading him as he walks. He appears confused. "Why didn't you join us to see off our guests? Your brother seems to have disappeared as well."

I swirl the whiskey around in the glass, drawing my father's attention to the liquid. "You shouldn't drink."

I move away from the window to my father as he walks toward me. "It is understandable, Rajaa ... nerves.

First you are crowned heir and then propose marriage to Daya."

I find fault in his statement. "I didn't propose to Daya, Baba, you did."

He stops walking, seeming to be stunned by my words. "You would eventually propose to her, Rajaa. The Amir and I made it more convenient."

"For who? You?"

"No! For you!" he yells back at me.

I take a drink of the whiskey, silently thanking Ella for pouring a hefty dose. As I savor it, then pull the glass from my lips, I contemplate the game my father has chosen to play with me and realize where Zaid has found his innate ways of strategizing. "Why me?"

"What do you mean?" he asks, his tremors returning as his head shakes.

"Why did you crown me when it has always been expected for Zaid to succeed you?"

My father moves away from me and finds the back of the chair to rest his free hand, the cane not being enough as he stands to speak to me. "You will be a better leader."

I don't deny I am the better choice, but he is not answering my question truthfully. "I will not deny it being that Zaid is still in contact with Tariq under our family's noses."

I expect my revelation to surprise him, but he remains fixed on the ground below him, running his thumb over the top of his cane. "You knew?"

He refuses to look at me as the words he speaks draw bitter disdain. "While I am old, I am not blind, Rajaa. I thought he would change, as he groveled to me and the Amir that day you were gone, telling us as Allah as his witness, he would turn against the evil that had pulled him."

He shakes his head. "I knew his deceit wouldn't make it through the day."

He closes his eyes. "Your mother, he had her almost believing his atonement as he took hold of planning this celebration. His mind was completely set that he was going to be King."

He shakes his head. "The courtyard is below my room. I heard you and Zaid arguing. I heard everything."

He looks up into my eyes. "While I knew you were set on not marrying Daya because of this woman you have fallen in love with, I knew giving the throne to Zaid would be the greater downfall of our monarchy, one that would further throw the Middle East into chaos."

"So you decided to crown me heir and propose on my behalf in front of the press, hundreds of guests, the Prime Minister, and Cabinet present to witness it."

He strains to keep his head from shaking as his fury rises. He raises his cane and hammers it to the ground. "Yes, I did!"

"Yes, we did." My mother is standing at the open door, boundless and supremely transfixed on our exchange as she walks toward us, turning to me. "You chose a volatile lust for a woman, an impure bond that has clouded your path, Rajaa!" She takes the glass of whiskey from my hand and throws it across the room.

"No, my love for Ella has clouded *your* path!" I look between both my mother and father now. "If you think a public proposal will keep me from being with Ella, you are wrong."

My mother strikes me across the face, sending me stumbling back as her eyes widen and her mouth hardens. "You will marry Daya!"

I take my hand from the sting she has left on me. "If I marry anyone, it will be Ella."

I contemplate the trivialness of my parents' logic. "You are finding fault with my love for Ella, while your oldest son is cavorting with prostitutes, drunk and strung out like a fiend, while extorting resources from a Syrian Sheikh who will turn on him and our country in a heartbeat! You are turning on me, while he is masterminding his own reign! You think my forbidden love will destroy us all? Where is he?"

They stare at me, wordless to my uncontrolled tirade, as I step closer to them, maddened knowing he is running loose. "Where is your son?"

Neither of them speak, sending my mind into wicked place and possibilities a scorned man may hide while planning his retribution.

Ripping myself from their blinded eyes and deafened ears, I rush through the door in search of a madman intent on revenge.

Chapter 26

Ella

I startle awake with the feeling something has happened to Raj. Sitting upright, I look at the two-piece dress I wore last night with the veil strung on the hanger, the smallest amount of dawn drawing sparkle from the beading.

Last night, while the guests and royalty were staring up at the cascading firework display, Badir took me from Raj's arms and stealthy drew me out of the palace, bringing me home to safety. As I walk over to the window and peer out, I see Badir's SUV still parked where it was parked last night. He stayed and watched the house, watched for me, even after the Ba'ashirs and Ahmadis returned. I pretended to be asleep, not wanting to explain why I had left early, how I had gotten into the house. Now morning, I know Hoda will be waking with questions for me.

I'm not sure what answers to give her, as I'm still not sure what happened after we left the party. On the way home, I'd heard Badir's phone ring, his covert Arabic conversation giving little away.

The call had been quick, Badir claiming Raj called to make sure I was safe. It would have been a sweet gesture, if not for Badir helping me out of SUV while pulling back his suit coat, releasing the holster his gun was locked into. When we arrived at the Ba'ashirs', I found myself locked out without a key. He took out the most sophisticated lock-picking tool I'd ever seen, picked the lock and ushered me inside with strict order to lock the door. The urgency in his eyes scared me as he claimed he would be just outside the entire night. He kept his promise, and that has me even more worried now.

After I dress, I touch the fabric of the dress once more. Waking up with the sensation something has happened to Raj, combined with Badir's behavior last night, leaves me lost and I need something to hold onto that carries a memory of him. I pull the sheer, blue veil through the hanger just as Raj slipped it from my neck last night and tuck it into my bag before leaving my room.

Hoda is already working in the kitchen, getting food ready for the family. I notice Ismad, Uncle Naz, and the boys sitting in the living room eating around the coffee table. She hears me close the door to my room and turns to me. She puts down what she is doing, wipes her hands on her apron, and comes toward me.

"Where you go?" She keeps her voice low as she glances over her shoulder, making sure no one hears her line of questioning.

"I felt sick. Mareed."

"Mareed?"

"Naam," I confirm.

She looks me over. "Okay?"

I nod. "I'm better."

She nods, seeming to find satisfaction until she looks down the stairs then back at me. "No key."

Fuck.

"It was open. Fath."

"Fath!" Her voice is louder all of a sudden as she seems anxious and nervous. "Ismad!" She turns toward the room the men occupy, Ismad coming to the doorway.

"Naam. Oh, Ella, where were you last night? How did you get in?" His urgency is akin to Hoda's.

Hoda speaks quickly in Arabic explaining what I have said, then he turns to me, concerned. "Not locked? I remember locking the door."

I lower my eyes and shake my head. "No, it was unlocked. I just touched the knob."

That wasn't a complete lie. I did just touch the knob, after Badir picked it.

He looks between Hoda and me, his hands on his hips as he appears to retrace his steps in the mass exodus to the procession of trucks collecting us. Focusing on me now, he raises his eyebrows. "It is possible."

He explains to Hoda in Arabic.

She looks back at me as Ismad walks back into the living room to finish his food.

As I sit to the table, Hoda returns to her duties, preparing food more food for us. Ameena comes up behind me, hugging my shoulders. "Salaam."

I clasp her hands around my neck and lean into her. "Salaam."

She sits down next to me as Hoda turns to us bearing Shrak and two bowls of hot Fuul. "Shukran."

Hoda nods as she enunciates, "Welcome."

I wrap my veil over my head as Hoda hands me a small bag for lunch, just as she has done for the past two-and-a-half months now. She arranges and tidies my veil, finding something amiss with the way it sits. She glances at me as she does this, then pulls me to her, kissing me on both cheeks.

As I start to move from her, her hands hold me still as she looks at me. "Okay? No sick?"

I see worry in her eyes for me, something Hoda has never expressed. Feeling thrown off by her concern, I nod. "Naam."

She seems to find peace in my response as the wrinkle in her forehead disappears. "Wa-Alaykum as-salaam."

"Wa-Alaykum as-salaam."

Badir drops me a few yards from the courtyard like I have asked him to in the past. Before I open the door, he tells me. "I will watch you."

I thank him and open the door.

As I walk along the sidewalk, passing the local store owners opening their doors for the day's business, I notice one of the faces I hadn't seen in weeks—the man who pulled my veil from my head. I avoid his brief stare as he picks up a piece of trash from the ground, looks beyond me, then goes back into the store he came from. As I pass the open doorway, I walk quicker and glance back once, before entering reaching the guards standing at the courtyard entrance.

Entering the center, I walk toward the computer lab. I hadn't emailed my sister in days and on the way here, I told myself I should at least make contact. Just as I come to the door of the lab and see Ana at a computer, my name is called from behind.

"Ella." Tom is standing in the hall with a grim expression on his face. "Can you come to my office?"

I look back at Ana, knowing she heard Tom, and I am wondering if she knows what's going on. Her wide eyes tell me she doesn't have a clue either. I turn to Tom. "Now?"

He nods. "Yes, please."

I turn back toward Tom and walk toward him. Each step I wonder what he knows, what he has learned. Is this about me? Did something happen to Raj?

Tom motions for me to enter ahead of him. As I enter, I see the face of a man who is not supposed to occupy this world, the face of my father as he rises from the chair he occupies.

"What are you doing here?" is my greeting.

My father scoffs, seemingly embarrassed by my ill-mannered greeting, then sets his bitter glare on me. "Well, that is a fine greeting. I have come to bring you home."

"Bring me home?"

Tom shuts the door behind him. "Your father has been in contact with Prince Zaid. He has told your father and me about the apparent affair you and Prince Rajaa have pursued in secrecy. He fears that it has put you both in danger."

I don't think Tom means to convey the burden I have placed on him, but I feel the guilt of it still.

My father starts in, "I knew coming over here was a bad idea from the start." My father glances at Tom. "Nothing against what you are doing here, Mr. Stern, but my daughter's naive risk-taking behavior is not cut out for ventures like these, as you can see!"

He glares at me. "An affair with a Prince of Jordan. Do you not have any self-respect, Ella? Any shame to your actions? You have come to this country, traipsed around with a prince, swayed his code of conduct by seducing him into an affair!"

What the fuck? "Is that what Zaid has told you? That I swayed him into an affair?"

"Yes."

I laugh at him with sheer disgust. "And you believe him because he is fucking royalty, right?"

"What? Should I believe the daughter who has apparently spread her legs to a Prince of Jordan?"

"Fuck you!" I spit the words at him as his hand comes across the side of my face, sending me stumbling back, Tom catching my fall.

I stare at my father, shocked by what he just did. Still enraged, my father reaches for me to pull me to him. "Here, we are leaving."

Tom holds me protectively. "I think we need to calm down before that happens."

My father then tugs at his collar, refusing to look at either of us. "Yes, well, we have a flight to catch."

I find my voice through the shock and hate. "I am not going anywhere with you."

The door to Tom's office suddenly opens, Raj standing in the doorway. He takes in the scene, Tom holding my arms and my father hovering close. "What is going on?" He releases the door knob, appearing out of breath, like he had run to get to me.

The sound of children in the hallway creeps through the open door; the students have started arriving. I move away from Tom to pick up my bag, it having fallen when my father struck me. As I come up my father takes hold of my arm. "We are leaving this instant."

Raj steps in front of him, blocking the doorway as he closes it behind him. "You aren't taking her anywhere!"

I try to pull away from the grip my father has on me, but he digs his fingers in deeper, making me wince as he glares at Raj. "She is my daughter, and yes I am!"

Raj's shock is apparent as he looks between my father and me.

My father pauses for a moment to take Raj in. "I'm thankful that your brother thought of my daughter's safety, since you had no sense! And to think you will be King."

My father shoves Raj away from the door as I fight harder against his pull. "No! I'm not going with you! Raj!"

Holding my arm, my father opens the door to Tom's office and pulls me into the hall, Raj and Tom following behind us as I fight against him.

"Mr. Wallace," Raj starts to plead with him, but my father refuses his words, standing at the doors of the center with me in tote.

"Don't you dare speak to me."

As my father drags me down the hall, I look out into the courtyard and see the man who pulled my veil from my head all those weeks ago, the one I saw for the first time in weeks this morning, standing in the middle of the courtyard. As the children and families walk around me, staring at my father pulling me along, I look back at Raj as he and Tom follow close behind us.

"Raj, the man in the courtyard!"

Just as he turns in the direction of the courtyard, his eyes widen. He lunges straight for me and my father, taking us both down to the ground just as a flash of light blinds me and the resounding boom numbs all sound, setting a high-pitched ringing stationary in my head until it fades with me into the consuming darkness.

"Ella!" The sound of Raj's voice brings me to. I think I am still in between this world and another as I open my eyes and look into the safe haven of his golden embers while the screams, cries, and gunfire surrounds us. His voice is almost inaudible as I watch his lips.

"I love you, Ella."

Suddenly, I feel the weight of him lift from me, the blinding sunlight replacing his face. I command myself to reach for him, pull him back to me, yell for him to not leave me, but I am deadened to this world I am fighting to return to for him.

I love you, Raj.

"Ella." I can't think in the thickness filling my head to recognize the voice immediately.

"Ella." The strong accent makes me think of Raj, trying bringing me back to the natural world.

"Raj."

There is no response from my transporter. I sway side to side in his arms as he carries me. I mumble once more as I lay suspended in my deliverers arms. "Raj."

Fighting against the draw of peace in the darkness, my arms find some life as I touch the rough fabric of a soldier's gear. My eyes find new life, just as my body is beginning to, and I open them to see the face of the man who crossed Raj and me both. Zaid.

The moment I try to push against his chest, he hoists me up higher into his chest, forcing my head into his shoulder and bringing his mouth to my ear. "The risk was too great, Ella. They have taken him."

Weak beneath his grip, I stare helplessly over his shoulder as he walks away from the rubble and bodies that was once Makan Lil 'Amal. My cry for the small broken bodies of children, some maybe my girls, and the soul that captured mine in this very place meets the sound of sirens and yelling soldiers, not yet reaching this world caving in all around me.

As my heart breaks, my soul takes flight, set to wander in search of the one certainty, the one love that has been stolen in this darkest hour. The one love that crossed the stars to consume me, and the one I will risk stealing the moon to get back, no matter what.

عبر النجوم

عبر النجوم
النجوم
عبر النجوم
عبر النجوم

STEAL *the* MOON

BOOK TWO

Releasing September 2016

For exclusives and information on new releases,

http://www.venessakimball.com/#a__blank_cvjg

to join Venessa's newsletter and receive one of her books FREE as a thank you!

About the Author

Having always been passionate about the written word, Venessa Kimball embarked on writing what would become her debut novel, Piercing the Fold: a young adult urban fantasy series in 2010, with a 2012 release with Crushing Hearts Black Butterfly Publishing, it quickly finished out as a four book series. Venessa has also written a compelling teen contemporary series, the Evan series.

Venessa also writes New Adult and Adult romance under the pen name V. Angelika. When she isn't writing, she is keeping active with her high school sweetheart and three kids, chauffeuring said children to extracurricular activities, catching a movie with her honey, and staying up way too late reading.

Connect with her at:

www.VenessaKimball.com
http://www.facebook.com/venessakimballauthor
http://www.twitter.com/venessakimball

Other Novels Published by Venessa Kimball

YA/ Teen Urban Fantasy/ Sci-Fi series
the Piercing the Fold series

Piercing the Fold: Book 1
Surfacing the Rim: Book 2
Ascending the Veil: Book 3
Transcending the Legacy: Book 4

Piercing the Fold: the Complete Urban Fantasy Collection Boxed Set

YA/Teen Contemporary Fiction Series
the Evan series

Dismantling Evan: Book 1
Saving Gavin: a Novelette, vol 1
Resurrecting Gavin: a Novelette, vol 2
Reviving Evan: a Novella 1.5

Novels Published by Venessa Kimball Writing as V. Angelika

New Adult Contemporary Romance
Crossing Stars Duet

Cross the Stars (Crossing Stars Duet #1)
Steal the Moon (Crossing Stars Duet #2) - Coming Soon

Acknowledgments

I have said this a million times, and I will say it a million more: It takes a village to produce a novel. The village I have been blessed with has helped bring this novel from imagination to realization. It could not have been accomplished without the energy of so many behind the scenes; Rebecca Berto with Berto Designs for bringing the Cross the Stars cover to life; Kristina Circelli with Red Road Editing for her keen eyes; Imad Lyzzaik for making sure my Arabic translation and usage was up to par and while keeping the linguistic depth this cross cultural story calls for; and to Julie with JT Formatting for bringing all the elements together to fancy the readers' eyes.

Dawn Miller, thank you for being an extraordinary friend first and a meticulous critique partner second. Your critiques, opinions, and nudges to push the characters make my stories more compelling than I originally imagined they could ever be.

To my beta readers, I have always asked you for brutal honesty and you have obliged. Thank you for that!

To my launch team, Darlings, thank you for embracing and spreading the word about my writing and being my biggest cheerleaders on my writing journey. I am truly blessed to have fans as great as you! Special thanks to Tanya Rutherford and Jamie Deann for discovering the names of Ella and Raj.

Austin DD gals, I love you dearly. Thank you for the inspiration and motivation you infuse into the atmosphere every month at our gatherings. I owe you a cheese tray and antipasti tray next time my friends.

To the bloggers and community of readers that have put energy and time into posting and spreading the word about my writing, you have been the life line for my books as they make their way into sea of novels and novelettes. I have the utmost respect and appreciation for all that you do to spread the word for authors worldwide.

Much love to all of you,

~V

www.ingramcontent.com/pod-product-compliance
Lightning Source LLC
LaVergne TN
LVHW041058080826
845145LV00007B/1627

* 9 7 8 0 6 9 2 6 3 3 8 3 0 *